SARASWATTEE

KIT PURAN SINGH

Saraswattee

A Novel of India

SEATTLE · Madrona Publishers · 1982

Copyright © 1982 by Kit Puran Singh
Printed in the United States of America

Published by
Madrona Publishers Inc.
2116 Western Avenue
Seattle, Washington 98121

FIRST EDITION
10   9   8   7   6   5   4   3   2   1

Library of Congress Cataloging in Publication Data

Singh, Kit Puran.
    Saraswattee: a novel of India.

    I. Title.
PS3569.I5744S2   813'.54   82-7175
ISBN 0-914842-88-9   AACR2

To Vedavitri,
who has never seen me;
and whom I have never seen.

SARASWATTEE

ONE

SUCH a time it is now, as it was then, the first summer of the year, when in the brittle heat of the day the ber trees and the cactus sucked up their own shadows; when the sheep and the goats foraged not for the meager briars and shrubs but for whatever meager shadows not sucked up by the midday sun: and when mortal nights blew cold and brought frost to the earth and *only* the spirits of the desert, bedraggled creatures, knew the folly of human beings and the folly of their gods.

Spring had come and all the girls fortunate enough had matches made for them. When the harvest was over, and at the harvest festival, the fathers of girls with matches ceased to be summer shadows and rose up from the marriage ceremony, men.

But the unfortunate girls. Those with no matches. They faced yet another unmarried summer. And they faced it very much as the land faces this season; the land itself like a gigantic desert-beached fish, gutted and salted and stretched out in the sun to flake into dust; its scales the color of deep wine. They faced this season of the unmarried, very much as their fathers faced this season of yet another shame: summer shadows to their daughters. And the daughters: summer shadows to themselves. Unless, of course, some stray luck befell them. Or they were exorcised of their evil spirits.

"Little Husband," Saraswattee asked as she crouched down more tightly in their forbidden hiding place in the stone cleft between the granite breasts of Durga Kali. She fixed her eyes on the sacred volcanic crater and studied the bloodstains on the

3

cobblestones of the courtyard before the temple. "Little Husband, do *I* have an evil spirit?"

Gopi made no reply, he dark-skinned boy, darker yet in spirit—no no, not evil, not even mysterious, just withdrawn; elusive: he on a fair day a dark shadow on the far and purple horizon.

Gopi knew the legend well.

But not Saraswattee, curious child, stubborn girl, she did not know the legend. Not all of it—anyway.

But she was to know.

The girl fought to keep her eyes away from the one-footed monster who whipped her sister and she shifted her gaze from the bloodstains and studied the vapors. The vapors, legend said, were the breath—and the wrath—of Durga Kali, vengeful goddess, bloodvexed and bloodlusting slayer of evil; and of evil men.

Of this Saraswattee knew not yet. But she was to know—as she, Saraswattee, curious child, stubborn girl, was to come face to face with the son of the demon Mahisha, the very same way, ages and ages before her, Durga Kali had come face to face with Mahisha himself, he who enjoyed a boon from the gods that no mortal or demon nor even an immortal could slay him; only a woman could slay him: and he knowing delightfully well there exist nowhere in creation a woman who could slay a man—let alone a demon!

Of all this Saraswattee had no knowledge; knew not then, as she watched her sister struggle to stay on her feet, the demon son of the demon Mahisha was making his evil way through the desert to the shrine to confront her face to face.

Of this too Gopi had no knowledge. Nor did Durga Kali herself.

"Gopi," Saraswattee asked, "does Chinta have an evil spirit—does my sister have an evil spirit? How much longer is your father going to whip Chinta? How much longer can my sister stay on her feet?" Saraswattee moved her gaze over the five other girls sprawled in sandcaked tangled heaps on the blood-wet temple courtyard. "Are they dead? See what your father has done to Phooloo and Doolwah and Amakutty? And to Roopa and Sirju? Your father has whipped them to death. See what your father has done to Chinta? He has beaten her so much now she has shrivelled up like an old beggarwoman. Little Husband, does my sister have an evil spirit?"

Still Gopi offered no reply but kept his eyes fixed outside the volcanic crater and past the slums and shanties and the palatial ruins of legend-honored times gone by to the vast desert beyond. Saraswattee looked at the distant boy next to her. "Gopi! Why don't you answer me? For three days now you have not answered a question I have asked! Three days now your father has been whipping Chinta! Chinta will die! *Does my sister have an evil spirit?*"

Gopi turned and looked into Saraswattee's eyes and the girl beheld for the first time in those three days of the exorcism how far indeed into the desert of himself Gopi had withdrawn from her. This knowledge pained her. Because he had abandoned her just when she desired most to be one with him. She wanted to be one with him then because she had a pledge to ask of him. By this the third day of the whipping she had worried enough as to her fate, and her fear had driven her to chance her future in her own hands. Gopi sensed her urgency and instantly Saraswattee beheld herself mirrored tenfold times in the eyes of the boy and she could feel the reflections of his face echo through the prisms of her eyes and her fear eased and she grabbed his hands in hers and he asked: "What is it, Little Mother?"

Then, just as the girl was about to ask of Gopi his promise, the whip echoed on Chintamani's body and rebounded off the bouldered walls of the temple crater and pierced through the tiny pores of the girl Saraswattee and she knew a rage greater than her fear and she jumped up in full and defiant view in her forbidden sanctuary and before Gopi could pull her down she spun around and confronted the bloodvexed and bloodlusting slayer of evil; and her tiny black eyes mirrored the anger coiled up in her heart. Thus, with such angry eyes, did Saraswattee behold the goddess Durga Kali, she of the terrible visage; she of the terror-inspiring countenance: she the unquenchable thirster and insatiable ravisher of the lust of evil men.

Durga Kali. There she towered. From out the kilned earth of the volcanic crater. Fleshed of cast iron and breasted of granite. She loomed to the dizzy height of twenty mortal warrior men; her hair of bronze serpents wrestled and knotted about her angered head in bouldered chaos. She wore a necklace of skulls, and a sea of serpents lashed out of every pore of her body. In her cauldron eyes of red coals her carnivorous blood boiled. Her tongue she regurgitated in clotted blood and it stretched down to her granite breasts greater in length than two skinned mortals. With her tusked mouth hymen-ruptured, Durga Kali towered up into the desert sky with her mighty legs apart, and in the mortal pain of a woman in naked labor she pushed out of her womb the ancient and most sacred temple of Shiva. Thus, Durga Kali loomed up into the abode of the gods: temple-crotched. And with its tail ingrown in her navel, its massive body coiled around her waist and between the cheeks of her bottom; its head plunging out of her pubis ancient with muck and moss: her cobra phallus slithered forward erect. Yet she wasn't ready. Stood, impotent. And caught in the final shudder of mortal death.

Such a time it was then, as it is now, the first summer of the year, when gods desired death and knew not of their own destinies; when demons enjoyed rebirth and stalked the earth in vengeance: and when only the spirits of the desert, bedraggled creatures, knew the suffering and the pain of mortal children.

But then the tiny black eyes of Saraswattee became as venomed as the tiny black eyes of the cobra lingam and in that instant Kali looked upon Kali: Kali looked upon Kali with vengeance in her heart. And had not the cauldron eyes of the goddess been clotted up by the black void of the death she so desired, she might have seen with what hostile countenance her daughter Saraswattee looked up at her. Then Durga Kali would have indeed wished she had died and departed the mortal abode of men long long ago because she would have been shocked to see to what fate she had abandoned her children. But Durga Kali did not behold the black venomed eyes of Saraswattee, and the girl turned her back on the goddess and stared down at the temple courtyard from where the vapors rose and clouded up the sky and she whispered: "Don't fall, Chinta, don't fall, sister."

Gopi heard the urgency in the girl's voice. He withdrew his eyes from the far-flung desert and from the ancient sandclogged ruins and he stared down inside the volcanic crater. He fixed his gaze on Chintamani before the bouldered-veined temple of Shiva; erupted out, the legend said, of the womb of Durga Kali the moment before her immortal body of flesh and blood became transformed into an immense body of cast iron and granite boulders with serpents for hair and serpents for veins—with a mighty cobra lingam to slay evil and evil men.

Thus said the legend; and this Gopi knew.

As he also knew why Saraswattee did not want her sister to fall unconscious or dead to the temple courtyard. The way the other five girls had succumbed. Saraswattee did not want Chintamani to fall victim to the vile echoes of the whip because she knew if Chintamani fell, she would be beaten to be exorcised of her evil spirit. And Saraswattee was already long past the age when she should have found a husband. It was then, for the first time since the exorcism began, Gopi fixed his dense and desert eyes on his father.

But not Saraswattee. She fought off the evil snare of the monster who whipped her sister. Of all, he alone terrified her and tormented her sleep. As he terrified and tormented the nightmares of all the girls in the village. And so she shifted her eyes from Chintamani to Roopa and Sirju and Phooloo. She pulled her gaze from the villagefolk to the hordes of hated pilgrims to the hated Pundit Ayer—punditji, punditji, when will a match be made for my daughter Chintamani, what evil omen darkens my daughter's stars? chee, chee, chee, such an old girl, so close to her monthlies and not married yet, a shame and a disgrace on her father's head, she has an evil spirit, she must be whipped to be exorcised of her evil spirit, such a shame, such a disgrace, so close to her monthlies and not married yet, chee, chee, chee—but she couldn't stand the sight of the painted bony face of the painted bony pundit and she let her eyes roam over the landscape of the massive crater. She studied the black basalt walls. The solidified and contorted laval tongues and lobes of magma. The rocks and boulders and debris and mudflows. Raw and red. Black and brown and yellow and crimson. The floor of the crater padded thick and soft with sand. White streaked with yellow plaited with crimson and interwoven with vermillion. The floor embroidered with a quiltwork of multicolored pebble pathways, as if painstakingly and meticulously handcrafted—and yet, legend said, unmade by mortal hands.

And the precious stones. A vast and immense treasure cave strewn and littered with precious stones. Hunks of gold. Chunks of quartz. Ridges of topaz. Shards of agate. Pearls and sapphires and emeralds. Prisms of diamonds and fires of opal and flames of ruby. As if the gods and goddesses of madness and pleasure had held a harvest festival and danced so wildly their ornamentations flew off their bodies and scattered all over the earth. And yet the gems and the jewels belonged to only one goddess—Durga Kali: her necklace shattered by the god Shiva on this sacred shrine.

Once again Saraswattee glared at the goddess but she immediately paled and became purged of her anger. She asked: "Gopi, you notice a change about Durga?" The girl didn't wait for an answer. "Her face? Is her body hotter than usual? She is sweating so much!" Saraswattee's anger returned and she rebuked Kali: "Well at least you had time to play and get your necklace broken. You didn't have to worry about evil spirits!" With that said Saraswattee turned and suddenly found herself enveloped by great clouds of vapors and she quickly, instinctively, covered her mouth with her hands so as not to cough. The desert blew up mighty breaths of wind and the wind swooped down into the temple courtyard and sucked up huge puffs of vapors and spiralled the white clouds high above Durga Kali. Saraswattee stifled her coughs and squinted. The vapors were hot and itched her eyes. She inhaled the sulphur and fanned away the gushes of mists. The storm, so sudden. For a moment Saraswattee thought she might have angered Kali. But the wind died down and the desert recalled its spirits of sand. In the crater the great swirls of vapors began to reverse their upward spirals as if inhaled back in by the hot sulphur springs. When her vision cleared, and with her mouth swamped by the taste of sulphur, Saraswattee shifted her eyes from the scattered precious gems and she studied the source of the vapors. Among the gems and the jewels of the broken necklace, and scattered like cooking cauldrons on outdoor firesides, boiled nine hot sulphur springs.

The springs, legend said, were the sacred orifices of Durga Kali.

Of this, too, Saraswattee, curious child, stubborn girl, knew not yet. But of something else she alone had knowledge. And this was of a world—a universe: where the desert sun in the dusty sky shot its rays of light through the prisms of the pearls and the rubies and the emeralds and the diamonds of the broken necklace of Durga Mata and the diamonds and the emeralds and the sapphires caught the myriad rays of the desert sun and flung the reflections through the clouds of white vapors in a bazaar of rainbows. This was the universe Saraswattee now beheld. Here she would live. With Gopi. Here she would forget that other world. The world of the people. Down in the bloodstained courtyard. Before the sacred temple of Shiva. Such different worlds. Her world. And the world of people and pilgrims and pundits. Never to come together. To collide— but, suddenly, that monstrous foot hopped, kicked up sand, and the sand exploded as in her tiny black eyes.

Saraswattee jumped but there was no escape and she saw them, those hated feet: the dead ugly one; and the ugly living one. She no longer had the power to avert her eyes and she stood victim to those feet. Try as she could to shift her gaze to the wooden foot she was unable to take her eyes off the living one. Huge. So huge the girl felt that foot could squash her. And lumpy. Like a crocodile's back. She was terrified that the blobs of toes would break off. Jump at her. Her eyes moved up the leg to the monstrous torso. A hideous sheepskin garment wrapped the body. The belly was another great blob and the shoulders were packed high. The sheepskin was raw, uncured, with bloodstains in the seams. The man, Saraswattee thought, had grabbed five sheep, slit open their throats, peeled back their fleeces, stitched them together with his teeth, and stuffed the whole thing over him, sheep guts and all. She shifted her gaze to the face of Saheb Kahar. Lumps of cheeks stuck on to blob of mouth stuck on to bulges of dead sheep's eyes. His head was wrapped in a bloody sheepskin turban, strapped around the chin and throat as if to tie all the lumps together. Between the nose and upper lip grew a moustache as big as two gerbils, gutted, and stuck to the upper lip. Saraswattee glanced at the knotted leather whip in the ugly hands and back to the face again. She looked at the lumps of eyes, and her heart beat dhoom dhoom dhoom. In olden times, legend said, the goddess gulped down the blood of men and the flesh of one human delighted and pacified her for one thousand years and the blood of three mortal men satiated her lust and sedated her delirium for one hundred thousand years. This Saraswattee knew, as she knew an evil man when she saw one, only she was confused, didn't know anymore what were olden times, these times before the dissolution of creation, or times not yet come, times to come after the dissolution of creation. She, Saraswattee, curious child, stubborn girl, confused by time and legend. And something other. The beating of her heart. *The beating of the heart under her feet.* Then, in her heart of six cold winters, Saraswattee knew the terror of a scarecrow to little birds.

"Little Husband," she whispered, "your father is an evil man." Gopi returned his gaze past the shanties and the palatial ruins to the canyons and the gorges of the desert. "Gopi," Saraswattee continued, "you are good. But your father is evil. If Kali wasn't asleep she would slay your evil father. But Kali sleeps. And that evil man lives. Who will kill him? Will you kill him?"

The question did not surprise Gopi. He turned his head and looked into the black eyes of the girl. Around her small drooped mouth, her small oval face drooped. She was sad but serious. And he was surprised to find in those tiny black eyes of the girl before him there wavered no tears. No tears. Only fear. "Will you kill your father?" Saraswattee asked. Gopi understood her fear and he said: "Little Mother, you must not think such things. You must not talk that way. Yes. I know. My father is an evil man. Kali will slay him."

"Kali sleeps!"

"Then I will slay him."

Saraswattee glanced at the courtyard to see Gopi's father bring his whip down upon Chintamani and Chintamani fell to her knees and Saraswattee got to her feet again in full view of all and she whispered: "Don't fall, Chinta, don't fall, sister!"

But even if she had screamed her sister couldn't have heard. By now Chintamani stood almost blinded and could not see the girls lumped around her on the unburnt brick of the temple courtyard. It seemed such a long time ago since the last one had fallen. Such a long time ago since she heard the whip echo. Maybe they had stopped beating her. As she had stopped feeling pain. Even the blinking of her eyes she did not feel. All she knew of was a certain swollenness. Not of her body. But of the space inside her body. The space inside her head. Many a time, during forbidden sideglances on her daily pilgrimages to the temple where she would go to perform her duties and sometimes to ask a shy blessing, she would pause in her steps, stolen faltering, to observe the wind in currents sweep up the sand the color of tumeric and saffron into dust storms no bigger than a conch shell. These sandstorms she would let thrill her eyes as they tempted her feet, and she would stare down with fascination into the miniature whirlwinds. Whirlwinds within the universe of an atom. There she thought herself now. In the dust storm of an atom. Eye of dust. Blurred and twisted and warped. So she couldn't distinguish any more the villagefolk from the pilgrims. Nor Pundit Ayer from the evil Kahar Saheb. Could not see the blood on the ground or the girls sprawled around her, dying; or dead. In there too, the warped nucleus of an atom, she knew the certain swollenness. In there she knew the puffing up of the space within her, though she did not feel her swollen feet and toes, her swollen knees and elbows, her swollen hands and fingers. In there the blunt lashes had long deadened their echoes. The desert earth parched dry the blisters on her feet. Dust clothed her skin, and her torn cotton dress clung to her torn flesh in caked stains of sweat and blood. Sand, kicked up by the hated feet of Gopi's father—those horrible feet jumping around her, one of flesh and blood, the other of wood, two feet so hateful of each other that in her mind they had come to belong to monsters, both one-footed, hideous, loathsome, sometimes they circled her in opposite directions, terrified her even more, split her mind apart till she had forced herself to shut them out as she had long ago shut out the echoes of the lashes—the hot sand kicked up by those hated feet and blown on her by the wind had crusted over her wounds. Brine from her pores oozed around the edges of the sandscabs, thus she felt no pain—not even from her heart. Her long hair stuck to her body like black dried veins but she did not taste the hair matted thick with sand and oil, did not feel the weight of her cracked lips. Thus she crouched disjointedly forward her hands clutched together at her chest. Indeed a faint and ancient beggarwoman. You would not tell she was only thirteen years old. Two days ago. When they brought her and the other girls to the temple courtyard to be exorcised of their evil spirits.

Thus, Chintamani could neither hear nor see her sister. Of only one thing was she conscious. Wrath. A dry wrath. Because in her mouth her tongue flaked like the parched slime left by a snail in the slow wake of its slow journeyings through the desert. Wrath. Only wrath had sustained her to this the third day of the exorcism. And as pain and memory had been whipped out of her, so too instinct. She couldn't even *feel* where the goddess rose. Yet, with her body baked as in a potter's kiln, her eyes glazed like desert stones, her vision soldered together with dust and sand by the haze and the heat, Chintamani faced Kali. And as she had done so many times during the lingering two days past and two nights, she begged for the wrath of the benevolent one to erupt. Only now she prayed: O Durga Mata, no more, slay me then, let me die now, if you will not slay evil men.

Over and over Chintamani uttered that prayer in her shrivelled heart: O Durga Mata, benevolent mother, protector of the innocent, O Kali Mata, destroyer of evil, slay me then, your daughter, if you will not slay evil men!

And over the three days past, the tiny black venomed eyes of the serpent coiled up in the shell of the mighty cobra lingam of Kali stared at the girl as through blurred lenses. The echoes disturbed the death sleep of the serpent and the persistent pulses of the weak prayers caused the brain of the cobra to ache because the serpent had grown old and feeble and he awoke and found himself irked. He, the ancient and venerable sage Naga, awoke to find himself grumpy. He, the gentle and generous seer Naga, who always conducted himself with the equanimity of a vacuum, awoke to find himself in a sour mood. He, the patient and soft-hearted guru Naga, awoke to find his mouth clogged with bitter venom—the opium of evil men. And he suddenly remembered how in ancient times and times not thus far ancient, Kali would bid him go spit his bile between the eyes of such men as he now beheld before his drugged gaze in the temple courtyard. She, Kali Durga, would bid him go among men; because he—who prided himself no less than the serpent of serpents!—loved nothing more than to come face to face with an evil man and indulge in a brief but dignified conversation.

But now he had a headache. With his mouth full of bitter bile. And irked. Not at Chintamani. Not by her prayers. The mighty cobra Naga found himself angry at she who possessed him coiled around her waist and between the cheeks of her bottom and erect out of her pubis. Her desire for mortal death was to be honored and never never violated. This was why over the ages past instead of polite conversations with evil men he had been forced to swallow his own venom and inject the poison into the veins of

Durga Kali so that she might die and depart the mortal abode of mortal men.

Now the pitiful prayers of a daughter of Kali made him slither out of sleep into a headache and he found himself grumpy. Thus he had been forced to listen to the pleas of Chintamani; thus he had been forced to listen to the silence of Gopi: thus he had been forced to listen to the heart of Saraswattee. And he found himself in his old age given to grumpiness and moodiness. And reflection. What age did he awake in, when children were no longer holy and honored and were abandoned to defend themselves? What age, indeed, was this? Was Kali, after all, right to desire death and to depart the abode of mortals? And this his last mouthful of bitter bile. His last potion of venom. His very last opportunity to have a chat with that monstrous one-footed evil creature! Should he swallow his own poison and force it through his body like acid and inject it with his tail into the belly of Durga? Or should he defy Kali and risk her final wrath on his own head? Naga, irked by his headache, made bitter by the surfeit of his own venom, tightened his throat, shook himself fully awake, fixed his gaze on the one-footed Kahar; and he beheld the man filtered through the black lenses of his tiny lidless eyes.

Thus, Naga, the cobra lingam of Durga Kali, beheld the evil creature with a twisted smile on his face about to bring down his whip on the girl Chintamani—she who knew the legend well. And Saraswattee, curious child, stubborn girl, forgot where she hid. Barely waist-high-to-a-grown-man tall. Skinny and flat like split bamboo. Dressed in a brilliant red satin blouse and a shiny green ankle-long straw skirt. In open and resplendent view. Her eyes riveted on Chintamani. Her thin legs rigid so that her sister might fall no lower than her knees.

And Gopi. He dark boy; desert boy. Withdrawn and elusive. He too forgot where he and Saraswattee stood and what sacrilege they committed. He got to his feet in full and open view of the hordes of people in the temple crater. But his eyes were not on them. His gaze shot over Kali's right breast. To the northwest. Where a red desert storm spiralled up into the sky. But Gopi knew that was no desert storm. Because Gopi knew all desert storms. Dust storms. Sandstorms. Locust storms. Mirage storms. No. That was no desert storm. Something other than the desert and the desert wind stirred up that whirlrush of sand. Something commanded the desert and the spirits of the desert to brew up that blur of blood-red dust and blast it towards the shrine. For such a time it is now, as it was then, the first summer of the year, when demons made pilgrimages to holy shrines; when mortal men mistook demons for gods: and when it was absolutely forbidden for the human hands of a woman or a girl-child to touch the sacred body of Durga Kali, vengeful goddess, bloodvexed and bloodlusting slayer of evil men—and of demons.

Absorbed in the approach of the demon son of the demon Mahisha—Mahisha himself, in olden times, once known as Durga, the one and the same demon who delighted in a boon from the foolish gods that only a woman could slay him—absorbed in the approach of this pilgrim, Gopi forgot what sacrilege he and the girl next to him committed and to what death he exposed himself, and she; Saraswattee, curious child, stubborn girl.

TWO

SO, WHILE Naga kept Kahar filtered in the
opium of his tiny jet eyes, Gopi and Saraswattee stood to their full
height in the stone cleft between the granite breasts of Durga Kali.
Both oblivious of their sacrilege. They might have been trudging
through the plains, or sitting on a boulder, learning the secrets of
the desert by starlight—Chintamani never saw the desert by
starlight because she dared not step out of the house at nights but
only in the daylight and then only to go to the temple and
sometimes to allow dust storms to bewitch her—but Saraswattee,
she, inquisitive and at times inquisitorial, watchful but always
from afar, in corners, on the edges, in the distance, in shadows,
only her dark eyes more curious than she as she slipped about, not
playfully, even Saraswattee had not time for play, fear yes, but not
play, her silent black eyes watching watching watching, looking
here, looking there, asking asking asking but saying nothing to
anyone except to Gopi because no one but Gopi looked into those
eyes—no, Chintamani never saw the desert by starlight, but
Saraswattee saw the desert in all light as she followed Gopi
around, day and night she trudged around with him, sometimes
behind him, sometimes abreast of him, he, Gopi, older in unspoken
wisdom—older in his limbs, feet old for a boy his age and hands
old too but he older in his stern face carved with swift sharp lines,
sharp in the cheekbones, firm about his mouth, his face though
thus far alien to wrinkles already immune to smiles, Gopi, older in
all these things by trice his years numberable on the fingers of two
mortal hands added to four more mortal fingers, his years

15

unwritten, left to the opium-clogged memory of the village pundit to record—punditji, punditji, by the new moon, how old is my daughter Saraswattee? chee chee chee, too many years past the age when girls should be married, so close to her monthlies and not married yet, such a shame and disgrace to the father, chee chee chee—but Gopi older most of all in his black chiselled eyes, and he more silent than the desert, more distant, more withdrawn, unspeaking to all other but to Saraswattee, who, as Gopi sat on a rock, would take his face in her small hands, look into his eyes, and ask: *"Little Husband, do all little girls have evil spirits?"*

As many times she asked so many times Gopi never answered her question. Because he didn't know what she asked. He felt she asked more. Asked about the land. The desert. The grain fields and the plum orchards. All those things for which he had no answers, and he would look into the girl's eyes but say nothing. And she for the moment would forego her struggle and let it seep into his and become theirs and she would resume the desert silence and edge closer to the boy and lean against him she in weight not more than a handsack of millet and they would sit echolessly in the night the two a blur of shadows, neither casting a glance up to the stars Chintamani never saw.

And if the punditji had cast his eyes there on the bosom of Kali what spleen would he have vented on Saraswattee! She who had forgotten she was not supposed to be there. Was forbidden to as much as touch the body of the relentless pursuer of evil men—let alone climb all over her. If a boy-child should touch that sacred body, Gopi himself, ah Gopi, it was none other than Gopi who taught Saraswattee to climb up there, she tagging around behind him the rag-doll shadow she was and Gopi showing her which serpent to grab hold of, where to slip her foot, and she not afraid one bit to fall or of the great height or of the numerous serpents on Durga's body and Gopi knowing full well if they caught him they would strip him naked, shave his head and trim his nails, bathe him in milk, stain his body with ashes, intone mantras over him, and plunge a knife into his heart—all in front of the slayer of evil so that she might be appeased, might not spit her wrath on them. But a girl-child! What would they do to a girl-child caught in desecration of the sacred body of their goddess? Who knows? Who can tell? In all the genealogy of the village, graveyard after graveyard after graveyard, from the day of its founding to this very day, no girl-child had ever touched with her mortal hands that forbidden body—men did and came to their fate, boy-children did and suffered a knife in their bosoms, but a girl-child!—but such a time it was then, as it is now, the age before the dissolution, when men no longer looked to their gods and goddesses; when mortals looked not to the forward of them: but when humans just looked upon the earth as if with eyes on their behinds.

Gopi watched the dusty approach of the demon. Then in a sudden moment his breathing became puzzled, reversed; inhalation confused with exhalation. For such a time it was also. A time when humankind inhaled and exhaled counterclockwise to the inhalation and exhalation of the gods. Kali Durga too suffered this dizzy puzzle of respiration. But then, she, slayer of evil and of evil men, stood netted in mortal death.

But as it was instantaneous so too was it momentary and Gopi felt the puzzlement of his breathing vanish and he saw the ruins outside the gush of the volcanic crater. So many layers of ruins. As if a nest of snakes had taken a distaste to the place and crawled out of their skins and slithered off through the canyons and the caverns of the vast desert. Stone walls and bouldered embankments. Granite columns and marbled colonnades. Palatial swings and palatial gates. Marble avenues and marble promenades. Ruined palaces upon ruined kingdoms inside ruined civilizations—such an ancient wreck of legends lay about the land. And on top of the ruins—next to pillars and under collapsed archways and inside the cracked halls of cracked palaces—slums and shanties. And the ruins of slums and shanties. Black jute tents. Heaps of sticks and wood. Ragged mats on the tattered earth. In these the pilgrims encamped. Squatted. Such a land of ruins. And of pilgrims. Maybe there came another pilgrim, thought Gopi, and glanced at the sandstorm as it whirled towards the shrine. The boy returned his gaze to the ruins and the shanties. In the harsh sunlight they all lay abandoned. Deserted. Devoid of mortal shape and mortal form. Yet the wrecks and the slums exuded such infestation of human life. Such an overwhelming pervasiveness of mortality inhabited the land. A leper colony—but devoid of lepers: infested with just leprousness. And something more demonic: *a premonition of mortal beings undead.*

And that other phenomenon the boy had begun to observe recently. That phenomenon of substantial things casting no shadows on the land. The huts and the hovels. The slums and the shanties. The broken walls and the ruptured avenues. The collapsed pillars and dislocated columns. The hazy sandclogged wreck of the legend-honored palaces—all bequeathed no shadows to the land. Substantial things casting no shadows. Is such a phenomenon possible? Maybe. Ghosts offer neither shadows nor greetings.

Gopi looked at the goats and the sheep among the boulders and pillars. Untended, the animals straggled about and foraged for any meager midday shadow available. But there lurked none. The ber trees had already absorbed their shadows. So too the kumat. The animals crept about, tucked themselves into whatever shade offered by the rocks and the archways, now too, noiselessly and imperceptively, sucking up their own shadows. Gopi glanced at the dust storm and decided it was created by something mechanical. A jeep. A landrover. And he heard the faint strain of the vehicle and he could tell that whoever drove through the desert like that did not know how to drive through the sands of the desert.

That decided, Gopi realized he and Saraswattee stood in full view but even then he didn't panic and pull Saraswattee down. The boy looked at his father. Chintamani still crouched on her knees, her head bent, her hands clutched before her chest. His father hopped around the girl, cracked his whip. Dust scattered. Gopi glanced at Saraswattee. The girl searched among the throngs of people packed in the volcanic crater. "Who are you looking for?" Gopi asked. Now it was Saraswattee's time for silence and she did not answer. "Who are you looking for, Little Mother?" Instead of a direct answer the girl just spoke her thoughts. "Look at that," she said, "look at all those strangers. I can't even tell who is from our village and who is not! Pilgrims. Hundreds. Thousands. So many pilgrims! Where do they come from? Where do they return to? What do they get here?"

"Another one is coming."

"Where?"

Gopi pointed to the sandstorm in the desert. Saraswattee shaded her eyes, tiptoed, squinted. Gopi knew how much the hordes of pilgrims irritated her. Such disruption they caused—coming and going. As if life was just a sandy traffic of holy men and holy women who made pilgrimages to holy places to seek more holiness and when they left the holy places they left the ruins of their slums and shanties and the ruins of the remains of their food and the ruins of their spit and the ruins of their defecation littered over the ancient wrecks.

Saraswattee dismissed the approach of yet another pilgrim and resumed her search among the people in the temple courtyard. Because of the people she beheld the crater to be a mammoth gash in the belly of the earth with the top half of the earth lopped off, scooped out, crushed, and scattered over the plateau and the plains in a whirlwind of debris. People people people. Pilgrims pilgrims pilgrims. Pundits pundits pundits—brahmins! The brahmins of her village. And the hordes of brahmin pilgrims who out-numbered the pilgrims of other castes. High-caste brahmins. Higher-caste brahmins. Highest-caste brahmins. Low-caste priests, lower-caste priests, lowest-caste priests. Big-headed brahmins, pin-headed brahmins. Pot-bellied ones, thimble-bellied ones, no-bellied ones. Brahmins who were permitted to face east but not west; brahmins for whom it was a sin to walk forwards but a blessing to walk backwards. Brahmins for whom it was pure to defecate but impure to clean themselves; brahmins for whom it was just simply unholy to defecate. Saraswattee didn't like brahmins. She suspected them of everything.

But her eyes raced through the hordes of pilgrims clustered in groups by caste and subcaste and sub-subcaste. She sought out her villagefolk. Her eyes fell on the huddle of outcast menfolk of her village. She studied the faces as she sought to find one. But her father was not there among the untouchables of her village. In desperation Saraswattee glanced over the womenfolk. The brahmin women clustered apart. Smug. Scornful of the temple prostitutes opposite them. Scornful of the lower-caste womenfolk. All— old faceless women, young faceless girls, naked faceless children— all, on the bare earth where they had thrown themselves, fallen, dropped. Where they wept and mourned and grieved. Beat their hollow chests and breasts of skin as they poured dust and dirt over their heads and their bodies. In shame, in disgrace. In atonement, in self-chastisement, in self-scorn; for theirs was the greatest sin of all, not being born women but being born low-caste women: outcast

women: excrement. But her mother was not there among the untouchable womenfolk. Nor her sister, Madhuban.

"Where is my father?" Saraswattee asked, and now Gopi
searched among the people. "Why is my mother not among the
womenfolk? And Madhuban, where is Madhuban?"

Saraswattee bent her head, peered directly down below her.
Between Durga Kali's outstretched legs, rough-hewned and
bouldered, its roof stacked with rocks and built up to a vertebral
tumble, the temple of Shiva rose. Behind the temple and behind the
goddess, the western end of the crater was littered with the huts
and tents of the temple prostitutes. But there was no one behind
the temple. Saraswattee was about to glance south to the village
when the mighty cobra lingam caught her eyes. The body of the
serpent was jewelled. Made of scales of decorated glass. It
glistened in the sunlight and appeared textured like the plumes of a
peacock. Deep inside the dark glass body coiled a red vein. Like a
vein of blood. Saraswattee blinked. The vein of blood looked alive.
Seemed to slither forward and then slide back. Again and again the
girl blinked. Quickly she glanced up at the face of Durga Kali; and
Naga, serpent of serpents, seized the opportunity to regain the
composure of a vacuum. Saraswattee thought again something
about Kali had changed. Still, she wasn't sure. Quickly she glanced
back down but this time Naga kept still, his jet eyes fixed on
Kahar—lidlessly. But out of the top of his eyes he could see
Saraswattee. He saw her doubt, beheld her confusion. Then
Saraswattee herself decided it was more urgent to find out where
her father and mother were than to figure out if the serpent was
alive or not. Naga kept his equanimity; and his intent. Kahar
circled Chintamani but made no attempt to strike her. He just
cracked his whip and grinned.

On the ground before the temple the outcast women wailed and
beat their breasts and their heads and poured dirt and dust over
themselves. As she knelt Chintamani repeated her prayer. And
again this caused Naga, the patient aged sage, to lose his
composure and to become more and more irritated with Durga
Kali. She the ravisher. She who was once wildly, procreatively,
virile. And bloodlusting. Now impotent. As her flaccid will. Victim
of mortals. Victim of the lust of evil men. So many sewers of the
evil of mortals she had had to suck up. From the day of creation to

this day. So many sewers of the lust of humans she would have had to suck up. From this day to the very end, the dissolution of creation. If she lived on. Kali didn't want to live on in a body of granite and cast iron. No more, no more! Tired. Sick. Surfeited of mankind. Of humanity. Once upon a time and a long long time ago, she loved this place. Dear to her heart. Sacred to her being. But no more. No longer. No more were men the beloved of her heart. Her heart! If only her children knew. She no longer had a heart. Once it was two-faced and twin-bodied. One face, the right, bulged ripe with milk, the succor of mortals. The other. The left. Weighed clogged with black blood. The lust of evil men. But now, within her cast-iron chest, gorged on a surfeit of evil, her two-faced heart had turned into an ogre. And had turned on her. In bilious rebellion. In gluttonous revenge. Within her own being an ogre had been created. A monster of evil. And she stood—towered up into the abode of the gods, not just a once virile goddess, but alone; and dying. Trapped in a body of granite and cast iron by her own folly.

Thus, Kali had become. And faintly she heard her daughter's pleas—this the ancient cobra Naga did not know!—in her vast head they echoed. In her immense rotting brain. Through the collapsing cavernous cells. Where a tangle of serpents sloshed, bled white of their venom. Chintamani's voice echoed but Durga fought off those pleas. Once she bore the cries of her children. She had had to bear them for all eternity, and an infinitesimal moment more. But no longer. Soon it would be over. The ogre within her chest had become all-powerful. She, an immortal, had succumbed to mortal choice. She who once desired blood now desired oblivion. To depart from the wicked and vile abode of men. Once she had been angry with the Goddess Saraswati for her abandonment of the abode of mortals. But now she understood why Saraswati departed. And even though the knowledge pained her soul, Durga struggled to deny the cries of her daughter, as Chintamani herself had exorcised her own mortal senses so she wouldn't suffer pain.

Now too, as she relinquished the fight with the monster that once beat as her heart, Kali began to abandon the struggle to retain, to regain, her memory. What was the use of it, the past? Let her memory precede her body into oblivion. What good anymore to ask, how long ago was it she confronted the demon? One celestial day, one kalpa? Two kalpas? Yet, up to that age such a fierce battle had she fought to regain her memory. As if to regain her memory was to recapture her past. As if to regain her past was to recapture her former formidable self—yes yes, to come face to face with *the demon Durga* once more, to take his identity, to take his powers, to take his name: become again Durga Kali! Vengeful goddess! And destroy evil men for all eternity and for an eternal infinitesimal infinite moment more!

What Kali didn't know—so much her senses, her mind, her will, had been consumed by the two-faced ogre in her bosom—what she didn't know was there existed no need for her to ravish her genealogy, no need to ravish the genealogy of humankind, to confront the demon. The demon was within one stride of her legs. On his way. *To her.* At that moment. Through the desert. In the form of his son, Mahisha—like father, like son: same name. But then, truly, Kali didn't know the demon had a son. Of this, the legend did not tell. But she was to know.

And then what? Would she strive to undo her wish for death? Would she be able to triumph over her desire? Who knows? Who can tell? If it is futile to predict the ways of mortals, why attempt to predict the follies of gods? Kali wished for death. And death was on its way. Already it had inflamed her head with an ague. Already it had atrophied her limbs. Already it had impregnated her womb with nausea. Thus she stood: agued, dizzy, nauseous. And she strained her eyes to look down on the land, to look down on the temple courtyard; to focus her senile vision on her daughter Chintamani. Mother and daughter. To whom death had become a thing to beseech.

But the serpent Naga, striving to maintain a cool head, looked at Chintamani. The vapors swirled up, did not cloud his view. After a while, he rolled his eyes upwards and looked at Gopi and Saraswattee where they stood in the stone cleft between the granite breasts. As the serpent of serpents he could see all and he beheld the cauldron eyes of Kali blinded by clots of blood. His heart ached for his beloved goddess and he wished then to come into mortal combat with the ogre in her chest. Suddenly, as when a conquering demon hammers the golden gates of a besieged palace with a mighty battering ram, the two-faced ogre within Kali's chest struck out: dhoom! dhoom! dhoom! Saraswattee jumped. Quickly she glanced up at the goddess. Sweat oozed out of every pore in the massive head. The blood in the cauldron eyes boiled alive, seemed to ferment sourly. A dense breath of steam issued out of the ochre cave of the ruptured mouth. Saraswattee squinted and looked closely at the regurgitated tongue. Yes, something about it had changed! But what? She glanced over the granite breasts and the cast-iron torso. Again something was different—the sweat, so much of it. And the heat radiated by the body. Not like the heat of the sun. But like the heat radiated from a fevered mortal body. So too the beats of the heart under her feet. Or was it her heart beating so?

Saraswattee glanced at Gopi. He, his eyes still on his father, seemed to be unaware of anything unusual about the goddess. Maybe indeed it was her heart. Certainly, she sweated. Her red armless satin blouse and green ankle-long straw skirt leaked. So too her dark skin. For a moment more Saraswattee listened, studied the face of Durga Kali. Yes. She was right. Something about Kali had changed. What was happening to Durga Kali? But as Saraswattee reflected, Naga froze. He was not the only member of the body of Durga Kali alive! Within her chest the ogre of her heart had picked up his idle thoughts to do mortal battle and had banged out his acceptance of that challenge. The serpent listened, and cold beads of sweat oozed out his body.

"Gopi!" Saraswattee said. "Something is happening to Durga Mata."

Gopi did not even as much as look at the goddess. He vacantly asked: "What?"

"She is sweating more than I have ever seen her sweat."

"Sweating?" Again Gopi didn't look at Kali Durga.

"Yes. And feel her body. Feel how hot it is?"

"It is a hot day today, Little Mother. No clouds in the sky. And the wind is blowing up a lot of steam."

Saraswattee fixed an angry gaze on the boy. He didn't seem to care. He had gone into one of his empty-headed moods again. And at a time like this! Saraswattee hissed: "It is not that kind of heat!"

"What kind is it?"

"The heat of a human body. Here feel my body. That kind. Here. The kind of your body too. And listen to her heart beat."

"Little Mother—"

"Listen!"

Gopi listened, heard his own heart beat. Saraswattee saw his eyes withdraw into the desert of himself. "Durga Kali is coming awake!" she said. "And she is going to take vengeance on your father and slay him! She is coming alive! She is going to change her body of stone and cast iron into the body of the true Kali! I know it. I can feel it. She is going to turn into flesh and blood and slay your evil father. Then you won't have to kill him. *Kali will slay your evil father!*"

"Yes."

"And you must promise me something."

"What?"

"Promise me you will promise to do as I say."

"I promise." Gopi stared into the girl's eyes and was surprised to find tears. Fear. And tears. Worry about her fate. Frightened about her future. Would they beat her? Did she have an evil spirit? "What is it you want me to promise, Little Mother?"

"Look!" Saraswattee shouted and pointed in the direction of the village. Gopi spun around to see Madhuban burst out of a yard into the pathway to the shrine. As she ran Madhuban shouted: "Sister! Deedi! Sister! Deedi!" Madhuban ran wildly through the cluster of huts and hovels. Her feet kicked up sand. She startled the dogs and the goats. She shouted: "Deedi! Deedi! Sister! Sister!" No sooner had Madhuban run past five stone houses when her mother burst out of their hut and ran after her. Padma ran, fell to a walk, ran a few steps again, fell again to an urgent walk, her weight a hindrance to her anxious feet. Ahead of her, Madhuban did something she would not have done if the pundit was about. From her own outcast quarter of the village she cut straight through the brahmin section. Padma saw her daughter but couldn't stop her. Instead she made her way among the huts of the untouchables. Madhuban's cries echoed throughout the temple courtyard.

"Gopi, what is happening?"

"I don't know."

"Why is Madhuban running as if she has gone mad?"

"Something has happened."

"Come on. Let us go down."

"No. We cannot."

"Why?"

"Don't you see? We will be caught."

"I don't care!"

"They will kill us."

"They are going to kill me anyway!"

"You must not talk like that." Gopi and Saraswattee stared into each other's eyes. The boy wished he could offer her more consolation. Ease her fear. Dry her tears. He could dry her tears—but what about her fate?

"Sister! Sister!"

"Why is Madhuban calling out like that?"

"You stay here. I will go down and find out."

"But they will catch you."

"No. Not if I go alone. You hide here. I will go down Kali's back. No one will see me."

Both Gopi and Saraswattee saw Madhuban race up the stone steps on the south wall of the crater. Padma ran not far behind. Then Saraswattee beheld something that surprised her. Sutnami. Her father. Her father stumbled forward towards the shrine, a bedraggled creature. But Madhuban climbed the crater wall. The crowd in the courtyard began to part. Gopi's father began to laugh. Saraswattee and the boy stared down at Kahar Saheb. He had his whip over his shoulders and it hung like a dead serpent. He had his hands on his waist and he acted as if he not only knew what had happened but knew it would have happened. At first he chuckled. His chest shook. Then he coughed spells of evil laughter. But then, seeing his father at his most evil, Gopi remembered his idle promise to Saraswattee to slay his own father. He had answered her out of the distance of himself. But as his father laughed on, the boy asked himself, what would he do if his father lifted that whip against Saraswattee?

Gopi evaded the question and observed no one looked up at Kali. When he felt it safe he stepped out of the cleft and, taking hold of one skull at a time, he crawled up Durga's chest to her shoulders. He was about to go over when he suddenly hid down.

"What is it?" Saraswattee asked.

Gopi made no reply but continued to squint over Kali's shoulder towards the northwest.

"*What is it?*" Saraswattee whispered in her urgent anger.

"Jeep," Gopi answered.

Saraswattee didn't understand. Neither did Durga Kali. Like Saraswattee, Kali became pensive. Perplexed. Saraswattee thought, Jeep? And Durga wondered what had happened to the ogre within her chest. Gone. It had vanished! Kali was astounded. Confused, baffled. Ever since the dawn of the present yuga, age—the age of Durga Kali herself—the left body of her heart had expanded, grew like a malignant and cancerous tumor gorged on black blood. Such was the growth of this tumor of evil, she herself became poisoned. Her flesh, her blood, her senses, her will—all became infected. For this was the age. The epoch of the triumph of evil over good. The yuga of the triumph of wrong over right. When justice lay on the earth like a shattered vase and evil crawled in the veins of humans. When meanness and cruelty and unkindness encrusted the land like scabs of salt. This was the time when violence erupted even in every family like a rash of volcanoes. This was the era when leaders of nations became dacoits and plundered their own nations and when these nations turned upon their own children. This was the age, at the end of which, like a black void, the dissolution. Thus her heart had become a power of its own. Breathed an existence onto itself. Infested with its own vile life. And plunged into carnivorous destruction of her body, her being, her soul. Eating her blood. Beat by beat. Pulse by pulse. Grew and grew. Into a dark force. A destructive demonic power—like the total counter-gravity of the universe coiled up inside her. Till at last she cried for release. Desired death. Because this evil force twisted within her counter to the natural circulation of her blood; counter to the heavenly rhythms of her soul. So much that if she screamed in pain the universe would shatter instantaneously and echolessly. When, suddenly, it was gone. The evil ogre within her. Vanished. Left in its place its opposite: a void. Kali felt her viscera relax. Felt the pull on her brain slacken. Felt the faint trickle of blood through her veins—she could even hear the trickle of blood as it struggled for its natural course in the natural rhythms of her body. Kali listened. Concentrated. She had to eavesdrop on her very own heart! Inside her, deep within the void it had exhaled around itself, the ogre listened too. As Saraswattee listened. But the heartbeats had disappeared. Or was it *her* heartbeats vanished? She put her hand on her chest. Her

heart pounded. She looked up at Kali. All the sweat had evaporated. No vapors issued from the mouth. The granite breasts and
cast-iron chest were also dry. Brittle. Saraswattee jumped up, grabbed the first skull she could reach, and scrambled after Gopi. Once
more, in her new desperation, she had forgotten where they were.
Gopi looked back, reached out, grabbed the girl and pulled her
against the stone neck. Under the bouldered head they pressed
against each other. Gopi glanced behind him but the breasts of the
goddess shielded them from view. Pressed against Gopi, Saraswattee felt his chest, felt hers, looked up at the head, the neck, the
shoulder. Again she tested her heartbeat, tested Gopi's heartbeat.
Gopi's heart was normal, less frantic than hers. But not a sound
came from Kali. Not the faintest throb or vibration. His eyes on the
desert, Gopi seemed unaware of the stillness of Kali. Saraswattee
clutched him, pressed her chest against his. From the northwest,
beyond the ruins and slums, beyond the gorges and canyons, the red
ghost of dust whirled.
   "Little Husband, a pilgrim?"
   "I do not think so." Gopi reflected. There was a distortion about
the red ghost of dust that bequeathed to it a menace—*a human
menace*.
   "Who then?"
   "I cannot say, Little Mother."
   "Why do you say maybe not a pilgrim?"
   "The jeep. The way he is driving the jeep."
   "Yes. You are right. Evil."
   "Deedi! Sister! Deedi!" echoed Madhuban's cries.
   The engine of the jeep strained against the clouds of sand. Gopi
and Saraswattee listened to the clogged whine. Durga Kali con-
centrated. The ogre within her chest listened. And so too now,
frozen Naga, the ancient and venerable serpent of serpents, poised
his aged ears.
   "Little Husband, don't go down now. Stay with me. Bad things
are happening. Evil is coming to our village."
   "Why do you say so?"
   "I can feel it—Kali feels it too!"
   "Stay and hide. No harm will come to you. I will return soon."
Gopi pushed himself up and swung a leg and straddled Kali's

right shoulder. Just as he was about to go down, Saraswattee scrambled up and flung herself at him and cried: *"Little Husband, what is to become of me?"*

And as lucid as the day upon the land, and as far as he could see, Gopi heard the girl. Now he knew she asked not about the fields and plum orchards and the desert and all the other things for which he had no answer. She asked about herself. She. Saraswattee. Curious child. Stubborn girl. When did she first start trudging after him? Why? What was she to him? What was he to her? Even though they were the children of two brothers, that's how he felt. He was Gopi. She was Saraswattee. Not cousins. Not blood relatives. Not brother and sister. Not even boy and girl. Just Gopi; just Saraswattee: just mirages in the desert.

As they looked at each other Gopi realized a new thing. Consciously, he questioned himself. Never before had he asked of himself or anybody else, questions. He had answers. Or discovered answers for questions he didn't consciously pose. Like the time in the desert he discovered the curvature of the earth. Discovered the earth was round. When he had never asked, is the earth flat like the desert, or is the earth shaped like Durga's orifices? Then Gopi beheld Saraswattee differently. She was no rag-doll shadow. She had tiny fingers, small lips, a round face, never plaited her long black hair. Against his body he felt the heat of her own body. He saw how sharp and clear her eyes shone. He saw her fear. He understood her question. She was not his shadow. Neither was she her own shadow. Indeed, no shadow was she.

Saraswattee, too, stared back at the boy. His ribs and bones as hard and bare as the branches of a stunted kumat tree. He himself as scrawny as the desert. But as resilient. His armless cotton vest frazzled. So too his jute pants. A film of salt covered his black skin, his lips were cracked, the broad flaps of his nostrils showed no sign of breathing. So stern his mouth, his face; sterner yet his eyes. His hair was stacked on his head like the sheaves of dried grass on the roof of a mud hut. She herself cut his hair that way. Neither did Gopi ask her nor did she ask him. But every once in a while she would come upon him where he sat on a boulder and cut his hair with a knife.

For a long moment Gopi and Saraswattee sat opposite each

other on Kali's right shoulder. And the desert imposed its silence on the universe. So much so that even the approach of the demon Mahisha became quieted out of that existence. Gopi and Saraswattee looked at each other. And in their own configuration of silence the breaths of white vapors exhaled and expanded upwards and consumed the crater, and the desert blew in a warm wind and spun the vapors and spiralled them upwards into the abode of the gods and then wove the white vapors into a sari of mist and the wind wrapped this silken garment around Durga Mata and spun it over her head and draped it over Saraswattee and Gopi like a veil embroidered with the frazzle of rainbows.

Earlier before, Saraswattee had found Gopi far withdrawn from her into the desert of himself. Now she saw how close he was to her and she could feel the reflections of her face dance in his eyes. She became happy.

She said: "Gopi, you must marry me."

And once again the girl did not take Gopi by surprise. Because just before she spoke, he knew what her words would be. And, once again, he had no words for her. He thought of who they were. Who was he? Who was she? What was she to him? What was he to her? What he found was, not that they were the children of Kahar and Sutnami. He found they were not cousins—blood relatives. Not brother and sister. Not Gopi; not Saraswattee. Not even mirages of the desert. But a boy and a girl. Just a boy. And just a girl. And so he had nothing to say.

But Saraswattee, curious child, stubborn girl, needed no words. She slipped a hand in her bosom and took out a thali. Not made of silver or gold. But her own homemade one. Made from two chips of desert shells and strung together by a thin string of dried vine. The girl held out the thali to the boy and he looked at it. He had never thought about a thali before. What it was. What powers did it possess. What authority it wielded. What identity it bestowed. That tiny piece of homemade ornamentation would not only exorcise Saraswattee of whatever evil spirit she might possess; it would give her a face: transform her from a shadow of no substance into a shadow of substance.

"Here," Saraswattee said, "tie this around my neck now. Marry me."

Gopi took the thali and tied it around the girl's neck.

"Now we better get off here before we are caught, Little Husband."

"Yes."

"You go down. But don't stay there too long."

Saraswattee leaned over and watched Gopi climb down Durga's back. After a while she fixed her eyes on the approach of the jeep and the whirlwind of red dust. No pilgrim, that one. Pilgrims were puny in heart and body and soul. There was nothing puny about the steadfastness and purposefulness of that arrival. And Kali slept! Which left only she, Saraswattee, curious child, stubborn girl. And Gopi, he, dark-skinned boy—*her husband*.

When Gopi disappeared Saraswattee turned, scrambled down the necklace of skulls, jumped into the stone cleft, and stared at the courtyard. Madhuban raced among the villagefolk, rushed at Chintamani, threw herself on her knees, collapsed against her sister and broke into sobs. Chintamani neither responded nor resisted. She just let herself be hugged. Madhuban clung to her sister as if it was she being flogged. Clung to her sister as if she sought protection from invisible blows. Chintamani stared at the blood on the ground. When Madhuban caught her breath she tugged at Chintamani and cried: "Deedi, a match has been made! Sister—you are to wed—a match has been made!"

THREE

THE puzzlement stirred up by Madhuban created a diversion and only Saraswattee beheld the army jeep eased to a silent stop in a silent rush of dust on the north bank of the sacred shrine. Saraswattee rose to her full height. She crossed her arms over her chest and tightened her face. Then she squinted. So often she would practice to view things with the serenity of Gopi's face. With the dignity of his distant eyes, and with his ancient detachment. But she was an impatient girl. And blessed with something of a bad temper. She always ended with her face tight in a knot and her eyes screwed up on the catapults of her temper. Thus, now, she viewed the arrival of the stranger in his army jeep. Needless to say, she had *not* once again forgotten where she stood. As she became suspicious, so too she became defiant. She was conscious of the thali on her bony chest. She felt the dried vine around her neck. She was married. She had a husband. She had found a greater protection than Durga Kali herself.

This Kali Durga slowly realized. But who was she to blame? Hadn't she denied the cries of her daughter Chintamani over the three days passed? Didn't she desire death and crave to abandon the abode of mortals? And in that choice, hadn't she, the defender of the innocent, deserted the children? When men are evil and gods choose to die, what are children to do? Her children had trusted to her and she had betrayed them as her heart had betrayed her and now sloshed in ambush for vengeance on her within her very own bosom. Durga Kali knew a greater pain than the pain inflicted on her by the ogre within her breast: the pain of the abandonment of gods and the loneliness of abandoned gods. What pain the children must have suffered! What loneliness must have haunted the children! Then, too, Durga Kali knew a greater death than the death she desired. Because an unloved god is truly a dead god. Saraswattee trusted only to Gopi. He was her god. As Saraswattee was his god. This realization was a terrible blow to Kali. She immediately surrendered to the quarrel of dizziness in her head.

Thus Saraswattee alone beheld the arrival of the demon Mahisha. And though she didn't know he was the demon Mahisha, she just didn't like the man. With her face tight and her eyes squinted and with her arms across her flat chest she watched the red dust settle over the army jeep. The windscreen became coated with a drift of sand and this darkened the inside of the jeep, but the figure in it became more solid and Saraswattee bit on her lips. The stranger had his eyes fixed on Durga Kali. And though she couldn't see the eyes, she could feel that gaze because it matched hers exactly—and hers was not a benevolent gaze. Whether the stranger saw her or not didn't matter. Her immediate question—though not urgent—was: why would an evil man make a pilgrimage to a holy shrine?

When the dust settled and when the stranger was satisfied with his thoughts, he opened the door of the jeep and made his way to the top of the jagged north wall of the volcanic crater. Saraswattee's eyes fell on his footsteps—not only his feet in brown army boots—*but on his footsteps*. They were sure, those footsteps. Certain. The terrain was rocky and bouldered. Humble pilgrims picked their way through that land with prayers on their lips. The stranger kept his eyes fixed on the temple courtyard. Yet his footsteps didn't fumble. Didn't falter. Didn't even dislodge a stone or a pebble. When he stood on the topmost rock outcrop and stared down at the people thronged in the temple courtyard, Saraswattee knew he was no stranger to her village. She could tell by the contempt on his face and behind the shadows of his eyes he had made a pilgrimage backwards in time and place. He had retraced his genealogy. He knew exactly what his eyes beheld. And what was to follow. Because he had beheld that scene many times before.

He was a handsome man, the stranger. Long-limbed and broad-shouldered. Muscular and well-proportioned. Bigger in size than

that monster Kahar, who happened to be the biggest man in the
village. But handsome; not ugly like Kahar. His cheeks shaved like
the wings of a locust. And as smooth as the smoothest desert
pebble. Though not hard, Saraswattee was certain—soft: soft like
the desert sand. And his well-trimmed, well-combed, well-parted
black curly hair made her Gopi's hair a disgrace. And what a royal
black and bushy moustache the stranger sported. Saraswattee was
certain that any of the dead maharajas of all those wrecked ancient
palaces would have given their ruins for such a moustache. Army-
booted; and khaki-clad. Handsome hunter-styled khaki jacket
with flap pockets. No doubt about it. A handsome stranger, indeed. Saraswattee didn't like him one bit.

And the girl knew what his thoughts were as he stared down at
the courtyard and fixed his eyes on Chintamani. But it was here the
stranger suddenly plunged Saraswattee into doubt. Disgust flashed
into his eyes. Disgust, not at Chintamani, but at what had been
done to Chintamani. To the other girls. And more: contempt for
the ugly sheepskin-clad Kahar. And even much more: scorn for the
painted village pundit!

Saraswattee became confused and stared at the stranger and
then followed his gaze to Chintamani and she saw Madhuban grab
Chintamani and shake her and shout: "Deedi! Deedi! A match has
been made!" Chintamani's glazed eyes stared at the bloodstained
bricks. "Sister!" Madhuban repeated in alarm. "You are to wed. A
match has been made. A husband has been found. *You are to
become a wife!*"

Again no response came from Chintamani. No recognition of
her sister. No recognition of herself. And for a moment the people
became wrapped in a suspicion of disbelief. Even the painted
pundit didn't appear to believe what his ears heard. The womenfolk stayed on the ground. Became hushed. Confusedly hopeful.
They stopped grieving. Stopped pouring dirt over themselves.
They looked up, glanced shyly at each other, stared at Chintamani.
They seemed afraid to breathe. Afraid the news might be false. Yet
they all hung on to it—and prayed it might be true.

Padma ran down the steps and collapsed in the arms of Matti,
and a group of women grabbed her, supported her, and fanned her
with the tails of their headcloths. Madhuban took her sister's face
in her hands, saw the swollen lips and cheeks, beheld the kilned

eyes. Light seemed to bounce off the pupils—not permitted to penetrate to her brain. Madhuban became terrified that her sister had been beaten till she was now demented and she cried, "Sister!"

But suddenly the pundit lost his own surprise and confusion and exploded: "O Durga Kali! Such is your power! In this universe none other is greater! Praise be to the goddess of the terrible countenance, she of the necklace of skulls, she of the horrible visage, she of the serpents and the regurgitated tongue, she who breathes death to evil, she who destroys evil men, she who drinks the blood of all who disbelieve and are sinful and lustful and are the doers of foul and evil deeds and corrupt practices and who dwell on superstitious customs and evil evil deeds! Behold the truth of Kali, the slayer of bad thoughts and bad men! See her supreme power and omnipotence! The evil spirit has been exorcised! *The evil spirit has been exorcised!* The girl is now cleansed, purified, a match has been found, behold the power of religion, let all men see the supreme importance of priests and brahmins! Offer oblations to Kali! Offer gifts to her priest! Sacrifice in thanks to Kali Mata. Give blood to she who delights in blood! Sacrifice the sheep! Cut its throat! Offer its blood to Kali! Offer an oblation of blood made pure and holy by my words, blood turned into ambrosia, O Durga! Durga! Durga! lawba dandayi namah! hrang! hring! spleng! rhing! Kali! Kali! Kali! Salutations in thy name, accept this blood. Drink! Drink! Drink! Be pleased, be pacified, enjoy this blood, become intoxicated, O Mahamari! reng! spleng! deng! greng! Namah! namah! namah! Om rheng! treng! hrang! dang! bang! crang! jang! drink! drink! drink! blood! blood! blood! all hail Kali, the destroyer of evil men! behold the power of her priests! rheng! hreng! blang! cleng! om namah! namah! *namah!*"

Oh what a migraine did the noisy nonsense harangue of the bony painted pundit give to the ancient and venerable serpent of serpents Naga, who, his brain now aged and airy, repented his resolve and blackened out his consciousness and went fast asleep. Slowly his throat slacked. And the bitter venom in his mouth began to trickle backwards inside his belly.

But where her cobra lingam went fast asleep into sweet oblivion, the pundit's harangue shocked Kali awake. She rolled her cauldron eyes. The words of the pundit echoed in her head and infuriated the nest of serpents in the cells of her brain. The serpents arose and

hissed and their fangs ruptured her death sleep. The more the
words of the pundit reverberated in the cave of her skull, the more
infuriated the serpents became and they lashed out in a fury and a
rage until Kali's brain began to burn as if inflamed by the fires of
her memories. Suddenly the oblivion snapped. Her vision cleared.
Her eyes fell on the slit throat of the sheep and she beheld the gash
as it splurted blood and her own eyes rolled in the death agony of
the eyes of the sheep and Kali stared in horror at her first view of
mortal men in ages.

At the moment Kahar slashed the throat of the sheep,
Saraswattee dropped in terror in the stone cleft. The stranger
flashed his eyes up at the massive stone head as if to behold the
reaction of the goddess to the blood sacrifice. From where she hid,
Saraswattee, like Kali, couldn't take her terrified eyes from the slit
throat of the sheep as it gasped for breath and its blood gushed out
into a silver goblet.

The stranger, too, knew the legend well—knew the legend more
than all else. But he had not read it in the worn pages of some
tattered scriptures. Nor had he heard it told by some wise master
or venerable sage. He had heard the tale at his father's feet right
there in that very courtyard. Before the temple of Shiva. As Kali
gazed down upon him many many years ago when he was a boy
but never a devotee of hers. He had returned a man. And still not a
devotee of Kali. But in his ears he could hear the echoes of his
father's voice tell how once upon a time ages and ages ago in the
beginning, sweet time had ripened the body of the creator of
creators, Narayana, and from his primeval vital fluids Brahma was
born. And Brahma created the seven worlds in half a day and
retired on his bed of lotus flowers. Soon, he will close his eyes,
sleep, and all creation will dissolve. Until then, Shiva, with his
beautiful and beloved wife Parvati, looks on the earth. In the
beginning, mankind was the sweetheart of the gods. In the earliest
days of creation. And for a long long time after that. But even then
evil stalked the earth. And demons, like men, get ideas. This is
what happened to the demon Durga. One day he decided to pray,
to perform tapas—sacred austerities. So he got up on his one big
toe and stood thus for six million years. All the while he mumbled
the sacred syllable: Om. Neither ate he, nor voided. He kept his
eyes closed, his thoughts pure. Indeed, a miraculously remarkable

feat for a demon! But demons, like mortals, are full of surprises. Be that as it may, of such intensity were the demon's austerities that the earth caught fire. The forests ignited and the oceans began to evaporate at a terrifying speed. Pandemonium erupted like the flames of the fires. Then the god of the oceans and the god of the jungles and the god of the animals together with the host of lesser gods joined in with the multitude of mortals and a tumultuous clamor echoed up to the abode of the Supreme Creator as all cried: "Save us, O Brahma, save us, appease the demon, or the seven worlds will be destroyed!"

Brahma rose on his lotus bed and the heavens lit up. The Supreme Creator looked down to the earth and asked the demon Durga: "What do you want?"

The demon shouted in delight: "IMMORTALITY!"

Immortality! The Supreme Creator became absolutely astounded. Such a perplexity engulfed him. He had found himself in a predicament that even he didn't know how to extricate himself from. Because there existed a law of the universe that if a creature—be this creature an animal or a human or a demon or any other creature in the universe—should forsake evil and embrace good and should pray and fast and perform such austerities as the demon Durga had performed, then not only are the gods obligated to answer your prayers: they are under compulsion to grant your wishes. Even Brahma, the Supreme Creator, existed subject to this law.

This the demon Durga knew very very well.

Thus the Supreme Creator found himself victim to his own decree. Because not only humans hunger and thirst after immortality but demons too. But to grant immortality to a demon? That evil may live on for all creation and eternity? To grant immortality to a demon is to grant immortality to evil. This the demon knew. This Brahma knew. "No!" Brahma said. "It cannot be done. Your wish cannot be granted. Ask another boon and it shall be so."

But the demon Durga was clever indeed. He rolled his red eyes as his behind pleasured him with an itch. And as his behind itched, so his brain ticked. He had anticipated Brahma's folly, and he laughed. How demons can laugh! The Supreme Creator was not impressed—in fact he became bored, eager to get back to his bed of lotus, and to some ambrosia. All the while he laughed, the demon rolled his eyes in treachery. At last he shouted: "I want superhuman might and power."

"Granted," said Brahma.

"I want to be the most invincible warrior and the mightiest unvanquishable conqueror."

"Granted," said Brahma.

"I want wealth and riches and kingdoms beyond compare."

"Granted," said Brahma.

The demon could hardly keep his pious demeanor. He rolled his eyes in glee and said: "I want every woman I desire!"

Oh! how his behind delighted him! It was impossible to keep his pious pose!

"Granted," said Brahma.

The demon suppressed his laughter and shouted on: "I want the power to transform myself into whatever shape or form I choose. I want the supreme and magical power of illusion!"

"Granted," said Brahma, absolutely indifferent to the plight he had inflicted on humanity.

"Finally," the demon shouted, "if I am to die no mortal or demon or immortal must have the power to slay me. *If I am to die only a woman must slay me!*"

"Granted," said Brahma, and he reached for a goblet of ambrosia, lay back on his bed of lotus petals, and the light vanished from the heavens.

Then the demon Durga flung away all pretenses of piousness and his evil laughter echoed throughout every single atom in all of creation. He had reason to rejoice. He had reason to laugh. The joke was on the gods; the joke was on the Supreme Creator. *For he had tricked the Supreme Creator into granting him immortality!* Because, where in all creation there exists a woman who could slay a demon? Where in all creation there exists a woman who could even slay a mere mortal man? Such a time it was then, as it is now, thought the stranger, when gods were fools and men believed in nonsense. He had sat and listened at his father's feet. He had to. Not only because he was of the brahmin caste. But because his father happened to be the village pundit. But even then, as a little boy, he never believed in the legends and the tales. They were all lies. They were still lies. And weighed down upon the land like all the ancient wrecks and ruins of civilizations upon civilizations.

No, when the stranger looked upon Kali's face it was not to see her reaction to the blood sacrifice. He stared at her full face so that she might see his scorn and contempt. And disbelief. He didn't believe in her legend. He didn't believe in her. He didn't believe in any Supreme Creator who had allowed himself to be tricked by a demon into granting him immortality. Why believe in a Supreme Creator who could be so easily tricked by a demon? Better to believe in such a demon!—which indeed he did—though he denied it to himself. But the demon Durga had got his vengeance. And now he, Mahisha Narayana—such was his mortal name—had returned to his childhood village for *his* vengeance. Not the vengeance of any god or goddess. *But his vengeance.* Because he believed in neither gods nor mortals—to tell the truth, though he loathed Kali, the stranger loved the demon part of the legend with a secret delight. But then, Mahisha Narayana didn't know he was the demon son of the demon Mahisha Durga.

But he was to know.

As Gopi was to know. He. Dark-skinned boy. Desert boy. Who, from behind the temple, studied the stranger. As Saraswattee studied him. Only unlike Saraswattee, curious child, stubborn girl; he, Gopi, sensed a different kind of menace than the menace of evil Saraswattee beheld. But the harangue of the pundit shattered the air and drove the kind serpent Naga into a deep slumber. Durga Kali awoke to the horror of the slit throat of a sheep. So too this interminable amalgam of gibberish filled up Chintamani's eyes with an evil light. Her gaze flashed on the pundit and a spell of sacrilege seized the girl. She abandoned her soul and allowed herself to become disgusted by the pundit's wayward toes and misaligned ankles and hairless shins and emaciated thighs and kneecaps that jerked like his knob of a navel. When was the last time the pundit washed his loincloth, stained with grease and food? She knew the man ate more food than anybody else and yet he had a belly no bigger than a scab. His ribs were hungry. Ravenous. He had a snake-egg head with no hair and a skeletal face juggled into a puzzle and camouflaged by a patchwork of ceremonial streaks—white, red, yellow—all as emaciated as his ribs. His life-thread was twisted and knotted and dirty with grime. His gumless teeth stuck out from his jaws like slabs of limestone.

The man seemed as hideous as his navel. Seemed to have been turned inside out from that very navel—such that his eyes got crossed. Chintamani fixed her vicious gaze on those crossed eyes of the pundit. They seemed to rage at each other, the pupils now stuck to the bridge of the nose, as if eating away beneath the nose to attack and devour the other—punditji punditji, why can't a match be made for my daughter Madhuban, what flaw exists in my daughter's fate? chee, chee, chee, such an old girl, so close to her monthlies and not married yet, a shame to her father, she has an evil spirit, she must be whipped to exorcise her evil spirit, only then will a match be made, shame shame shame, such an old girl, so close to her monthlies and not married yet, shame, disgrace, chee chee chee.

Chintamani was astounded by her sacrilegious vision and thought, how strange indeed. They had brought her to the temple to be whipped and exorcised of an evil spirit. And here. Now. After being whipped. As she looked at the cross-eyed pundit holding on to his beads and holy gourd and vomiting his mantras. She felt herself become possessed of an evil spirit. Indeed it was an evil spirit—mean, bitter, infuriated, vengeful—because what else would make her dare think the pundit was a dacoit? And more: she realized he had asthma.

The girl could hear his mantras scrape against his lungs and she didn't think he was going to make it to the end of his invocation and wished he didn't make it, wished his ugly navel would fold over him, suck him up, blot out his mismatched eyes. With no bother for her heresy, with no prayer for forgiveness for her thoughts, Chintamani flashed her eyes at Kali and mother and daughter stared at each other face to face. But as Kali's was the horror; so too the sorrow. Not only had she lost Gopi—no, she had never really had Gopi, did she? But she had lost Saraswattee. And now Chintamani. This was the biggest blow of all. Because of everyone in the village, of everyone in the eternal traffic of pilgrims, none loved her more than Chintamani.

As Durga Kali looked on Chintamani, so too Saraswattee. Only now she was eager to jump down from her sanctuary and rush into her sister's arms. Chintamani had fallen no lower than her knees: Chintamani had stayed on her feet: Chintamani did not have an evil spirit. And a match had been made. A husband had been found. Chinta was to wed. Now Saraswattee's anger turned on herself. How to slip down the goddess without being caught?

For a moment longer than Durga Kali could bear, Chintamani stared at her and not a word of prayer entered her heart. All Kali beheld was the mean glint in the eyes of her daughter. And she pained. As Chintamani now felt the pain in every pore of her body. She saw her swollen feet and swollen knees and swollen hands. She felt her swollen cheeks. Her swollen lips. Her swollen eyes. There was pain in her fingertips, pain in her ankles, pain in her breastbone. Chintamani thought of the pundit's asthma and that eased her agony. She flashed her eyes at her uncle Kahar and that increased the evil in her spirit. Even though the sheep lay dead in his hands, her uncle still held the slit throat stretched apart. He looked at her, laughed. Chintamani stared at the bloodstained knife in his right hand. Around his neck hung his whip. Blood dripped from the whip. Chintamani glanced at the silver goblet full of blood. And it was easy for Gopi, who followed her eyes, to know what her thoughts were.

As the mothers of the other girls tried to revive their daughters, Chintamani fixed her eyes on her sister. Madhuban became cautious, hesitant. Chintamani's eyes pressed. Madhuban whispered: "It is true, sister. A match has been made. A husband has been found. You are to wed. You are to become a wife." Madhuban threw her arms around her sister and wept. Chintamani looked at the bricks. She seemed in doubt. In disbelief. There was something impossible about what Madhuban said. Indeed, if a match had been made it had to be a miracle. But above all else, whether the news be true or not, there was one thing Chintamani desired to know with urgency. She pushed Madhuban back, took her by her shoulders, looked in her eyes and asked, "Sister, how was the bride price paid?" Madhuban dropped her eyes to the ground. Chintamani became stern. She lifted her sister's head, shook her angrily, and insisted, "Answer me! How was the bride price paid?"

"No bride price was paid, sister," Madhuban whispered.

"What?"

"No bride price was paid, deedi!"

The news of the match hadn't stunned the girl. But this did. Chintamani turned around in her astonishment. Her eyes searched

among the menfolk for her father. But her father was not there.
Then she looked at her mother being helped by the womenfolk.
Maybe a match had been made. But without the bride price being
paid?

"No bride price paid?" she asked detractedly.

"No," Madhuban answered.

"Any gifts offered?"

"No."

"No gifts?"

Madhuban sobbed.

"Any offerings, an offering of fruits?"

"Sister, oh sister!"

"No fruit? A plum?"

"No!"

"Then some dhubba grass? Tell me! Say yes! SAY YES! Some
dhubba grass? *Some flowers?*"

Madhuban looked at the ground. Chintamani needed no further
answer. She sank back. She felt like the sores over her body. She
had always felt herself to be a sore. As a daughter. As an unmarried girl. Now, a loathsome festering sore even as a wife.
There was no horror known to her greater than being given away
in marriage without a bride price. Not even being left unmarried
all her life. Or a widow. It was unthinkable. Unacceptable. She
would have none of it. She would rather die. She would take her
own life—"Madhuban!" the girl shouted. "Why was the match
made? How was the match made? Who was the go-between?"

"There was no go-between, sister," Madhuban whispered in
shame.

"WHAT?"

"No one intervened, it was done—"

Chintamani felt the evil spirit possess her absolutely and her
eyes again became demented. The crowd parted and her father
stumbled through the courtyard. He looked dazed. Chintamani
wished her father to walk to her and to take her in his arms and
explain all these things of life. But her father came no further than
the edge of the cobblestone courtyard. Kahar laughed and flung
aside the dead sheep. Chintamani kept her eyes on her father. He
was thin and short. Smaller in stature than his younger brother.
But in no way as hideous looking. Sometimes she thought there

never was any resemblance. Because not only was her father fine-featured: he had a dignity about him. A humility and a dignity she loved. But now that which she loved was gone. Her father stood before her a broken man. A shell of a man. A shell of a man broken in his soul. His humiliation had been greater than hers. For she was just one girl. He had three unmarried daughters. And now, again, his degradation was still greater than hers. She had been given away in marriage without the bride price being paid. *But he had to give her away in marriage without being able to pay her bride price.* All this Chintamani understood about her father. She understood because she knew the legend; she understood because she knew the life. He, her father, was as much victim as she was. But there was a consolation. He loved her. And she loved him even above Durga Mata.

But then a greater terror seized Chintamani and she grabbed Madhuban and shouted: "Who?"

Madhuban bowed her head and didn't answer. Chintamani shook her sister violently and again shouted: *"Who? Who is to be my husband?"*

"Gopi," Madhuban whispered.

Chintamani reentered the nucleus of the atom she had inhabited when her uncle whipped her. Once in there she thought nothing, felt nothing, saw nothing. She didn't even know her eyes again flashed up to behold the face of Durga Kali. She stared up at the relentless destroyer. But Kali had again succumbed to her desire for oblivion. The pundit had ceased his harangue and the serpents in her head ceased to burn her brain with their fangs and more and more of the venom of her cobra lingam trickled back into her veins as within her chest the ogre of her heart hung in the void of its own vacuum so that Durga Kali had nothing to struggle against and she certainly didn't want to behold the horror of blood sacrifice. Besides what was there to fight for? She had lost Saraswattee to Gopi. She had lost Chintamani.

Saraswattee watched her sister and she became more annoyed with herself because she heard what Madhuban said and there she hid trapped. And there was Gopi who moved away from his hiding place and walked in full view in front of the temple. Chintamani sensed Gopi's approach. She suddenly snapped out of her trance and looked at her uncle and the pundit and the villagefolk. She settled her gaze on her mother being consoled by Matti—Gopi's mother. Padma and Matti. Two women so unlike in every way. And yet held together by a secret bond only they knew about. Not even she, Chintamani, the oldest daughter, could penetrate that bond between Padma and Matti. And Matti. So old and wrinkled. But piercingly bright-eyed. Chintamani thought of her as a senile star. Chintamani beheld all the womenfolk of her village as senile stars. Because, at one and the same time, there was something about them defiantly alive—and something: dead.

Chintamani looked at Madhuban and asked; "Gopi?"

"Yes, sister, Gopi."

"*Gopi?*" Chintamani asked in her secret terror.

"Yes. Gopi."

Chintamani repeated the name as if in prayer. She didn't know what was the greatest horror to her. Being left unmarried all her life. To become a wife without her bride price paid. Or this unexpected unwanted match. To seek an answer Chintamani faced Gopi and the boy beheld the revulsion on her face. But they both knew Chintamani's rejection of Gopi had nothing to do with the fact that they were cousins. What did they know of blood and its peculiar composition, they who didn't know of the weave of their future? What difference did blood make to them, they who knew so little of who or what they were? They both knew the legend well. They both knew all the rituals and the customs and the ceremonies. Of the past they knew; and of tradition. They both had witnessed, over and over, the plotting in marriage of related blood. Observed it they had. Accepted it they had. Custom and tradition confirmed it. The pundit sanctified it and celebrated it—the cross-eyed asthmatic pundit himself, sixty years old, had married his granddaughter of birth and breath only six months. No. Theirs was not the right to question—certainly not Chintamani's. Hers was only the duty to succumb. But Gopi? She hated Gopi.

Gopi knew this. He knew why. But this was of little importance now. He had tied a thali around Saraswattee's neck. *He had married Saraswattee.* And this marriage made a difference to him because it made a difference to Saraswattee. Chintamani had had her exorcism. Madhuban would be whipped next. What would he do when Saraswattee wept under the whip of his father? But who was Chintamani? What difference did it make if Chintamani hated him? All their lives they had seen each other in the village. Never had they spoken a word to each other. Then, there: that was the first time they ever looked at each other—the first time they ever looked into each other's eyes. Chintamani existed. She didn't make a difference. She didn't make the earth any softer to till. He existed, he didn't make a difference, he didn't make the earth any softer to till. Chintamani existed, he bore her no hate, wished her no wishes, blessed her no blessing. But then he bore himself no hate, wished himself no wishes, blessed himself no blessing either. At another time he wouldn't even have questioned this match. It would have made no difference to him. To be married or not to be married. To marry Chintamani, or marry another. Such things just happened. He worked the land, they would find a bride for him someday, he would continue to work the land. But now it wasn't all that simple anymore. Suddenly it became like the day he discovered the curvature of the earth, discovered the earth was round. All kinds of complications turned up. Here again, the complications. Marriage was important to Saraswattee. To Saraswattee marriage was a matter of life and death. And he was going to honor his pledge to her. That thali had become as symbolic to him as it was real to Saraswattee.

But how to defy his father? It was clear to Gopi his father had forced this match. Why, he didn't care. How did he confront his father and say no? Saraswattee had asked him to slay his father and he consented. Suddenly Gopi realized he consented to something he had to commit. He stared at the bloody knife in his father's hand. He looked at the slit throat of the dead sheep. He beheld the goblet of blood before the temple of Shiva. The boy studied the blood. Yes, there was blood amongst them. Between he and Chintamani. Between he and Saraswattee. Between his father and him. And as he studied the silver goblet of blood, Gopi wondered: How much of the dry and brittle desert was soaked in blood?

FOUR

"Marry them!"

Everyone faced Saheb Kahar. His wooden leg longer than his blood leg, he rose up in the air lopsided. He slapped his whip in his hand and his huge eyes glared as he shouted again: "Marry them right now!"

The villagefolk and the pilgrims stared in horror at Kahar Saheb. Saraswattee watched the ragged hordes and wished they would just fall into the hot sulphur springs and be burnt up and give her a chance to climb down the goddess and rush to Gopi and Chintamani. She had little time for the stranger now, but he just stood on the north wall, his eyes on the temple courtyard. His evil would make its entrance soon enough; and soon enough she would deal with his evil. But for now. To get down Durga Kali. To Gopi. Who discreetly glanced up at her and their eyes met and hers told him she wanted to get down and his told her to stay up there, to hide, too much transpired, it was now very easy for someone to glance up at the goddess, and she would be caught. But all Gopi could see was the defiance in the black eyes. He began to ease backwards. If he didn't slip away and climb up to Saraswattee, she was going to climb down. And be caught. The sacrificed sheep and its blood in the silver goblet stood proof to her fate if caught. Besides, there rose his father. He who had lost his leg because of his evil and his greed. He who had made his own wooden leg out of a kumat stump. Now Gopi became fully convinced that his father had indeed *forced* the match and he wondered, why? With no bride price paid, what had his father to gain? What was so urgent that he insisted on the marriage then and there?

"Marry them, punditji!"

Once addressed the pundit came to his senses but his eyes lost what little control they had and mirrored his astonishment and confusion. "But how can this be?" Pundit Ayer said as he tried to tighten the slack ligaments of his eyes. But to no avail. At one and the same time his wayward eyes questioned everyone thronged in the temple courtyard. "How can this be? It is not the time of the harvest festival. Besides the horoscopes have not been checked. Who knows if the match is a good one? The stars have not been consulted. An auspicious day must be set!"

"Aye, punditji!" Kahar said as he hopped toward the pundit. "Don't talk to me about stars and horoscopes. Marry them now or this won't be an auspicious day for you!"

"But how can this be?" the pundit's eyes appealed to everyone.

"My husband," Matti came forward, "you have tempted fate enough. Please do not insult the gods any further. The match has been made. The marriage will take place together with all the other marriages at the harvest festival as is the custom."

Kahar's face twisted with a rage that his wife should address him in public. Before strangers. His whip lashed out and a cloud of dust exploded before Matti's face. "How dare you speak to me in this manner!" Kahar thundered. "What say have you in this matter? Keep your place—and keep your mouth shut!"

Gopi did not look at his mother. He studied the rage on his father's face. The vengeance in his eyes. Like the land and the desert, so too his father and his mother. They were there; they existed: they made no difference. To tell the truth the land and the sands of the desert made more difference to him than did his mother and father. He understood the land; he knew the desert. But then the land was something to understand and the desert was something to know. What did one need to know about one's father and mother other than they were one's father and mother? What had made him feel the desert, and yet not know the texture of the wrinkled skin of his mother? But now. That rage on his father's face. That hate in those eyes. The rage and the hate were not spawned simply because his mother stepped out of her place. The hate—and that evil lust for vengeance!—had been festered up by something else. And the something else, decided Gopi, had to do with the reason why his father forced the match—and why he now demanded an immediate marriage.

"My brother," Sutnami spoke up to Chintamani's relief, "you have gotten what you long wanted and waited for. The match is made. Neither you nor I can undo it. The marriage is as good as performed. I have paid. And even though your older brother, I bow to you and beg you for forgiveness and beseech you to cast no further shame and disgrace on our family name and on the memories of our ancestors."

Kahar hopped over and confronted his brother and hate became transformed into scorn and contempt and he laughed and his laughter pierced through the weak brain of the gentle serpent Naga and the cobra tightened his throat and with his eyes open he began to hypnotize himself into sleep again in his now chilled bejewelled glass body.

"Aye, punditji," Kahar threatened, "do my bidding. Marry them now!"

"But how can this be?" The eyes of the pundit ran amok in the temple courtyard.

"Father," Chintamani said, "I do not want this match."

"Daughter! Beti!" Sutnami cried. "What are you saying?"

"I do not want to marry Gopi."

"Daughter!" Padma shouted and ran up to Chintamani and shook her. "What is the matter with you? Do you know what you are saying? Your father has done his best. Do you want him forever to live with his head bowed?"

"I do not want to marry Gopi. I hate Gopi!"

"What has hate got to do with marriage? Chinta, you have always been the most polite and obedient girl. What has suddenly gotten into you? Do you indeed have an evil spirit? Daughter, what has hate got to do with marriage? Or love? What has love got to do with our fate? Isn't it enough that we are women? Why add the further burdens of hate and love on to our shoulders? Beti, this is not a moment for such things. Hate—or love—will come later. This is a moment for duty. This is your moment of highest and most sacred duty. *This is your moment to make your father a man!*"

Chintamani looked at her father. Sutnami stood before her with his head bowed. A broken man. Summer shadow to his daughter. She, Chintamani; his daughter: who had the power to transform that shadow before her into a man. Such an odd revelation to Chintamani. The power. She had always looked upon herself as a shame and a disgrace. A sore on her father's forehead. And she had always thought it her duty to erase that sore from her father's fate. A duty—not a power! And yet a power is what she suddenly felt. Maybe indeed an evil spirit had taken possession of her soul because she discovered the pundit had asthma and wished his navel to suck him up into oblivion. To have three daughters, thought Chintamani, and to love them all. In her village—what a godly feat! Yet, hers was the power. Or was she under a delusion? Possessed by an evil spirit—which she indeed felt in her heart. Why was the match made? How? Her father and her uncle hadn't even met face to face. Who decided? And why? Was the decision made between her father and her mother? That was impossible. Was the decision then made between her father and her uncle before she was brought to the courtyard to be whipped and exorcised of her evil spirit? Was that why her uncle whipped her with a hateful personal vengeance—and Chintamani knew those lashes came not just from the ritual of exorcism but from a black heart full of hate and warped into vengeance. So there was no intermediary; the match had been made: *but why no bride price extracted?* Bride price! Bride price—the sun, the moon, the stars, the universe, the oceans, the earth, gold, gold bangles, gold bracelets, silver, silver pitchers, silver goblets, brass, brass plates, brass bowls, a million rupees, half-a-million, five hundred, one, a cow, a goat, a bull, saris for everyone or a few, flour, rice, wheat, perhaps a piece of land, a promise of labor—Malik! Malik! lend me five rupees that I may pay my daughter's dowry, I bind my labor to you for eternity—a chicken, a donkey, a sheep, mother's jewelry pawned, a body, a soul, a limb, a bull-cart, a promissory note, a deed, a title (Maharaj, Sadar, Takor, Patel, Sarpanch, Brother? Father?), a pledge to enshrine the benefactor as a household god, history, tradition, a coconut, a grindstone, a bed, a chair, a flower, a blessing, a curse, a plum—*bride price*! What was she worth? What was her equivalent? What would it really take to give her a face? A husband? Or the due bride price? Which carried the greater value? Was there any value to she herself? Or did she acquire some arbitrary value only in relationship to some promised bride price? Why question now, when she had not questioned before? Her father was poor. She never hated their poverty. She never hated her father for his poverty. It was because he couldn't attach some gold to her fingers and toes to give her some worth, make her an attractive bargain, that no match could be procured for her. It was because he couldn't pay her bride price that she had remained so long a shame and a disgrace on his head, a shame and a disgrace to her sisters, a shame and a disgrace to all womanhood. Till in time she had come to see herself as a sore. She without bride price was nothing. It was not she that mattered. *It was the bride price.*

This the girl came to realize. All along she had only seen herself in relation to an allotment of some money. She never thought of herself as a bride. The bride price washed the stain off her. Removed from her the stigma. As fathers with sons had the power to wipe the sores off the foreheads of fathers with daughters who could pay for such an honor. *No one would have her even for free.* Yet for her a match had been made. A husband had been found. She was to wed. She was to become a wife. And she found herself possessed of an odd power.

Chintamani glanced at her uncle and then at her father. She didn't understand it. Her uncle hated her father. Her father never returned that hate. Just bore it. Lived it. Now she hated them both. As she hated Gopi. All her life she had witnessed—suffered from—the feud between her father and her uncle. What was the cause of their feud she didn't know. When and where it began she couldn't tell. She knew it raged long before she breathed life. It had a life that preceded hers. She had inherited it. But not a day passed without Kahar hurling curses at her father. They had never come to blows, at least not as far as she could remember. But the bad blood between them frothed so gangrenous that even when they passed in front of each other's homes, Kahar would cross the road, hawk, and spit.

Yet they had consented to match their children in marriage. What had transpired? No blows. No spit. No forgiveness. No embraces. No bride price. Not even any petty haggling and wrangling over life-lines and the position of stars. Why? How? Why or how, it was unbearable, she wouldn't have it, it was unacceptable, a sore unmarried, a sore married. It was too much.

A horror. There was an evil spirit in her. The pundit was a dacoit.
She would rather die. She would kill herself. The pundit had
asthma!

Indeed an evil spirit had come over her. What was she thinking?
All her life she wanted to be married. Ever since she could
remember, she was ready. Whatever was in her power to prepare
herself, make her more attractive, she did. She was never rude,
never disobedient. To all she was respectful. Willingly, she helped
her mother with the household duties. She learnt to sew, to darn,
to embroider, to decorate, to wash, to cook. All the women com-
plimented her on the way she was such a fast learner, on the way,
even at such a tender age, she could keep a house so well and could
cook such tasty food that even the pundit's sour belly belched with
satisfaction after eating a meal from her hands. Even though all she
had to wear were rags she took pains to keep herself clean and tidy
and presentable even on short notices—though the notices never
came. She did her duties before the temple. Everyone commented on
what a good wife she was going to make some lucky fellow. Yet the
years came and went, and left her in rags, unadorned; a disgrace to
her father; a sore unto herself and to her womanhood. What was she
doing wrong? Where was the lucky fellow? So much she yearned to
fulfill this duty. Not power. A duty. An obligation. Life as she had
experienced it in her village spun out into knots of marriages. Over
the years she had seen so many marriages. Big ones, small ones.
Quiet ones, noisy ones. High-caste marriages, low-caste marriages.
Everybody got married. Everybody's brothers and sisters got married. Everybody's cousins, nieces, aunts, uncles, grandsons, grand-
daughters, got married. To her then, her life, her head, was one big
knot made up of all the small knots she had witnessed tied around
the bedi—the marriage mound. She knew no other more sacred duty
than marriage—other than being a dutiful wife when she did become one. So what was she thinking now? She knew nothing of
birth, high or low. She knew little of herself. She knew only duty.
Duty she had longed so much to fulfill. Now she wasn't sure
anymore. Nothing made sense. She felt as if someone—the pundit—had bound her eyes with a black band and spun her around.
Around and around she spun. Afraid to make a step one way or the
other. Lest she tumbled into one of the hot springs. Afraid to grab
for someone. Lest it turned out to be her own blindfolded self. Alone

she was; she didn't want to be blindfolded too. The pundit had crossed eyes, his holy gourd was full of food, he had asthma, and may the lucky fellow fall from his horse into quicksand!

"I will not marry Gopi," Chintamani said and she glanced at the boy. Even though he admired Chintamani for her rebellion, Gopi showed no emotion. He just looked at the girl. Chintamani became shocked. She suddenly understood why she hated Gopi. She hated Gopi because she hated Gopi's father. You see, hate too, has its own genealogy. This Chintamani discovered as she stared at the boy. She hated Gopi because she hated his father because his father hated her father because her father hated his father because she now hated them all. Well. Where does it end? Who knows? Who can tell? Where does it begin? Who knows? Who can tell? Such a time it was then, as it is now, when it appears better to travel in circles than to ask questions. But Chintamani was shocked. To discover she didn't really hate Gopi. Then came her greater dilemma. Yes, she had forever yearned to fulfill her duty and become married and have her father rise up from the sacred fires a man. That was still her most sacred wish. But the girl asked her mother: "What is to become of Saraswattee?" Her mother turned away and she and Matti looked at each other and however much they wanted to avert their eyes they couldn't. What is to become of Saraswattee? How could Chintamani know only a moment ago Saraswattee had asked of Gopi: Gopi, what is to become of me? And how were Chintamani and Padma and Matti to know their secret wish—plot—had already come true. Because in their hearts —unspoken—all three had decided that someday Gopi would marry Saraswattee. And now Chintamani was to marry Gopi.

"What is to become of Saraswattee?" Chintamani asked.

"A husband will be found for her," Matti said.

"How? Where? When?"

"Fate."

"Fate?"

"Yes. Fate. Do not suddenly become so brash! Why question now, you who have never questioned before? You who are the most beloved of the benevolent one, where is your faith in Durga Mata?"

Chintamani flashed her eyes upon she of the awe-inspiring countenance and this time Kali beheld Kali. Same as Saraswattee saw the vengeance of Kali radiate out of Chintamani's eyes and Saraswattee became proud because her sister had become as defiant as she and she took this to be a good sign because two defiant sisters could create greater havoc than one defiant sister alone by herself. And Saraswattee wished she could shout down to her sister and say no need to worry about Saraswattee, Gopi has taken care of Saraswattee and as Gopi has taken care of Saraswattee so too will Gopi take care of Chintamani.

All this Durga Kali heard echo in her skull but then she, Chintamani, who had declared rebellion, reconsidered. She had reduced the power she thought she had to nothing. Now she had to do something. But what? What were her choices? Indeed, did she have the leisure of choices?

She could kill herself. In that instance she would be cremated without ceremony and the soul of her father would be eternally damned—and Saraswattee, what would become of Saraswattee?

She could execute her rebellion. Refuse to marry Gopi. In that instance she would either be murdered, or be beaten and dragged and tied down before the marriage mound—and Saraswattee, what would become of Saraswattee?

Or she could succumb. Actively succumb—what a choice! To succumb as an act of will! In which instance she would be dressed. Made to sit next to Gopi. Marry Gopi before the sacred flames —and Saraswattee, what would become of Saraswattee?

"Auntie!" Chintamani cried. "What should I do? What is my duty? Should I accept and perform my duty to my father? Or should I refuse and protect my sister?"

"Your first duty is to your father, Chinta," Matti said.

"And what is to become of Saraswattee?"

"Saraswattee will become whatever Saraswattee is."

"She will be beaten and killed by this evil demon with the ugly face and the wooden foot!" Chintamani screamed.

"Daughter," Padma shouted.

"What is this?" Kahar asked. "A panchayat of women? Are we to stand here while women talk and make decisions? Pundit! Are we to listen to our women?"

"The women must shut up!" the pundit said. "You women have no say in this matter. This is men's business!"

"Then marry them now."

"But how can this be done? The horoscopes—"

"Punditji. Have you consulted your horoscope lately? Is this to be your inauspicious day?"

"But but—"

"Enough! Perform the marriage ceremony!"

"I will not marry Gopi!" Chintamani shouted.

"So, my elder brother. *You are not a man after all,*" Kahar said to Sutnami.

For a brief moment Chintamani saw her father's dignity flame up and she thought for once he was going to confront his younger brother and make him observe tradition and bow down and honor his elder brother. But it was not to be. Once again her father allowed her uncle's scorn and contempt to shatter him and he slumped his shoulders and his dignity vanished and he mumbled: "Marry them."

And again Kahar's evil laughter echoed throughout the volcanic crater and Naga the serpent of serpents constricted his throat even further as he made a superhuman effort to meditate on sleep.

"I refuse to marry Gopi," Chintamani insisted.

"Then let your father live in shame and disgrace and walk the earth forever with his head bowed," Padma shouted.

"Father!" Chintamani cried. "Why? Why have you consented to this match? If I marry Gopi, who will marry Saraswattee? What should I do, bestow honor on you and death on Saras?"

But her father neither looked up nor answered.

"Why worry about Saraswattee when her fate is already decided?" asked Padma. "Look at your father. See what you are doing to your father. You are bestowing death to your father this moment. Look! Refuse this match and your father is dead!"

"Then I will kill myself!"

No sooner had the girl spoken when her mother slapped her and Kali's head shifted and the volcanic crater shook and the desert and the ruins rocked in the throes of an earthquake. The villagefolk and the pilgrims clustered together. A clamor filled the crater and rose up to the goddess and echoed O Durga Kali forgive us, spare us, be appeased, it is only the rebellion of one little foolish girl who is possessed by an evil spirit, but we will force her to obey your will and we will make atonement, spare us O benevolent one and do not wreak your vengeance upon us because of one little girl possessed of an evil spirit! The clamor became frenzied but the earth shook on and the ruins collapsed everywhere and the pundit's eyes scattered as he intoned: "O Durga Kali! Slayer of evil and of evil men! Be appeased! Lawba dandayi namah! spleng! deng! reng! greng! Offer oblations of blood to the drinker of blood! Quick. Another sheep! Bring another sheep! Cut its throat! Offer blood—"

Suddenly the earth became as still as a grain of sand in harmony with the motions of the planetary systems. Kali would have destroyed the earth then but she couldn't stand another harangue of nonsense from Pundit Ayer. She kept her peace—for the moment. A silence greater than the silence of the desert descended upon the temple courtyard. The people stared at each other to find themselves alive and amazed. They gazed up at the goddess Kali Durga and Durga Kali glanced down upon all and quickly completed in her mind the genealogy of a few and concluded the day of their deaths and then she closed her eyes to concentrate; to meditate: to pulse her consciousness through the brain of her cobra lingam, the aged and ancient serpent of serpents Naga, who now slept as only an old serpent could sleep.

"An evil girl," said an old woman.

"Disobedient," whispered another.

"Possessed of an evil spirit!" decided a third.

But the pundit seized his opportunity and condemned Kahar: "It is your sin! You who will go against the dictates of custom and tradition. You who will go against the dictates of the high priest of Durga Kali. The horoscopes must be matched. The stars must be consulted. An auspicious day must be found. Durga Kali must be propitiated with offerings. Her blessing must be sought. Gifts must be offered to the high priest of Kali Durga. His blessings must be beseeched!"

Kahar began to hop to the pundit. As he hopped his way, Matti rushed to Chintamani, put an arm around her shoulders, and said: "Chinta, take a look at the women. Take a good look at the women. See them on the ground? See them prostrate on the earth? Look how they have poured dust and dirt over themselves. Look how they have torn their clothes. See how they have flattened their already flat breasts with their blows? Look how they have torn out their hair. Why, Chinta, why? Look at their faces. Like cold damp black empty fireplaces. Empty of hope. Wearied of hopeless resignation. Teeth without smiles. Skin without flesh. Flesh withdrawn from flesh. Behold the public chastisement, the universal degradation. It is decreed by custom and tradition the disgrace of one woman is the disgrace of all womanhood and the public humiliation of one woman is the universal degradation of all women. For ours is the greatest sin of all. You know why? *Because we think ourselves sin.* Yes. Look at us. The debris of our village. Look at us. See what you—and even Saraswattee—will become. Look at us, our downtrodden eyelids weighted down by the menstrual slime of our menfolk!"

"Auntie, what are you saying?"

"If you will not accept for your father, will you not accept for us?"

"And Saraswattee?"

"That we may rise up with honor and pride?"

'Look at the beggarwomen. Look at the little girls made into beggars. Like lepers! Is that to be the fate of Saraswattee?"

"Chinta. You. By a single act of yours. You can lift all these women to their feet!"

"See the prostitutes. Look at the temple prostitutes. So many. So filthy and degraded."

"The filth and degradation of men."

"Less than lepers!"

"The sores of men—the sores of the souls of men."

"But is that to be the fate of my sister Saraswattee?"

"You foolish girl. Is not Saraswattee a woman?"

"What do you mean?"

"Look at all the women."

"I see them. I see their shame and degradation. I see their faceless hope. I know what they are—what they are made into."

"And is not Saraswattee a woman?"

"Yes! Yes!"

"Then to accept for yourself is to accept for Saraswattee. To accept for yourself is to accept for us all. But do not accept for yourself. No. Don't be so proud, so vain. Raise us women to our knees. Keep Saraswattee on her feet. Lift your father on your shoulders—*you are not his burden, he is your burden!*"

Chintamani looked into Matti's eyes. Dark. Deep. Black.

Whatever made her behold Matti as a senile star? Matti. Like a
sister to her mother, Padma. And now mother to she, Chintamani.
But even as she looked into the old woman's eyes, the heart of
Chintamani rebelled. She wished there were better reasons to do
things for. Saraswattee was the best of reasons to die for. What
other reason existed? Chintamani looked at her father. She
squinted, studied the man before her. Then she realized if she
persisted with her rebellion her father would succumb to her
wishes! But she also realized that even beyond her concern for
Saraswattee there existed a greater wish. She ached to perform her
most sacred duty as a daughter. She desired to fulfill her most holy
obligation as a daughter. She longed to sit down before the
marriage fire that her father might rise up a man. And not out of
duty. Not because she had the power. But because she loved him.
And that was the best of reasons to transform her father into a
man. Never had she ever intended to call the cross-eyed pundit a
dacoit, she was really sorry he had asthma, and may the lucky
fellow not fall from his horse into quicksand.

Matti saw the light fill up the girl's eyes and quickly she removed
her veil from her head and draped it over Chintamani and then
Chintamani beheld a miraculous thing. As one, all the womenfolk
rose to their feet. Suddenly they no longer seemed senile stars.
Magically they had been transformed—into women. And another
miracle occurred: they all looked upon her as if she too had been
magically turned into a woman. And in that moment, in the prayer
of their eyes, she had been transformed not just into the ceremony:
she was the worship.

She looked at her father. He lifted his head and returned her
gaze. The girl felt radiant. And she beamed her love to her father to
transfer its glow into his skin that he might light up and no longer
loom a shadow upon the land. But the dignity she loved about her
father did not return and infuse his soul with the love he bore for
her. Then Chintamani, she who knew the legend well, didn't know
if she had made the right decision. She felt the evil spirit repossess
her heart.

But it was too late for further rebellion. Either from her or from
the pundit. Because Kahar had his whip coiled tightly around the
bony neck of Pundit Ayer and for once his crossed eyes uncrossed

and he stared before him in a straight line as he lamented: "But how can this be?"

"It will be because I say so."

"But the goddess—the earthquake. It was a sign of her displeasure. No offerings were given to her. No gifts offered to her priest. The horoscopes—the stars. The earthquake. A sign. An evil omen!"

Saraswattee rose to her feet, watched the crowds part, watched the stranger walk down the stone steps and make his way to the temple courtyard. The villagefolk stared in worshipful silence as the stranger eased his path before Kahar Saheb with the pundit coiled up in his whip. The stranger created a diversion and Gopi glanced up at the goddess and caught Saraswattee in full and resplendent view. She had her eyes fixed on the demon—though neither she nor Gopi knew him as such. What a look in her eyes. Such an intensity. Such reflection. It was as if she were locked in the performance of austerities. Gopi fixed a desert gaze on the stranger. And he saw with Saraswattee how sure and certain the footsteps were. But he didn't attach the same meaning to this fact as did Saraswattee. With Saraswattee too, Gopi beheld the brown army boots of the stranger kick up no dust—indeed there shone no dust on the clothes or the brown skin of the man. But again Gopi did not attach the same premonition to this phenomenon as did Saraswattee. The stranger made his way to the courtyard and stopped three feet away from the strangled pundit. He clasped his hands to his chest and said: "Namaskar." He kept himself in the prayer of greeting until Kahar Saheb released the pundit and then all suddenly returned the greeting. The stranger dropped his hands, relaxed, and smiled. For a while he did nothing more. Just stood. And waited. Waited for something. From the pundit. From Kahar Saheb. From Sutnami. From Padma. From Matti. From—only the villagefolk. These were the people Gopi saw the eyes of the stranger seek out. And to each his eyes posed questions: Do you recognize me? Do you know who I am? I dare you rustics to see me for who I really am! But no. You are too blind, are you not?

And Mahisha Narayana became pleased. Because no one recognized him. Not that he expected anyone to. He had left the village when he was eleven. He returned in his forty-fifth year.

Mahisha Narayana became courteous. No one could feel the scorn and contempt in his heart. No one could feel the coil of vengeance he came ready to unleash. Instead, on all, he radiated a bliss. He said: "Peace, brothers and sisters."

For a while no one knew what to do or say. Then Sutnami answered for the village and said: "Peace, brother. Greetings. Welcome to our village and our holy shrine." This brought the pundit to his verses and he remembered not only was he the headman of the village, he also was the highest caste brahmin. He quickly said: "Yes, yes. Greetings. Welcome to our village."

"Please forgive me. I couldn't help but witness. You have some dispute. Can I—"

"Dispute indeed!" Pundit Ayer intoned. "Today is an auspicious day for our village. An evil spirit has been exorcised from a girl and a match made. But this unholy and irreligious low-caste Kaharsaheb, the father of the boy, insists that the ceremony be performed immediately. But how can that be? The horoscopes have to be checked, the stars consulted, an auspicious day selected—besides all our marriages are celebrated in one mass ceremony at the harvest festival. Besides our deity has not been propitiated. And her priest has been offered no gifts! Things must be done in accordance to custom and tradition. Things must be done in accordance with the teachings of the scriptures and the priestly caste. These low-born will never learn. They forever violate the scriptures and tradition. Why barely before you arrived Durga Kali showed her displeasure by shaking the earth to pieces! She gave a sign. An evil omen!"

"Aye punditji," Kahar said with scorn. "Look before your very eyes. Behold a stranger come to our holy shrine. Behold how rich this stranger is, how handsome. Now doesn't tradition and custom say there is no better omen than the arrival of a rich and handsome stranger? Behold, punditji, a rich and handsome stranger has come amongst us. A good omen, indeed, is it not?"

Pundit Ayer found himself caught in the logic of his own folly. Not just a good omen stood before him. But fate. Against that the pundit had no argument. Mahisha Narayana could not suppress his laughter. What irony. A good omen. He. Mahisha Narayana. Who had returned to his childhood village to wreak havoc and vengeance. He, Mahisha Narayana, greeted and welcomed as a good omen. That in itself was a good omen for his plan. As was that girl. The one about to be married. Young. And beautiful. And unable to take her eyes off his face. He, Mahisha Narayana; rich and handsome stranger: a good omen.

Despite his scorn and contempt, the laughter of the demon was pleasant and cordial. The temple courtyard became animated with good cheer and happy greetings. And as Saraswattee watched Mahisha Narayana, Gopi watched the stranger fix his eyes on Chintamani. Gopi beheld Chintamani, she who couldn't take her eyes off the stranger; she who in her forbidden dream had stolen the liberty to pray that for her a rich and handsome bridegroom would come from far far away—on a horse. Mahisha Narayana hadn't come on a horse. But he had come with a plan for vengeance. That plan did not include a young bride. Suddenly it did—perfect for his evil design stood the girl Chintamani. She who knew the legend well and thus knew it was forbidden for a woman—let alone a girl!—to stare in such a manner at a man.

FIVE

T HEN, with no will of his own, Mahisha Narayana glanced up at Durga Kali and his handsome brown eyes became transfixed and paralyzed by the tiny black venomed eyes of Saraswattee, curious child, stubborn girl.

Half the village menfolk were caught in discussion about the unusual marriage; the other half basked in the blessings to be had from the arrival of a rich and handsome stranger. The womenfolk fussed around Chintamani in excitement and adoration. The beggars and the pilgrims and the temple prostitutes stood on the periphery of their prayers. And Naga the serpent curled up in sweet slumber. Durga Kali sank deep into meditation to awaken the consciousness of her messenger coiled in the shell of her cobra lingam.

Thus only Gopi witnessed the stranger transfixed by the tiny black venomed eyes of Saraswattee. And the girl stared at the stranger for one celestial day—which for mortals is only a moment. Then she dropped to the bottom of the stone cleft.

But Mahisha Narayana stood paralyzed. Even though Saraswattee caught herself in time enough and disappeared from view, the image of her eyes still pierced the demon and he beheld them as if they were real. No illusion. Real live black venomed eyes. And suddenly his body leaked a thick black sweat so much so the ground around him became soaked dark with a shadow. A dizziness swamped his head and the earth darkened and in his mind time and place careened off course and out of rhythm and he had a vague recollection that only a few days ago he had set out on a mission in an army jeep from the base of the twentieth century. But he had taken more than a trip back to the desert. He had journeyed through the wrecks and ruins of time and place. And he found himself in a land littered by sandblasted wrecks of ancient palaces and sandclogged ruins of ancient civilizations. He found himself in a time and a place where time and place hadn't changed from the eternal moment of creation. He stood in a land where history and tradition were the past: where history and tradition were the present: where history and tradition were the future. A land where this future coiled entrapped by customs and rituals. And didn't he know all those ceremonies and superstitions? Hadn't he lived them? Hadn't he lived among a people who burnt widows with their dead husbands? Hadn't he lived among a people who made widows out of children? His own father, Pundit Narayana, once had half that village held in bonded labor—men, women, children: slaves. And all he had to do was to look around at the little girls with big bellies. The little girls with babies at breasts of bare nipples. There stood the boys and the girls maimed and let out to be beggars. All around thronged the temple prostitutes and all he had to do was to drag one or two or three right there behind the back of the goddess and purge himself of lust and step back before the goddess—purified: his lust left to rot the body of a woman. Such a time it was then—*as it is now*? Who knows? Who can tell? Certainly not the stranger. He had a vague recollection of the knowledge of another world—one called the nuclear age. But it was only a vague recollection and might have been a bad dream. Because there he stood. Paralyzed in reality—paralyzed by reality? No, he had not just made a journey backwards through the desert. He had stepped back into legend.

And that legend now possessed him and he could feel the sweat ooze out of his body in a thick black slime, the kind of thick black slime, legend said, the demon Durga sweated after he tricked Brahma into granting him immortality and then flung off his clothes with his pretenses of piousness and went on a rampage for he had been granted all the boons he asked for and he became an invincible warrior and a mighty conqueror and swept through the seven worlds in such whirlwinds of death and destruction and kingdom after kingdom fell at his buffalo foot and then there were no more kingdoms left to be plundered and ravished and he had all the mortal women he wanted—he would plunge into binges of orgies with the wives of the conquered kings and princes and with any woman he wanted because lust was his primeval nature and he loved his primeval nature most of all and when he went on a rampage of death and destruction, he indulged in orgy after orgy and as he pleasured himself ever so much his massive black body swamped the earth with the eruptions of his black sweat until every molecule of the seven worlds stunk of the smell of his lust, very much as Mahisha Narayana found himself suffocated by the stench of the thick black sweat that oozed out of his body and his dizziness further engulfed him and his knees sagged and he staggered into the opium of a faint and Gopi shouted: "Something is wrong with the strangersab!"

Then everyone looked at Mahisha Narayana and beheld how wet and black with sweat he had become and quickly all eyes followed his up to the goddess and they beheld she of the terrifying visage, she the slayer of evil and of evil men, she the bloodvexed and bloodlusting ravisher of mortals, she the disillusioner—the enchantress. And all became suddenly very humble and holy and voices rose up and gave praise to Kali and said hail Kali Mata, all praise to Durga Mata, see her power, she has possessed the stranger, she has enchanted the visitor, she has purified our guest, the stranger is pure and holy and is the beloved of Durga Kali and he stands before her sweated out of his lust, bleached of mortal desires but Kahar broke the incantation and shouted: "What is the matter with you peasants? Don't you see our guest is about to faint? He is a stranger to our land. He is not accustomed to the heat. You fools, you have allowed our guest to suffer heatstroke! Bring an umbrella. Put up a tent. Bring fans. You, mother of Gopi—go and bring tea!"

"Yes! Yes!" said Pundit Ayer. "You rustics forever forget your obligations of hospitality. You of low birth will never learn. Such a rich and handsome stranger. An umbrella! A tent! Fans! Bring tea!"

The villagefolk bustled around Mahisha Narayana and a red sheet was strung up on four poles and a tent made and a stool brought in and Kahar Saheb ushered their guest to the seat and three village men fanned him with the long ends of their grimy brown turbans and Matti rushed in with tea and Kahar took the tea and offered it to the stranger and Mahisha Narayana took the tea and sipped it and a cool wind rushed into the crater and dampened the vapors of the hot springs and the demon felt better—the hot tea cooled his head.

Gopi glanced up at the goddess. Saraswattee was still completely hidden. The boy was certain the stranger had seen the girl. What would he do when he recovered fully? Would he tell what he saw? But there was little time for questions, and even less time for plans. His father hopped about and shouted: "Prepare for the marriage ceremony!"

"Yes!" said the pundit. "Today is an especially auspicious day. No need to wait for the harvest festival. Bring forth all the children, bring forth all the brides and bridegrooms who have been matched. You among the pilgrims to our holy shrine, you who have arranged matches for your sons and daughters, prepare for the mass marriage ceremony. Send runners to the nearby villages, bid all those with grooms to bring forth their grooms. Spread the news. Our village is blessed. This is the most blessed day in our village. Most most holy and auspicious! All praise to Durga! All thanks to Kali! Om namah! namah! namah! Reng! Deng! Bleng! Peng! Greng! Kleng! Offer oblations to Kali! Offer gifts to her high priest! Clang! Bang! Hang! Dang! Om hari om hari om hari!"

And the serpent of serpents, so old and grumpy and moody now, did something he never did before: he began to talk in his sleep. And he mumbled reng deng beng cleng, alright, punditji, we will have a little chat about that amalgam of nonsense soon.

But the village became festive and Mahisha Narayana recovered to find Chintamani with her eyes still fixed on him. He glanced up at the goddess and squinted. Furrowed his brows. But the tiny black eyes were gone. The tiny black eyes had disappeared. He searched the massive face of Durga Kali. His eyes roamed over her bouldered breasts with the heads of serpents for nipples. He beheld the tiny jet eyes of the serpents. Diligently he studied the necklace of skulls. With disgust he beheld the red raw regurgitated tongue and the red raw cave of a tusked mouth. Quickly he shifted his gaze to the serpents of hair wrestled and knotted about the granite head and he beheld all the black eyes of the many serpents. He became confused. Plagued by doubt. He didn't know if he had seen the black eyes of a little girl up there. Or because of the heat and the haze he thought he saw a little girl up there and what was the matter with him, he was a man of science, he knew the effects of heat in the desert, he knew all about the science of mirages, it was the heat and those damned primitives, barbarians, with that revolting slit throat of a dead sheep and a silver goblet of blood and all those whipped and brutalized girls and that even more revolting and horrendous face of that ugly hideous statue with all those damned serpents of stone with tiny jet eyes!

Gopi watched the change come over the stranger. For the moment he knew Saraswattee was safe. He had to sneak away and bring her down. But there was something he had to do before and he rushed over to where the demon sipped his tea under the makeshift red tent. The three men fanned him with the tails of their turbans. Kahar turned and saw his son. But Gopi said to Mahisha Narayana: "Strangersab, I do not want to be married—" Kahar's hands flew out and the whip struck Gopi across the forehead and down his left cheek and a thick black welt puffed up and Saraswattee jumped to her feet, scrambled up the necklace of skulls, and disappeared down the back of Durga Kali.

Mahisha Narayana did not protest. Nor did he look at Kahar. Instead he stared at the boy who lay on the bloodstained cobblestones. For the first time since she laid her eyes on the rich and handsome stranger, Chintamani now looked at Gopi. The boy seemed unpained by the blow. Indifferent to the black welt on his face. As his father was indifferent to him. Then Chintamani realized what a sin she had committed. To stare so brazenly at a man—and a stranger. And she who was already betrothed! About to be married that very next instant! Immediately a prayer entered her heart and Chintamani whispered: O Durga Mata, forgive me.

Mahisha Narayana stared at Gopi. The boy raised himself up from the ground. Mahisha glanced from Gopi to Chintamani. He knew soon those two were to be husband and wife. He had heard Chintamani's refusal of Gopi as a husband. And now the boy had appealed to him to prevent his marriage to the girl. But he had not come to interfere in an isolated ceremony of his old village. He had come to destroy the entire ceremony of life as he had left it there and again found it unchanged. And as Chintamani fitted neatly into his plans for vengeance, so too now he decided that the boy

Gopi fitted in even better. So he didn't interfere on Gopi's behalf. To do that was to work against his own purpose. What he did was to fix a most understanding and most benevolent gaze upon the boy Gopi. Gopi looked up into those eyes and became puzzled. He saw the understanding. The sympathy. But he saw no promise to prevent the marriage. Then he thought the stranger was a stranger to their ways and he had been a fool to appeal to the stranger and Saraswattee was right and his father was an evil man and had to be slain—had to be slain before the marriage took place.

"Away with that girl!" Kahar shouted. "Prepare her for the ceremony!" Padma rushed to her daughter and took her hand but Chintamani resisted. She resisted because she knew the eyes of the stranger were on her. And though she didn't want to sin anymore by returning his gaze, she wanted to stand there under his eyes forever. But then Matti intoned the marriage song and sang of a rich and handsome bridegroom who came from far far away on a horse to claim his young and beautiful bride. There was nothing Chintamani could do and she allowed Padma and Matti and the womenfolk to lead her away as they all sang of the rich and handsome bridegroom—and his horse.

The pundit and the village men thronged around the stranger. Gopi got up and was making his way towards the temple when Saraswattee whispered: "Gopi!" The girl was hidden behind the womenfolk bathhouse. Gopi stopped. When Saraswattee saw he wasn't going to come to her she rushed out and pulled him and pushed him to sit down on the left foot of Durga Kali. She got on her knees and looked at his face. She reached up and touched the welt. Gopi neither resisted nor showed pain.

"Is it hurting you?"

The boy didn't answer.

"Are you in pain?"

Again he didn't answer. Saraswattee shook him and shouted: "Answer me! Is it hurting? Are you in pain?"

"No."

"Then you must be made of stone! Fool, why did you go to that evil man?"

"Little Mother, he is just a stranger."

"He is evil!"

"He is an educated man. I can tell. He knows things."

"And I know things too. So he is an educated evil man!"

"If you say so."

"I say so. And why did you want to anger your father?"

"To stop the marriage."

"You think by making your father angry you could stop the marriage?"

"So I will slay him."

"Aye Gopi! Is this the time to talk such nonsense?"

"What time is it for?"

"A time to be happy. A time to celebrate!"

"Celebrate?"

"Yes, fool, celebrate. Why do you want to stop the marriage?"

When Gopi looked at the thali on Saraswattee's chest she followed his gaze and lifted the thali and the sun glinted off the desert shells. "Pretty, eh?" the girl said. "Why did you want to stop the marriage, Little Husband?"

"Because I am already married to you."

"Yes. You married me. We are married. You are my husband!"

"Then how can I marry Chinta?"

"Why not?"

"I tied a thali around your neck."

"Then tie a thali around Chinta's neck too."

"Who ever heard of one boy marrying two girls? Little Mother, such things are not done."

"Gopi, why did you marry me?"

"I married you because you asked me to marry you."

"No. You married me because you love me! Not so?"

"Aye, Little Mother, what do you know about such things?"

"I know. You love me, not so?"

"I do not know about such things. I married you so they wouldn't beat you."

"That too. But you married me because you also love me."

"If you say so."

"I say so."

"So be it."

"And you will marry Chinta too!"

"What are you saying?"

"You will marry my sister."

"Little Mother, what are you saying? Such things are not done. We will be in enough trouble when they find out I married you secretly."

"They already know."

"How come?"

"Aye, Gopiwalla, we have always been married!"

Then Gopi looked into Saraswattee's eyes and saw the truth of what she said and he realized that, yes, in the eyes of the village, as she, Saraswattee, curious child, stubborn girl, trudged after him and ate his lunch and cut his hair and sat with him in the desert by starlight—in the eyes of the village he and Saraswattee were married. The boy was shocked: *deep inside himself even he had accepted it.*

"It is as you say, Little Mother. We have always been married."

"In spirit."

"Yes, in spirit."

"So now you can marry Chinta."

"What kind of logic is that?"

"My logic."

"It is wrong. No. It will not be allowed."

"You and I have always been married. In one way. In spirit. Now you can marry Chinta in another way."

"In what way?"

"In body."

"What are you talking about?"

"Aye, Gopi, you of the wisdom of the desert, did your father's blow suddenly make you a fool?"

"It is possible."

"All the blows in the world to that head of yours could not make you a fool. So don't play the fool with me now. You will marry Chinta."

"I will marry Chinta and then our marriage will become null and void."

"Our marriage will not become null and void because it will never be known."

"Then they will find another husband for you."

"Never!"

"Then they will whip you to exorcise you of your evil spirit."

"NEVER!"

The girl jumped up and faced Gopi and the boy looked up at her. She said: "Never will they whip me! Not as long as Gopi is alive!"

Suddenly Gopi realized he had had that kind of conversation many many times with the desert and with the spirits of the desert and somehow in those silent conversations the conclusions always made sense and here what Saraswattee said made sense though he didn't know what to make of the sense.

"Little Husband, have you ever not done my bidding?"

"No."

"Then you will marry Chinta."

"If you say so."

"I say so."

"Then I will marry Chinta."

"You are a good boy, Gopi. You will make Chinta a fine husband—Chinta! They are dressing Chinta! Why are we wasting time here for? Come, let us go and see Chinta dress to become your bride."

"No, Little Mother, I don't want to go. I will stay here. You go."

"Alright. But you stay away from your father—and from that evil stranger—and besides, he is not as handsome as you."

Saraswattee took Gopi's face in her hands, watched the harsh chiselled face, the chipped desert eyes. She said: "He has the handsomeness of clothes, Little Husband, and the handsomeness of skin. You have the handsomeness of the desert, and of the things of the desert. Now I must go. I don't want you to be sad. This is not a day of sadness for you. You are to be married. Today is a day of happiness for you. As it is a day of happiness for me to see my sister become your bride. You promise to be happy?"

"Yes."

"Some promise. I might as well go ask the desert to be happy!"

"I am happy, Little Mother."

"I know. You are happy in your way. Alright. So be it. But stay here. Sit right here till I return. Don't go wandering off in the desert. You hear? You have a wedding to attend. I am going to see Chinta be dressed as your bride."

Gopi watched Saraswattee disappear behind the womenfolk

bathhouse and just as he was about to withdraw into his distant eyes the girl reappeared like a mirage and stood before him with her hands on her waist.

"What, Little Mother?"

"Another pledge."

"I promise."

"Good!"

With that the girl bolted but stopped at the bathhouse and looked back and said: "Do you want to know what you have promised?"

"What?"

"You have pledged to marry my sister Madhuban too!" And with that she disappeared and Gopi fixed his eyes on Mahisha Narayana as the menfolk sat around and questioned him. What a puzzle the stranger was to him. But Saraswattee emerged from her cover of the bathhouse, ran among the huts of the temple prostitutes, dashed across the open crater to the south steps. On the southern wall she stopped and glanced back at the courtyard. She beheld the stranger and Saheb Kahar and the menfolk. On the outer edge squatted her father. She glanced up at Durga Kali, back down to the temple, back up to the cobra lingam. She glanced at Gopi already far into the oasis of his desert and then she beheld the vapors spread and as they spread the precious stones shot their rainbows through them. Most of the pilgrims had returned to their shanties. With the exception of the men in the courtyard, her universe was at peace. Someday she would arrange it so that there never will appear any priests and pilgrims and brahmins in her universe. With that decided, the girl ran through the village past the stone houses to her home. She ran openly. Her red blouse and green skirt flashed in the sun. Now there echoed festivities in every house. The wind blew up the dust, rattled roofs, and the pots hanging from the slate eaves. Saraswattee ran through the main pathway until she came to her house. The front yard was empty but she dashed for the fenced backyard. The two rear windows and back door were crammed with girls and the womenfolk. From inside came voices and laughter. Saraswattee tried to squeeze herself among the girls in one window and then in the other. But she couldn't get through. Then she had no choice but to crawl between the legs of the women thronged in the back door.

The girl crawled her way among the legs into the house but found she couldn't stand up. There was no room. So many girls and womenfolk had crowded themselves inside. The stone floor pained her knees but she pushed her way through to a table and climbed up on it. Because the roof was low, she could barely stand upright. But she had never seen her home that full of people before. There were women in the kitchen and in the bedroom. And in the center of the living room, surrounded by all the women—stood Chintamani!

Was that Chintamani?

Saraswattee couldn't believe her eyes. How changed Chintamani looked. So transformed. Saraswattee gasped and her hands clasped her mouth and her eyes shone with excitement and wonder. Chintamani didn't see her yet, since she held her eyes down. Padma, Matti, Madhuban, all stood in admiration of the bride. Even Amakutty, Doolwah, Phooloo, Roopa, and Sirju—the whipped girls—pressed in among the girls in the windows and looked at Chintamani with eyes aglow with excitement and admiration. Saraswattee held her breath—enthralled.

Then, an even greater silence came upon the room and all became still. For a long while nothing but Chintamani's eyelids moved. Her eyelashes fluttered because the girl knew she was being admired. She became afraid, trembled, held her breath, suppressed a blush. The withheld breath became as if brittle, and Chintamani's eyelids trembled even more. Matti went up to the girl, placed a hand under her chin, and lifted her head. Chintamani pressed her head down, kept her eyelids shut tightly. Matti whispered: "How beautiful." Still yet Chintamani suppressed her blushes. Again Matti whispered: "How very beautiful." Chintamani kept her head down, afraid because of the fragility of her breathing. In her free hand Matti held up a mirror. "Look," she whispered again.

Chintamani didn't lift her head.

"Look, daughter," the old woman coaxed, "raise your eyes, look."

Slowly, as for the span of the forty-three million, two hundred thousand mortal years it takes the creator to open his eyelids, indeed, so much time it seemed Chintamani took to raise her eyelashes and behold the form in the mirror. The girl took one glance, and dropped her eyes. But creation didn't dissolve. Not for her. In that one glance she had seen it all and her heart began to beat like a tabla drum. The girl trembled. Afraid. Frightened that if she stared again the image she had caught a glimpse of in the mirror would have disappeared.

"Look, daughter," Matti coaxed again, "do not be afraid. Look and see."

Chintamani shuddered. Fragile. Waited for her breathing to quieten down. Prayed for her trembling to drizzle out of her body. When she felt sure enough again, brave and bold enough, she looked into the mirror. The image did not disappear.

And this time the girl could not take her eyes off the image reflected before her. To either side of the mirror, holding it up fully, stood Padma and Matti. Opposite to her, on the table at the far side of the room, crouched Saraswattee. Though she could not see the reflection in the mirror, Saraswattee herself wasn't sure if what she beheld was her real sister—or perhaps a mirage. With her eyes caught by the image Chintamani still hadn't seen her sister yet. But both stared, as if at another person, mesmerized; enchanted. Saraswattee could not take her eyes off that face. That figure. The womenfolk had bathed Chintamani. Anointed the wounds on her body. Applied hot poultices to reduce the swelling. They had decorated her feet, her hands, her arms, her face, with henna and vermillion dyes woven in intricate patterns of flowers. They had decorated away the cuts and bruises on her body and the pain in her soul. They had dressed her in a red sari, the likes of which Saraswattee had never seen before. Made of the finest silk. Embroidered with fretworks of gold. How colorful it was! How beautiful! At that moment, like Saraswattee, Chintamani could not ask herself: Where did the sari come from? To whom did it belong? Who paid for it and how much? Enthralled, enchanted as was Saraswattee, she wasn't even aware of passing her hands ever so lightly over her face to authenticate the thrust of her forehead and the curve of her jaws, to authenticate the smooth rise of her cheeks and the faint indentation in her round chin. And as Chintamani touched her face, traced her features; so too did Saraswattee. Because if she discovered the same features, the identical face: it could only mean she, Saraswattee, curious child, stubborn girl, was as beautiful as that girl there with her eyes enchanted by an image reflected in a mirror. And as Saraswattee couldn't believe her eyes, thus too Chintamani doubted what she beheld in the mirror. Could not believe the girl there with her reddish dark brown complexion and with the darkened eyebrows and darkened eyelids and with her hair plaited with flowers and with a garland around her neck was her; couldn't believe the girl there with the bangles and the anklets and with the nose ring and with the pendant suspended on her forehead was her; couldn't believe the girl there decorated with the henna and the vermillion and dressed in that red embroidered sari—the girl with the moist red lips—could be Chintamani.

She didn't give a thought as to where the jewels came from. It was the first time she had seen herself in a mirror. Seen a reflection of herself. There was no mirror in their home. They were too poor for that. Besides, with all the cooking and the washing to be done, there was no time for such frivolities. In her excitement she wasn't even shocked that a mirror had been produced as if by magic, and as if by magic too, had transformed her—she, Chintamani, who had only heard the name Chintamani, who had only answered to it emptily and out of habit, but who had never really known there was a real Chintamani—now, she, as if by magic, had suddenly materialized; Chintamani becoming Chintamani: Chintamani becoming beautiful Chintamani.

The girl was frightened by her surge of vanity and she withdrew from the reflection and dropped her eyes and prayed: O Durga Mata, forgive me. Matti reached out, pulled her forward. Chintamani raised her eyes, stepped into the beautiful Chintamani again. In her heart she humbly prayed: O Durga Mata, let me be true.

Matti began her song again. The song of the bride. The song that celebrated the arrival of the handsome adorned bridegroom, on his horse, accompanied by music and the greatest host ever. The older women joined in the singing. Padma wept. Madhuban wept. A group of young girls laughed and giggled and rushed in front of the mirror and Chintamani peeped here and peeped there to get a view of herself and as she shifted so too Saraswattee peeped here and peeped there to find her. See her. Have her sister reflect Saraswattee.

With her reflection in the mirror a young girl teased: "Aye, how beautiful."

Other young girls joined in the game.

—Aye, what eyes. What they behold!

—Aye, what lips. How sweet!

—Aye aye, such glances, piercing my heart!

—Hai hai hai! my heart patak patak patak beating!

—Hai hai hai! oh my sweet, my love, my master, when will you come? oh my heart pains so!

—Aye aye aye! How I am perspiring! How my heart beats so, how impatient I am, hai hai hai!

—Oh! Where are you, lover, why do you tease me so?

—Hai hai hai! tonight, when the moon rises, under the cyprus tree, I will bathe in perfumes and anoint my body with oils and fragrances, I will sing, aye aye aye, I will beat my drum, he will come, he will take me in his arms, my bangles will shake, I will let him have his delight, hai hai hai!

—Aye!

The young women teased, their elders sang. Chintamani showed her fake displeasure. Saraswattee wished her sister to stay put. But it was time to escort the bride to the courtyard and Padma took away the mirror and Chintamani beheld her sister Saraswattee perched like a newborn bird startled out of its shell and gazing with amazement and wonder upon her new world.

When she saw her sister Chintamani suddenly thought she had become vain and inconsiderate indeed. But Saraswattee beamed at her in enchantment. And there, from her neck, hung a thali! This sight made Chintamani forget her guilt about having forgotten Saraswattee and she cried out: "Deedi!"

Room was made for Saraswattee to get to Chintamani and Madhuban rushed at them and the three sisters hugged and kissed each other but only Madhuban wept. And Chintamani knew why Madhuban wept. Now came her turn to find a husband. Or be subjected to the ordeal of an exorcism. But there was Saraswattee with a thali and it was forbidden for a girl to tie her own thali around her neck.

"Saras!" Chintamani said, as Madhuban now looked up in alarm. "Where did you get that thali?"

"Chinta," Saraswattee beamed, "you look so beautiful. You are the most beautiful bride I have ever seen. Such a beautiful sari. And how pretty they have decorated your feet and your hands and your face. You are most beautiful!"

"Saras! Who tied that thali around your neck?"

"Don't worry, Chinta. Gopi is a good boy. He will make you the best husband."

"Mataji! Come and look at Saras!"

Padma turned and looked at Saraswattee and saw the thali and gasped and instinctively she reached out a hand to rip the thali off. Matti grabbed her hand and the two women stared at each other. "Saras," Padma asked, "where did you get that thali?"

"Someone gave it to me."

"Who?"

"Someone."

"Look, Padma," Matti teased, "your youngest daughter has a secret love!"

"Matti, this is no time to joke."

"Don't you know who tied that thali?"

Padma's eyes opened in alarm as she understood. Matti's eyes bid her to keep yet another secret.

"Who?" Madhuban asked. "Who gave you a thali, Saras?"

"Someone. And don't worry, Madhu. I have arranged for a thali for you too."

"See," Matti said, "Saraswattee has become matchmaker."

"She has become demented, Matti! What are we to do?"

"It is fate, Padma."

"And how many secrets are we to carry in our souls?"

"As many daughters as we carry in our wombs."

"What secret, Mother?" Chintamani asked.

"The secret of wisdom," Matti answered. "Come. Enough of this talk. We must escort Chinta to the temple. Such a beautiful bride. And so lucky to win my son—oh Gopi! Where is Gopi? I have forgotten all about Gopi. He is not washed and dressed. Oh dear, he will sit next to this beautiful bride in his rags and with dust on his skin!"

"Don't worry, auntie," Saraswattee shouted. "You bring Chinta. I will take care of Gopi."

"Wait!" shouted Padma, before Saraswattee bolted away. Padma brought a brass plate. On it she placed a square of camphor. She struck a match and set the camphor afire. Then she held out the plate to Chintamani. Chintamani circled her hands over the flame, circled her hands over Madhuban, circled her hands over Saraswattee. She saw the girls who had been whipped with her. Once more Chintamani passed her hands over the flame and blessed in turn Doolwah, Amakutty, Roopa, Phooloo, and Sirju. Then Saraswattee pushed her way through the crowd and went in search of Gopi.

Matti and Madhuban led Chintamani outside. The older women helped Padma. The girls teased and sang. Outside, the village did look as if already it was the harvest festival. Like a marketplace or bazaar. From almost every house and hovel came a wedding party, and music and songs echoed through the sand-storms. Chintamani stopped and looked back at her home. It was built of mud and stone and had a slate roof. And it looked as windblown and echoless as every other house. Sandblasted and sandclogged. As windblown and echoless as the desert itself. She would return to that house after the puja. Not until after she attained puberty would she go to the home of her husband. Husband! Gopi! But her thoughts were more of her father. That was his home. He was her home. Today she wished to make her father a home unto himself.

Chintamani allowed herself to be led along the dry dusty path. Streams of colorful wedding parties flowed past her. But she had walked that path all her life. Over and over, she had made that pilgrimage. It was like an old journey. But something was different: it was an old journey in new clothes.

Once in the courtyard, Chintamani faced the temple. Inside its ample darkness, a single flame burned. It was hot and muggy in the courtyard. Inside the temple would be cooler and fresher. And nicer. She had longed to be married inside the temple. But hers was a low-caste marriage. And low-caste marriages were not permitted inside the temple. Chintamani glanced up at the goddess, the beloved of her heart. She offered thanks to Kali Durga. She asked of Durga Kali her blessings. Kali beheld her daughter and memory of she herself as a woman flooded her brain and she blessed her child and returned with a fever to awaken her aged senile messenger.

But Chintamani knew not of this. Nor did Saraswattee who was beside herself with anger before Gopi where he sat on the left foot of the goddess. "Look at you!" Saraswattee shouted. "Just look at you. Look at how all the other bridegrooms are dressed up in rich and colorful satins and velvet and brocades and with such fine turbans. You wouldn't even let me comb your hair—it is impossible to comb that hair of yours! Who ever saw a bridegroom in rags? At least come to the spring so I can wash some of the dust and dirt off your hands and feet. But no, it is too late now. Go. You are the only one missing. All the other brides and grooms are seated in the courtyard. Look at Chintamani. Isn't she the most beautiful bride ever? You are very lucky, Gopi. You could wash up after the puja. Now go!"

The courtyard was indeed crowded and colorful. Multicolored saris and multicolored turbans. The flood of white cotton and the throngs of sandalled feet. The concentric circles of saffron life-threads. The stacks of foreheads stained with white dots or with dots of ash or with spots of pot-black or with henna and vermillion. Gopi and Saraswattee stood, looked, studied. They beheld the sudden flush of brides and bridegrooms as in a royal but ancient game played with only kings and queens. And so richly dressed the kings and queens. Elaborately decorated; extravagantly ornamented. A palatial and royal flush of kings and queens, indeed; and none older than fourteen. In fact, Gopi, at fourteen, was the oldest groom. And no less than two dozen brides sucked at their mother's breasts; and already fast asleep. And Gopi beheld the scene of the mass child-marriage as did the stranger—a horror. But where Gopi became sad; Mahisha Narayana seemed pleased.

But Saraswattee saw Kahar hop towards Gopi and the girl pushed the boy forward and she disappeared behind the temple and Gopi picked his way among that resplendent and radiant royal flush of child-brides and child-bridegrooms and Matti bowed her head in shame because she had forgotten about her son, had neglected him—but when wasn't it that way? She carried a bigger shame than just the sight of him. And when the ceremony was over that greater shame would be transformed into a sin. But of this Gopi did not know. As he knew not why he didn't really know his mother. The boy picked his way among the dozens of brides and

grooms. Chintamani sat in fear. When Gopi slipped down beside
her and she saw his rags and his tattered hair and the starkness of
his black skin and the starkness of his vacant eyes, the girl felt the
revolt swell up her heart and she wished she had ranted and raged
and demanded a rich and handsome bridegroom on a horse but
there was nothing she could do but lift her eyelids and stare at the
rich and handsome stranger. And she did. Only this time she
caught the rich and handsome stranger with his eyes fixed on Gopi.
And there was something evil about the way Mahisha Narayana
stared at Gopi.

But then Mahisha Narayana switched his gaze to her and she
quickly dropped her eyelids and the pundit heaped ghee into the
fire and the flames leapt up and the pundit leapt into his asthma-
clogged chants and Chintamani felt the flames of the sacred fire
catch her toes and the heat of the flames began to engulf her body
as Mahisha Narayana kept his eyes on her. Chintamani became
conscious of the heat of the sun, the lack of wind, the spread of the
vapors. She was aware of her hated uncle. She was aware of the
annoying chants of the cross-eyed pundit, of the flames of the
sacred fire, of the presence of Gopi next to her. She was conscious
of the eyes of the stranger on her. She couldn't tell how long the
ceremony had progressed, but it, like the sulphurous heat, became
unbearable. She dared ease her eyelids upwards and stare transfix-
ingly at the cross-eyed pundit who sat opposite to her, across the
fire. The smoke shielded his nakedness better than did his loincloth and life-thread. The mask of his face seemed peeled. He
existed apart from, indifferent to, his irritating chants. He might
have been talking in his sleep, snored, he had asthma, he picked his
nose. His eyes confused her. Made her strain her own eyes. Gave
her a pain in her forehead. Made her feel dizzy. His chants whizzed
on like the buzz from a nest of wasps. Yes, the pundit's head was a
nest of wasps. In there, trapped, the wasps swarmed in loops,
moaning their anguished prayers for escape. On and on. Loop over
loop into loop. Unending, unable of escape. The pundit heaped
some sugar in the fire, said something nasty to it, the coals hissed in
anger, hissed steam, Chintamani jumped, looked up.

The eyes of Mahisha Narayana caught hers. The girl stared back
for a moment more, and then dropped her eyes. The pundit cursed
at the fire, spooned ghee into it, the flames hissed, circled her toes.

Her toes tingled. She smelt attar of roses. Again her heart beat like a tabla drum. With the tips of her fingers she delicately rearranged her sari.

To keep herself from looking up she concentrated on the decorations on the back of her hands. In her mind she rewove the patterns. She painted round seeds, blood-red, planted them over her body. With her eyes she colored vines. She made them burst into flowers. She dyed stars red. Her fingernails she polished over and over until they were a dark purple. Her hands and feet were hillsides. On them orchards bloomed. Red vines and hedges grew and crawled over her hands and feet and between her fingers and toes. The flowers smelled sweetly. Again Chintamani rearranged her sari. She shifted, mentally checked herself to see if she was in the proper lotus position. She would sit correctly. She would be a model bride.

The girl turned her hands over. She opened her palms. Two henna stars unfolded. She had seen lilies unfold that way. Suddenly. In a cup. With dew. She had cut open plums that way, quickly, hurriedly, sliced them downwards five sharp times; and as quickly, as hurriedly; she would peel them back, peel them open, so that their juices squirted, ran down between her fingers, wetted her face and her lips.

Chintamani remembered when she had first glanced into the mirror. Then she had experienced plain left-out nobody Chintamani transformed into beautiful Chintamani. Looking at her hands, Chintamani saw the beautiful Chintamani again. She had always thought that when she sat down before the sacred fire she would experience herself be transformed from Chintamani the girl to Chintamani the woman—the wife. Now she indeed experienced a transformation but didn't know what it was. Whether it was the transformation of Chintamani the girl into Chintamani the woman. Or whether it was the transformation of Chintamani the wife into Chintamani the adulteress. When she had accepted the match the womenfolk had looked upon her as not just the puja but the worship itself. Maybe she was becoming the worship—but the ceremony was over.

SIX

*S*ARASWATTEE rose up in the stone cleft and stared down into the courtyard as the vapors spread and she wondered what was the matter with that Gopi who sat and stared into the sacred fire on the marriage mound when the ceremony was over and everyone had gotten to their feet.

But Gopi looked into the fire and watched the flames turn over and roll like the sacred pages of a text of scripture. As the flames turned and unfolded he tried to read them. That he might understand why he who always knew the coolness of the desert night in his soul should know now the heat of that sacred fire in his body. Suddenly he who could understand all understood nothing. Most of all: himself. This perhaps most plagued him then as the flames of the sacred fire evolved before his eyes. Why himself? What had he to do with himself? What had he to do with anything or anyone? Why this sudden consciousness when he had never thought of himself before? And why was this preoccupation more painful than his preoccupation with the desert and the things of the desert?

In just that one day he came to know Saraswattee. Understood Chintamani. Recognized the evil of his father. The nonsense of the pundit. He saw blood sacrificed and came into a realization of it as a horror. The exorcism of girls because they were believed to be possessed by evil spirits revealed itself to him an abomination. And even though he knew he participated in a mass child-marriage ceremony, even this act didn't cause him as much confusion as the effort to understand himself. To understand what he felt there as the heat from the sacred fire burned through his body.

He could relate that heat to something—Chintamani. Even up
to that moment he never said a word to the girl. And yet, for the
duration of their marriage ceremony, he sat next to her. Close to
her. Their bodies almost in contact. And it was not like when he
sat in the desert. Not even when Saraswattee sat next to him or
between his legs as they watched the sun set or beheld the desert
moon claim the sky. No, that experience there, before the marriage
mound, had been a different one. He knew she hated him—even as
the pundit intoned his chants he could feel her revulsion of him. He
saw her eyes play over the decorations of her body, saw her open
the palms of her hands and beheld the henna stars there unfold like
plums sliced in five pieces and could see the fine spray of their
juices in Chintamani's mind. He knew she had wandered off in a
faraway enchanted garden and he knew who stalked behind the
vines of henna and the hedges of vermillion. The stranger. The rich
and handsome stranger. With his city clothes. With his royal
moustache. All through the ceremony Gopi kept his eyes on
the flames of the fire. But it was through those very flames the
eyes of Mahisha Narayana shot their gaze to Chintamani.
And throughout the ceremony the stranger kept his eyes on
Chintamani; and Gopi beheld her struggle to keep her eyes down:
when she wanted to return the gaze. This Gopi understood least of
all. And what he felt in his body the boy didn't know. Because he,
dark-skinned boy, withdrawn and elusive, he who knew the
secrets of the desert; didn't know then the secrets of the human
heart.

Kahar hopped behind Gopi and kicked the boy with his wooden
leg and Gopi got up and glanced at Mahisha Narayana who deliberately forced the eyes of the boy to survey the scene around
them. Gopi looked with Mahisha Narayana at the mass-marriage
ceremony. With its magic flush of child-brides and child-
grooms—most of them now fast asleep. And it was as if Mahisha
Narayana said to Gopi, behold Gopi, take a good look, this is
your village, this is your people, this is your life, this is your
legend—behold and understand the evil of all that is yours.

Chintamani stood with her back to Gopi. She waited for him to
tie his thali around her neck. Matti went up to her son and held out
a thali. The gold shone in the sunlight. Gold; unlike the desert
shells of Saraswattee's thali. For the first time in his life Gopi stared

into the eyes of his mother. He saw tears there. When he had always thought those eyes were never capable of tears. He saw pain too. But that didn't surprise him. So strange, their relationship. Mothers with sons deified their sons. His mother didn't glory in him. But that never mattered to Gopi. What always struck the boy strange about he and his mother was the way his mother carried herself about the village. *As if she was his shame.* As if he was her father. She his daughter. Thus she the shame and the disgrace. The sore on his forehead. Sore to him; scorn to his father.

Gopi glanced at his father. He saw the ugly hideous face, the rough-hewn and cracked wooden leg. He beheld the whip coiled like a thick fat scaled serpent. Asleep around his father's neck. The terror of the village his father; and the serpent of his whip. He promised Saraswattee to slay that man. But he would never slay his father because his father would never whip Saraswattee. Thus the end, and the nature of his relationship with his father. The end; and the nature. Where fathers with sons gloried in their sons, Kahar was indifferent to his son—so indifferent he didn't even care to demand the material equivalent of a son in the form of a bride price. And why had he forced the match on his brother?

Gopi took the thali from his mother and glanced up at Durga Kali—and at Saraswattee. As he tied the gold thali around Chintamani's neck the boy realized it was a mechanical gesture. That act had none of the meaning of the homemade thali. And where the thali on Saraswattee made her free, the gold thali on Chintamani made her sink. As if he tied a ton of granite around her neck. Chintamani watched the gold glint on her chest. Indeed the thali did weigh like a ton of stone on her bosom. Tears filled up her eyes. Because she was now a wife. But her husband was not a rich and handsome stranger who came on a horse. No, her husband was Gopi—whom she now really hated.

Love, or hate, would come later, her mother said; and hate came: even hate towards her father. Because she had succumbed to the match out of her love for him. Had hoped he would rise up from the marriage mound a man. But he didn't. He now seemed less a man than when he sat down next to her. Chintamani screamed: "Father! Look at me!" Even then her father would not lift his eyes and look at her. The girl shouted: "Why won't you look at me? I am married now! I am a wife! I have done my duty! Am I still a shame and a disgrace on your forehead? What am I to do that you might rise up a man?"

"Ha ha ha." Kahar erupted into laughter and confronted his older brother. "Ha ha ha. Some man. My elder brother, some man you turned out to be in your old age. Behold your daughter. A wife. Wedded. Behold your son-in-law. If your married daughter cannot make you a man then maybe your son-in-law here might make you a man. Ha ha ha! You are doomed. You will forever be a disgrace unto yourself. Never will you be a man. Nothing will ever make you a man. Not this the marriage of your eldest daughter. Not the marriage of your second daughter. Nor the marriage of your youngest daughter. Never before the eyes of these people will you ever rise up a man. And forever in the eyes of our dead mother and father and in the eyes of all our ancestors you will always be a shame and a disgrace and the souls of our deceased mother and father and the souls of all our deceased ancestors will be forever doomed because you will forever be a shame and a disgrace, even after your death! Ha ha ha!"

Then before anyone could stop him Sutnami lunged at his brother and grabbed Kahar by the neck and began to choke him and the wooden-footed man rose up lopsided into the air and his evil laughter echoed because his elder brother was slight of stature and his hands were frail and weak and hardly made an impression on the windpipe and Chintamani became horrified to see her father degrade himself thus and bring disgrace on her on this her wedding day and she damned her marriage, deemed her marriage an unholy one, and she encouraged the evil spirit to fill up her head and thought how she had asked Durga Mata to let her be true and how she had wanted to sit up a model bride but now no more, the pundit had crossed eyes, his life-thread was grimy and dirty, he had asthma, may the lucky fellow fall off his horse into quicksand—and yes! yes! she would stare at that man because he was a rich and handsome stranger and in her stolen dream—her sin—she had prayed for a rich and handsome bridegroom and even though she was a wife she would look into his eyes and may her soul burn in the fires of a dozen rebirths!

"Brothers. Brothers," Mahisha Narayana said as he pulled away Sutnami. "Peace. Let there be peace and love between us. Today is a happy day in your life. You, my brother, you have married your son. And you, my brother, you have married your daughter. It is a happy moment in your life. A blessed day. A time not just to put aside personal grievances and family feuds—but an auspicious occasion to absolutely forgive and forget. Forgive and forget and bless each other."

"Indeed!" Pundit Ayer shouted. "So well spoken. And so true. But those of low birth will always be of low birth and act like those of low birth. Shame shame shame. Two brothers. Fighting on the auspicious day of the marriage of your children. Do you know what you have done? You have cursed your children. Instead of giving them your blessing for a happy future, you have cursed them by your actions. And now their marriage is doomed!"

"Punditji!" cried Padma. "What are you saying?"

"It is not me," Pundit Ayer said. "It is your husband. By his actions he has doomed his daughter's marriage to tragedy! Never to be consummated!"

"My husband," Padma begged, "what has come over you? Didn't you know what you were doing? Did you not make the final decision? Why must you add sin to sin to sin? What is to become of your children? Punditji, what can my husband do to make atonement?"

"He must offer a sacrifice of seven sheep to Durga Kali. He must offer purified food cooked in purified butter to me for the rest of my life! And he must make a pilgrimage to the holy river Ganges and there take a holy bath and wash his sins and evil deeds away!"

"All these things will be done," Padma said. "Now will you please remove the curse from this marriage? I implore you to bless this marriage, punditji, all you have decreed will be done, I beg you in the name of Durga Mata, please bless this marriage."

"Of course, Pundit Ayer," Mahisha Narayana said, "you must show your generosity and bestow your forgiveness. Only you can remove the curse. In the name of Durga Kali, and as her high priest, bless the marriage of these children."

Pundit Ayer's eyes rolled in the frenzy of pride and power and he became haughty and full of condescension and immediately humbled everyone and he beheld how all instantly bowed to him and he dispensed a blessing with the flick of his index finger and thumb and Padma fell at his feet and kissed them and the crowd became festive again and greetings and blessings were exchanged and the wedding parties began to flow out of the courtyard to the village and the slums and the shanties among the ancient wreck of legend-honored ruins.

Saraswattee watched the people and the pilgrims and the wedding parties disperse in all directions and she longed for the day to see that place devoid of every single human body besides she and Gopi. She stooped down and propped her chin with her hand and watched the menfolk of the village convene a panchayat in the courtyard. They bestowed the position of highest authority and honor on Mahisha Narayana and sat at his feet. To humble themselves before him. To seek his good favor. And his many blessings. She watched her father sit at the edge of the circle of village men; she saw Gopi stand before the temple of Shiva: she beheld Chintamani hide behind a hut of a temple prostitute.

"See," Kahar said as he bowed to Mahisha Narayana under his red tent and now fanned by three men with jute fans. "What did I say? Did I not say the stranger was a good omen? He has brought peace and forgiveness to our village."

"Om hari," Pundit Ayer said, "hari om. What, may I ask, is your name, brother?"

"My name is Mahisha. Mahisha Narayana."

Again Gopi watched those eyes seek out the shock of recognition.

"Narayana, Narayana," Pundit Ayer said, "ah yes, we had a pundit by the name of Narayana, yes, Pundit Narayana—ah! so you are of the brahmin caste?"

"Yes."

"And of the highest!"

The demon son of the demon Mahisha radiated blessing and bliss.

"Like myself! Quite like myself! Welcome welcome, brother, it is always an honor to meet with one in one's own subcaste. Might you have relations in our village, Mr. Narayana?"

"No, I don't think so. But pundit, you know, Narayana is quite a common brahmin name."

"Not common! Brahmin, yes, but not common!"

"Of course. Forgive me."

"You are of the city. That I can tell. You are forgiven. No need of a brahmin to ask forgiveness. And you are an educated man, I can tell. Have you crossed the dark oceans in search of polluted knowledge?"

"No, punditji. I have never left the land of my birth and crossed the oceans to any other foreign land."

"Good good. Then you are not polluted. Good good good!"

"You are of the army, Sab?" Kahar asked.

"Yes. I am an army engineer."

"Ah!" Pundit Ayer said. "A man of science?"

"Yes, Pundit Ayer, you can say that. A man of science."

"A man of the new science?"

"Yes. A man of the new science."

"Excellent indeed. We brahmins must always take the lead. We are the creators and the keepers of knowledge and wisdom—old or new. And we must always be the creators and the keepers of knowledge and wisdom. Too many of the low-born are being educated today. That is not good. And the wrong kind of knowledge and wisdom. Not the new science, like you. Are you sure you are not related to Pundit Mahesh Narayana?"

"No punditji. I was born and grew up in the city."

"I was trained by Pundit Mahesh Narayana himself. The best!"

"What has become of Pundit Narayana? Is he dead?"

"We don't know. Many many years ago he departed our village with his son Mahisha Narayana—did you say your name was Mahisha Narayana?"

"The same. *Mahisha Narayana.*"

"What a coincidence indeed. But of course you are not that Mahisha Narayana. That I can tell. Mahisha Narayana had been trained for the priesthood and is probably a saint by now. He was a most brilliant boy and knew every word of all the sacred scriptures by heart before he was even five years old. A saint. He wouldn't have joined the army and become a man of the new science. Mahisha Narayana was a man of the ancient wisdom and has joined the ranks of sages and saints—most probably!"

"I am sure."

"And what is an army engineer doing in a village like ours?" It was Sutnami who spoke. The minute Mahisha Narayana heard the question he knew the real leader of the village. Pundit Ayer was just the highest caste brahmin and the keeper of the shrine. Kahar was the village tyrant. But real power and authority lay with the small fragile man with the humble posture and the humble eyes. Pundit Ayer might decree and Kahar might terrorize. But the men of the village sought the final say of that low-caste peasant Sutnami. The demon was happy to know his real enemy from the start. He also realized if anyone recognized him as Mahisha Narayana, son of Mahesh Narayana, it would be Sutnami.

"Aye brother!" Kahar said. "Is that a question to ask our honored guest?"

"What impertinence," Pundit Ayer added. "Indeed is that a question to ask our honored guest? Mr. Narayana you must forgive these ignorant peasants. They are only ignorant peasants. What is your mission to our village of Nagar?"

"Why punditji," Kahar said, "doesn't an army engineer have the right to visit the shrine of Shiva and pay homage to Durga Kali and seek her blessing?"

"Of course. I was not suggesting otherwise. I was merely posing a question that is solely my prerogative!"

"Brothers, brothers. No need for harsh words—"

"You have not come for a holy bath then—"

"Of course the Engineersab has come for a holy bath."

"Aye Kahar, can't you keep your place and let our guest answer for himself?"

"What kind of engineer are you?" Again it was Sutnami. Mahisha Narayana fixed his eyes on the defiant little man. He said: "I am a specialist—"

"What kind of specialist?"

"An energy specialist."

"What kind of energy specialist?"

Mahisha Narayana kept his anger hidden and answered: "I am a specialist in geothermal energy."

"Geothermal energy," Kahar shouted at his brother. "You hear that? Our guest is a specialist in geothermal energy."

"Geothermal energy!" Pundit Ayer marvelled as his eyes betrayed their consternation and rolled all around in their sockets. "What lexicon you men of the new science possess!"

"Only words, punditji."

"More than words! New gods! New myths!"

"Ha ha, punditji, you flatter me. New gods. New myths. The gods and the myths, like the words, are the same."

"You mean geothermal energy means the same as Durga Kali?"

"No no, not quite. Energy yes, but of different kinds."

"Oh. I thought for a moment you were about to include our goddess in your new science."

"No, not at all. They are quite separate things. Perhaps, Pundit Ayer, you are right, we men of the new science do serve new myths, new gods."

"You mean you are not a devotee—"

"Most certainly I am. I am a devotee of your goddess Durga Kali." Mahisha Narayana glanced up at the goddess and the hundreds of tiny black eyes flashed back at him. He stared at the goddess. Scorn and contempt powerful in his heart. As powerful as the force of the universe of counter-gravity with which the ogre within her chest had reversed Kali's respiration. Counter-pulsed the circulation of her blood. Disoriented the heavenly rhythm of her soul. But as Durga Kali—now released from this dark centripetal force—meditated: thus too the ogre within her chest kept his silence and listened. To pulse the heartbeats of Mahisha Narayana. And discover if that heart pounded in harmony with the evil heart of the demon Mahisha Durga, he who though he delighted in an idle boon from the gods that no woman could slay him—had his neck split by a woman.

Saraswattee stared down at Mashisha Narayana and again the myriads of black eyes netted him in his genealogy and for another moment the heat of the sun blurred the crater with mirages and a dizziness once more swamped the head of the demon and sweat oozed out of his body and he felt the earth under his feet shift. Gopi and the village men beheld the demon in confusion. Then suddenly Mahisha forced his eyes away from those two black eyes on Kali's bosom and he smiled and said: "The heat." All tried to laugh but could not. Mahisha Narayana looked at Pundit Ayer. He had to be more careful in his words. Well aware was he of the convoluted logic of pundits! He had better not let himself be led into saying something that would cause suspicion or have him denounced. Not yet—anyway. "Of course, Pundit Ayer, I am a brahmin, and I am a devotee of your deity Kali Durga."

"Om hari," Pundit Ayer said, "hari om."

Mahisha Narayana looked around, studied Sutnami, fixed his eyes on Gopi. Nothing more than the convoluted logic of the pundit had the land tied up and twisted in all manner of barbarous rituals and superstitions. And it was precisely that brahmin logic he had come to destroy. A difficult task indeed. No sense in making it any more difficult. As a matter of fact, with those ignoramuses and primitives, trapped by their customs and ceremonies, it was impossible to do anything. Even to make the simplest change. Let alone wreak total destruction on their evil ways and unscientific wisdom. Yes. He would need all the help he could get. And he would wreak such a transformation the end result would in no way resemble their outmoded outcoded outlandish original. He would wreak such a transfiguration and realign their cosmos that progeny would not know the difference from progenitors. Yes. He was a man of a new science. New myth. New religion—new cosmogony! And he stood in the oldest civilization that ever existed. Evolved of the oldest scriptures in the world. Yet not just mired in the quicksand of the past but constantly in regression—in the guise of rejuvenation. Mired in the past; and rotten to the core. Indeed. This universe created by Brahma in his waking half-day and which but for a span of forty-three million, two hundred thousand mortal years, nay, Brahma himself, the Supreme Creator who lives for three hundred and eleven trillion nought and forty billion years with however many oughts and noughts—yes! the Supreme Creator together with all his creation; he: Mahisha Narayana would destroy in less than a single minute of mortal time. He would catapult their sacred motherland—myth, shit, and primitives—straight into the twenty-first century.

Poor Brahma. With his lingam of oughts and noughts!

And that boy there. Gopi. He. Desert boy. He would help. Thus decided Mahisha Narayana.

And Durga Kali came awake. Because her meditations had been penetrated by the most profane and sacrilegious thoughts ever. And she decided no mortal could think such thoughts. Make such brash conclusions. To destroy the universe. To bring an end to creation. If a mortal, then a brash mortal indeed. But more likely: a demon. Or Brahma himself. Was it that age then? When Brahma was about to close his eyes? And bring an end to the age of Kali? Was Brahma, then, in the body of one of those mortals before her in the temple courtyard? If so, which one? In which of those mortals had Brahma manifested himself and come to conclude his final act of dissolution? That handsome stranger? Or the desert boy Gopi?

"Engineersab," Kahar said, "are you not well? Would you like some more tea? You sweat so!"

"It is the heat."

"Yes yes. The sun. This is the hottest summer we have had in one hundred years! Would you like some more tea?"

"No no. I am fine."

"Perhaps a sulphur bath? There is nothing better to cool the brain and restore the senses like a wonderful bath in the breath of Durga Mata."

"Yes yes," Pundit Ayer agreed, "prepare the bathhouse for our honored guest."

"No please. I am in good health. I will become accustomed to the heat in a while. After all, I belong in the army."

"When will you depart from our village?" Sutnami asked.

"Aye brother, watch your place," Kahar said.

"What impudence to our honored guest—and a high-caste brahmin at that!" said the pundit.

"Mr. Narayana," Sutnami asked, "what has your geothermal energy to do with our shrine?"

Mahisha Narayana flashed his eyes around and all followed his gaze as the hot sulphur springs exhaled their steam and vapors and the vapors expanded upwards and Durga Kali herself inhaled the strong powerful smell of sulphur and it refreshed her brain and quickened the flow of her blood through her body and her vision became clearer and more lucid.

"Aye Sutnami!" Pundit Ayer shouted. "You ignorant peasant. How can such a thing of the new science as geothermal energy be related to our shrine? Our shrine is the source of cosmic energy—not geothermal energy! And cosmic energy has nothing to do with geothermal energy. Cosmic energy is cosmic energy! And geothermal energy is geothermal energy! Look around you. Behold the breath and the wrath of Durga Kali. You see any geothermal energy in this sacred crater?"

Sutnami said: "For the creator and keeper of knowledge and wisdom, punditji, you are very blind indeed."

"How dare you, you low-caste peasant? How dare you talk to

me like that? Have you forgotten only a moment ago you were on your low-caste knees before my power? Have you forgotten I have the power to damn your soul to eternal rebirth? Shall I spit out curses upon your head till they fall on the very last of your future but yet unborn offsprings? Why don't you set out on your pilgrimage to the holy Ganges and leave us alone to conduct our affairs? Besides, I am getting hungry and I want my meal before the sun sets! No one but me has the authority to question our guest. Whoever has a question ask it through me. Mr. Narayana is our guest and as such he is welcome to stay as long as he pleases. Mr. Narayana, how long do you wish to stay in our village?"

"Only for a few days, Pundit Ayer."

"Engineersab, will you be my houseguest?" Kahar asked.

"How can that be? How can a brahmin be the houseguest of one who is of the lowest caste? A brahmin can only take food and water from another brahmin. Mr. Narayana will be my houseguest."

"Please brothers, no need to fuss. I have an army camp set up only a few miles from here—"

"An army camp, Mr. Narayana?" the pundit asked, his eyes in disarray.

"Yes. Only some other engineers and technicians. No real army camp. No need to worry. I will drive back and forth every day."

"What is your mission back and forth to our shrine every day?" Sutnami asked. "How many holy baths do you need?"

Mahisha Narayana found himself without an answer. He would have to deal with that peasant Sutnami much sooner than he had anticipated. But he had been a fool. He had trapped himself. Instead of dispelling suspicion, he created suspicions. It would have been better to spend a few days as a pilgrim in the village. He would have all the freedom to do what he wanted to do.

"Why don't you set out on your pilgrimage, elder brother?" Kahar asked. "You have a long long way to go. And the more holy baths a person can take the better, is that not so, pundit?"

"That is so."

"Thus the Engineersab is free to come as many times as he wishes from his camp to our shrine to visit or have baths."

"That is so. Certainly. Mr. Narayana you are free to come and

go as you please. Stay here if you wish. Be my houseguest. Or camp
out. Either way, our shrine is yours."

"Brothers," Sutnami said to the menfolk, "in your name I ask
the Engineersab again. What has his geothermal energy got to do
with our hot sulphur springs?"

Again Mahisha Narayana had no answer. And this time all the
menfolk waited for one. As Gopi waited. Eager already to learn the
wisdom of the new science. Mahisha got to his feet. The men stood
up simultaneously. Saraswattee saw Chintamani squeezed herself
tighter behind the hut of a temple prostitute. Mahisha pushed his
way through the crowd and Kahar hopped behind him as his whip
dragged on the ground. Mahisha confronted Sutnami but the little
man wasn't cowered. Before Mahisha could speak, Sutnami said:
"And brothers, I ask you, is it so strange that Mahisha Narayana,
son of Pundit Mahesh Narayana, though schooled to become a
priest, is it so strange that that Mahisha Narayana should instead
join the army and become a man of the new science?" By his
question Sutnami suddenly roused the menfolk to dissension and
the pundit hustled over and his eyes jerked about as he tried to
focus them on the stranger and he asked: "What are you saying?
That Mahisha Narayana is this Mahisha Narayana?"

"It is possible, is it not?" Sutnami asked.

Pundit Ayer's eyes became terrified and he asked: "Are you that
Mahisha Narayana?"

"Do I look like that Mahisha? All of you who are of the age,
take a good look at my face. Am I that Mahisha? What did he look
like? What did his father look like? *Did the boy resemble his
father?*" When all agreed yes he did, Mahisha asked: "And do I
resemble your Pundit Mahesh Narayana?"

The men became silent as they studied the demon's face. Pundit
Ayer said: "Absolutely not! The boy was the very image of his
father. Today he would be exactly like his father. No this Mahisha
is not that Mahisha. Besides that Mahisha is a saint—most
probably! Sutnami. You take a good look at our guest's face and
answer your own question. Does he look anything at all like
Pundit Mahesh Narayana?"

Sutnami couldn't answer and he realized he had lost his
opportunity to confront Mahisha on the issue of geothermal
energy and the hot sulphur springs. Mahisha was clever enough

not to press an advantage. He, like his father who had the power of delusion and could change shape and form, believed more in the creation of diversions and he asked: "This Pundit Mahesh Narayana, what became of him?"

The village men became sullen, evasive. Pundit Ayer said, "He went away."

"Why?"

"A tragic incident."

"What tragic incident?" Mahisha asked, as Gopi beheld his face swell and darken.

"A very evil occurrence," Pundit Ayer said. "Something to do with his wife."

Mahisha Narayana felt the lust for vengeance begin to possess him and he began to ooze sweat again and he knew he had to act fast or betray himself then for in his ears suddenly there echoed and reechoed his mother's screams as the flames engulfed her flesh and he moved quickly and confronted Gopi and said: "Ah, young man, you are the fortunate one who got yourself a most beautiful bride. Congratulations. What is your name?"

"Gopi."

"Ah, Gopi. A nice name." Mahisha turned to the pundit and said, "Pundit Ayer, with your permission, I would like to explore your holy shrine a little bit."

"You are a brahmin," Pundit Ayer answered, "you don't have to ask permission. Come and go as you please. The shrine is yours. You have my blessings and my permission."

"I will be your guide, Engineersab," Kahar offered.

"No no," Mahisha said, "no need to bother yourself. Gopi here will be my guide, not so, Gopi?"

"If you would like," Gopi answered.

"I would like that," Mahisha said, "thank you. And thank you, my brothers, for your welcome and your hospitality."

"When you are done, come to my house to dine," Pundit Ayer concluded, and he and the menfolk began to disperse. Kahar hopped away in displeasure. Chintamani hid behind the temple and her eyes followed the stranger. Then Saraswattee thought she would stand up in full view and shock that evil man as she did when his eyes caught hers. But she decided against it. She would wait. She had to see what Chintamani was up to. And she had to know more what that evil man wanted from Gopi. The girl was so angry with Gopi. He who was wise about the desert. And yet blind about the menace of Mahisha Narayana—some saint!

"Well, Gopi," Mahisha said, "are you ready?"

"Ready for what, Sir?"

"Why, a contest."

"What contest?"

"Your legend against my legend!"

Gopi knew exactly what Mahisha Narayana meant. But not Saraswattee, curious child, stubborn girl, even though she was fated to come face to face with the demon Mahisha who now stalked the holy grounds of Durga Kali in the mortal footsteps of a man in the guise of a good omen.

SEVEN

TELL me, Gopi," Mahisha Narayana said as he studied the volcanic crater vacantly, "what kind of a place is this?"

"Why, it is a shrine. The sacred shrine of Shiva. The beloved abode of the goddess Durga Kali."

Mahisha fixed his eyes on Gopi and knew immediately he had either underestimated the boy's foolishness—or his faith. "The beloved abode of the goddess Durga Kali, is that right?"

Saraswattee concentrated, turned an ear to Durga's mouth where there echoed faint resonances of voices but she could only pick out a word here and there because the voices scraped all interlooped and jumbled.

Mahisha led Gopi around the basin of the crater along the pebble walkways—the pebbles, black and gray and brown; polished with a metallic lacquer. The vapors rose, sometimes clouded Mahisha and Gopi from Saraswattee's view; sometimes shielded Chintamani as she hid behind the puffs of vapors and stalked Gopi and Mahisha.

"So tell me, Gopi, tell me more."

"Once upon a time a long time ago, after Brahma had completed the work of creation in one half of his celestial day, and having completed the seven worlds, he retired on his bed of lotus. Then Lord Shiva, with his beloved Parvati—"

"Ah Parvati. She had not yet acquired the terrible visage. The terrifying countenance. She had not yet gained fame and renown as the most fierce warrior. Parvati, the beloved of Shiva, not yet known as Kali, the bloodvexed and bloodlusting slayer of evil and of evil men."

Gopi looked up in confusion at Mahisha and Mahisha smiled reassuringly and said, "Go on, Gopi."

"Lord Shiva with his beloved Parvati embarked on a long journey to survey the works of creation, to survey the creation of Brahma. And together they journeyed from world to world until they had inspected the seven worlds and Lord Shiva was pleased with the works of creation and gloried in the existence of the seven worlds. Then they came upon this place. The mountaintop called Nagar. Here they came to rest for a while, and to quench their thirst."

"Ah yes. To rest. And to quench their thirst. This was then a beautiful and lush mountain range with fertile valleys, not so Gopi?"

"It was."

"And what happened? What made the mountains crumble? What made the valleys barren? How was a verdant and fertile earth transformed into the sands of a barren desert?"

"Lord Shiva had come to Nagar because he knew it was the sacred and beloved abode of the Goddess Saraswati."

"Yes yes. Another goddess. The Goddess Saraswati!"

"Saraswattee?" Saraswattee whispered as she cocked her ear to Durga's mouth. "Why are they talking about me? Aye, Gopi, don't let that evil man use my name in his mouth!"

"So what happened, Gopi?"

"Well, Lord Shiva came to Mount Nagar to discover the Goddess Saraswati had deserted this place. She had abandoned the abode of men."

"Yes, Saraswati picked up and left. She could no longer abide humankind. So she just picked up and left. And Lord Shiva came to find the region a desert and devoid of water and he was thirsty and so he got mad!"

"You know the legend, Sab?"

"Only bits and pieces. Tell me more."

"Parvati beheld her Lord become angry because he had not known Saraswati had abandoned this place and there no longer was any water and he was very very thirsty and he got angry and threatened to destroy this world—the abode of humankind."

"What a temper, ah, Gopi? Just because he was thirsty. Destroy the entire world of men—just because he was thirsty!"

"Because he didn't know the Goddess Saraswati had departed this place."

"Oh I see. Did Shiva destroy this place?"

"When Parvati saw the anger rise up in her Lord and beheld him turn blue and was about to destroy this world she ran quickly to him and begged him not to and she pacified him and made him sit under a tree and went in search of water to quench his thirst—"

"And she quenched his thirst, didn't she?" Mahisha said with anger and began to tremble with rage and the black sweat oozed out his body and Gopi became confused and afraid. "Yes!" Mahisha shouted. "She quenched his thirst! She satiated his—his—she satiated—his—thirst! And this sand, all this red and yellow and crimson sand, ah Gopi, this sand is the sweat off the bodies of Lord Shiva and his beloved Parvati, right? The sweat of their bodies transformed into a desert of sand after Parvati had found water and quenched the thirst of her Lord and Master Shiva!"

Gopi couldn't tell what had come over Mahisha but the man became not just angry but possessed—demented. It seemed more than the legend angered him. And more than his presence there too. Something about him. About his past. About his history—his genealogy.

Suddenly Mahisha recovered and though he couldn't stop the sweat he regained partial composure and looked at Gopi and smiled and said: "Forgive me Gopi. I forgot myself. And I get carried away."

"But why, Sab?"

"I am impatient, Gopi. Impatient with archaic knowledge and impotent wisdom. Impatient with rituals and ceremonies and customs and superstitions!"

"Impatient with the legend?"

"Yes, impatient with the legend!"

"You do not believe—"

"Of course, I don't believe!" Mahisha stunned himself with his conviction.

"But you said you were a devotee—"

"I am a devotee of nothing but the truth. The legend is a lie. Lies lies lies. All lies, Gopi." Thus spoke he who chose to delude himself.

"What are you saying, Sab?"

"Lies, Gopi. All lies. But I am a devotee of truth. And of science. I am a man of science. *Empiricism!*"

Such a big word Mahisha Narayana used! Indeed. Empiricism! What does it mean? Who knows? Who can tell? Certainly not Gopi, he of the desert wisdom; and of the puzzled heart. But then, did Mahisha Narayana know his own heart?

"Gopi, you know what a volcano is?"

"A volcano, Sab?"

"Yes. A volcano."

"No. I do not know."

"You know what earthquakes are?"

"When the earth shakes."

"When the earth shakes! Excellent. Excellent answer indeed! Not long ago the earth shook here, didn't it?"

"The wrath of Durga Kali."

"Oh that's what that was. The wrath of Durga Kali."

"Yes."

"So when the earth shakes it is the wrath of Durga Kali?"

"So says the legend."

"And what does the legend have to say about volcanoes?"

"Nothing."

"Why?"

"I do not know."

"Of course you do not know. As you don't know what a volcano is. Would you like to know what a volcano is?"

"Yes. I like to know things."

"Of course you like to know things. I could tell that from the first moment I saw you. A desert-wise boy, I said, and one who would make the best man of science. So here, Gopi. Let me show you what a volcano is. Grab hold of my fist. Put your hand around my fist. Come on. I am a human being, not one of the demons of your legend. I wouldn't hurt you. Take it. Clasp your hand around my fist."

Gopi stared at the right hand held out to him and Saraswattee whispered no Gopi do not take hold of that hand but Gopi reached out and clasped his right hand over that fist and immediately winced because it was colder than the coldest desert night he ever experienced and felt harder than any granite boulder he had stubbed his toe against and he pulled to free his hand but his hand became stuck to that cold stone fist and Mahisha Narayana—who felt his hand warm and human—laughed because he thought the boy expected the universe to blow up and he said: "Now, Gopi, imagine your hand to be the crust of the earth. Did you know that the earth had a crust? Well it does. A crust like your hand around my fist. And my fist is the core of the earth. But there is an inner core, Gopi. My heart. Imagine that my heart is the inner core of the earth—you feel your heart beat? Yes? It is soft and pulses with a power—and it is also hot. Very hot, Gopi. You feel the heat of your heart? Well imagine the heat of my demon heart to be a million—a trillion trillion times hotter than your heart. Such is the heat of the core of the earth. But the earth is flawed, Gopi. The earth is cracked and full of fissures and flaws. Think of your veins, Gopi. You feel your veins, Gopi? They are like the cracks and the flaws in the earth's formation and the heat and the power of your heart—the blood in your heart is forced by the core through your veins, the cracks in the earth, the flaws—you feel the force and the power and the blood pushed out of my demon heart ha ha into my fist, Gopi?"

And Gopi felt a force and a power swell up Mahisha's fist and the boy wanted to pull his hand away because he feared that force and power in Mahisha's fist would explode and blow him apart but he still couldn't withdraw his hand and he began to sweat and to tremble as his heart pounded down into the desert floor and he felt the earth shake under his feet as Mahisha's eyes bulged and his face twisted and turned black and his body seemed to expand and he shouted: "You feel the force and the power of the blood—magma, Gopi, it is called magma, because the core of the earth is so hot the earth becomes molten and this molten earth is now gushing from my heart through my veins to my fist which is your Mount Nagar, which in olden times was a volcano and suddenly one day because the magma pushed up with such power and such force the mountaintop blew up, the volcano erupted— like this!"

Mahisha Narayana exploded his fist and Gopi was lifted off his feet into the air and fell to the ground and Saraswattee watched waves of sand and sunlight bounce off the horizons and roll across the desert and thunder towards the shrine and there came bafflement of echoes as again the land shook in the tremors of yet another earthquake. Saraswattee beheld the desert shift. As she had that time before. When her mother slapped Chintamani. She beheld the shacks and the slums and the ruins and the village tremble and shake and the people scattered and ran wildly or fell to their knees and again a clamor filled the air and again Saraswattee marvelled: marvelled that the body of Durga Kali didn't shake, didn't vibrate. Saraswattee crossed her arms over her chest and she and the goddess Durga Kali remained perfectly still. As that time before. The girl felt pleased and safe and wise that at both times when the earth shook she had taken refuge in Durga's bosom. But poor Gopi. Both times he had had to suffer the terror of the wrath of Durga Kali and she felt fear for the boy as he lay on the ground and the earth shook. She felt no pity for Chintamani who scampered out the crater like a bride driven crazy by a wild-toothed bridegroom. But she took pleasure when she beheld fear seize Mahisha Narayana and she whispered good good, you evil man, taste the wrath of Durga Kali, this is only a taste, wait until she vents her real vengeance on you, then I will see how you will scamper around as a scared rabbit and Gopi you fool I told you to stay away from that evil man, well you are wiser now, so be it.

Then the earth became still. The grains of sand settled back in their niches in the desert. The villagers and the pilgrims blessed Durga Kali and rose to their feet. Gopi too got up and fixed his eyes on the man before him while the wise and venerable Naga, serpent of serpents, slept on and on in sweet slumber undisturbed by even the dust that settled in his ears.

It took Mahisha Narayana a long while to regain his composure but when he did he glanced at Gopi and saw the boy beheld him in a new way. Fear, yes. But also doubts. And suspicion. A suspicion that revealed the boy thought Mahisha Narayana was not Mahisha Narayana but someone else—a demon!

Mahisha laughed and said: "Gopi, it was only a coincidence!"

But Gopi's face stayed darkened like a desert night.

"What is the matter with you? You think I did that? You think I caused that earthquake?" Mahisha became astounded. "And I thought you were a wise boy. Now I see you are as legend-bound as the rest of them! Gopi, don't be a fool. Look at me. Come and touch me. I am only a human being. A simple man. It was pure coincidence. And what a coincidence! Nothing like an actual demonstration, is there? Gopi, that is how a volcano erupts! Now you understand. Come, come with me around this crater. Once this was a mountaintop. But inside it was flawed—had a fault. And it capped magma. As this crater now caps immense heat—and steam. Anyway, the force inside the mountain became greater than the resisting force of the mountain and the volcano erupted. Look around you, Gopi. What you see is called a volcanic crater. The top half of the mountain was blown away. Look outside. All those rocks and boulders and mud slides and ridges and hills of debris are all that is left of the mountain that exploded. And here we are in the crater. The volcanic crater. Look look, Gopi, these big black rocks are rocks of basalt. This thick ridge here is solidified lava—just like those ridges down the sides of the mountain. These are lumps of quartz. Here are clumps of igneous rocks. Talc, emery, agate, feldspar. All the end product of excessive heat!"

Mahisha Narayana pulled out a black handkerchief from one of his flap pockets and mopped the sweat on his face and around his neck. Gopi stared at the land formation. The big words of the stranger resounded in his ears. Something felt flat and dead. And the boy didn't know if it was the words of Mahisha. Or the crater—the land—suddenly sucked dry of legend. He asked: "And the precious stones? The gems? Where did the diamonds come from?"

"Ah Gopi. The necklace? The necklace of Parvati after she had become Durga Kali and played a game with Shiva and her necklace got broken and the gems and jewels scattered about the crater?"

"So says the legend."

"So says the legend. Heat, Gopi, heat. The source of everything. The creator of everything. Such immense heat in the core of the earth, Gopi, that it could turn mud into glass! Heat. Energy. Power. Force. You experienced the power and force of that earthquake. That is the kind of power and force I am talking about. There are more than two thousand minerals known to science, Gopi—lick your hand, go on lick your skin, here, see, look I lick my skin, just another experiment, Gopi, another demonstration, okay, what do you taste?"

"Sand."

"And what else?"

"Dust."

"Yes yes, but what else?"

"It is salty—"

"Salt! Ah! Salt, Gopi. Did you know salt is a mineral? Did you know those salt flats outside this crater comprise a mineral? The mineral halite. Common table salt. The kind your mother seasons your food with. You know the symbols and signs of your myths and legends and religion. Well in my religion the symbol for common table salt is NaCl. Say it, Gopi. Don't be afraid. It is just another mantra. NaCl."

"NaCl."

"You see? Just another sacred syllable in my scriptures. Try it."

"NaCl."

"That is right. Na stands for sodium."

"Na stands for sodium."

"Cl stands for chlorine."

"Cl stands for chlorine."

"Common table salt is made up of the elements sodium and chlorine in equal amounts. NaCl."

"Common table salt is made up of the elements sodium and chlorine in equal amounts. NaCl."

"Ha ha ha. There, Gopi. You are already a man of the new science. You love wisdom and knowledge. You are willing to learn. You have a desire not just for truth but to comprehend the entire universe! Now, let's take a look at this clump of diamond—"

"Sab! It is forbidden to touch the sacred gems and jewels of Durga Mata!"

"Is that right?"

"Yes, absolutely sacrilegious."

"What will happen if I do?"

"Your hand will wither away!"

"Let's see then. Look I have picked up a clump of diamond. Let's see if my hand will wither away."

Gopi stared in horror to see Mahisha's hand wither away before his eyes. But Saraswattee stared in horror at the violation. Such a violation. That such an evil man should touch with his evil hand the sacred gems of Durga Kali. With all the anger the girl could coil up in her she stamped her feet against Kali's chest to make sure Kali beheld the violation and the heart beneath her feet suddenly beat out dhoom! dhoom! dhoom! And as suddenly, too, Kali broke out into spasms of sweat. But Mahisha's hand did not wither away and Gopi, for the first time in his life, doubted the veracity of the legend.

Mahisha noted this and felt triumph and knew he had Gopi in his grip and his plan for vengeance took a twist even he hadn't anticipated or expected. He said: "Behold, Gopi. Diamond. The most precious of precious stones. The greed of men. Men kill for this, Gopi. Men sell their souls for this chunk of stone. Yes, stone! Chunk of stone! And composed of what, Gopi? A single element. Carbon. That's right. One single lousy element. Carbon. And how is it made, Gopi?"

"I don't know."

"Heat."

"Heat?"

"Yes. This here. This diamond. This is mud turned into diamond by heat—excessive heat! You don't believe me, do you, Gopi? Remember the core of the earth? The molten core? Made molten by heat? Well that same heat turns earth into glass, turns stone into diamonds. Oh yes. True. Magic. Mystery. The very stuff of legend. But also the very elementary truth of science. Science, Gopi. Empiricism! If your legend told the truth my hand would have withered long ago. But I hold a chunk of stone in my hand. Not the sacred jewel of some legendary goddess famous for her anger and her wrath. All this. This entire volcanic crater is just carbon—and common table salt!"

Gopi bowed his head in humiliation and disillusionment.

"And heat, Gopi."

Gopi felt the coldness of a desert night engulf him and he longed for mystery.

"And steam."

"Steam?"

"Energy."

"What kind of energy?"

"Geothermal energy!"

Gopi's gaze fixed on Mahisha in exactly the configuration Saraswattee beheld the demon. Then Gopi asked the question Sutnami had asked: "What has geothermal energy to do with our shrine?"

"Ha ha ha. Come with me, Gopi. I will show you. Facts. Truth.

Not legend. Not lies. Come let us take a look at these hot sulphur springs—"

"The springs, legend says, are the sacred orifices of Durga Kali."

"Sure sure. Sacred orifices. I must say legend has a nice way to put things. Holes in the ground. Sacred orifices! And the vapors, the vapors, legend says, are the breath of Durga Kali."

"And the wrath."

"Yes. The wrath. We must not forget the wrath of she of the terrifying countenance. She, Kali! Slayer of evil and of evil men."

Saraswattee stood and watched Gopi allow himself to be led around the courtyard and be subjected to an inspection of the sacred orifices of Durga Kali and the girl kept her hands folded over her chest and watched the springs exhale their vapors and watched the vapors expand and stitch out the mazes of rainbows and then Mahisha had Gopi in the middle of the courtyard again and Saraswattee listened to the echoes of voices in Durga's mouth.

"Gopi, those holes in the ground are nothing but holes. Hot sulphur springs. Not sacred orifices. Just hot sulphur springs. Full of heat. And those vapors are not the breath nor the wrath of anybody or any god or any goddess. Steam. Those vapors are just clouds of steam. Holes are holes, Gopi. Sulphur springs are sulphur springs. Heat is heat. Steam is steam is steam. Such are the simple facts of science. Empirical truths. But it is not as simple as that. It becomes a little more complicated. Steam is steam is energy. Geothermal energy! That is the connection between why I am here and your shrine. Gopi, outside this shrine, outside this volcanic crater, outside these ruins of a desert, encircles an entire new age—the twenty-first century! And right here, right under our feet, trapped by just a thick cap of rock, boils enough energy to launch this land of ours straight into that twenty-first century out there!"

"Sab, what are you saying? What do you intend to do with our holy shrine?"

"Gopi, look around at your village. You see all those hordes of pilgrims. The millions and millions of hollow emaciated bodies. The bones, the stunted growth. You see the children of the pilgrims. You know the children of your village. Their stomachs swollen not by excess of food but swollen by surfeit of undernourishment! Lack of food, Gopi. Hunger. You yourself have tasted hunger, haven't you? We are a land rich in lies and legends. We are a land weighted down by archaic and barbarous customs and superstitions. Look at all those ruins! Where did they come from? Ruins upon ruins upon ruins. Kingdoms fallen down upon kingdoms fallen down upon kingdoms. Civilizations collapsed upon civilizations collapsed upon civilizations. Why do civilizations collapse, Gopi?"

"I don't know."

"Because of ignorance. Because of barren rituals. Because of the desert of the past. Because of the forever future of superstitions and more superstitions and more superstitions. That is why civilizations collapse. And look at all those slums and shanties upon these ruins. What do you see, Gopi?"

"Ruins."

"Exactly. I knew you were a bright boy. You see ruins. Our civilization is poised to collapse into ruins once again."

Gopi halted on the eastern wall of the crater where Mahisha had led him. He glanced around at the ancient ruins and the recent ruins of the slum dwellings of the pilgrims. He studied all the thousands of people his eyes beheld. The emaciated bodies. The sunken faces. The swollen bellies of the children. So many people. So many many people upon the land. To the boy it appeared that Mahisha had left out a reason why civilizations collapsed. But he couldn't figure out what that reason was. Mahisha said: "We are more than just a land of the poor, Gopi. We are a land of the poverty of the poor. And the poverty of the poor goes beyond lack of food and clothes and shelter and wealth. The poverty of the poor goes straight to the human mind and human intelligence. That is why we need bright young boys like you. You are the future, Gopi. And the future is out there. Beyond the desert. The twenty-first century. You can become the pilot of this planet and launch us into the future. Before our civilization collapses again! Now. The time is now! We must do what is necessary now. Enough of myths and legends and superstitions. The truth. It is the time for the truth. The truth and the future. Gopi, are you ready for the truth and the future?"

Gopi and Mahisha stared at each other and the sun sank behind Durga Kali's back. Saraswattee beheld Mahisha and Gopi stand on the far eastern wall. The girl did not behold that Durga Kali cast no shadow upon the land. But that evil man—what mighty words he uttered!

"Are you ready to lead us into the future, Gopi?"

"Me, Sab?"

"Yes, you."

"I am only the son of a peasant. The low-born son of a low-born laborer."

"That may be so. But you are intelligent and observant. And you hunger and thirst for knowledge and wisdom. Are you ready to lead us into the future?"

"What can I do?"

"Well, to begin with, I need an assistant. Would you like to be my assistant?"

"And assist you in what?"

"My work."

"What is your work?"

"To launch us into the twenty-first century."

"That seems to be the work of the gods."

"Then become a god!"

"I do not tempt fate, Sab. I know my place."

"And your place is in the future. With me. Join forces with me. I can teach you a lot. You can learn new truths, new interpretations. Science, Gopi. Science! You can learn all about math and physics and chemistry and geology and about energy—geothermal energy. How about it? New ways to see the old!"

Gopi turned away from Mahisha and glanced upon Durga Kali. His eyes fell on Saraswattee but he betrayed no emotion. He saw behind Durga Kali, the earth flamed red, as if the horizon was on fire. And even as he noted Durga Kali bequeathed no shadow to the land the boy again betrayed no emotion. That didn't befuddle him as much as the knowledge of Mahisha. Durga Kali fixed her cauldron eyes on the boy. She realized what danger she was in—what danger Gopi found himself confronted with. If the boy turned to the man of science, would he be wrong? But she was guilty of a greater wrong. She, slayer of evil, herself guilty of evil. To have desired mortal death. To have abandoned the children. To have allowed her two-faced heart to become an ogre within her chest. To have bid her mighty cobra lingam plunge its bitter venom into her veins till now they were clogged more with poison than with blood.

As Kali Durga glanced upon Gopi she saw the doubts in his eyes. She knew the suspicions in his heart. What agony raged under that serene countenance! For at that moment the boy doubted both she and the stranger. At that instant the boy suspected both the stranger and her. He doubted and suspected both science and the legend. Yet how he longed for truth. The truth of all things. He desired truth—as he desired wisdom and knowledge. He had the knowledge and the wisdom of the desert and the legend and the scriptures. Now he stood torn. Because the new science of the stranger attracted him and tugged at his heart. Which way would the boy go? To whom would he turn? Would he turn his back on her as she had turned her back on him? As she had turned her back on Saraswattee? As she had turned her back on her beloved devotee Chintamani?

"What do you say, Gopi? The truth and the future? Will you become my assistant? Will you help me in my work?"

"You are a stranger to my village. If you require assistance, it is my duty to offer it to you."

"Good for you Gopi. Good for you indeed. Such good customs, such hospitality. Come. Let us go. Let us explore. Let us investigate. Let us learn!"

Gopi didn't have time to think or to decide. Nor did Durga Kali have time to figure out what was really happening. Saraswattee watched Mahisha lead Gopi among the ruins and hurry the boy towards the limestone valley and the dry riverbed to the north.

To the right of the old sandy riverbed, on a sand dune covered with shrubs and bushes, sat Chintamani. She stared into the sad sun. And its rays glittered off her brilliant red sari and her jewels and adornments. Saraswattee began to scramble down the goddess.

Once in the limestone valley the stench swamped Gopi and Mahisha. Mahisha bent down, picked up a piece of rock, held it out to Gopi, and asked: "Do you know what kind of rock this is?"

"Earth."

Even though it was exactly the answer he expected, Mahisha became stunned. For a moment his consciousness blanked out. Dizziness engulfed his head. He puzzled over the piece of rock in his hands. Struggled to recognize it. Identify it. Call it by its scientific name. But he couldn't. And though neither he nor Gopi observed the phenomenon, as Mahisha struggled to regain his consciousness, his skin became a shade darker and the hair over his body thickened an inch longer and he aged a full five years. Then he flung the rock aside and said absentmindedly, "Yes. Earth."

Gopi followed Mahisha and Mahisha waved a hand over the valley and asked: "What kind of land formation is this?"

"Desert?"

"No Gopi. This is a limestone valley. Sedimentary rock. Pillars and columns of limestone. Pillars and columns like a million skeletons—ah yes, what does the legend say about these pillars and columns of limestone?"

"They are the skeletons of the armies of the demon Mahisha."

"Yes yes. Armies and armies of soldiers. Petrified in their boots. Where they stood. Bleached white. Turned into stone. Just by the sight of she of the terrible and terror-inspiring face!"

"Yes. So says the legend."

"And the stink. The stench of those skeletons. The foul air of the terrified soldiers just before they turned into limestone skeletons, right?"

"According to the legend."

Mahisha Narayana stood astounded by the persistence of the legend. Seeping through the bowels of the earth. Saturating. Befuddling the brains and the imagination of a people. And in the very doorway of the space age, transforming an entire civilization into a limestone skeleton.

"It is not as the legend says, Gopi. What you see is not history. Not legend. What you are seeing is the simple work of wind and water. Erosion. Just as your brain and imagination has been eroded by legends and lies, so too the land has been eroded by wind and water. We must not let the land suffer further erosion from religion and superstitions. We must save the land from the erosion of the wind of religion, save the land from the erosion of the swamp water of superstition. If we don't, it will all be destroyed. All turn into desert."

"It is still earth, Sab. *The desert is still earth!*" Gopi wished to tell Mahisha something else about the desert. Something he had discovered about the desert one night. But suspicions about

Mahisha began to trouble him. He felt he owed it to the desert to withhold from Mahisha certain secrets of the desert.

"True, Gopi, true. The desert is still earth. A profound answer. I see you are well-grounded in your legend. But you are willing to learn. To experience. To experiment. That is a good thing. There is hope for you."

"I understand what you say about the wind. I myself have seen the work of the wind. But the water? Where is the water?"

"Ah. The water." Mahisha chuckled and led Gopi to the wide but dry riverbed that snaked through the desert like a red scar. He bent down, picked up some sand, cupped it in his hand. He said: "Tell me about the Goddess Saraswati."

The boy fixed his eyes on the dry red sand in the hands of Mahisha Narayana and as if in prayer he said: "Saraswati. The Goddess Saraswati. Fair and beautiful. The rays of the moon are her hair. The sun is the golden tikka on her forehead. The stars are her eyes. She, Saraswati, is the goddess of speech, of memory, of intellect. She, Saraswati, is the goddess of poetry, and of truth. River of knowledge and of wisdom and of learning. She, Saraswati, dwells in the heart of those who would have her. She, Saraswati, goddess of truth and wisdom and learning, dwells on the tips of the tongues of all those who would know her."

And as Gopi told of the Goddess Saraswati, the girl Saraswattee where she hid behind a pillar of limestone spread out her hair and looked for the rays of the moon. She, Saraswattee, curious child, stubborn girl, touched her forehead to see if she could find the sun there. She held out her hands as if they were mirrors that they might reflect the stars that were supposed to be her eyes. She, Saraswattee, curious child, stubborn girl, twisted her face and stuck out her tongue to see if she, Saraswattee, dwelled on the tip of her very own tongue!

While she went through her antics, and while Gopi intoned the legend of the Goddess Saraswati, unobserved by Gopi or the demon, Mahisha darkened another shade and the hair on his body grew another inch and he aged another full five years and when Gopi was done the sand in Mahisha's hands vanished and he stood and stared at the empty but now blackened palms of his hands and didn't know why he stared at his hands that way and had only a vague recollection he might have picked up some sand and he, like

Gopi, thought he had just let the red sand slip through his fingers and take to the wind.

"Ah yes, Gopi, and what happened to Saraswati, she the goddess of learning and books and poetry and literature?"

"Here where we stand. This was her abode. Here once in this riverbed the flood waters of a river flowed. And it was the river of truth, the river of knowledge, the river of learning. The waters of this river were her hair and her hair flowed through the land and nourished the earth and made it bear trees and fruits. Birds of the air came and quenched their thirst. Animals of the land came and quenched their thirst. And mortals came and sat on her banks and sought her wisdom and wrote songs and poetry and there was happiness in the land because mortals knew and understood the rightness and wrongness of all things."

"And what happened Gopi?"

"The people."

"What about the people?"

"They abandoned the ways of books and learning and turned to evil ways."

"What did the people do?"

"They polluted and poisoned the pure waters of the river Saraswati."

"And?"

"The Goddess Saraswati grew sad. She became brokenhearted. She became sorrowful and wept. She wept for humankind who had abandoned poetry and learning and literature. Then she collected her books, picked up her body, and rooted out the flood waters of her hair from the earth."

"Thence the desert was born."

"Thence the desert was born."

"And later came Shiva and Parvati. Shiva, whose job it was to keep an eye on creation lest it should disappear, he didn't know the Goddess Saraswati had deserted this abode."

"No."

"He came, full of thirst, expecting water, found a desert, became possessed of anger. Then came the other destruction?"

"Yes."

"The destruction wrought by Parvati and which turned your village into a shrine!"

"So says the legend."

Gopi watched Mahisha Narayana tremble with rage and he wasn't sure if the man had indeed aged and darkened or if it was his rage that made him look blacker and ten years older than when he first set foot in their shrine that very day.

"Is it not true, Sab?" Gopi asked.

Mahisha bent down and grabbed handfuls of red sand and stared at the sand and said: "Sand. It is all sand!"

Then Mahisha Narayana flung the sand in the air and stormed through the desert in long angry strides—furious that he was a mere mortal.

Saraswattee stepped out of her hiding place and she and Gopi watched the wind blow the sand through the red light of the desert sun. They studied the sand, as if they could see it one grain at a time. In the sun the sand became transformed; became no longer sand: became light. In this light of red sand grains Durga Kali shifted her eyes and beheld her children. She beheld Chintamani the bride on a sand dune, the desert sun in her jewels and in her hair. She beheld Saraswattee walk beside Gopi. She studied Gopi. And, she realized the menace of the stranger. She shifted her gaze to the stranger and watched his long strides through the desert evening. Who was he? Who was that stranger? Who was that man? Whoever he was he had an evil intent. He was about to make her legend a lie. He was about to transform Gopi from a devotee of hers into a disbeliever. Because, if the children didn't believe, it meant that she Durga Kali didn't exist.

EIGHT

SUCH a time it was then, as it is now; a time not
of gods and demons: but a time of evil men. That the stranger was
an evil man Durga Kali had no doubt. She recalled his brash and
vainglorious thoughts. His lustful boast to catapult her sacred
land—myth, shit, and primitives!—into the twenty-first century.
The twenty-first century! Was it that time already? Was this the age
of Kali then—Kali yuga? When men were evil and the earth verged
on dissolution. When nations coveted nations and destroyed each
other in the name of their gods. When the leaders of nations
banded together. Or in separated bands of dacoits. And plundered
their own people. Like the demon Durga had plundered. Ravished
their own nations and squandered the treasuries of their people on
further death and destruction. When entire peoples, leaderless, lost
hope and direction and became blind to even each other and took
to evil ways. Such an age it was then; when humankind lost instinct and intuition: when humankind lost the innate *feel* of the
rightness and wrongness of things.

But how long ago had she given up? When had she, Durga
Kali, lost hope and could no longer suffer the lust and evil of
humankind? A blank. Such a blank from that moment to this. No
recall. No memory. And yet for the salvation of the children—her
own salvation!—she had to regain her memory. Restructure the
past. So she might chart an infinitesimal future moment more for
herself to right the wrong she committed by her ungodly act of
abandonment of the children of mortals; and the abandonment of
godhood.

111

When gods relinquished godhood, false gods replaced them. Or demons. Or vain evil men! That stranger plagued her. She had heard his thoughts but she couldn't recall his name. If she had his name she could ravish his genealogy and come face to face with him and melt his heart with the thrust of her eyes for his brash and vain boast. And yet, was he a mortal man? Mortal men made such vain and proud threats and came to a sudden halt. Gods had no need of idle threats—they just destroyed if destruction was called for. Demons were notorious for such pronouncements—and then sneaking away to plot.

Durga Kali and Gopi and Saraswattee watched Mahisha Narayana stride across the sands, go to his army jeep, pull open the door, throw himself in, slam the door shut, start his jeep, and fling the desert in disarray as he smashed his way through the sand. Durga Kali followed the trail of the whirlwind. Who was the stranger? Man, god; or demon? If he was the manifestation of Brahma, would Brahma resort to the lowest and vilest forms of destruction: the destruction of belief? And even more loathsome and ungodly: the destruction of the delight and the wonder and the innocence and the beliefs of a boy—of children? No. Absolutely not. That stranger could not be the reincarnation of the Supreme Creator, Brahma.

Then who was he? An evil man—or a demon? But a demon? In this age? In this age of only a human population of mere mortal evil humankind? Durga Kali became seized by spasms of urgency and fear. Sweat oozed out of every pore of her massive granite and cast-iron body. Out her mouth she exhaled hot clouds of breath. She rolled her eyes, spun the blood through her skull, disturbed the tangle of serpents in the cavernous cells of her brain—the tangle of serpents that constituted the repository of her memory and her bad temper. She had to find out who the stranger was because it was impossible to destroy someone with no name. It was because he had lost his name that the demon Durga no longer existed and no longer plagued the gods nor humankind. She had to find his name—Naga would know, he, guru and saint, wise and venerable, keeper of the genealogies of all humankind: she had to wake him up. But the old and weak serpent seemed dead! Was he dead? Had he obeyed her so absolutely? Durga Kali felt the anger cloud up her head. She would wreak her vengeance on that lazy viper of hers and he would never know what clouted him—he who prided himself the serpent of serpents!

And what had become of the ogre within her chest? That monster, once her two-faced heart? Why had he released her veins and her vital organs and her vicious serpents from the fatal grip of his death lock? Her head was less dizzy. Her blackouts were less frequent. The tightness in her chest lessened and she could breathe easier. Her blood trickled in the normal flow of circulation. And the celestial rhythm of her soul vibrated through her body and she began to regain strength and vigor and vitality—and her taste for the lust of evil men.

Durga Kali closed her eyes and began to meditate and pulsed her vicious consciousness through her veins and her vital organs and began to knock on the brain of Naga, the ancient cobra. But just as he awoke sour and grumpy, the tapping in his brain ceased. The ogre within Durga Kali's bosom suddenly realized what she was up to. Quickly he paralyzed the lower portions of her body and a deep oblivion swamped the serpent of serpents. Then Durga Kali felt her consciousness bounce back into her own brain and she thought she had lost the blissful art of meditation and she tried harder and harder to pulse her emissary into wakefulness and vengeance. But there was no way a single thought of hers was ever going to seep through that heart of hers. Because the ogre had already picked up the vibrations he listened for and knew that he was the heart of the demon Mahisha Durga. Reincarnated right within the bosom of Durga Kali. And his master had come to claim him. To claim his demon heart and wreak vengeance on Durga Kali.

On the sand outside the crater, Saraswattee, oblivious now of the evil stranger who had driven away, ran among the desert bushes and picked wild berries for herself and for Gopi. Gopi crossed the bed of the lost river Saraswati and stood up on the opposite bank. He studied the volcanic crater and the ruins and the limestone valley. Mahisha Narayana befuddled him even more. He remembered the way he could not remove his hand from the man's fist. He remembered the force and the power he felt coiled up in that clenched fist. He relived the explosion of the second earthquake. And he had no doubt in his mind that in exactly such a way volcanoes exploded and perhaps, yes, that was how the volcanic crater of the temple of Shiva and the abode of Durga

Mata might have been formed. But if that was true: what of the legend? How did Durga Kali come to stand there and rise up to such massive heights into the abode of the gods? Did mortal hands build that statute? Or was it as the legend said when Lord Shiva grabbed her by her hair? And did she not, just before her flesh and blood turned into a body of boulders and cast iron, did she not give birth to the temple of Shiva very much as a woman gives birth to a child? If not, did mortal hands build the temple between the outstretched legs of Durga Kali? What then, of the legend? Was all a lie? And if the legend was a lie, did it matter that once in the desert he had discovered the earth was round, he had discovered the curvature of the earth? If legends were lies then the land was flat and that was that. Then there was no truth, even of the desert; or the spirits of the desert.

With her skirt full of purple berries Saraswattee came up to Gopi and filled her mouth with the ripe wild berries and asked: "Little Husband, why are you so troubled?"

"Little Mother, what if the legend is a lie?"

"*What?*" Saraswattee became so shocked she put her hands on her waist and all her berries spilled to the sand. "Look what you made me do! Now get down on your knees and help me pick up my berries!" Gopi joined Saraswattee on her knees and he sank in the hot sand and began to help her gather her berries. "Not a single berry for you, Gopi. Don't you put one of my berries in your mouth—not as long as you ask such stupid questions."

"But what if the legend is a lie?"

"Then you are a fool, that's all."

"I just don't want to know lies. *I want to know things. I want to know the truth about things*."

"I will tell you the truth about one thing. That blow to his head by his father has made Gopi a fool."

"I know what lies are. Lies always take care of themselves. But truth. Sometimes I feel truth is so foolish—so fickle."

"Adhey, Gopiwalla, such big words the stranger has taught you. But maybe it is the other way around. Lies are fickle and foolish. And truth—truth is like a bloom in the desert!"

Gopi stared at the berries. Gods love truth, demons hate truth; mortal men crave truth: yet they lie so much. What did the stranger want from him? In this contest. Of legend against legend. Myth versus myth. What?

"Didn't I tell you the stranger was an evil man? Didn't I tell you to stay away from him? See what he has already done to you? Confused your mind. An evil man!"

"How do you know he is evil?"

"Because he has no god!"

Gopi glanced up at the girl to find himself transfixed by her angry eyes. *The stranger has no god.* The statement shocked the boy. But he realized Saraswattee was right.

"He is handsome, Gopi. And he has learning and education. But he has no god."

"He is a man of science."

"And don't men of science need gods?"

"Maybe not."

"Then men of science are very lonely, Gopi. Do you know what loneliness it must be to exist without a god? What's the use of all his big fancy words if the stranger has no god other than his evil self?"

Gopi thought of what the girl said. Indeed Mahisha Narayana had knowledge and learning. But what must it be like to live without a god? Mahisha Narayana was a man of the new science. But he had no god. Saraswattee was right: what loneliness to exist without a god! To have knowledge, but no god. To have science; but no higher good. What was the point of science? Knowledge without a higher good could not be put to *any* good.

"Little Husband, a man of science without a god can only be vain and evil. And your stranger is given to such vanity. Given to vanity—and a mission of evil—with his science as a weapon!"

Gopi became stunned by the maturity and lucidity of Saraswattee's thought and vision. Vanity and evil. Yes, Mahisha Narayana was given to vanity. And there lurked a shadow of evil within the soul of Mahisha Narayana. What did he come to their shrine for? What was he really after? Mahisha Narayana knew their shrine and village as Gopi knew the desert. And to know a place in such a manner you had to be born there. For you to know the earth it must give birth to you. Was that why the eyes of Mahisha Narayana dared the villagefolk to recognize him? Had he been born there? Was this Mahisha Narayana that Mahisha Narayana the menfolk talked about? The son, who, said the cross-eyed pundit—punditji punditji, when will a match be made for my daughter Madhuban, what evil lurks in the birth of my daughter Madhuban, chee chee chee, such an old girl, so close to her monthlies and not married yet, such a shame and a disgrace on her father's head, she has an evil spirit, she must be whipped to be exorcised of her evil spirit, shame shame shame, such an old girl, so close to her monthlies and not married yet, a disgrace, chee chee chee—was most probably a saint by now? Mahisha Narayana was a man of the new science but there certainly existed nothing saintly about him. But none of the older men could recognize him. In fact, they all concluded that this Mahisha could not be that Mahisha. Why then, did the eyes of Mahisha Narayana dare all to be shocked into a recognition? And shocked into a recognition of what? The village men had indeed acted strangely. Nervous. Evasive. Almost guilty. What had happened to Pundit Mahesh Narayana that he had had to leave his birthplace of Nagar and depart? What evil incident was the wife of that pundit guilty of? What had she done? What evil had a wife of a pundit committed?

Gopi began to get more confused. There existed too many gaps to allow him a certain span of coherence. He could ask his father-in-law—his father-in-law! He, Gopi, dark-skinned boy, married? A married man? At fourteen. A husband; and with the responsibilities of a husband. What were the responsibilities of a husband to a wife—*two wives?*

The boy glanced at Saraswattee. She dusted the sand off her wild berries. A happiness, like the sight of the sudden flight of birds, swept through Gopi. Saraswattee herself the flight of birds. How much he liked her. Suddenly the boy realized he couldn't think of the desert without Saraswattee. He glanced at the thali on her chest.

"Aye, Gopi, don't be so immodest!"

"What are you talking about, Little Mother?"

"Love."

"Love?"

"Yes. Your love for me. Don't let it spill out all over the place like the sand and the sunset. Keep some of it in your heart. As I keep my love for you in my heart."

Gopi switched his gaze to Chintamani where she still sat on the sand dune. In her marriage raiments and jewels. And, with the desert sun caught and netted all over her, she looked more beautiful. A sudden sadness fell over the boy.

"Why are you sad now? What is the matter with you? There were times when for weeks I couldn't get a shadow out of you. Now you keep changing all the time. One minute happy, the next minute sad. One minute in love, the next minute out of love. How beautiful is Chinta! See. Even more beautiful than the evening sun. Don't you love Chinta too?"

"Little Mother, what are you talking about?"

"Love."

"What is this love talk?"

"Love talk. Don't you love Chinta too?"

"Chinta hates me."

"All that will change. She is just a little foolish right now."

"Little Mother, we have done wrong."

"What are you talking about?"

"I have done wrong."

"Adhey Gopiwalla, shall I too hit you on your head?"

"I married you and Chinta."

"I made you marry me and Chinta. You did no wrong. You are just a lucky boy. And wait till you marry Madhuban."

Gopi stared at Chintamani as if he didn't hear Saraswattee. Chintamani. His wife. Who hated him. Hated him because his father hated her father whom she loved above all. Why did his father hate her father? What was the cause of the feud between the two brothers? And why had his father forced the match between he and Chintamani?

Whatever the reason it was bad. Wrong had been done to Chintamani. Injustice had been done to Saraswattee. Evil had been done to Doolwah and Amakutty and Sirju and Roopa and Phooloo—and all the little girls ever whipped to be exorcised of evil spirits they never possessed. Gopi began to experience the innate inherent wrongness and rightness of things. And then he felt he understood some of the things Mahisha Narayana talked about. Rituals. Customs. Ceremonies. Superstitions. The way these things could be evil and could weigh down a civilization until that civilization collapsed. The whipping of girls to exorcise them of evil spirits. Child-marriages. The demand of a bride price was an abomination. The power of priests and brahmins was excessive and abused. *The ritual of a blood sacrifice was evil.*

Could this be the mission of Mahisha Narayana? To rid the land of wicked and evil rituals and customs? To free the land from the strangulation of tradition and superstitions? Outside this crater, Mahisha Narayana said, outside this desert, there circled the twenty-first century. The future—and truth. And Mahisha Narayana wanted him to become his assistant and help him in his work. But what really was that work? How did he plan to accomplish his goals? What was the dark nature to Mahisha Narayana?

Gopi studied the vapors as they rose up from the crater and spread in the air before Durga Kali. Geothermal energy. What had geothermal energy to do with Mahisha's work? How did Mahisha plan to use geothermal energy to achieve his end? What were his ends? Gopi remembered how Mahisha had stormed away. Flung the red sand in the air. Said, all was sand; just sand. Such a finality to what he said. And now Gopi sensed such a finality to Mahisha's ends. A finality to ends. A final—end?

And he Gopi, dark-skinned boy, desert boy, withdrawn, elusive: he a means to that end? Alien words reechoed in Gopi's head. Science, Gopi. Investigate. Experiment. New ways to see the old. Volcanoes, volcanic crater; volcanic ash. Basalt and igneous rocks and sedimentary rocks. Chemistry and physics and mathematics and geology. NaCl. How would a knowledge of the chemical composition of common table salt rid the land of the wicked practices of child-marriages and the abomination of blood sacrifice and the evil of whipping little girls and turning children into beggars and forcing women to become temple prostitutes? What good was the highest discoveries and truths of science and the twenty-first century if human beings failed to *feel* the innate rightness and wrongness of their lives and of the things around them?

But for the human beings to trust to their hearts again and know instinctively and intuitively the wrongness and rightness of things so much time seemed to be needed. And Mahisha Narayana was infected by a belief not much time existed—not much time was left. Perhaps this mania, this obsession, was what Gopi had sensed as demonic about Mahisha Narayana. Because suddenly, he of the patience of the desert, began to feel the urgency of time; became possessed by the sensation that indeed not much time was left and life couldn't go on in the swamps of tradition and superstition but

something had to be done and done immediately because
regardless of how many millions of pilgrims possessed the earth
they were unholy and it was not the universe that had to bestow
holiness on them but they had to purify themselves and bestow
holiness and sacredness upon the universe because such a time it
was then as it is now when humankind had to cleanse itself.
Perhaps, this was what Mahisha Narayana came to do. And do it
fast. And Gopi. He. Dark-skinned boy. Desert boy. He who knew
the legend well. Would he help Mahisha Narayana in his work?

"You are thinking of that evil man again."

"Yes."

"He has possessed you."

"Why do you say that?"

"Because since his arrival you have changed so much."

"You changed me, Little Mother, up there on the goddess. When
I tied the thali around your neck."

"I changed you for the good. That evil man changed you for the
bad. What were all the things he told you?"

"Things of science."

"And you believe the things he told you?"

"Some of them."

"He told you the legend was a lie?"

"Yes."

"And you believe the legend is a lie?"

"I did not say that."

"Do you now believe the legend is a lie?"

"I do not know what to believe!"

"I will tell you what to believe."

"What?"

"If you don't become my desert-wise Little Husband very fast, I
want you to believe I will become very angry with you very fast!"

The boy looked at the girl and thought it was good she was still
so young and still beheld things the way he once beheld things. She
was evolving into the wisdom of the desert and of the things of the
desert and soon he wouldn't have to worry about her because then
no one would have to ask what will become of Saraswattee
because Saraswattee will know the answer for herself and will
answer for herself.

"Here, take these berries to Chintamani. I will go and gather more for the two of us." Gopi took the berries but hesitated. "Go on. Take the berries to her. No fruits were offered on this her wedding day! You go give her fruits that she may become happy and may have a blessed future!"

Without protest Gopi walked across the riverbed of the lost Saraswati and made his way among the clumps of reeds while Saraswattee went through the berry bushes. Gopi stopped seven feet away behind Chintamani. For a long while he stood silent, the berries cupped in his hands, and held out like an offering.

Chintamani sensed the presence behind her and glanced around and transfixed Gopi with such a stare of anger and hate the boy felt and looked stupid. Chintamani beheld the handful of berries and tears filled up her eyes and she said, "Go away! I don't want your fruits!" Gopi didn't know what to do and he wriggled his toes in the sand as the berries tickled the palms of his hands. Chintamani returned her gaze to the sunset and wept and said: "I prayed for a rich and handsome husband. To come from afar. On a horse!"

Gopi became even more stupid and he withdrew into the desert of himself and felt far far away from the purple berries cupped in his hands. Chintamani stared into the sunset as she wept. She didn't think she might have done wrong—might be doing wrong. She had had a dream. A boy on a horse. The chance to bestow honor and pride on her father. To compensate. To apologize. To make atonement for having been born a girl. And yet she didn't hate having been born a girl. This puzzled her. She accepted it. Not because it was her fate. Simply because it was so: she was a girl. In her mind there was nothing wrong with that. In her body there was nothing wrong either. She felt no different for being a girl, she felt no different from being a girl, she felt no difference from anyone else. Now she found she didn't mind being a girl. In fact she discovered she liked it—if, then and there, someone was to have asked her: Chintamani, in your next life, do you want to be born a boy or would you still want to be a girl? The girl would have been scandalized. What preposterousness! What presumptuousness! What tinkering with human beings! Thus she would have reacted. She wanted to be a girl. When the time came she wanted to be a woman. When the time came she wanted to be a wife. She wanted to be a good girl. When the time came she wanted to be a good woman. When the time came she wanted to be a good wife. She wanted to learn. When the time came she wanted to learn some more. When the time came she wanted to share that learning. She wanted to cook. When the time came she wanted to cook nicer more delicious things. When the time came she wanted to eat some of those nice delicious things. She wanted to dream. When the time came she wanted to live her dream. When the time came she wanted to share that dream with someone. She wanted to honor her father. When the time came she wanted to care for her father. When the time came she wanted to love her children's father. She wanted to recognize her mother. When the time came she wanted to see and know her mother. When the time came she wanted to be a mother. She wanted to think. When the time came she wanted to think some more. When the time came she wanted to think again. She wanted to feel. When the time came she wanted to feel for herself. When the time came she wanted to feel for others. She wanted to love. When the time came she wanted to know what love was. When the time came she wanted to be loved. She wanted to be a girl. When the time came she wanted to be a human being. When the time came she wanted to be a good human being.

She wanted a lot.

And why not?

She wanted even more. She wanted all of the above and a little bit more for her sisters!

Chintamani flashed her eyes upon Gopi once more and the boy knew she beheld him as the sole cause of her misery and her agony. Her father didn't matter. Her father's poverty didn't matter. His father was of no consequence. It was him. He was the total cause of her being nothing. She was nothing. Gopi was the cause of that nothingness. Gopi was the effect of that nothingness. Gopi: cause and effect of nothingness. Desirous of being human; she beheld Gopi as inhuman.

And ugly.

She said: "I want a handsome husband. Not an ugly boy like you. Not a black boy like you. So ugly and so black!"

But Gopi didn't feel hurt. Didn't feel insulted. He was far from that girl. Deep within himself. But even from within there he wished she would accept the fruits from him on this the day of her marriage. And he understood now why she looked at Mahisha

Narayana the way she had. She had had a dream. And Mahisha Narayana stepped out of that dream. The rich and handsome stranger she had dreamed of as a husband. The boy wished he had known of her dream before. Then he would not have consented to the match. Instead he might have rebelled with her; fought for her: fought for her dream.

Now it was all hopeless. There existed nothing he could do. He couldn't undo the marriage. Or maybe he could. He could expose his secret illicit marriage to Saraswattee, couldn't he? That would make his marriage to Chintamani null and void. Then she would be free—or dead. They might all be dead. But that was a way—a chance. A chance to make Chintamani's dream come true. Then she might marry the rich and handsome stranger. And didn't he look at Chintamani the very same way Chintamani looked at him? Now that Gopi knew what her dream was he knew Chintamani liked Mahisha Narayana. He had stared at her that way. Maybe because he thought her beautiful? Thus they stood. Gopi and Chintamani. They who knew the legend well. Married. Husband, and wife. But that meant one thing to Gopi. And another thing to Chintamani. Neither *felt* married. Gopi didn't feel like a husband. Chintamani didn't feel like a wife. As far as she was concerned she was not married. Was not a wife. She still wanted her dream. Even just a part of her dream would do. She was ready—willing!—to prune down her dream some. Dampen down some of the color. Lessen the music. Reduce the size of the wedding party of the bridegroom. Tone down some of the dazzle. Blot out some of the glitter. She was willing to do with even less. She didn't mind if her bridegroom walked, left his horse at home—didn't even have a horse. Just as long as that ugly black boy before her with his stupid berries wasn't her bridegroom. He could eat his berries—and his thali.

The thali! Chintamani dropped her eyes on the gold ornament. How she had longed for that thing. Lived for it. Pained for it. Was beaten and ostracized because before this she didn't have it around her neck. To show. To signify. To identify her. Chintamani. Wife. No longer a shame and a disgrace to her father. No longer a sore. And now she had it she didn't want it. Hated it. As she hated Gopi. Who didn't have a horse. Who didn't come from far away. Suddenly she became possessed with the urge to grab the thali, rip it from her, and fling it away. Yet she knew if she did, never again could she show herself in the village. Or anyplace else. Then she would certainly have to kill herself. With the weight of the thali around her neck and with tears in her eyes she said to Gopi: "Why are you looking at me like that? What do you want? Go away!"

Suddenly Chintamani realized she had spoken to Gopi—was speaking to him. She didn't die. He didn't disappear. Neither felt any mystery or magic. Yet she had spoken to the boy. For the first time in her life. And though he hadn't said a word it had been a conversation. A conversation of sorts. The stupid ugly black boy with his hands full of purple berries! Chintamani glanced at the palms of her hands. Her tears had smudged her decorations. She knew she had messed up her face too. What did it matter? With an ugly husband like that boy. "I don't want your stupid berries," Chintamani said and again looked west. She brought up her knees and clasped her shins with her hands. The sun sank low. Dust clogged the air. The sunset was as beautiful as her sari. Sari! From where had the sari come? To whom did the sari belong? And the jewels! The mirror! Chintamani gasped. What had she done? What was she doing? What a sin had she committed! Indeed they had whipped an evil spirit deep into her soul. There she sat. In borrowed wedding clothes. On her marriage day. On a sand dune. Next to a black ugly boy. With dreams of a rich and handsome stranger on a horse riding out of the desert sunset into the desert of her life. When she should have been at home. Sequestered away like the other brides. Celebrated. Blessed. Worshipped. This—and all she had done was heap shame upon disgrace and sin upon sin.

"So Chinta," Saraswattee said, "you suddenly came to your senses?"

"Saras, why do you mock me so?"

"Because you are foolish."

"Yes, I am foolish."

"Gopiwalla, you didn't offer the fruits as a gift to Chinta?"

"She doesn't want the berries."

"I am not accepting any gifts from such an ugly black boy!"

"Chinta! Who are you calling ugly and black?"

"That boy there. Can't you see?"

"Gopi? Such a good and handsome boy?"

"Gopi? Handsome?"

"Yes! And good! I suppose you think the stranger was hand-some?"

"Yes. Didn't you see him?"

"I saw him. But he isn't as handsome as my Gopi."

"Then something must be wrong with your eyes, sister."

"No. Nothing is wrong with my eyes. Your eyes. You will soon see something is wrong with your eyes. Why don't you like Gopi?"

"I hate Gopi!"

"Why do you hate Gopi?"

"Because I don't like him."

"Why don't you like him?"

"Because he is black and ugly and has ugly hair."

"Sister! Don't you dare call Gopi black and ugly again! Do you hear me?"

"Yes, I hear you."

"Find other reasons to dislike him. But he is not black and ugly. And I like his hair just the way it is. One day when you fall in love with him you will see what a good and handsome boy he is."

"What do you know about love, sister?"

"I know love is not a rich and handsome stranger."

"Why do you mock me?"

"Why do you mock yourself?"

"You are very unkind to me."

"You are very unkind to Gopi. Remember, he is your hus-band."

"I wish I could forget that."

"Then forget it. And you had better run home before our father finds out what you have done. Go now and leave me and Gopi because we wish to be alone by ourselves."

Chintamani jumped up, gathered her sari to free her feet, and then rushed off. Gopi and Saraswattee watched her climb the north steps and disappear down into the crater. They watched until she reappeared on the south wall and then again disappeared, this time in the village. All around the crater and amongst the ruins the hordes of pilgrims were cooking or eating or already stretched out for the night.

Saraswattee went and sat on the dune and spread her berries before her. After a while Gopi slipped down beside her. Neither spoke. Saraswattee ate her berries, Gopi stared into the sunset.

After a long moment Saraswattee said, "Chinta is beautiful, eh, Gopi?"

The boy didn't answer.

Saraswattee spread out her hair, stuck out her tongue, held out her palms before her as if they were mirrors.

"Little Husband, am I as beautiful as Chinta?"

Once again the boy offered no answer.

"Aye, Gopiwalla, now don't turn into the desert, you hear me? Answer me. Am I as beautiful as Chinta?"

"Little Mother, you are more beautiful."

"Sure. If I had asked the desert, that is exactly what the desert would have answered."

"But I mean it, Little Mother."

"I know. But you mean it in a different way."

"Yes."

"That's fine."

Saraswattee popped berries in her mouth. Gopi watched the sun flake into dust. Saraswattee edged closer to Gopi. After a while she leaned fully against him and together they let the night come, experienced the desert change its skin. It was going to be cold, Saraswattee could tell. She could tell because Gopi had taught her how to tell. For a long long while they listened to the desert transform itself.

When the sun had almost disappeared, Saraswattee got up and pulled Gopi to his feet and said, "Come let us go to our place. Time to eat and then to sleep."

"The whipping is over now Little Mother, we can go to our homes."

"No. We are going to spend one more night in our secret place. Then we will go to our homes."

Gopi made no protest but followed the girl as she walked among the clumps of bushes, climbed up the northern steps, descended inside the crater, and made her way across the courtyard as the vapors rose without their drizzle of rainbows. In the middle of the courtyard Saraswattee bid Gopi wait for her behind the temple and made her way to his house. Kahar Saheb sat in the front yard, puffed smoke out of a chelum. The girl watched the big eyes, watched the wooden leg, watched the coil of the whip around the thick neck of her uncle. She slipped in the back door. Matti was not home. Saraswattee went into the kitchen and dished out food for she and Gopi, bundled up the food, and picked her way back to the courtyard.

Gopi stood behind the temple. Between the legs of Durga Kali. The courtyard lay deserted. All the temple prostitutes were in their tents. Then with Saraswattee in the lead, they began to climb up the body of the goddess. Saraswattee climbed, as Gopi had taught her to climb. From serpent to serpent. Gopi behind her. The girl climbed up the right leg, swung around the waist, climbed up the back to the shoulder, and then eased herself in the stone cleft. Gopi joined her and together they looked around. Songs and music echoed from a few homes. The pilgrims were mostly bedded down for the night. The desert had closed itself around tightly, secure against the cold of the night. In the crater, the clouds of warm vapors rose. There blew in only a slight breeze. The cross-eyed pundit made his way south of the village to the spring for his evening bath. He hawked, spat, kicked a dog away from his path. There seemed to be no activity in Saraswattee's house. But Kahar sat in his front yard and puffed on his chelum. The vapors in the crater rose, spread out, engulfed the shrine and the goddess in a white mist. In the sky above, stars began to appear. Gopi and Saraswattee climbed up the necklace of skulls and slipped into the tusked mouth of Durga Kali.

The cave of the mouth of the goddess exuded warmth. A reddish light lit up the throat and reflected throughout the mouth. Gopi and Saraswattee listened. For the past three nights, echoes of frightening and horrendous sounds vibrated inside the chest and belly of Kali Durga. From the brain echoed the sounds of hisses. But this night there resounded only silence. No sounds came up the throat. No sounds vibrated down from the brain. There came the smell of incense. And the goddess seemed in sleep—or at peace.

To keep the food warm Saraswattee placed the cups and bowls on a tooth. Then she untied bundles, rolled out rags and straw, and made up their bed. Once that was done, she and Gopi sat down on their bed in the floor of the mouth and Saraswattee dished out their food.

For a while they ate in silence, then Saraswattee said, "Little Husband, you know a lot of nice things about me."

"What, Little Mother?"

"You know nice things about me."

"How do you mean?"

"I heard you tell the demon stranger a lot of nice things about me."

Gopi realized the girl was talking about the legend. The legend about the lost river Saraswati. She, goddess of knowledge and wisdom and learning. Saraswati, goddess of truth and poetry and literature. And suddenly Gopi felt, yes indeed, he had spoken of Saraswattee, she, curious child, stubborn girl.

"I like the things you said. The rays of the moon are my hair. My eyes, the stars. You really believe that?"

"I do."

"You know more nice things about me?"

"Yes."

"Plenty? A lot?"

"The legend."

"Good. Will you tell me more? Will you teach me all the legend?"

"Yes. But you will also learn for yourself."

"Good. You are a good boy, Gopi. Black but not ugly. Very handsome. I like you. You like me?"

"Yes."

"We were married today. Durga Kali was our witness."

"I hope we have her blessings."

"It is a blessed marriage, this marriage of our spirits."

"Yes, Little Mother, it is."

Then they were done eating and Saraswattee put away her utensils and they washed their hands and faces in clouds of steam puffed out of the throat of Durga Kali. When they were done they lay down to sleep in their bed on the floor of the cave of the mouth of Kali Durga. The red light enveloped them. Saraswattee curled up against Gopi. She yawned. The boy realized she was tired. He didn't feel the approach of sleep. As if to herself, Saraswattee whispered: "Little Husband, when it is time to hold our public marriage ceremony I want you to wash—take a long good bath. Then I want you to dress up. Put on a beautiful silk gown and wear a crown decorated with jewels."

Saraswattee yawned; Gopi studied the red light of the cave. He showed no surprise to discover that she too, Saraswattee, curious child, stubborn girl, had a dream. What surprised him was that he, Gopi, dark-skinned boy, never had a dream. And he thought all people were like him and lived flat lives without beautiful dreams. But there he was. With the revelation that little girls especially, dreamt beautiful dreams of faraway places. Saraswattee yawned again and she mumbled: "And come on a horse!"

Then she was fast asleep. Gopi stared into the red light of the cave of their secret place. And he didn't know when he slipped into the beautiful colors of the dream of Saraswattee, she, curious child, stubborn girl—and rode through the desert with her on a horse.

NINE

IN THE morning Gopi awoke to find himself alone. The boy jumped up. He crawled to the back of the mouth and to the edge of the throat of Durga Kali. On his hands and knees, he stared inside. Deep down in the throat the light was blood-red but Gopi couldn't see far. From Durga's belly there echoed boiling and bubbling sounds. Gopi feared Saraswattee might have rolled in her sleep and fallen down the cavernous insides. He whispered: "Little Mother." From Durga's belly bounced up the echoes: *Little Mother Little Mother Little Mother.* "Saraswattee," Gopi called. *Saraswattee Saraswattee Saraswattee*—a voice echoed back at him.

Gopi looked up at the dark cave of the skull of Durga Kali. A tangle of hisses coiled around him and he began to sweat. He whispered: "Little Mother?" Then the echoes came: *Yes yes yes yes?*

"Little Mother?"

Yes.

"Little Mother, where are you?"

Here here here.

"Where?"

Here Gopi here.

"Where, Little Mother? Are you inside?"

Yes yes yes.

"Little Mother, did you fall in?"

No Gopi no.

"Where are you?"

I am here here here here here.

Gopi glanced all around and scrambled about the mouth of Durga Kali. The voices echoed everywhere. From outside the mouth. From deep inside the throat. From the dark cave of the skull. *Gopi Gopi Gopi. Here I am. Here I am. Here I am. Come come come. Up here Gopi up here. I am up here up here up here.*

Gopi sweated like the cave of the mouth sweated. Clouds of hot vapors puffed out the throat, swamped the cave, engulfed the boy, exhaled out the mouth of Durga Kali. Gopi slipped on the sweat. He sat on a tooth and listened. He felt fear. He listened to the hisses of the serpents in the brain. He listened to the boiling and the bubbles emanating from Durga's belly. The breaths of vapors swamped over him, flowed out the mouth. Gopi didn't know if he were awake or still asleep. Caught in a dream—or trapped in a nightmare. He called out: "Little Mother!" The whispers returned to him: *Yes yes yes yes?* "Where are you?" *Here here here here.* "Where?" *Up here Gopi up here.* "Where, Little Mother?" *Come come come. Here here here. Up here up here up here.*

Then Durga Kali's breaths came thick and hot and Gopi found himself caught in currents of respiration. The vapors swirled around him and he felt trapped in a desert storm. The boy let himself be pushed by the white breaths and scrambled out Durga's mouth and down the necklace of skulls into the stone cleft. He looked around. The desert lay shut out by a mist. Frost coated the walls and the floor of the volcanic crater. The mist netted the early rays of the dawn and there was little movement among the pilgrims or in the village. Durga Kali herself was wrapped in a sari of frost, polka-dotted with the tiny black eyes of the serpents. She rose up tall and mighty and might have been out for a morning walk and had become enchanted by the early morning desert and paused in reflection on the past of the universe and the future of her life. What would that day bring? What had she to do? What would be left undone? But at that moment there existed no urgency. The universe mirrored peace. She was content. Her breath rose up from the springs in the crater and spread with little effort. There was no wind, only a chill, and Gopi rubbed his arms and whispered: "Little Mother, where are you?"

Here here here here here.

Gopi spun around. The echoes had come from within the mouth. And not in Saraswattee's voice. Or it could be, because the girl had fallen deep inside, her voice appeared altered. Gopi began to scramble up the necklace of skulls and into the mouth when Saraswattee said: "Aye, Gopi! What is the matter with you? Where are you going?"

The boy glanced up. Saraswattee sat on top of Kali's head. In the lotus position. Her elbows on her knees and her chin propped up in her hands. Her eyes lit up with delight. The blue sky looked like a veil just above her head. She seemed pleased to have had Gopi worried about her—pleased to know he too, desert boy, could be possessed by fear.

"You were frightened?" she asked.

"Yes, Little Mother."

"Why? Of what?"

"I thought, I was afraid you fell down."

"Me? No, Little Husband, I wouldn't fall down."

"But what are you doing up there?"

"Sitting. Come up."

"You will be seen, Little Mother."

"No one is awake. Aye, Little Husband, look, all is asleep, only me and you and Durga Rani are awake. Come up, you can see farther from here. You can see everything from here. Come, Little Husband, do not be afraid."

"I am not afraid, Little Mother. Not to climb up. But they will catch us."

"Let them. We wouldn't go down."

"Come, Little Mother."

Suddenly Saraswattee tightened her face and then jumped to her feet. To Gopi she shot up all the way into the sky. Into the high abode of the gods. He squinted. Shielded his eyes. Looked at the girl who had no fear whatever of falling. Saraswattee gazed at the village. Gopi turned. The goats and the sheep bustled, eager for the freedom of grazing. On the main path, heading for the spring to have his purifying bath, walked the pundit. A rag was draped over his shoulder and as he trudged alone he coughed, spat, mumbled "Aye aye, Rama, hari om."

Saraswattee put her hands on her waist.

"Little Mother," Gopi whispered, "come down."

"Have no fear, Little Husband," the girl said, "he can't see me, his eyes are no good. Besides, he is going the other way."

The girl put her hands to her mouth and shouted: "Punditji, punditji, here I am!"

Then she dropped to her belly but could hardly stifle her laughter. Gopi crouched down. The echoes of her voice seemed to shatter the pundit and he trembled and glanced all around and called out: "What? What? Who called?"

"I did!" shouted Saraswattee.

Around and around turned the pundit and his eyes scrambled ahead of him.

"Who called? Where are you? What do you want? Who is it?"

"Me! Durga Kali!"

"What? What blasphemy is this? Who utters this wickedness? Is this a game? To provoke a high priest on his way to his holy bath? My curse on you. May you stumble and fall!"

"My curse on you too, you cross-eyed hungry-bellied pundit! May you stumble and fall!"

"Shoo! Little Mother. Look, the villagers are coming out of their homes. Come down."

"They can't see me—look! look! ha ha! the pundit has stumbled and fallen flat on his face. He tripped over a goat!"

Gopi glanced down to see the pundit sprawled out on the sand and a goat climbing over him as it sought to free itself and then villagers ran to the pundit's help. "You see, Gopi? You see what power I have? One word from me and the pundit crumbled!"

"Come down, Little Mother, come down."

Then something else caught Saraswattee's attention. Madhuban. Madhuban was sneaking through the backyard. Quickly Saraswattee scrambled down to Gopi in the stone cleft.

Madhuban ran to the fuel pile and hid.

"What is Madhuban up to?"

Madhuban waited. After a while, from other houses, appeared Phooloo, Doolwah, Amakutty, Sirju, and Roopa.

"What are they up to?"

The girls waited. Watched. When they felt safe and unobserved, they ran through the backyards to the temple courtyard.

"It's a good thing I caused the pundit to fall down. Otherwise they would have been caught."

The girls collected in the courtyard and stood up before Durga Kali. Gopi watched. Saraswattee watched. And Kali Durga, awakened by Gopi's voice and Saraswattee's pranks, watched. The girls brought pure water and fresh flowers and fruits. These they offered to the goddess and their voices rose up in prayers as the girls beseeched the benevolent one to be kind today and grant them their boons. Gopi listened. Saraswattee listened. Durga Kali listened.

As the girls prayed, the desert slowly changed. The sun rose, burnt the mist away. Quietly the village came alive. The pilgrims awoke, stirred, lit fires. At the spring Pundit Ayer poured water over himself. Smoke rose from the kitchens. The smell of curry filled the air. Dogs barked. Women appeared in their backyards; moved in and out their houses. The pundit stumbled back towards his house, hawked, spat, mumbled, "Hari om, om hari om." Kahar stepped out his hut, sat on a stump in the yard, lit up his chelum. Padma appeared in the backyard, collected fuel dung, reentered the kitchen. Matti scoured a pot in her backyard. Some boys began to take out the sheep and the goats. Dogs rushed about, barked. The sun rose high.

The girls in the temple courtyard prayed on and Kali Durga listened. When the girls were done they ran behind the temple and hid.

"What are they waiting for? What do they want to see?"

"Shoo, Little Mother."

"They are up to something—"

"Look."

Saraswattee followed Gopi's eyes. Sirju's father made his humble way through the village. The old man in his dhoti and ragged turban climbed up the wall, crossed the courtyard, bowed before Durga Kali, and offered up his prayers.

"What a pitiable looking man," Saraswattee said. "Does Nandassab expect to have his boon granted with such grimy clothes and weak prayers?"

Behind the temple, Madhuban and her friends watched. When he was done with his prayers, Nandass turned and made his way out. No sooner had he left when Amakutty's father, Akpar, appeared before the goddess and bowed and offered his prayers. Then he went north. In turn came Doolwah's father and Roopa's father and Phooloo's father. They all stood before Kali Durga, bowed, clasped their hands, prayed.

"What a pitiable bunch of men," Saraswattee said. "If I was a goddess you think I would grant such men their prayers?"

"You are being too harsh."

"Harsh? Look Gopi, these fathers are less than fathers. They have sunk too low. Prayers don't crawl in the dirt. Kali may be asleep but not in the dirt. What use are their prayers? Soon Madhuban will be whipped."

"Look, your father is coming."

"He too?"

Saraswattee watched her father make his way through the village. She was disgusted. What had become of her father? Why was he so broken? "Look at him. Like a lizard. He is walking as if the weight of the entire temple is on his shoulders!"

Sutnami stumbled through the village. When he reached the house of his brother, Kahar, without raising his head, laughed and spat.

"Gopi! What is it between your father and my father?"

"I don't know."

"Why don't you know?"

"Whatever happened between them happened before I was born."

"It must have been very bad."

"Yes."

Sutnami stood bowed before the goddess and Saraswattee became utterly disgusted. "Look at him. And he is not even offering up a prayer. He is just standing there. Out of habit. Dejected. Despicable. No pride, no hope, no life. No prayer! What has happened to my father? Chinta is married. I am married. How does he expect to find a husband for Madhuban when he can offer up no prayer? What sin has he committed that he should stand before Durga Kali so?"

And Durga Kali beheld Sutnami stand before her as if indeed he was just dirt wrapped in skin. His heart was flat and no prayer echoed out his lips. Bleached of lust, bleached of life, bleached of prayer. Neither a proud man nor a human man. No man. What could she the preserver do for such a creature? What could she the destroyer do for such a human being? When had mortal men been reduced to the debris of nothingness? And what was his sin? Even Durga Kali couldn't remember because she had so long ago relinquished control over the fate and the destinies of mortal men. But if this is what mortal men had been reduced to, then indeed it was time for the dissolution of creation. And as she could feel no pity for the man before her; she could not grant him a boon he did not ask for. As he stood, thus Sutnami went; and when he was gone the girls returned before their goddess and prayed again and their prayers granted Durga Kali life. Their prayers rekindled her will. Their prayers inflamed her with a passion to live. Gopi and Saraswattee watched Sutnami stumble through the ruins as he went in search for a bridegroom for his daughter Madhuban.

"Will he find a match for Madhuban?" Saraswattee said, mostly to herself.

"I do not know, Little Mother," Gopi answered.

"He didn't pray."

"He prayed, Little Mother."

"No, he didn't pray."

"In his own way, he prayed, Little Mother."

"Durga will not be pleased by that prayer."

Gopi didn't answer her.

"How can Durga grant him anything if he doesn't please her?"

Again Gopi had no answer.

"He will never find a match for Madhuban that way."

"He will, Little Mother."

"He won't. But I have."

They looked at each other but neither spoke of his promise to marry Madhuban. The boy knew Saraswattee was serious. Chintamani appeared in the backyard. She hugged a goblet under her arm. But instead of going to the spring, she took the opposite direction. Gopi and Saraswattee watched her make her way around the crater, behind the goddess, through the limestone valley, and to the sand dune where she sat the previous evening. There she stood up and stared to the northwest.

"What is the matter with Chinta?" Saraswattee asked.

Gopi withheld his answer.

"What is she doing there?"

"I don't know."

But Gopi knew. Knew she was looking for Mahisha Narayana.

"She is looking out for something," Saraswattee said.

"Yes."

"The evil one?"

"Yes."

"Little Husband, I do not like that man. He is bad. He is evil. Chinta must not be with him. You must tell her so. I will tell her so!"

"We must go, Little Mother, I have work to do in the fields. Come, let us go."

"No. I am not going down."

"We must be careful from now on. The stranger will come and go every day. The village men will be watching him. They are suspicious about him. Besides, he has already seen you once. If he catches you up here again he will make trouble. I know that."

"He will make trouble because he is evil—that I know."

"Well come. Let us go down. And while the stranger is in our village we must not come up here."

"I will come up here. That is the only way I can keep a good eye on him."

"Let us go."

"Yes, let us go. I have a lot to do today."

Saraswattee followed Gopi down to the temple courtyard. Once on the ground they made their way to the village. Gopi turned off to go to his work in the plum orchards. He asked: "What have you to do today?"

"A lot."

"What?"

"Things."

"Okay you go do what you have to do. I will be in the fields if you need me."

Gopi stood and watched Saraswattee make her way through the village. She became preoccupied. After a while he made his way home, picked up his hoe, and went to the plum orchards. He glanced up and saw Chintamani shield her eyes as she looked to the northwest. The boy wanted to go to the girl. He bent his back to his work.

Once in her home, Saraswattee began to pack up her things. Padma worked in the backyard and Madhuban came into the house and asked, "Saras, what are you doing?"

"Packing."

"Why, sister?"

"Because that is what I have to do."

"Why do you have to do that?"

"I don't have time for too many questions. Help me pack, or be quiet."

Madhuban sat down on a stool and watched Saraswattee bundle up all her clothes and her personal things. When she was done, she swung her bundle over her shoulders and went outside. Madhuban followed her. Saraswattee stopped in the front yard. Chintamani came through the gate. The sisters looked at each other. Saraswattee stared at the empty water jug and said: "I see you brought a lot of water."

"Saras, why do you mock me so?"

"Why are you behaving like such a fool?"

"What do you mean?"

"The spring is in the opposite direction to where you were."

Chintamani looked at the ground. Madhuban said, "Saras has packed up her belongings."

It was then Chintamani noticed the bundle on Saraswattee's shoulders. "Packed up her things? What sister, have you become a mendicant? Are you going on a pilgrimage?"

"No."

"Then where are you going?"

"I am moving in with Gopi."

"What?"

"You heard me. I am going to live with Gopi."

"Gopi?"

"Yes, Gopi. You remember the ugly black boy? Well, I am going to live with him."

"Sister, what is the matter with you?"

"Nothing that is as bad as the matter with you. When you have come to your senses, and when it is your time, you will join Gopi and me. In the meantime, Chinta, beware. That stranger is an evil man. I will be keeping a very close eye on you from now on."

With that Saraswattee went out the gate and took to the sandy path. Madhuban called out: "Maji! Look Saras is leaving home!" Padma came to the front yard to see Saraswattee trudge her way to Gopi's house.

Saraswattee walked into the house as Matti came out of the kitchen with a tray of yellow peas in her hands. "Oh, Saras, it is you?" Matti asked.

"Yes, it is me."

"Where is Gopi?"

"He is in the fields."

"Did he eat some food at your house?"

"He ate no food."

"What have you in your bundle?"

"My clothes. I have come to live here. I am moving in with Gopi. Yesterday I too married Gopi. He is married to Chinta and me. Soon he will marry Madhuban."

Matti stood in the door of the kitchen and watched Saraswattee. The girl went to the bed and rested her bundle. Then she untied it and spread out her things. She folded her clothes and put them away. When she was done she said, "Give me the peas, auntie. Go sit. I will cook for Gopi."

Matti got down on her knees and took the girl's face in her hands. She understood. A tiredness fell over her and she sank back on the floor.

Saraswattee went to the fireside, put in some fuel dung, lit it. She fanned the fire until it blazed. She put a pot of water to boil. That done she opened the flour pan, measured out some flour, and began to knead dough. That done she washed her hands, peeled two potatoes, chopped them up. When the fire died down she got on her knees, fanned it, blew with her breath, and coughed as the smoke burned her eyes and made her gag.

All the while Matti sat on the floor and watched her. The girl worked busily, expertly. And she talked. She said: "Gopi and I will live here. We will build a bigger fireside. Gopi will build it. Then I will cook there for him. Soon Gopi will marry Madhuban. I will cook, Madhuban will wash, and Chintamani will gather fuel and take care of the vegetables. Then no one will beat us. Gopi is a very lucky boy."

In the doorway Padma stood. She heard her daughter talk, watched her busy herself at the fireside. After a while she walked in and Saraswattee looked up from the flames at her mother. Padma stood behind Matti. The fire brightened their faces, cast their shadows through the house. Saraswattee looked at her mother but said nothing.

"Sister," Matti said, "have you heard your daughter speak?"

"Yes, sister," Padma answered.

"What is to be done?"

"Whatever it is her fate to be will be done."

"No more?"

"No more."

"And why?"

"Because it is so."

"Can it not be different?"

"Sister, are you not too old to question now?"

"Am I?"

"I am."

"Why are daughters born?"

"That they may bear men's sons."

"And in return?"

"Suffer."

"Yes, suffer. Adhey, Saraswattee, you hear what is to be your lot?"

Saraswattee, her face close to the fire, stared at the two women.

"Well," Matti said, "your daughter has made her own match."

"A good match it is. Gopi is a good boy."

"So she has your blessings?" Matti asked.

"What more do I have to give?"

"Yes, you are right. It is a woman's place to give birth and blessings. And to suffer in return."

"Not to question."

"Not to question."

"And what about our sin?"

"Look. Are we not paying for it? Saras. Chinta. Soon Madhuban."

"So much penance for one sin?"

"In our lives, sister, neither the penance nor the sin matters anymore."

"What matters?"

"That we may die before our daughters come of age."

Padma turned and left. Saraswattee watched Matti's face. After a while the woman got up and went outside. Left alone, Saraswattee busied herself again. She boiled peas, made chapatis, and curried potatoes. When she was done she dished out food for herself and Gopi and left the house.

She made her way to the fields, where she knew Gopi would be working. When she got there the boy was nowhere around. She rested the food down, placed her hands on her waist, and called, "Gopi, Gopi, aye Little Husband."

She heard the sheep bleat but did not hear Gopi's voice. With the food once more in her hands she crossed the fields, made her way through the plum orchards and worked her way to the pasturage. Other boys tended to the goats and the sheep. But Gopi was not to be seen. Saraswattee began to run through the pasturage to the eastern entrance of the courtyard. She reached the steps, bounded up, and then stopped. At the top of the stairs loomed her uncle Kahar. With his whip. And lopsided wooden leg.

The girl cried out and dropped her food. She stood paralyzed. Her uncle played with his whip and he chuckled. His eyes rolled like the eyes of the sheep whose throat he had slit with his knife. Saraswattee couldn't take her gaze off those eyes, couldn't move, couldn't think. In her mouth her tongue searched for spit that she might swallow, feel something, come to her senses.

"You!" her uncle shouted. "Where did you get that thali? Who tied that thali around your neck?"

Saraswattee could neither sweat nor tremble.

"Are you married? Answer me! Are you married to wear a thali?"

Tears filled up the eyes of the girl and she remembered the whipping.

"Do you have an evil spirit? Only a girl with an evil spirit will tie her own thali around her neck. I will have you whipped."

Saraswattee saw Chintamani fall, beheld Kahar slit the throat of the sheep.

"You will be whipped for this evil deed. Come here. Bring me that thali!"

Kahar raised his whip, pushed his wooden foot down. He pushed too hard and the foot missed the step and he lost his balance. Saraswattee saw the huge frame loom down on her and suddenly came to her senses and jumped back. Once she moved she didn't wait to see her uncle crash to the ground over her food. She turned and bounded away as fast as she could. She ran north, among the granite boulders. She ran wildly, carelessly; tripped and fell; but rose up again. When she reached the sand dune neither Gopi nor Chintamani was there. The girl stood up baffled, tears down her cheeks. "Little Husband?" she called. No answer came.

She took a moment to catch her breath and when she did, she ran through the limestone valley to the north wall where she stopped and looked down.

In the courtyard Pundit Ayer and the village men thronged before Mahisha Narayana. Her uncle hopped his way to them. Gopi hid between the temple and the menfolk bathhouse. On the opposite wall, in full view, stood Chintamani, her eyes on Mahisha Narayana.

Saraswattee ran along the wall. Behind the goddess, the army jeep was parked. Saraswattee paid no mind to the jeep but scrambled up the wall and into the crater. She ran between the legs of the goddess and flung herself at Gopi. She sobbed. Gasped for breath. Gopi held the girl and when she caught her breath he took her face in his hands and asked, "Little Mother, what happened?"

"Your father," the girl said and her eyes flashed to the courtyard.

Gopi followed her gaze, saw his father. His face became stern.

"The bad man," Saraswattee said, "he tried to hit me. He said I have an evil spirit. He wanted to beat me, Little Husband. He wanted to take away my thali!"

"No, Little Mother, no. He will never take away your thali."

"You promise?"

Gopi looked at the girl.

"I promise," he said.

"I cooked food for you," Saraswattee said.

"You did, Little Mother? Why?"

"I wanted to, Little Husband."

"And where is the food?"

"Your father—I lost it."

"It is alright, Little Mother, don't worry."

"I will cook again. From now on I will cook all your meals, Little Husband."

They looked at each other.

"As you wish," Gopi said.

The boy glanced at Chintamani and Saraswattee followed his gaze. Chintamani seemed to be in a trance. To be lost. But there was pain on her face as she stared at the stranger. The girl seemed oblivious to where she was, seemed unaware—could care less even —that her uncle glanced from her to the stranger and from the stranger to her.

"Engineersab," Pundit Ayer said, "are you finding what you seek?" Before Mahisha Narayana could answer, a villager, Badraj, asked, "What are you looking for?" Mahisha fixed his eyes on the untouchable and suppressed his contempt. Even with Sutnami gone, the menfolk might still make trouble. He answered: "I am looking for the source."

"The source?" Pundit Ayer said. "An excellent quest for a brahmin!"

"Thank you, punditji," said Mahisha.

"Is the source you are looking for here?" Badraj asked.

"In this region," answered Mahisha.

"Of course it is here!" Pundit Ayer shouted. "This is the shrine of Shiva. The source is here! Only a brahmin would know that!"

"I have to make some surveys, do some experiments," Mahisha said as he studied the men. He was glad Sutnami was absent.

"What surveys? What experiments?" Pundit Ayer asked in sudden alarm.

"Nothing serious, punditji. Small things."

"He will desecrate our holy shrine," Badraj shouted.

"A brahmin can never desecrate," Pundit Ayer pronounced. "How can that be? How can a brahmin desecrate what is impossible for him to desecrate?"

Mahisha Narayana looked at Pundit Ayer and his wayward eyes. Indeed, he thought, had the foolish pundit hit on a truth? Can it all not be desecrated? Was the legend that inviolable?

"The punditji is right," Kahar said. "Durga Mata will not allow her sacred shrine to be desecrated. The Engineersab knows that. He is an educated man. A man of science. He too knows the legend well, is that not so Malik?"

"Yes," said Mahisha Narayana. "I too know the legend. That is why I am here. Punditji, with your consent, your permission, I would like to do a few tests around these springs, take a few water samples, nothing much."

"No! No! No!" the village men shouted. "It is forbidden to do such things! It is evil. He is up to evil work!"

"Shut up," Pundit Ayer said. "How can that be? A brahmin can do no evil—Engineersab, you are free to do whatever tests you want. No one will trouble you as long as you have my blessings. May God be with you and your work. Come to my house for lunch when you are ready."

Pundit Ayer dismissed the men and stumbled away. Kahar glanced at Chintamani, glanced at Mahisha Narayana. Then he chuckled. Mahisha picked up a crate full of test tubes, thermometers, and other equipment. He began to walk east. Kahar hopped behind him. "You are after the precious jewels, not so?" Kahar asked.

"What?" Taken by surprise, Mahisha glanced at Kahar. He looked at the man and felt a resurgence of his scorn. Kahar pointed to the precious stones and said, "Gold, Sab."

Mahisha Narayana looked at the scattered rubies and pearls. After a while he said: "Maybe."

"I knew it. And diamonds too?"

"And diamonds too."

"Durga's jewels?"

"Yes, Durga's jewels."

"Of course, Engineersab, are you not afraid to plunder the sacred gems?"

"No, I am not afraid."

"You are not afraid because you don't believe in the legend, is it not so?"

"It is so."

The two men looked at each other.

"I too am willing to not believe in the legend. Malik, how do I not believe?"

"For you it is easy. All you have to do is not believe."

"Is that possible? A man like me? A peasant? One of the lowest caste? Ah, Malik, it is not that easy. It is not easy for a peasant to not believe. A peasant must believe because that is all he has. If he does not believe then there is nothing else—unless of course, his disbelief gets him gold and diamonds instead of death and damnation."

"Death and damnation comes to all, believers and non-believers."

"And gold and diamonds only to non-believers?"

"Yes."

"But how can I not believe? How can I become a non-believer? I have not your wisdom, your knowledge, your science. I do not know your religion."

"For men like you no religion, no science matters. You need no wisdom, no knowledge. All you need to know is that the legend is all lies."

"If the legend is all lies, then I am nothing!"

"If the legend is all lies, then you just don't believe. That is all. In other words, you are a non-believer. That simple. Believe, or not believe. For you proofs do not matter. Death and damnation come anyway. Why not possess gold and diamonds along with it?"

"And the wrath of Kali?"

"Kali's wrath will fall upon her own self!"

Kahar trembled. He felt the earth tremble under his feet. The way Mahisha Narayana had spoken. Such words. Such defiance. Such hate. Kahar suddenly realized Mahisha Narayana had come to the shrine for more than the gold and diamonds. Maybe he had indeed come for his geothermal energy. But what was geothermal energy to him? Kahar. A low-caste peasant. Landless. Without food or wealth. Poverty-bound and hunger-infested. When all that wealth lay scattered before his eyes. It was because of those riches—because of the legend he had lost his leg. The curse of the legend. But maybe Mahisha Narayana could destroy the legend and the curse would be null and void and all that wealth and riches could be his—his alone!

"What will it be, Kali's wrath," Mahisha Narayana said, "or gold and diamonds?"

"How can I be of service, Malik?"

"First, silence your brother. Keep him quiet and away from me. Silence the village men. There will be other things later."

Again the two men looked at each other. Suddenly Kahar felt the scorn Mahisha Narayana had for him. But what did scorn matter to him who had been despised all his life? Mahisha Narayana would use him. He would use Mahisha Narayana. What had the holiness and the sacredness of the shrine ever gotten him? He had been born there and still no blessing of the sacred place had fallen on him. When he was born there! By birth alone he should have been blessed. Instead all he was was a low-caste dog without land or money or even a decent bed to rest his head on. No reward for him—when he was the one to do the bidding of the pundit and whip evil girls and exorcise them of their evil spirits. But he would get his reward. And his vengeance. The man of science would get his geothermal energy. And that would be the end of the legend. Then he would slaughter the first man to touch his wealth—his wealth!

Kahar turned away but did not cast a glance on Kali, but Kali completed his genealogy and then resumed her search for the genealogy of Mahisha Narayana. Narayana. What a name. The name of the very creator of Brahma. And Mahisha! She knew a certain Mahisha once. Mahisha Durga. He who enjoyed a boon from the gods that only a woman could slay him. And with his prodigious genitals flashing throughout the seven worlds, what death and destruction he wreaked. When he had raped and vanquished the world of mortals, the vain demon turned his evil on the lesser gods and smashed their kingdoms one after the other and took their wives to his buffalo pens where he indulged himself with the wives and consorts of the gods and degraded and desecrated them. Soon he had vanquished all the gods and took over their palaces and their treasures. And yet his lust for death and destruction could not be satiated. Such was his evil he ploughed through the seven worlds and ruptured graveyards and cemeteries and cremation mounds and got hold of the spirits and their skeletons and proceeded to violate even the dead and all the ancestors of the dead until even the spirits lifted their voices with the mortals and with the gods and beseeched the Supreme Creator for help and for the death and the destruction of the demon Mahisha Durga.

Mahisha Durga.

And here, before her very eyes, in her most sacred abode, stood a mortal with the names of the highest god and the vilest demon. Mahisha Narayana. She would ravish his genealogy. Graveyard after graveyard after graveyard. And discover his true identity. Then she would confront him. Come face to face. With he who dared boast that the wrath of Kali would fall upon Kali herself!

But she could do nothing until she discovered his true identity and as she ravished his genealogy, Mahisha laughed because his plot for vengeance was succeeding with the least effort on his part. He had the blessings of Pundit Ayer. And he had that monster Kahar Saheb to take care of Sutnami and the village men. There stood the beautiful young bride Chintamani with her eyes on him.

Indeed, he was a good omen. He had arrived at an auspicious time—his auspicious time. Mahisha laughed and walked around a cloud of vapors and came face to face with Gopi.

"Ah, Gopi," Mahisha said. "My assistant. How are you?"

The boy studied Mahisha.

"Are you ready to learn? To investigate? To experiment?"

The puzzlement of the desert boy grew. Had Mahisha become ugly?

"Look, Gopi, who is that?"

"Why, Sab, that is our deity, Durga Kali."

"And the legend says no mortal hand can touch any of the things in this crater, right?"

"It is so."

"But yesterday I picked up a diamond of hers. Look. I still have my hand. And I am alive. Am I not? If the legend told the truth, how come I am still alive?"

What had changed about Mahisha? Did he have that much hair on his arrival?

"Maybe, as I said yesterday, the legend is a lie."

"The legend is the truth!"

"Great. Excellent. Spoken like a true devotee of Durga Kali. Well, would you like to champion her?"

"Champion Durga Kali?"

"Of course. Look at her. She is all made of stone and cast iron. She cannot defend herself. She needs a champion to defend her."

"Defend her from what?"

"Why from me, Gopi."

"You?"

"Yes."

"Why?"

"Because I have come to destroy her!"

Then Kali, she the ravisher, she the relentless pursuer, she who once slew the demon Mahisha Durga and took his name: she Kali: shuddered. As she had desired mortal death, so too now she became possessed by mortal fear. And she fixed her gaze on Gopi. With doubt in his heart, Gopi stared back into the eyes of Mahisha Narayana. Gopi, desert boy, he knew the legend well—but did he really believe in Kali?

TEN

ND to think, she Durga Kali, bloodvexed and bloodlusting slayer of evil and of evil men, didn't really know Gopi—didn't even know for sure if Gopi was a true devotee of hers. She couldn't remember once when the boy asked of her any boon. And here. Gopi. Dark-skinned boy. Desert boy. He: defender of she who was once the defender of the innocent. He: devotee of she who had ceased to believe in herself? He: champion of she who was once the champion of the mortals and the gods against the demon Mahisha Durga. And was Gopi a match for such a threat? What weapons, besides his silence and his desert wisdom, did Gopi possess to stand up against unknown science? Mahisha Narayana! What a name for an evil man. Could Gopi confound his science and his gods? But, such a time it was then, as it is now, when even gods had to place their lives and their faith in the hands of mortals and pray for their salvation because in the hands of their devotees lay their immortality and Durga Kali whispered yes yes yes, Gopi, you are my hero, you are my champion—*verily you are my god.*

Durga Kali stunned herself. But had no time to celebrate her joy. Because Saraswattee made her way through the vapors to confront the evil man. Kali had to stop the girl because she needed Saraswattee close to her. On her bosom. So that Saraswattee's consciousness would be available to her and that she could use Saraswattee as a medium to exist. Until she came into her own. Thus, Saraswattee found herself enveloped in a cloud of vapors and couldn't move. She parted the vapors with her hands and they parted. She could even see through the vapors. She could see the evil man before Gopi. And she wanted to confront him. Come face to face with him. And kick him in the shins for what he had said. *He was going to destroy Durga Kali!* So she was right. The man was evil. He was a demon. And he had come to destroy Kali Durga. She tried to tell that Gopiwalla this. To warn him. But he wouldn't believe her. And there he stood alone before the demon. While she had become all entangled in the breath of Durga Kali and could not extricate herself. She fought with Kali's breath. Tried to push herself forward but could not. Saraswattee became filled with a wrath and she kicked against the web of vapors. She stepped back and found she could walk backways. So she tried to walk backways towards Gopi but found herself up against an invisible wall. She stepped forward and could move. She spun around and ran into the invisible wall. She backstepped. No invisible wall! The girl turned and glanced up at Durga Mata. This time Kali beheld Saraswattee mirror her own rage. She remembered how Chintamani had looked upon her thus. Saraswattee retraced her steps and Durga felt the girl climb up her body and she caused the vapors to swamp the crater and give cover to Saraswattee and then Saraswattee, she, curious child, stubborn girl, slipped into her bosom and together, goddess and rebel devotee, fixed their eyes on Mahisha Narayana.

As Gopi had his eyes on the man before him. But more than what the demon said perplexed the boy. Mahisha Narayana had changed. Mahisha Narayana had been transformed. The stranger who walked into the shrine only the day before was handsome and had light brown skin. The man who stood before him was still somewhat handsome. But he was almost black. Gopi knew the heat of the desert darkened the skin of human beings. He had seen many a light-skinned pilgrim leave the shrine holy and well-roasted. But to become that dark in less than two days? And his skin itself had thickened and hardened. And his hair. Such a tangle of hair sprouted from the head of Mahisha Narayana. Tufts of black hair stuck out his ears and nostrils. Gopi had not noticed this before. Maybe he hadn't looked at Mahisha carefully. Gopi couldn't tell if the hair on the black body had lengthened, or if the man had arrived that covered with thick hair. And didn't he look younger on that first day? Younger—and rich and handsome. A good omen! And yet, a moment before, when the villagers questioned him, none of them had expressed any shock. Or surprise—to show they felt Mahisha Narayana had suffered a transformation and now appeared bulkier and darker. With more hair over his body. And looked not forty-five but fifty-five and his skin no longer smooth but leathery and wrinkled.

But, perhaps, the greatest astonishment was Mahisha himself. Mahisha saw Gopi study him. His eyes followed Gopi's over his own body. Mahisha showed no surprise at the changes in his body. As a matter of fact, Mahisha noted no change in his appearance. Then Gopi darkened with doubt. He could not tell if he was under a spell. Or suffered a delusion. His doubt weakened his resolve and unravelled his will to do battle with the evil man who had so openly boasted he had come to destroy Durga Kali.

"Ha ha ha," Mahisha laughed. "Did I shock you? Are you astonished to hear me say I have come to destroy your goddess?"

"I do not believe you."

"Ah. A good start Gopi, a good start."

"No one can destroy Durga Kali."

"So I see you have decided to be her champion. And I can see you think I am an evil man."

"Yes. You are an evil man."

"I am not an evil man, Gopi—I am a man."

"Then a man with evil intent."

"Evil intent? I do not see my work here as evil. It is for your good—the benefit of your people. Steam is steam is energy. That's the only legend I know."

"Then why not take your steam? Why threaten to destroy the goddess?"

"To free the people, Gopi—to free you. To free your mind and your intelligence and your imagination from the traps of tradition and the swamps of superstition and liberate—generate even greater energy! The energy of the human mind free of the quagmire of the past. The energy of the human intellect free of the pitfalls of tradition. The energy of the human imagination liberated from the debilitation of souls of superstition!"

"Will the destruction of the gods bring about all this? Free mind? Pure intellect? Purified imagination?"

"Yes, it will. Just think of the human mind bounded by nothing!"

"The human mind bounded by nothing turns to thoughts of destruction—destruction, yes, of bad customs and evil superstitions. But also destruction of good, good things, good people—destruction of the gods."

"I have chosen well, Gopi. You are indeed a worthy adversary. Your Durga Kali there is going to be well-defended, that I can see. But I will destroy her nonetheless."

"Such hate. Such evil desire for vengeance. From a man of science like you? A man of knowledge and wisdom and learning?"

Mahisha Narayana flashed his eyes on Gopi and the boy felt the hate scorch his soul. Did that boy sense he, Mahisha Narayana, loathed his mortal nature?

"Does science and knowledge and wisdom and learning inevitably lead to destruction?"

"Ah Gopi, so young and so wise. The desert has made you wise. Introspective. And philosophical. All good weapons to fight me with."

"Who are you?"

"Mahisha Narayana."

"That Mahisha Narayana?"

"Yes. That Mahisha Narayana."

The boy stared into the eyes of the man before him as Saraswattee squinted and Durga Kali reflected: *That Mahisha Narayana? Which Mahisha Narayana?* But she had a name and a lead and a frenzy seized her as she began to ravish her memory and plunder Mahisha's genealogy, graveyard after graveyard after graveyard. But Gopi was not surprised. No panic or frenzy, not even fear, seized him. He said: "You have come for vengeance."

"Yes. Vengeance. I have come for vengeance!"

"What did they do to your father?"

"They forced him to leave his birthplace."

"Why?"

"Because of their customs and superstitions—"

"What did they do to your mother?"

Mahisha spun on Gopi and his hands flew up to clamp themselves around the boy but Gopi stood his ground and beheld the eyes of the demon bulge out and become like lumps of clotted blood. Mahisha caught himself, saw his hands tremble, and though the echoes of his mother's screams vibrated through his body he tried to regain his composure. He realized he had to be more tactful with Gopi. He had to be less open. He had to be more diversionary—and he had to shatter Gopi's beliefs fast.

Mahisha calmed down. Regained his composure. But Gopi beheld his eyes remain as they had been transformed: big lumps of clotted blood.

"I am sorry, Gopi. The memory is too painful. What these people—what your people did was horrible. Inhuman!"

"They are your people too."

"No more."

"You were born here."

"But I left here a long time ago. And I am not the same person I was then. I am different. I am another person. But soon I will return to what I was. Then you people will see who I really am!"

"You are not afraid I will expose you?"

"No I am not afraid you will expose me. You are too wise for that. You know I have come for vengeance. You know I will use my science to gain my revenge. And you know my vengeance means the destruction of your goddess. All this you know. But you also know your villagers are helpless and cannot prevent me. More. You know—feel!—you feel you are the only one who can stop me. Yes. Your belief fills you with pride. Your faith makes you brave. You will do battle with me because you think your legend can destroy my science. Not so Gopi?"

Gopi maintained his silence. Saraswattee watched, saw Chintamani slip into the crater, hide behind the breath of Durga Kali. Kali Durga ravished her memory. Such urgency. She had to discover Mahisha's true identity. Confront him face to face. Bid her faithful servant spit his venom between those evil eyes.

"So Gopi, are you ready to do battle? The war is on."

Again Gopi maintained his silence. But Mahisha's face became bloated and his blood-red eyes bulged in pride. He felt his lust for vengeance crawl thick through his veins. His heart grew within his chest. And its enlarged pulses beat through his body. Mahisha Narayana thought, what irony that he should feel the wrath of the avenger seize his body and madden his will and make him sweat with his lust for war—"Ha ha ha, Gopi. War. War indeed. Fact against fiction. Intellect against emotion. Sense against superstition. Truth against lies. Empiricism against legend. Body against soul. Man against god. *Science against myth*."

Gopi beheld Mahisha become demented. Delirious. Mighty; omnipotent. He spun around and faced the goddess and Saraswattee dropped down and Durga Kali shuddered as she and Gopi beheld Mahisha's chest swell and he seemed to grow to an iconoclasmic height with his surge of omnipotence and again Durga Kali was plunged into doubt and she asked herself could that man really then be a manifestation of Brahma? He, Supreme Creator, who with the knowledge of her desire for mortal death, reincarnated himself in mortal flesh and blood? And come to wreak vengeance on her and destroy her because she turned her back upon the children?

But Gopi knew more doubt than fear. This Mahisha Narayana was that Mahisha Narayana. What had they done to his father? What had they done to his mother? What evil had the wife of a pundit committed? *And who was that Mahisha Narayana? What was his real nature? Mortal? Godly? Or demonic?* As Saraswattee said. As Saraswattee tried to warn him. Gopi glanced up at the goddess and knew exactly where to look for those two tiny black eyes and his eyes told her that he was unsure and he didn't know who Mahisha Narayana was and that he might be a demon after all and those two black eyes of Saraswattee flashed back in anger at Gopi and said I told you so fool, I told you to stay away from that evil man, I told you that he was a demon, now you had better come to your senses and call upon your spirits of the desert and destroy that demon or else I will stand up in full view and shout: aye, you, demon!

"Enough time wasted, Gopi. Come on. Time to do battle. Truth against legend. Myth against science. Why don't we begin with the sulphur springs—or as the legend says, the sacred orifices of Durga Mata. Come on. The sacred orifices of Durga Kali are a good place to begin. To experiment with. To investigate. To explore. Here, let's begin at the top. Let's start with her eyes. You and me, man of science and man of legend. Stare into the eyes of lies. Eyes of deception. Behold the eyes of delusion."

While Mahisha Narayana stood triumphant, Gopi stared into the two hot sulphur springs—the eyes of Durga Mata. Oval pools of the most sparkling and most pure water. Deep; clear: lucid. Alive: human. Beautiful and tender and pervasive. How many times had he looked into those eyes and beheld their love and peace and solitude? Such human eyes indeed. Such mirrors. With such reflections of the soul of the benevolent one. And as he stared into those eyes, Gopi felt Kali stare back at him, overwhelm him with her warmth and humanness. With her reflections—reflections? Gopi rushed up to the eyes, bent over, peered down. And there. Indeed. Reflections of his face flashed back at him from the pools of water. When never before this had he ever seen a reflection of himself in those eyes. And more. Mahisha Narayana peered deep down into those eyes to see what had caught Gopi's attention and made him become so alert and agitated—but Gopi beheld no reflections of Mahisha Narayana in the lucid pools of the eyes. Whether Mahisha Narayana was aware of this or not Gopi did not know. But he, dark-skinned boy, like Chintamani when she looked into the mirror for the first time: Gopi had never seen a reflection of himself before. So that was how he looked. With his hair stacked up like thatch on a grass hut. No wonder Chintamani thought his hair ugly. But Gopi had no time to think of ugliness or handsomeness. The reflection of himself in the eyes of Durga Kali became like a revelation into the true nature of Mahisha Narayana. No mere mortal was Mahisha Narayana. And it was going to take more than his desert wisdom to defend Kali. Why didn't *his* face cast an image in the pools? But then: why did his own face reflect for the first time?

"So Gopi. These sacred orifices must indeed possess secret powers. Why, look at you. Just one glance into the eyes of your goddess and you seem like a new man—a magical transformation has come over you. Indeed, I must be careful. What am I up against? What power? What mystery? What magic? Indeed, those eyes make me feel mortal. My science seems about to evaporate in the smoke of ideas. Me, and not the twenty-first century, will vanish! Ha ha ha. We will see. We will see. Gopi, look again into those eyes. Study the water carefully. What do you see?"

Gopi studied the water, studied his reflection, wondered why Mahisha cast no shadow upon the water.

"You don't see water, do you Gopi? You see the eyes of your goddess. You see the legend."

"I feel the legend."

"Indeed. An excellent answer. I feel the legend. A splendid answer. Indeed, a magnificent answer. I feel the legend. I suppose, Gopi, that that makes the legend true?"

"For me, yes."

"A true peasant. A true son of the land. A true child of the earth. Feeling is believing. Water is no longer water because you feel it is something else! Don't trust to fact, believe the senses. You feel a thing is true and so it is true. A peasant's philosopher—a pauper's philosopher. You see Gopi, you and I are scientists together, we are the same, only our methodology is different—but we will arrive at the same answers, I guarantee you. Trust me. We will arrive at the same conclusions. The equation is the same. Naturally the solution must be the same. Whatever the method of solving the equation—this is itself a mathematical truth, a scientific truth, you see, already we are on the same track, the same side. There is hope for you. I feel, therefore I believe! A splendid conclusion. Here, Gopi, take one of these test tubes, dip out some water."

Gopi looked at the crate but did not take one of the test tubes. Mahisha Narayana laughed, selected one himself, and rested the crate down. When he reached out to dip into Durga's eyes, Gopi shouted: "No! It is forbidden to touch the sacred orifice that way!"

"Come now, Gopi, how are we to arrive at a solution? How are we to arrive at the answers? How are we to discover the truth? We must engage in a method of proof. This is not an act of desecration. It is an act of verification. Consider all we do from now on as an experiment. An impartial experiment for the sake of discovering truth."

"No! No!"

"So you will not learn? You have no desire for wisdom? For knowledge? Is your belief that weak? Is your faith in your beloved goddess that weak?"

"No!"

"Good then. Now I will make a deal with you. I challenge you. A friendly challenge. But a challenge with the best and purest motivations and goals—truth. You believe in truth, Gopi?"

"Yes."

"Then I challenge you to enter this experiment with me."

"No!"

"Come come. What have you got to lose but your fallacies? Your superstitions? Consider what you stand to gain—truth, wisdom, knowledge. A new pair of eyes! Is all this not worth it? Can you not defend your goddess? Will you let me destroy your goddess without you making an attempt to defend her?"

Gopi felt his body tighten. He stepped back, turned to face Kali and glanced up at her.

"That's right, Gopi. Look up at her. Say: Durga Mata, I am your son. I am your devotee. On your behalf I accept this challenge to defend you against this, against this demon, if you will, Gopi. Demon! Go on. Say to her, Mother Durga, you who are the disillusioner, you who detest evil and untruth, you who bring men to truth, bless me Mother, give me your permission, give me your protection, bestow on me your wisdom and your knowledge that I may accept this challenge and defend you, accept this challenge and defend truth against this demon—defend you against this demon!"

And though Mahisha didn't know it, thus indeed did Gopi pray. Never before had Gopi ever prayed. Not like that, not in words, not in prayer. He worked the land, tended the fields. He sat in the desert, discovered the curvature of the earth. He walked with Saraswattee. Held her hand. Answered her questions the best he could when he could. Till this day he had not thought of himself as a champion of the relentless bewilderer of evil men. Indeed, until this day the boy didn't know he really believed in the legend. Now he found himself not only with the knowledge that he believed all along, but that he would always believe. Consciously, within himself, he accepted the challenge. Became the defender of his beloved Durga. And as he stood there, Kali gazed upon him in prayer. She was grateful. Pleased. Honored. For what was she if she didn't have Gopi? What was she if she didn't have Saraswattee? What defenses without them did she have against the demon Mahisha—demon. Why, that man had called himself a demon! Maybe indeed he was one. What if he was a demon in the guise of a mortal man? Could Gopi then stand up to him? And there she was, fool, thinking the man might be a manifestation of Brahma. Would Brahma, even in the guise of a mortal, refer to himself as a demon? Would Brahma reincarnate himself and appear as a demon to wreak death and destruction over her for her sin? What had become of her? Was she a fool? Was she in the throes of dotage? Had she grown that senile? Had she relinquished so much of her mind and her memory and her omniscience that she stood there like a senile mortal plagued by dotage and unable to tell if a man was a man or a demon was a demon or a god a god? What all this fumbling about manifestation of Brahma? Was that man who he said he was: Mahisha Narayana? Or was Mahisha Narayana a reincarnation of Brahma? Or was Mahisha Narayana a demon? And yet she couldn't tell. Desirous of mortal death she had been reduced to a mortal. With a mortal mind. With the memory of a mortal. With the senses of a mortal. There, as she stood, Durga Kali, was more of a mortal woman than a famed and renowned goddess. Thus the emotions, the passions of a woman seized her, possessed her body. Then a sudden excitement took hold of her. A sudden delicious possession of love engulfed her. Swamped through her body. As it had done Parvati that day. Oh! Her oversight! How could she have known? But it was the same, the very same thing Parvati had experienced that day. So long ago. A creation ago. And here she was, Kali. Goddess. Experiencing passion again—experiencing love again. Love for a mortal. She a god. But why shouldn't it be that way? What was wrong with that? Wasn't that the way it should be? For so long men had displeased her. For so long the evil ways of mortals filled one face of her heart with black blood. For so long she had turned away, grown cold, numb, asleep, drugged with the evil of humans that this evil ate into her body. Ate into her soul. Oh how mortals filled her with rage. How humans filled her with wrath. And yet. To love a mortal again. Kali found the eyes of Saraswattee on her and she knew the girl's thoughts as the girl wondered why she, Durga, behaved so, why her body trembled that way, not in fear, but in delight. Saraswattee, she, curious child, stubborn girl. And a girl not to be messed with. Not by a mortal. Not by a demon. Not even by a god. As if to remind Kali of this Saraswattee gave her such a look of disgust the goddess felt scolded and lamely followed Saraswattee's eyes to Gopi. But with this knowledge: *She, Kali, believed in Gopi.*

"Accepted," Mahisha said. "Good for you. I knew you couldn't refuse such a challenge. Even without your goddess behind you, you are too much a seeker after truth to refuse to discover truth."

But Mahisha's words sounded flat. Dry. His face became twisted. He studied Gopi closely. *Then he realized that Gopi did, indeed, absolutely, purely, believe in the legend. In the goddess.* Mahisha felt his own voice stammer inside of him and he looked away from Gopi, looked into the eyes of the disillusioner.

He saw water—did not see Kali stare back at him.

"So," he said, "Gopi, to work. To our experiment. To discover truth. Gopi and his goddess versus Mahisha Narayana the demon. And yet both sides the defenders of truth. What a coincidence. What irony! So Gopi, you look into this water and you see something else—you feel something else. Not water, but truth. A fantastic truth. Well. Do you know why this water is so clean? So clean and pure? Of course, as legend says, because it is the soul of Durga Mata. Imagine that. This water, this spring water, a soul. The soul of your god. Is the soul of your god so easily seen, so easily had? Gopi, no plant, no algae forms in this water because it has a very high mineral content, that is why it is so clean. So pure. These pools do not reflect the soul of your goddess. This water is pure because of its very high mineral content."

Gopi stared into the water, saw Kali reflected there.

"You don't believe that, do you? And even if I did a chemical analysis right before your eyes and showed you the minerals, you still wouldn't believe me, would you? Your legend will say the minerals are the blood content of your goddess. What chance do I stand? What chance does truth stand?"

"I will believe, if you prove it to me."

"Prove it to you? Yes. So you will. We will see."

Mahisha bent down, picked up a handful of sand, and prepared to throw it into the water.

"This water," he said, "the soul of your goddess, if I throw this sand into this water I pollute it. Is the soul of your Kali so easily polluted?"

It was clear Mahisha was disappointed in the boy's responses. He had expected Gopi to become terrified, to protest. But Gopi stayed calm and said: "The sand belongs to the body of Durga. What belongs to the body cannot pollute the soul."

"Arrgh!" Mahisha shouted as he flung the sand away in disgust and asked: "What kind of reasoning is that? Is that logical? Is that scientific?"

"Yours is the way of logic and science. Mine is the way of the heart. It is all I have."

"And what of reason? Of logic? Of science?"

"If your reason and logic and science convince me I will believe. Other than that I will trust my senses, my heart, my soul."

"Remember Gopi, this works both ways. The deal works both ways. If my way is truth then you will believe in my way. If your way convinces me, I will believe in it. But I am ahead of you. I know your way, I once believed in it. Now I don't believe in it."

"Then bring me where you are."

"How can I, when this water is soul, and this sand is body?"

"You have not shown me it is any different. Yes, I see water but I also see something else. I see sand but again I also see something else. I lack the words to express myself. This is what makes me doubt, more than anything you have said so far. We are talking about different things."

"We are talking about the same thing! Here. I dip into this water, fill this test tube. There, Gopi. Have you tasted water? Have you felt water? Here feel this water and tell me if it is something else."

Gopi stared at the wet hands, the test tube filled with water. He didn't take it but said, "It is water."

"What?"

"In your hands it is water. *In your hands water is water.*"

Mahisha Narayana turned black. He stared at Gopi as if he would strangle the boy. For the longest while Mahisha Narayana stared at Gopi. Then he swallowed and said in a bitter mocking tone: "Splendid, Gopi, splendid. What is of the body doesn't pollute the soul, but what is in the hands of the demon does. If you keep this up you will have me convinced that I am indeed the very demon! You will convince me that I am something else. Then will my science save me? But, on with our experiment. Your legend says that this water is the soul of Durga Mata. Therefore it is not harmful to drink it, is it, Gopi? Good. My legend says this water has a very high mineral content and that it is poisonous. If you drink it you will die. Now Gopi, let's put our legends to the test. Here. Drink your legend and live. Or drink my legend and die. Here. Drink, if you believe your legend."

Mahisha held out the test tube to Gopi. The boy stared at

the sparkling water. Mahisha's hands became steady. His eyes bulged, bore down on Gopi. The boy folded his fists. The palms of his hands sweated. "Drink! Drink the soul of Kali!"

Gopi felt his chest tighten, felt his throat contract. He became dizzy, couldn't breathe. He wanted to take the water. Drink it. Yet he could not lift his hands. Or free himself from Mahisha's gaze. Mahisha pushed the test tube forward. Gopi leaned back. Mahisha erupted into laughter. He laughed as Kahar had laughed. Louder. More raucously. More sinisterly. And Gopi felt himself a disgrace. A disgrace to Durga. A dishonor to her. Already he had failed her. What else was left? Mahisha laughed as if mad. He flung his test tube against the crater wall and the stem broke and the water spilled. But neither he nor Gopi saw the water turn to blood and soak down the walls of the volcanic crater. Suddenly Mahisha rushed at Gopi, grabbed the boy and pulled him behind him as he ran madly about the crater. He dragged Gopi to Durga's ears, pinned the boy down closely to the orifices and said: "Ears! Listen! What do you hear? Whose voice do you hear, yours, Durga's or mine? This is not an ear. This is a hole. Only people and animals have ears. Things do not have ears. The earth does not have orifices. It has holes. One of which is your grave! Come, here, her nose, her nostrils, smell them. Let them smell you. Smell yourself. Smell your death. Her death. Is sulphur the stench of your god? You know what sulphur is? You know its chemical formula? Do you know sulphur has a chemical symbol? Come, come here is her mouth. Her big mouth! Look at the teeth. Look at her gums. Look at the inside of her mouth. Look well Gopi, look well. This is her mouth, not a hole in the ground. These are her teeth, not chunks of limestone. These are her gums, not mud! Look well, who is speaking? You? Durga? Call out to her. Beg her. Scream, Durga Mata! Kali Mata! Speak to me! Why don't you? eh? Who speaks lies? Me? Or you? Or your Durga? Lies! Lies! Lies! It is all lies, Gopi. Lies told by men who want to be gods. Lies told by gods who are nothing but demons. Lies told by priests who are parasites. Lies lies lies. Speak. Who is telling lies? You are, Gopi! Your goddess is! Your false goddess. Made of stone and cast iron. Her body untouched by the hands of men, no mortal hands, the legend says, have touched that body, no mortal hands built the temple, not brick by brick, stone by stone, boulder by boulder. No. Lord

Shiva and his consort Parvati came to this place and when they were rested and had quenched their thirst of each other Parvati was extremely pleased and this place became holy to her and she gave birth to the temple, no, no mortal hands touched her body, you know Gopi, don't you, how her body came into being, of course you do, for you know the legend well, you know the lies well, come, come, come my good boy, you who will learn, you who will gain wisdom, you who will be forced to see old things with new eyes. Look, look! What do you see, ah, yes, the holiest of the holy orifices. Look, don't be ashamed. Yes, her yoni. Behold the massive vagina of Durga Kali!"

Gopi and Saraswattee and Mahisha Narayana and Chintamani all stared at the largest and most sacred orifice of Kali Durga. An immense gash in the earth. Between the temple courtyard and the doorway of the temple itself. Wider in span than two mortal humans and greater in length than four. The outer edges outcropped with rocks and boulders stained purple and crimson. Ages and ages of sulphur coagulated around the most sacred orifice like an embroidered scar of gold. Inside, coated by frothy wet salt, the ledges and walls of mud. Ledges and walls of mud boiled by the steam and the heat, of the texture of sponge; and thickened with the muscles of ochre and vermillion algae. Mud: red and raw; mud: fleshy. Here, the pathway to the very womb of the earth and from whence issued the salty breath and the sulphurous wrath in clouds of vapors and steam like sprays of fine white hairs. The vapors moist with the warmth of the womb of the earth, saturated with the healing powers of sulphur and brine; intoxicated with the vital fluids of life: teeming with the abundant smell of a well-fished sea.

This. The largest and the most sacred of the sacred orifices of Durga Kali. Remember, legend said, it is wise to besiege her breath. To court her wrath is the wisdom of fools. Come. Clad, or unclad. Inhale the vapors of sulphur, soothing balm of brine. Let the steam envelop your joints. Let the heat detach the ligaments of your thoughts. No lust oozes in the private regions of your brain. Let the smell of this well-fished sea be the succor of your bones. No evil thoughts lurk in your pores. Come. Clad; or unclad. Let the vapors of the most sacred of the sacred orifices of Kali unhinge you from the skeleton of the pyre of your flesh. For to bathe in the sacred vapors, legend said, is to obtain the utmost of happiness: to attain the utmost in bliss eternal.

Durga Kali rolled her eyes and stared down. Saraswattee rose to her feet, crossed her hands over her chest, fixed her eyes on the most sacred of the sacred orifices of Durga Mata. On the opposite side from Gopi and Mahisha, and hidden from them, Chintamani held her gaze to the most sacred orifice.

But Gopi held his eyes down; away.

As he stared at the most sacred orifice of the ravisher of evil and of evil men, Mahisha Narayana once again began to ooze layers of thick black sweat. The hair on his head grew five inches longer and the hair on his chest and neck and hands and feet grew two inches. His skin turned basalt black and became scabbed in patches. His hands thickened and grew six inches and his feet fattened and lengthened three inches. His chest expanded out to another half its size and within it the black heart doubled in size and weight and in the number of valves and chambers. Where he had had no paunch, now he had a belly like a buffalo's and the cheeks of his bottom became the cheeks of the behind of a buffalo. And inside the crotch of his pants his testicles tripled those the size of mere mortals and his penis thickened and lengthened down to mid-leg. But no one there—most of all Durga Kali and Mahisha himself—noted the transformation as they stared into the most sacred of the sacred orifices of she, Durga Kali, ravisher of the lust of evil men.

Still caught in his frenzy and madness, the black sweat in blobs over the courtyard, Mahisha Narayana grabbed Gopi and shook the boy and screamed: "Behold! Behold the most sacred orifice of your beloved goddess. Her sacred yoni. Her holy vagina. Her—her vile most sacred orifice! From whence you came. From whence she came. To where you will return. And so will she. Her yoni. A hole in the ground—a grave. Is this your Durga's body? Is this your Kali's sacred parts? Is this her private regions? This her breath and her wrath? This her pubic hairs and labias? God! What madness! What insanity! To bathe in these vapors is to attain bliss eternal. To what bliss eternal, eh? When the land is barren and destitute and thirsty for every drop of energy. The hungry children. The starving millions. And this the most sacred of the sacred orifices of your superstitions! I will tell you what this is, Gopi. I will tell you. Your goddess squats on one of the greatest sources of wealth. She squats on one of the richest potential stores of energy. She. Her rituals and religion. Her strictures and superstitions. She squats on progress stifling it. She squats on the very future. Why, Gopi, look around, look at all the orifices. See with your own eyes. This is one of the most obvious geothermal fields there is! You don't have to do any experiments, explorations. No complicated experiments are needed. The truth is obvious for you to see right before your very eyes. Right here on this mountaintop there is enough geothermal energy to thrust the entire world straight into the twenty-first century, superstitions and all! That's right Gopi. In this very spot on which we stand, there is enough energy to blast your land into the future. But your goddess squats on it. You don't believe me do you? eh Gopi? You won't believe with your own eyes, this is the richest geothermal field ever. All the geological, hydrogeological and chemical conditions are apparent to the coldest sceptic. It is a sin! Yet you fools worship it. Waste it. Well, I neither want to worship it nor waste it. I simply want to use it. Your religion is just like one of these springs, only it has spent itself, has squandered its resources—is dead. Cold. I will not let dead weight weigh down progress. *I will not let your goddess squat on the future.* Goddess indeed! Her breath and her wrath. Why Gopi, look at those vapors, what are they? Are they a mystery? Are they mythical? Are they legendary? Are they magical? Or are they fact? Fact, Gopi. Fact of science. Fact of truth. Fact of fact! Let me tell you what my legend has to say about these vapors. My legend, Gopi, says these vapors are steam. Where does steam come from? What makes steam? The answer is simple, Gopi, steam is nothing but water, H_2O, in its gaseous state. But the great thing about water as steam is that it is energy. Power! It can move mountains! That is why this mountain moved. That is why this mountain will move again. How then is steam made? Steam is made when water is heated. Gopi, when you go home tonight, watch your mother boil water. From the boiling water rise vapors. Are those vapors the breath and the wrath of your Durga? No! Those vapors are steam, simple as that, Gopi. Is that proof enough for you? Well, you ask, where does the water come from in this desert? Is the water in the belly of the earth? Yes, Gopi, the lost Saraswati. That other goddess. That goddess of wisdom and knowledge and learning. Well learn from her. Ask her to bless you with knowledge because I am going to enlighten you. The Saraswati didn't pick up her body and her books and ascend to heaven. No. All that happened is the Saraswati River lost its bed, went underground. Simple as that! The land caved away, the water sank. Same as you would sink if the earth under your feet disappeared. That is how the Saraswati disappeared. Simple. No magic. No mystery. Simple fact of simple geography. The river went underground. The land turned into a desert. Another simple fact of geography. Gopi we are not even dealing with science yet. No physics, no chemistry, no mathematics. Now, you might ask, where does the heat come from? But we already know, don't we? This earth we live on is round—do you know that? How could you? How could you discover anything on your own? Truth to you is what religion says! But the heat. You remember the fact of the earth's crust? You remember the core? Molten into magma? Molten and red hot. Boiling red hot. The kind of hotness that could melt even your dead gods! Boiling red hot and full of molten magma, the stuff of which volcanoes are made. And so this place, Gopi, the earth's core is so hot that if you fell into it you would turn instantly to steam yourself! That is how steam is made. The water of the Saraswati runs underground, falls into open fissures, into hot open sores, bubbling, boiling, listen to it, you hear it boil and bubble and steam? Yes, that noise is not your goddess's belly noises. It is not the boiling of the earth's bowels. Water falls into the hot molten core, turns into steam. As simple as that, Gopi. Your sacred shrine is nothing but a boiler. A natural boiler. A pot on a fireside! And your goddess is nothing but a cover, a cap. She squats on the future! But when this mountain blows she will go sky high, Gopi. Steam is steam is energy and there is enough of it here to blast your goddess straight to her heaven. And I am going to do it. Energy. Power. Heat. Gopi, heat is energy, you don't believe me, do you? You don't believe your eyes do you? Well come, come, here, *if feeling is believing then feel!*"

Before Gopi knew what happened, Mahisha Narayana grabbed him, dragged him to the orifice, pushed him down on his knees, snatched his hand, and plunged the hand deep into the thick red mud of the most sacred of the sacred orifices of Durga Kali.

Then Kali screamed. In her head. A mighty silence descended upon the earth. Kali screamed and came to bloodlusting and bloodvexed life. None but the ogre in her bosom heard that scream. The mortals of the earth heard only the silence upon the land. Kali's scream vibrated through her body; rebounded within her skull. The tangle of serpents in her head hissed and raged and the cells of her brain ruptured and blood gushed down her throat into her chest in a red shower. And the sound of this shower of blood became like the soul of an unseen waterfall and this was the sound the mortals of the earth heard. And as all stared in silence; within her immense body of granite and cast iron: Kali came back to her former virile and vengeful life. Then Kali transfixed the most lucid eyes on Mahisha Narayana.

But she was not the only one. Her scream shattered the slumber of Naga, wise and venerable sage; serpent of serpents. The scream exploded in his old head like a volcano and he suffered instant rebirth and he opened his lidless eyes and fixed his venomed gaze on Mahisha Narayana and became as impartial as a vacuum.

ELEVEN

ND it was because of the utter silence that befell the temple courtyard, as Kali's scream rebounded and reverberated through every cell of her body, the villagers and the pilgrims thronged the crater walls and stared down at the group around the most sacred orifice of the goddess. Gopi. On his knees. His face stained with tears. His eyes fixed on his right hand— scalded red and raw. Mahisha Narayana glanced up and saw Chintamani. On the opposite side of the sacred orifice. The girl stepped back into the mist. Dropped her eyes. Then Mahisha Narayana became conscious of the enormous weight of his testicles and the enormous length of his penis. Suddenly he realized he was prodigiously endowed. And this realization pleased him. Filled him up with lust. For a woman. Lust for the body of a woman. And as he stared at Chintamani across the most sacred orifice he began to laugh and the shattered ogre within Kali's chest collected its senses. The shower of blood rained down and the ogre spun himself into his whirlwind of evil but suddenly found himself locked in a death grip. Kali had awakened. Kali had come fully alive. Kali, bloodvexed and bloodlusting slayer of evil and of evil men, vibrated with her passion for vengeance.

Then the ogre within her chest realized where he erred. When he released his death hold on Durga Kali he allowed her vital organs to function in their natural manner and her respiration had been restored and so too the natural circulation of her blood. The ogre could feel her lust for vengeance as blood splattered over him. He knew as soon as that scream dissolved, Durga Kali, destroyer and

165

ravisher of mortals and demons, would bid her cobra lingam spit his bitter venom between the eyes of his master the demon Mahisha Durga and once again slay him. The ogre reached down his hand of claws into the belly of Durga and clinched a vicious grip around the tail of the cobra lingam where it coiled around Kali's womb. Naga, the serpent of serpents, felt the sharp claws slice into his body and he lost his equanimity and impartiality. But with Mahisha Narayana still filtered through the black lenses of his jet eyes, he muttered: *Mahisha Durga!*

Then Durga Kali stopped screaming and fixed her eyes on Mahisha Narayana and asked: *What?*

Mahisha Durga, Naga said with irritation.

The demon? Kali asked. *Mahisha Durga, the demon?*

Yes.

But that is impossible. I slew the demon. Took his name. Took his identity. Became Durga Kali!

All very true, said Naga with even greater irritation. *But there he stands before you. The demon Mahisha Durga. Returned for vengeance.*

That is impossible, Kali said in anger as her consciousness bounced in the serpent's brain and caused his migraine to return. *Demons are not granted the gift of reincarnation! How could he return?*

Bid me bite. Don't ask me academic questions. Bid me bite and I will bite!

Then Durga Kali realized her faithful servant had grown old and testy and was angry with her and had awakened in a bad mood. But she herself happened to be in no mood for insolence. The demonic laughter echoed in her ears and only further maddened her. She said: *Silence, you old viper. Before I vent my wrath on your head. Demons are not reincarnated!*

Maybe it is his son.

The demon did not have a son.

Bid me bite and I will bite. I have no time for rhetorical or philosophical discourse. Bid me bite and I will bite. Or I shall bite on my own bidding. Mahisha Durga. Here I am. You old nemesis! Look! Here I come between your eyes!

And Mahisha Narayana found himself paralyzed by the tiny black eyes of the cobra lingam. He couldn't move a muscle. As if already the venom of that serpent benumbed his nerves. In his head echoed the name *Mahisha Durga! Mahisha Durga! Mahisha Durga!*

And just as Naga was about to transform his body of glass into the live body of a serpent and spit his venom between the eyes of Mahisha Narayana, Durga Kali crushed his will and her consciousness echoed in his ears: *Rebellious old viper, be patient! What if you are mistaken? I slew the demon Durga and took his name and his identity and here I stand Durga Kali! What if that creature is the reincarnation of Brahma who has come to destroy me for my sin? Will you be that impatient to rashly slay the Supreme Creator by mistake? Then think what your fate will be! And the fate of the seven worlds! I need your good counsel right now, not your impertinence and bitter venom! What if he who stands before us is Brahma?*

Whereupon, Naga, serpent of serpents, immediately recoiled into his vacuum of impartiality and Durga Kali again became possessed of a frenzy and tore through her memory in her hunt for the true identity of Mahisha Narayana and as she had hunted down the demon in olden times, so too now she plundered all the genealogies of mortals and gods and demons, graveyard after graveyard after graveyard, and she beheld the utter death and destruction wrought by the demon Durga as he ravished and plundered the seven worlds and in her head now echoed the prayers and the supplications of the mortals and the gods and the dead as they lifted their voices and called upon Brahma and Shiva and Vishnu. The three supreme gods stood in the heavens helpless and paralyzed. And as the clamor arose and they beheld the demon Durga deal out further death and destruction, then Brahma and Vishnu and Shiva cowered in fear and became like babies and whimpered and withered and whelped and then crawled to she: Kali. Known then neither as Parvati. Nor Kali. And not yet taken the name Durga.

But she: *Devi!*

Devi the sexless one. That which is outside creation and from which creation comes. She, Devi, whose heart is the universe and whose loins are the earth. She, Devi; formless. And as she was formless and sexless: so was she fearless. The mother of all creation and from whose loins came even the supreme triad of

Brahma and Vishnu and Shiva. Who all three now stood before her cowered like babies and withered and whimpered and whelped: *O Mother of all creation! Help us! Save us from the demon Durga!*

And Devi stood on the pinnacle of creation and became disgusted by Brahma and Vishnu and Shiva as the three supreme gods squabbled among themselves because it was known to all three as it was to all creation that the demon Durga could only be slain by a woman and Vishnu said to Brahma, send your wife Saraswati; and Brahma said, what? send my beautiful Saraswati? she is the goddess of knowledge and wisdom and learning and poetry and literature, what match is such a one against the demon Durga? send your wife; what? asked Vishnu, send my wife Lakshmi? are you crazy? Lakshmi is the goddess of wealth! the demon Durga would ravish and plunder her instantly! she is no match for the demon Durga, let Shiva send his wife Parvati; what? asked an enraged Shiva, my beautiful Parvati? against that demon Durga? have you lost your mind? I am not sending my beautiful wife to do battle with no demon to have him ravish her! let Brahma send his wife Saraswati! he was the one who blundered in the first place, he is responsible, he let the demon trick him and he granted the power of invincibility and the power of illusion to the demon, let Brahma send his wife because he was the one who granted that the demon could be slain by only a woman!

Devi, creator of creators, she who was formless and fearless and sexless, watched the gods squabble among themselves and she let her gaze roam over Parvati and Lakshmi and Saraswati. And each she assessed. Truly, Lakshmi, goddess of wealth, was no match for Durga. And Saraswati. Of all the goddesses and of all the mortal women ever created Devi loved Saraswati the best because she was gentle and kind and was the patron of learning and wisdom and poetry and literature, attributes which Devi herself prized above all else. In battle against brute force and base evil, what match could the gentle and kindhearted Saraswati be? Devi fixed her eyes on Parvati. Parvati was more mortal than god. And she was a bit of a flirt. She had courage but she lacked strength. While the gods squabbled, Devi reincarnated herself in Parvati. She, the fearless one, the formless one, the sexless one; she Devi: sneaked into the body of Parvati. Neither Brahma nor Vishnu nor Shiva knew this. Nor did Parvati herself. In this, Devi was immediately guilty of an oversight: she didn't foresee the position she would find herself in later in the body and sex of the beautiful Parvati. But she had already taken form and shape and she left an illusion of herself for the gods to squabble before. She also left an illusion of Parvati for Shiva to cuddle. Then she, Devi, now Parvati, put on her armor, took up her weapons, and stalked the seven worlds as she hunted the demon Durga.

Thus now Durga Kali stalked her memories and her past because she had to come face to face with the demon Durga and as she ravished her genealogy, graveyard after graveyard after graveyard; Saraswattee scampered down the back of the goddess to run to her Gopi. Who still crouched on his knees. His hand peeled of its skin. And red and raw like the mud of the most sacred of the sacred orifices of the goddess. As Saraswattee climbed down, Pundit Ayer rushed down the steps into the courtyard and Kahar hopped behind him. Chintamani stepped further back into the cover of the vapors. Mahisha Narayana, released from the paralyzing stare of the cobra lingam, looked at the pundit and Kahar. He glanced up at the goddess as he tried to hide in his soul the echo of that name: *Mahisha Durga, Mahisha Durga, Mahisha Durga.*

Mahisha Narayana became troubled because he too knew the legend well. Knew that Mahisha Durga was a demon of death and destruction. But though he had come to wreak death and destruction, he was Mahisha Narayana; son of Pundit Mahesh Narayana: he was not the demon Mahisha Durga. But then immediately he thought: What if I *am* the demon Mahisha Durga? Would not that be indeed sublime? He had come for death and destruction. Certainly as a demon the effects of that death and destruction would be the ultimate: dissolution. Dissolution. Dissolution of creation! Suddenly a mighty pride filled up the chest of Mahisha Narayana and his eyes lit up and he said to himself not only mortals and demons wrought death and destruction but Brahma himself when he dissolved creation wrought death and destruction and might not he, Mahisha Narayana; instead of being the manifestation of the demon Mahisha Durga: might he not be the reincarnation of the Supreme Creator himself—Brahma? Such a time it was then, as it is now, when mortals and demons bethink themselves gods and plunge the world in a downhill slide and wreak death and destruction everywhere and without reason and demons who have a chance to be decent and do good deeds embrace their baser nature and bethink themselves supreme creators.

"What is this, Mr. Narayana?" Pundit Ayer asked, as the villagers and the pilgrims stared down in silence. "What has happened to the boy Gopi?"

"Nothing, punditji. Only an experiment."

"A what?"

"An experiment in truth. The discovery of truth. Certainly as a brahmin and a priest you approve of experiments for the discovery of truth?"

"Absolutely!"

"Then the boy Gopi has just discovered a certain truth. Ask him, Pundit Ayer, what truth he has just discovered."

"Gopi," Pundit Ayer asked, as Mahisha Narayana made his way behind the temple and between the legs of Durga Kali, "what is this truth you have just discovered?"

But Gopi just stared at his scalded hand. Tears streamed down his face. He wept not because of pain. He wept because that hand he held seemed an alien hand. An evil thing. Not his. Not of flesh and blood. Hand of failure. Hand of desecration. Hand of defilement. Yes, he had violated his goddess; violated the body of Durga Kali. But the boy knelt gripped by a greater terror. What horrified Gopi most was that he had felt heat—he had felt mud. When he thought he would have experienced something other than mortal heat and mortal mud.

Pundit Ayer moved away to join Mahisha Narayana where he stood between the legs of Durga Mata in a horror of his own. He had made his way and halted between the outstretched legs of Durga Kali and looked up at her massive cast-iron bottom to behold two tiny black eyes transfix his. He felt as he did when he had walked into the courtyard that first day and glanced up and had been transfixed by two black eyes. Then he thought he had seen a little girl on her feet in the stone cleft between the breasts of the goddess. And once again, Mahisha Narayana thought he had seen a little girl peep out at him from behind the right hip of the stone goddess. But how could that be? What would a little girl be doing there? How would a little girl get there?

Saraswattee had little time to hang from the hip of Durga Kali and enlighten Mahisha Narayana. As soon as she caught his eyes she swung back up and crawled around to Durga's belly and heedless as to whether the clouds of vapors shielded her from the eyes of the villagers and the pilgrims she crawled over the belly, grabbed hold of the cobra lingam, swung down from it, dropped to the temple, scrambled down the far slope of the roof, and dropped to the ground not far from where Chintamani hid in the vapors.

"Engineersab," Kahar said to Mahisha, "what is the matter? You look like you have seen a demon. Why those are only stone serpents. Certainly you are not afraid of stone serpents, you who do not believe the legend?"

"What?" Pundit Ayer asked. "Who does not believe the legend?"

Mahisha Narayana recovered quickly and glanced at the sulphur spring behind Durga Kali and asked: "This is the ninth orifice of Durga Mata?"

"Indeed," Pundit Ayer said, "the ninth orifice, and as sacred as the rest of the orifices of our deity."

Mahisha Narayana fixed his eyes on the round black hole thick with black molten lava and suffocating with the stench of sulphur. And again he thought. A hot sulphur spring. A hole in the ground. The holy and sacred anus of a goddess! Mahisha Narayana regained his evil intent and began to take measurements by his footsteps of the distance of the ninth orifice from the feet of the goddess and from the west wall of the crater. Kahar hopped about. Pundit Ayer's eyes scrambled to keep up with the footsteps but what he saw only netted him in further confusion.

From the side of the temple, Saraswattee noted the strange behavior of Mahisha Narayana. Then she ran to Gopi. She threw herself on her knees and lifted the boy's hand and knew exactly what to do. Quickly she scooped out some mud from the most sacred orifice and heaped it on the ground before her. Chintamani eased forward. Saraswattee spread out the mud, blew on it. When she felt it cool enough, she began to paste the mud over Gopi's hand. As she worked, Gopi looked not at the girl, but at the hand. Once again it was being transformed. Saraswattee transformed it. In her hands the pain froze. The temperature of that part of his hand became lower than the temperature in the rest of his body. But if the pain left, his confusion did not. True he had felt heat before. The desert heat. The heat of his body. The heat of the food he ate. True too, he had felt mud before. Mud in the fields. Mud in the desert after a sudden flash of rain. Mud on his feet, between his toes. But it was not the same heat, the same mud. Or maybe it was. Only he had expected to find it different. Did he believe in the legend so absolutely, so blindly, so much in a straight line, as he had once believed the earth was a straight line? And if it were different, what made the difference? What made the heat in his body different from the heat in Durga's most sacred orifice? What made the mud on his body different from the mud in Kali's body? Why was the heat in Durga's body, heat; and why was the mud, mud? Yes, indeed, he found it heat and mud. Yes, indeed, he expected to find it not heat, to find it not mud. Gopi looked at the vapors, looked around at the other orifices. Was it as Mahisha said? Were the orifices only holes in the ground? Were the vapors just steam? And was steam *just* steam? What did he grapple for! Mahisha knew so many words. Yet Gopi suspected his words. They seemed to be as flat as he had once thought the earth flat, and Mahisha's words struck him as wrongheaded, misguided, dry, brittle. Yet the heat he felt in Durga's body felt flat, and the mud he felt also felt flat. Flat as steam is steam is steam is water is heat. Wait. *Flat as steam is steam is steam is water is heat?* Heat. Something was wrong in that equation—not wrong: different. Steam is water. Water is heat. How could that be? Yes yes, through the wisdom of science he understood how it could be in one way. He understood the scientific principles. But something happened to water when it became steam. Something happened to water when it became heat. A transformation took place. What transformation? How? Why? What did he grapple for? What was that transformation taking place in his hand as Saraswattee tended to it? Indeed it was being transformed. Already he was beginning to not see it as alien to him, as the hand of failure and desecration and defilement.

What made the difference?

Gopi watched the girl as she busily tended to his hand. Carefully. Lightly. She applied the mud as a poultice. Saraswattee worked, all her concentration on the hand she held. Chintamani looked at her sister, looked at the little fingers as they brushed on the mud as gently as a light breeze would sweep over her, inhaling away the thin film of perspiration on her skin. Chintamani watched her youngest sister. She. Saraswattee. Curious child. Stubborn girl. Chintamani realized, despite all the fear and the agony and the pain and the damnation of being a girl, life was as simple as those fingers passing over Gopi's hand. Or as simple as when at quiet moments her mother would comb her hair or she would comb Madhuban's hair or Madhuban would comb Saraswattee's hair or she, Chintamani, would sit at her mother's feet and listen to her tell of the legend.

Once upon a time a long long time ago upon a long long long time ago.

Such were the prologues to tales; such were the epilogues to lives.

Chintamani. She. Who knew the legend well. She was thirteen, felt three hundred, lived thirteen thousand. Wisdom was not so many years. Wisdom is so many moments. So many moments she had had; so many moments she still had to live. She thought of her dream. The lucky fellow had indeed fallen into quicksand. The best thing about the dream was the horse. Only it didn't change. Remained a horse. The cross-eyed pundit had asthma. And the earth was as flat as a chapati. And Saraswattee loved Gopi. This Chintamani realized. As she watched her sister tend to the hand of the boy. No shadow-sister; she: no rag-doll girl. Saraswattee loved Gopi. She didn't love him as a girl or a sister or a mother. Saraswattee loved as a wife; Saraswattee loved as a woman.

Chintamani bowed her head. A shame to her sister. She felt the weight of the gold thali on her chest. She lifted her gaze, beheld the thali around Saraswattee's neck. She knew who had tied that thali. She glanced at Gopi. He had tied that thali for Saraswattee so that Kahar Saheb would not beat her. Then he had tied a thali around her neck. Made her his wife. So that she would no longer be a shame and a disgrace. That her father might rise up a man. And she had been so unkind to him. He who had taken care of Saraswattee all her life. Let her trudge after him. Bother him. Eat his food. Sit with him in the desert. Protected her; defended her. No one in that village had ever taken care of Saraswattee as Gopi. He had gone so far as to marry her in secret. Then he had gone even further. Married she herself. And she had been so ungrateful to him. Called him ugly and black. When he really wasn't all that ugly. True his hair was a disgrace but that was Saraswattee's fault. To cut the boy's hair with a knife! No, Gopi wasn't really ugly. And he, dark-skinned boy, loved that girl. Loved that girl as much as that girl loved him.

And what had she done by her marriage to Gopi? What had she done to Saraswattee's future? What had she done to that love displayed there by those two? How could one boy marry two wives—and two sisters at that? Why was fate so cruel to them? And why was she tempting this cruel fate even further? With her behavior. The way she looked at Mahisha Narayana. The way she followed Mahisha Narayana around. How could she have been so foolish? She was no flirtatious girl. No adulterous woman. No unfaithful wife! What indeed possessed her? To be an adulterous woman, to be an unfaithful wife—did she know what shame and disgrace she would heap on her father's head? She had better come to her senses. And fast! Mahisha Narayana was not for her. She was a married woman—a wife. Mahisha Narayana was an evil man—especially after what he did to Gopi. And Gopi black—no, not black, just dark-skinned. And not at all ugly. Even with his hair stacked up like thatch. She didn't really hate Gopi. What reason had she to hate Gopi? Just because his father hated her father? On the contrary. She had every reason to like Gopi. He was a good boy—as Saraswattee said. He was a handsome boy—as Saraswattee said. He defended and protected Saraswattee. He loved Saraswattee. As Saraswattee loved him. And as she was now, was now—liking Gopi.

Saraswattee held up the hand. Inspected it. She looked at Gopi and asked: "Little Husband, does it hurt?"

The boy shook his head no. Saraswattee reached up with her left hand and wiped the tears off the boy's face and said, "Don't cry then. Are you hungry?"

"No."

"Don't cry then. Are you thirsty?"

"No."

"Don't cry then. Did you do wrong?"

"I don't know, Little Mother."

"You didn't do wrong. Don't cry."

Saraswattee glanced up at Chintamani and Chintamani jumped as if under her feet the earth moved. With what eyes did her sister look at her! Such a stare. Stern. What admonishment! Chintamani whispered, *"Deedi!"*

But before Saraswattee could say anything, Roopa's father walked into the crater. Saraswattee glanced behind her and saw Madhuban and the other girls peep out from behind the temple.

Roopa's father stumbled up, faced the goddess, slumped, bowed his head, clasped his hands, prayed, gave thanks for this day, asked for another, full or empty, as Durga Mata pleased.

From all directions they came, the other fathers. One by one. As they had left. Sweaty and soggy, as the clothes on their backs. They came, they prayed, they gave thanks, they begged, they left. If they saw their daughters they didn't show it.

One by one, too, the daughters followed their fathers home.

Then Sutnami came. He came over the north wall. Struggled across the courtyard. Dragged his lathi. Before the goddess he stopped. As a goat or a sheep would stop while grazing. For no apparent reason. He stopped, but he didn't turn to face the goddess. The girls looked at their father. Chintamani horrified. Terrified. She had married that her father might rise up a man. And what happened instead? Her father appeared to be disintegrating into filth. Why? What was her sin? What was his sin? Why Sutnami stopped was indeed a puzzlement. He didn't stop to pray. He didn't stop to give thanks. He didn't stop to breathe, he didn't stop to beg. Why or how he stayed on his feet was an even greater bafflement. What gave him the signal to move on was another perplexity. But he moved on. Went home.

Madhuban came out of her hiding place with her head bowed. The sisters knew it wouldn't be long before another whipping began. Saraswattee sat back on the ground and they all stood where they were, neither speaking with their tongues nor their eyes. The vapors rose, the wind dropped, the shadows came. Outside the crater the sheep and the goats bleated as they made their way home. In the village, smoke rose from the kitchens. In groups the pilgrims dispersed. Madhuban went home, Chintamani to sit on the sand dune. For a while Gopi and Saraswattee sat in the courtyard. Then Gopi got up and made his way into the desert.

Saraswattee sat, her chin propped up in her hands. Later she would go find Gopi, be with him. But right now she had to find Chintamani.

Chintamani didn't look up when her sister came beside her. For a while both looked at the sunset, then Chintamani said, "Come, come deedi, sit with me."

Saraswattee didn't move. Chintamani remembered the look her sister had given her and she glanced at the girl. Saraswattee, her hands behind her back, seemed in thought.

"What is it, deedi?"

"You."

"Me?"

"Yes, you."

"How? Deedi, what?"

"What is happening to you?"

"I don't know."

"You have changed so much."

"I have, I don't know!"

"You like that man?"

"*What?*"

"You like that man?"

"Sister!"

"You like that man?"

"Please please deedi."

"You like that man?"

"How should I know, sister, what do I know about these matters? What are you asking me? What do I know?"

"He is a bad man."

"How do you know?"

"He is a very evil man!"

"Yes. He is a very evil man."

"You shouldn't have anything to do with him."

"No. I shouldn't have anything to do with him."

"He is a very very evil man."

"He is a very very evil man."

"Have you forgotten you are married?"

"Sister! What are you saying?"

"Have you forgotten you are married?"

"No, I have not!"

"Then what is the matter with you?"

"Don't mock me so."

"I am not mocking you. You are married. It is wrong of you to behave as you are behaving. It is wrong of you to look at someone else."

"Sister!"

"It is wrong."

"Yes, it is. But it is also wrong what you have done!"

"What is that?"

"Married Gopi yourself!"

"Why is that wrong?"

"How can two sisters marry one boy?"

"Three."

"What?"

"Three sisters."

"What are you talking about?"

"Gopi has promised to marry Madhuban too."

"WHAT?"

"You heard me."

"I thought I was the one possessed. Now I see you are the one possessed. I will have none of it!"

"Give me the thali, then."

Chintamani was stunned. She stared at Saraswattee's outstretched hand. Saraswattee was serious. Chintamani lifted her thali, looked at it.

"If you don't want it give it to me. I will give it to Madhuban so they won't beat her."

Chintamani dropped the thali, dropped her head on her knees, began to weep. Saraswattee went to her, sat down next to her. Chintamani wept on. Saraswattee sat in silence. When Chintamani stopped weeping she said: "You are right, sister. I am a fool. I have done wrong."

"Yes, you have done wrong. But you will change your ways."

"I will change my ways."

For a while neither sister said anything. Then Chintamani said: "You love Gopi?"

"Yes."

"Very much?"

"Very very much."

"How can three sisters marry one boy?"

"We will work it out."

"How will we work it out?"

"It has already begun to work itself out."

"Why do you say that?"

"You no longer hate Gopi."

"How do you know?"

"I know."

"You are right, I don't hate him."

"He is a good boy."

"Yes. He is a good boy."

"And you have begun to like him."

"What? Sister! How can you say that?"

"I saw your face back there. When I fixed Gopi's hand. I saw it in your eyes."

"Sister!" But to hide her blushes, Chintamani covered her face with her hands.

"You can cover your face all you want. I know."

"How do you know these things, sister?"

"Gopi taught me."

"And who taught Gopi?"

"The desert."

"Yes. You, Gopi, and the desert."

"Me, you, Gopi, Madhuban—and the desert!"

"And our father, sister, what is becoming of our father?"

"What is to become of him."

"Sister, you can be so harsh. Don't you love our father?"

"I love our father. But what can I do for him?"

"You can ask him what is happening to him. You can ask him what his sin is."

"How do you know he has sinned?"

"He is punishing himself for some wrong he has done."

"Done wrong to whom?"

"To his brother."

"Is that why they hate each other?"

"Why else can it be?"

"Our uncle is just an evil man. Anyway, it is your place to talk to our father. You ask him what wrong he has done. You find out what his sin is."

"Yes. You are right. I will. I will talk to our father."

"Tell him also there is no need for him to go in search for a groom for Madhuban. Tell him it is all arranged."

"No, sister, that's your task. You are the matchmaker. You tell him. Only tell me just when you are about to tell him, so I can go on a pilgrimage while he beats you."

"Nobody will ever lay their hands on me. Not on Saraswattee!"

"Yes. I have forgotten who my sister Saraswattee is. Well sister, it is getting late. I am going home to help our mother cook. Will you be coming home tonight? Or will you be staying over with *our* husband?"

"Why should I come to your empty house, when I have *our* husband to hug and sleep with?"

"Sister! You are so frivolous at times! I am going home."

Chintamani got up and began to make her way home. Saraswattee called after her: "So you don't think our Gopi too ugly after all?"

Chintamani giggled and without turning she said, "No."

"And you don't think our Gopi too black after all?"

"No—ha ha, sister!"

"And you don't think the stranger so rich and handsome—"

Chintamani spun around and Saraswattee shot to her feet and the two sisters simultaneously and instantaneously relived every single transformation suffered by the rich and handsome stranger taken as a good omen when he first stepped onto the sacred ground of their shrine.

TWELVE

ITH that sudden revelation the two sisters ran. Saraswattee swung east and began to circle the crater wall to the desert where she knew Gopi would be. Chintamani ran up the northern steps and stopped. Saraswattee halted and dropped behind a boulder. Then she beheld the tangled black hair of Mahisha Narayana rise out of the crater. There flashed the clots of his red eyes. His moustache had grown and thickened and looked more like the tips of the tails of buffaloes. Then the demon towered over Chintamani.

Saraswattee watched her sister step back, bowed her head, clutched her hands to her chest. She saw Mahisha smile. She saw him reach up and lift Chintamani's head and then both sisters beheld the transformations over that good omen of a rich and handsome stranger. Of his facial and head features, only his lips and ears hadn't grown in proportion. They had darkened but they hadn't grown. This made Mahisha hideous to behold. Both Saraswattee and Chintamani saw Mahisha himself wasn't aware he had become ugly and hideous—he still thought of himself as a rich and handsome stranger. And indeed Mahisha did. The only change he felt in his body was the experience of his genitals. This experience of his genitals—the weight, the size—was a new experience for him. Though he didn't think it as such. He thought it was Chintamani, the sight of that beautiful young girl, who made him aware of his prodigious parts and of the lust in his veins. Mahisha lifted Chintamani's gold thali off her bony chest. Chintamani dropped her head and her eyes fell on the thali as it lay in the thick black ugly fingers with the thick black ugly growth of hair between them. And as humiliation filled up Chintamani, thus anger became Saraswattee, and she grabbed a rock and flung it with all her might but she missed the demon by fifteen feet.

Saraswattee dropped behind the boulder. Mahisha saw the stone fly through the air. He dropped the thali and began to laugh and said: "Such a beautiful girl. So young and so beautiful. And married already. A wife. Ha ha ha!" Chintamani felt the scorn and the contempt. She felt the desecration. Tears ran down her cheeks. Mahisha walked past her, got into his jeep, and drove demonically through the desert.

With the desert in a turmoil, Saraswattee ran to her sister and Chintamani dropped to her knees and Saraswattee clasped her hands around her sister's neck and hugged her. Chintamani wept. Kahar hopped through the crater, stared at the jewels, stared at the girls. Saraswattee pushed Chintamani up and bid her run home. She stood on the wall and watched her sister run across the courtyard. The vapors rose. Kahar stared at the girl with his whip curled around his neck. But Chintamani ran without a glance at her father-in-law. When she disappeared over the other wall, Saraswattee raced down the steps and among the ruins and the pilgrims and ran until the ruins and the pilgrims were left behind. But she didn't stop until she came to Gopi where he sat on a boulder under a kumat tree.

In the west the sun began to sink behind Durga Kali but again she cast no shadow upon the land and even though she beheld the approach of night she knew there could be no sleep for her until she discovered how Mahisha Durga came to be reincarnated; and she continued to plunder her genealogy and leapt back into the history of creation celestial day by celestial day—four trillion three hundred and twenty million mortal years she bounded in a leap, for such a time it was for her: a time to come face to face with herself. But Saraswattee flung herself at Gopi and wept. The boy held her as he held his silence and his own counsel. When Saraswattee was done with crying, rage consumed her and she folded her fists and pounded Gopi on his head and shouted: "Such a hard head! Didn't I tell you the stranger was an evil man? Didn't I tell you the evil man was a demon? Now what are we going to do? He has come to destroy Kali Durga! Will you wake up now and defend her and destroy the demon before he destroys us?"

Thus they spent the night in the desert. Gopi sat on his boulder, his eyes bright in the darkness of the desert. Saraswattee crawled up between his legs and slept. From time to time she would awake, jump up, fold her fists, pound Gopi on his head, and shout: "This is no time to withdraw into yourself. No time to feel sorry for yourself. You did no wrong. You did not violate Durga! Wake up! You have to confront the demon in the morning when he returns!"

And indeed when the dawn came Mahisha Narayana returned and the villagers and the pilgrims awoke to a great rumble and rushed to the walls of the crater. From everywhere in the north and the west army jeeps and trucks pulled up around the shrine. The people rose like the dust of the desert and then like that very dust they settled down in silence and stared. Mahisha Narayana came out his jeep and stood on the northern steps in a tall shadow of triumph. Pundit Ayer ran down into the courtyard. Kahar hopped ahead of him to meet Mahisha Narayana. Behind Sutnami thronged the village men. Everyone stared at the jeeps and the trucks one at a time. Pundit Ayer's eyes saw it all at once and he became engulfed in bafflement. Gopi and Saraswattee pushed their way with the goats and the sheep through the crowds. As the goats and the sheep filtered themselves among the people, Gopi and Saraswattee stood up on the east wall. Saraswattee fixed her gaze on Mahisha Narayana. Gopi looked at the most sacred of the sacred orifices of Kali.

And for Kali it was a time for sorrow. Because there the demon Mahisha stood. In her presence. About to dictate her future. And there she rose. Trapped in a body of cast iron and granite. And trapped so far and deep in the past. The demon had arrived at a point in time and creation where she should have been. Despair filled her brain. Could she crash through the past and redouble and return an infinitesimal moment before her future arrived?

With the people she beheld all the strange things that had crashed through their life and their present. The twenty-first century; and the myths and the gods of the twenty-first century. And they, like her, stood unprepared for that future. Mahisha Narayana began to descend the steps and the ogre within the bosom of Kali beat dhoom! dhoom! dhoom! And each time the feet of the demon hit the earth, a layer of dust settled on the temple courtyard. The serpent of serpents still felt the claws of the hand clamped on his tail and then the demon halted in the bloodstained gaze of the lidless eyes.

Kali fixed her gaze on Gopi as the boy stared at the most sacred orifice. She knew his sadness. His sorrow. The boy himself stood engulfed by a sense of failure and futility. Plagued by a sense of desecration and defilement. And she wished she could enter his heart, fill up his body with her consciousness, and let him know he was guilty of no desecration of her, no defilement of her body. And he had not failed her, and to give in to futility now was certainly to abandon her to her future of doom and destruction just when she needed him most. What a champion he had been! How well he had defended her! With only his heart; and the wisdom of the desert. How he loved her; how she loved him: what a lover he was! She felt no shame, no disgrace. To feel the emotions of a woman. Why to feel shame and disgrace from the experience of the emotions and the passions of a woman was to feel shame and disgrace for being a woman—and she was more woman than a goddess then and loved it. But how to let Gopi know this? He. Dark-skinned boy. Desert boy. Withdrawn and distant in the oasis of himself. So he had touched her body. Knew it to be heat. Knew it to be mud. But there was something else, Gopi. The heat you felt was the heat of my body; my blood. The mud you felt was the mud of my flesh; the mud of my soul. And I am more than the heat of my heart; more than the mud of my soul. Only if you lost your faith in me shall my heat be heat and my mud be mud. New wisdom, Gopi. New knowledge. New learning. New religion. New myths and new legends and new gods. New eyes to see old things. *But to see the old things with the new eyes.* Don't just turn new blind eyes to old things. So much of the science of Mahisha Narayana you have already learnt. What will this new wisdom, this new science do to the boy of her heart, the love of her love? Will he assume a false face? Will the new eyes dazzle him such that he will see nothing but his own reflection? Will he become enamored of his new learning for itself? Will he serve this new power and in the end be consumed by it? Will his blood drink his blood and his flesh eat his flesh and his loins copulate with his own loins and he be dead long before the flames of the funeral pyre are lit? Will he fall in the gutters of his new wisdom and not find the truth? Will he fall into the quicksands of his new knowledge, and not find firm ground? Will

he travel in the images of his new learning; and never find a
straight path? And with his new eyes. With his new eyes: will he
look away? Or look back? Look to? Yes yes, Gopi, look at yourself, look at yourself but look at me too. *The gods ask; they do not
demand. The gods serve: they do not command.* The things she
had learnt. The things she was learning. Gopi would learn too.
Already he had learnt the truth of Mahisha. Already the boy had
mastered his science. Let him behold Mahisha's gadgets. The
paraphernalia of his new religion. Let the people—and the damned
cross-eyed pundit, doomed to die a most horrid death, the cross-
toothed gnat!—punditji punditji, when last did you see the sun
rise, ah, chee chee chee, what can one do, you live once, you die all
the time, it's all in the gods' hands—you lie! you painted-face
dacoit!—but no: the time will come when you will see in the
strangest way of all—punditji punditji, why is my daughter
Madhuban a shame, a sore? chee chee chee, she a girl, girls are no
good, girls are a disgrace, shame shame shame, shame to their
fathers, shame to their menfolk, lock them up, hide them away, let
them cover their faces, let them not be seen in daylight, let them
walk five steps behind men, let them never enter the temple, let
them be slaves, servants, let them serve and be of service in the
gutters of men's lust so that in the night in corners the priests and
the brahmins may uncross their legs and unravel their genealogy
and save their souls!—chee chee chee, such an old girl, so close to
her monthlies and not married yet, shame on the father who can't
pay the bride price, girls girls girls, shame shame shame, chee chee
chee—yes one day she Durga Kali will make that cross-eyed pundit see things in a manner he never expected, but for now she had
to get to Gopi, he, dark-skinned boy; lover: she had to enter his
body: she had to get him to reenter her soul. Unto herself she had
made a desert. From the desert of the land Gopi made an oasis for
himself. Kali fought to penetrate that oasis of Gopi. As she did,
Pundit Ayer and Kahar and Sutnami and the menfolk went from
vehicle to vehicle. Beheld the soldiers and strangers. And all the
paraphernalia of their religion. Naga kept his eyes on Mahisha
Narayana. But the aged serpent of serpents winced in pain as the
claws cut into his body. His vision became blood-clogged.

Of all the village men Pundit Ayer became the most confused.
But Chintamani kept her eyes on her father. Though his old dignity

did not return, her father was still the *real* leader of the menfolk. Perhaps this was his opportunity to confront that evil man and destroy his evil work and thus atone for his sin—whatever it happened to be. All stared in silence at the proud Mahisha Narayana. Then the pundit·asked: "What does all this mean?"

"It means the destruction of our sacred shrine!" Sutnami answered. "Brothers, didn't I tell you the stranger's geothermal energy has everything to do with the sacred orifices of Durga Mata?"

"But how can that be?" Pundit Ayer asked.

"Ask him," Sutnami shouted at the pundit. "Let him explain. He has come to destroy our energy—the energy of our deity, the energy of our beliefs, the energy of our life force!"

"Engineersab," Pundit Ayer asked, "why all this strange equipment? What do they do? What does it all mean?"

"Destruction of our shrine!" Sutnami said.

"Punditji," Mahisha Narayana said as he tried to keep his composure, "no need for alarm. No need for concern. No need for fear and worry."

"But what does it all mean? Why did you bring them? What do they do?"

"This is simple scientific equipment. Simple scientific apparatus. Nothing complicated or sophisticated. Simple. Very simple scientific instruments."

"But what has even simple scientific instruments to do with our shrine? What do these instruments do?"

"Evil!" shouted Sutnami. "Nothing but evil. Is he a good omen? Is he a pilgrim? Does a pilgrim come to a holy shrine for a holy bath armed with all such equipment of science? Brothers, this man is evil. Drive him out of our shrine now before he does any further desecration!"

"Yes! Yes! Yes!" shouted the angry menfolk. "He is evil. Drive him out!"

Gopi and Chintamani beheld Mahisha flash his red eyes at Kahar. Kahar began to hop his way behind Sutnami. Gopi descended the eastern steps and made his way towards his father. Saraswattee began to follow but then she stopped. So far the demon had never really seen her. If she appeared before him now he might realize he had indeed seen her twice on the body of the goddess and he might expose her sacrilege. From where she pulled back in the crowds, the girl stalked the demon with her eyes. As Gopi made his way to his father, thus too Chintamani made her way to stand behind her father.

"Engineersab," Pundit Ayer said, "this is holy ground. Only human feet are allowed to touch this earth. It is forbidden for these vehicles to be here."

"Come now, punditji, what kind of talk is that?"

"It is the truth!" Pundit Ayer shouted as his body shook. The village menfolk became more irate and pressed closer around Mahisha.

"Why are soldiers here?" Sutnami asked.

"Yes!" shouted the menfolk. "Why do you need soldiers if you are a pilgrim?"

"Soldiers," shouted Pundit Ayer. "And jeeps and trucks?"

"Sorry, Pundit Ayer. Please forgive me. I had no idea. You must know I have no intention of desecrating what is holy and sacred. I am a brahmin and a stranger."

"He is a stranger to our village," Kahar said. "Is this any way to treat a stranger?"

"My younger brother, it is clear to see you have joined forces with the evil stranger. And everyone knows why you have joined forces with him. Have you forgotten how you lost your leg?"

"And you my elder brother, have you forgotten I can twist your neck with this whip and snap your head off?"

"Better to do that brother, than to join forces with an evil man to do evil deeds. You cannot earn the jewels of Kali. Haven't you sinned enough? Why court the wrath of Kali?"

"Why do you court my wrath? Is my sin greater than yours?"

Sutnami became silent and dropped his eyes. Chintamani beheld her father recoil into wrinkles. He lost his anger against Mahisha and she knew he was going to withdraw from the protest. Gopi drew close to his uncle and fixed his eyes on his father. Kahar stared at his son and he beheld the distance of the boy. But he beheld something behind the distance. But what he saw didn't chill his heart. He had no doubt he would snap his son's neck without a thought. This, too, Gopi saw. But Chintamani was wrong. Sutnami shouted: "Not only has that man desecrated our shrine with his presence, he has desecrated our temple with his vehicles and evil instruments!"

"Pundit Ayer," Mahisha said, "like you, you know, I am a brahmin of the highest caste. Are you going to let these low-born peasants dictate to you? I didn't know my vehicles would be a desecration. If I did I wouldn't have brought them in. But now that they are here, certainly you can purify my vehicles, can you not?"

Pundit Ayer became doubtful, his eyes plagued by random motion.

"Get out!" the menfolk shouted. "And take your vehicles and instruments with you!"

"Shut up, you low-born peasants!" the pundit shouted.

"Surely, punditji, yours is the power to bless all, yours is the power to damn all. Damn me and I shall leave. But bless my mission. Bless my vehicles and equipment and I will bring prosperity to you and your village. Such prosperity and wealth as you have never seen! Listen people, all listen. I am not here to destroy your shrine. I am not here to destroy your goddess. I too believe in her. I too am a devotee of hers. I know her wrath. Will I court her wrath and have her slay me? No, I am not here to destroy your ways. I have come in peace on a mission for the future of our land. For your future. For the future of your children. These vehicles will only be here for a few days. All I need is a few days to do some tests and conduct a few experiments. Then I and all my men and equipment will be gone and you will not know the difference. I will be gone and your shrine and your customs and traditions will be safe and sound. I offer you great wealth and prosperity. I give you my word on this as a devotee of Durga. May she slay me where I stand if my words be untrue!"

Kali became astounded. She watched Mahisha grow in stature. He straightened his shoulders and his chest puffed out. Such brazenness! Such audacity! What impudence! To stand right before her and dare her to vent her wrath on him. To use her name. To claim to be a devotee of hers. He. A demon. A devotee of a goddess! But the presence and the stance of Mahisha was only a testimony of what she had become—of what she had allowed herself to become. And the way he looked at her. His eyes. His disbelief. His brash challenge. With his vain knowledge that she was made of stone and cast iron and had no veins. Daring her to slay him then and there and she impotent. Kali could see her devotees stand in silence for her to slay that man. They were puzzled. He claimed to be a devotee of hers. Not to slay him was to bless him. Bless his lies. Bless his mission of deception and vengeance. And still—impotent! Did it matter she didn't know his identity? Did it matter she didn't know how he attained reincarnation? Wasn't it enough she knew he was a demon? Did she know for certain he was a demon? What if indeed he was Brahma? Wasn't it the prerogative of gods to take upon themselves whatever shape or form they chose? Be it god or mortal—or demon? Hadn't she herself, the creator of creators, succumbed to the folly and taken the mortal body of a woman? No, she still had to ravish her genealogy and come out ahead of her future. That was the only way to slay evil for all eternity.

"Brothers," Mahisha shouted. "If my words were words of lies would I still be standing here alive? If I had blasphemed before your very deity wouldn't she have slain me before I finished even speaking?" The menfolk became doubtful. Pundit Ayer began to see the wisdom of the words of the demon and he shook his head. "Brothers, I have not come for evil. Let me do a few simple experiments and I will transform your lives for you. Such wealth as you have never seen. Such prosperity! No more poverty and hard labor and hunger for you and your wives and your children. What do you say? What harm can I do in a few days? How can I, a mortal man, destroy your goddess?"

"That is what you said you came to do." It was Gopi who had spoken. "He said to me he came to destroy Durga Kali!"

"Ah Gopi. My assistant. You who would learn and see old things with new eyes. Am I mistaken in you? Are you such a fool to take my words too literally? We entered a contest. Legend against legend. Myth against science. A contest of wit. An experiment. What did you feel in the most sacred orifice of Durga Kali? Not heat, as I said? Did you not feel mud? Or did you feel something else? Is our contest over? All this is still part of the experiment for the discovery of truth. If you really believe I have come to destroy your goddess then you are still welcome to defend her. Be her champion. Match wits with me. Show these peasants you, a peasant, can destroy a man of science with your peasant wisdom."

Before Gopi could reply, the menfolk shouted: "No! No! No! Go away. No experiments. You and your vehicles defile our shrine. You have brought soldiers to kill us if we stop you. We will defend our deity and fight you and your soldiers! Go away!"

"Aye, punditji!" Kahar shouted. "Are you not forgetting the Engineersab is a brahmin? Can a brahmin defile? Can a brahmin desecrate? If so then your hands are capable of evil too!"

"SHUT UP!" Pundit Ayer shouted to his villagers. "Shut up! Is that a way to behave? Is that a way to treat a brahmin? Haven't you heard the Engineersab declare himself to be a son of Durga Mata? Haven't you heard him ask her to slay him dead if his words are those of one who lies? I am the pundit. I am of the highest caste, the priestly caste, the learned caste. I am the representative of God! I will decide what is right and what is wrong. My word is law. The Engineersab has my blessing. He is free to conduct his work with my blessing. He is a guest in my home. He is a guest in our village. He is no different from any other pilgrim who has come to seek the blessings of Durga Mata and to partake of her boons. Engineersab, you have my permission and my blessings, may Durga speed your work and may it be fruitful and bestow on you the results you seek. May you be true to your vows to Kali or may Kali slay you if you are evil!"

Mahisha Narayana looked at the pundit but couldn't suppress his scorn. He chuckled. Befuddlement again entangled the eyes of the pundit. Then, as if to enlighten him, Mahisha Narayana led the pundit on a tour. Showed him. Explained to him all the pieces of equipment, tools, apparatus. What they were and what they did. How they worked. Mahisha Narayana explained: "This is surveying equipment, punditji, here take a look put your eye here, with this telescope you can see far, you can see the land and survey it, measure it, plot it, take readings. And this here is a hydrogeologist—I myself am a geothermal geologist, an expert in the field of geothermal geology—the function of the hydrogeologist is to discover thermal fluids in permeable zones and trace it to surface thermal phenomena. He is an expert in gradients, porosities, and permeabilities. He uses isotopes and knows the difference between magmatic and meteoric waters. This here is our geochemist. The geochemist analyzes the chemical constituents of thermal fluids and with these test tubes and other apparatus he will compute silica and magnesium and sodium and potassium ratios. Here is our geophysicist. These are his thermometers, thermocouples, geothermographs, platinum resistance thermometers and mercury maximum thermometers. With these he does his thermometry, deduces temperature gradients and heat flow and he studies electrical resistivity measuring voltages between electrodes. He also does seismic measurements, scanning of infra-red radiation, micro-seismicity and andromagneto-tellurics, and this—these punditji, are our bores and drilling equipment. Drilling equipment, punditji. *Drills!* "

Then the pundit, he who knew ancient Sanskrit, was duly impressed. And confused. As he had always been with his ancient Sanskrit. And yet his ancient and well-learnt verses, verses known by heart and for everything, never bore down on him as the verses of this chant. Pundit Ayer tried to focus in on Mahisha Narayana's face, to pin it down, scrutinize it, identify that face. Because here was a high priest. A high priest of another religion in the service of a new god as he himself, Pundit Ayer, happened to be another high priest in the service of another god. But Mahisha Narayana disturbed him. The words of Mahisha Narayana disturbed him. The verses and the chants of the religion of Mahisha Narayana disturbed Pundit Ayer. Somehow, in his tangled vision, in his opium-clogged brain, amidst his own confused chants and verses, amidst his own pettiness and prejudices; amidst his own misgivings and misconceptions and myopia: the cross-eyed pundit felt that Mahisha Narayana was a shamaan. A phony sadhu. The cross-eyed pundit felt that Mahisha Narayana was not a high priest but a witch doctor. The cross-eyed pundit in his befuddlement thought not that Mahisha Narayana was a demon: Mahisha Narayana was a dangerous man. Dangerous because of his science. Dangerous because of his words. Dangerous because of his knowledge. Then he who knew all the legends and all the sacred scriptures, drugged and stupefied by the verses and chants of Mahisha Narayana, stumbled his way to the courtyard where he sat down in a stupor.

And as he sat he desperately tried to focus his eyes. And he did. And he saw things in a straight line. Then with his focus straight Pundit Ayer took a close long look at himself. Who he was. What he was. Where he was born. He took a long close look at the people about him. He tried to discover things about them. Who they were. Who were their parents? Where did they come from? Where did they go? With his new vision Pundit Ayer studied the deity he served. Did he serve her well? Who was she? What did she want of him and of humanity? Pundit Ayer sat and tried to restructure his life, his past; tried to figure out what wrongs he had committed: what evils was he guilty of? He mumbled, repeated his own chants and verses. Tested them on his tongue. In his ears. To see if they rang true. Or false. But then he who knew Sanskrit and all the sacred scriptures only became more and more befuddled and he knew a great despair.

Mahisha went about his work. Kahar hopped behind him. Sutnami and the menfolk stood and watched. Mahisha directed his men to pitch tents. He instructed his assistants to set up workshops. He supervised his technicians as they erected their laboratories. From group to group he went. Issued orders. Checked results. Consulted with his specialists. Conducted his own experiments. The fathers of the girls came before the goddess. Prayed. Went in search of bridegrooms. They returned; prayed again: went home. The girls hid; watched. And Durga Kali leapt back from celestial day to celestial day, and at each leap the dusts of four trillion three hundred and twenty million mortal years fell on the earth and the shrine became more sandclogged and the ruins and the village became more and more echoless and windblown as ages and ages of pilgrims came and left and the villagers grew older and more wrinkled as they watched their desert and their ruins and their shrine be transformed day by day into something more and more ancient, more and more lost in the past; more and more like an archaeological discovery of which they and their deity were part of the artifacts: relics of a dead life.

And as the ages came and went, thus Kali stalked the past. But as the ages changed, thus too the demon Mahisha changed. Because he had the power of illusion. Because he had the power to transform himself into any shape or form or thing or creature. So as she hunted him down, so he eluded her. She caught him roasting a dead spirit on the spit of a skull and as she flung an arrow he turned into smoke and vanished. She came upon him in slaughter of a world of mortals and she flung a spear but he turned into a hawk and shot through the air to another world. But she stalked him, searched out the footprints of that creature with one buffalo foot and a human foot with only a big toe. She surprised him in a buffalo pen in an orgy with the wives of the lesser gods and she catapulted a thunderbolt, but the demon transformed himself into a sperm and crawled through to the center of the earth where he hid out and rested for half a celestial day while she sweated and tired herself out ripping the earth apart. A serpent. A mendicant. A woman. A cloud. A leaf in a river. The sheep dog in a herd of sheep. A saint. A newborn baby. Shape after shape after shape. Form after form after form. Illusion after illusion after illusion. Such that one day, suddenly, she came face to face with herself and before she could think, her spear flew through the air but she caught herself in time and caught the spear just before it entered her own throat. Thus the demon Durga eluded her. While he wrought his death and destruction. But it wasn't long before he realized there was a woman on his trail. A powerful woman. A warrior woman. A woman who occasioned him not a little fear. Who was she? Who was this powerful warrior woman who slaughtered the entire armies he sent out to her? And what powerful and mighty armies did he send! Armies of thousands; armies of millions. And she, Devi in the body of Parvati, not yet famed and renowned as Durga Kali, slaughtered his armies left and right—right there in Nagar an army of one million took one look at her and fouled themselves and turned into skeletons.

It was after she had ravished and depleted most of his armies the demon Durga decided to try a little tack—a little masculine approach. He began to woo her. Court her. Emissary after emissary after emissary he sent to her. Loaded with gifts of riches and wealth and heads on platters—and perfume! He sent fruits and flowers and beads and earrings and necklaces and the finest silken saris. He wrote songs and poems and these he sent to her with promises of his love. His poems made Kali puke; weakened her. But such love; his undying love—oh how he pined for her love, his emissaries said. He promised to make her his number one concubine; pledged to give her control over all his hordes of concubines. And with what descriptions of love-making he wooed her. Sexual pleasure as she had never known. He filled up the seven worlds with echoes of his sexual prowess—sent her clay replicas of his prodigious penis. Then, when the replicas of his penis returned to him shattered to pieces, the demon Durga decided he had better wise up: it was no ordinary woman who stalked him!

And she—whoever she happened to be—certainly wasn't after his prodigious penis.

No. She. Whoever she happened to be. Lusted for his demon life.

Then the hunt really began. And the seven worlds became transformed into mazes of illusions. And she, Devi Parvati, despaired of ever slaying the demon Durga and saving creation. She, Devi Parvati, despaired: as she, Durga Kali, now despaired of discovering the true identity of Mahisha Narayana so that she might confront him, stand face to face with him, slay him as she had slain the demon Durga; take his name; take his identity; become again: Durga Kali: bloodvexed and bloodlusting slayer of evil; and of evil men.

But the days and the nights went by and the crater became transformed into an ancient shrine: into the wreck and the ruin of an ancient shrine. The fathers came. Prayed. Went in search of matches. Returned. Prayed. Returned home. Their daughters watched and waited and waited and watched. Madhuban became dark and skeletal. Chintamani busied herself at home with her mother and her chores. Gopi abandoned the fields; abandoned the land. He, dark-skinned boy, sat far and alone in the desert and he sought to discover the answers for which he searched. During those days Saraswattee too busied herself. She kept house for Gopi. She cleaned the rooms, swept the yard. She washed clothes; she cooked food. At mealtime she took food to Gopi in the desert and sat and forced him to eat or if he was too stubborn and wouldn't eat she ate all the food herself. At nights she slept with the boy in the desert. Or, when she could, she bullied him to return some nights—it was safe only at night now—and sneak up the goddess and sleep in their bed of rags in the red cave of the mouth of Durga Kali.

This Saraswattee loved best. Because it gave her a chance to be with Kali Durga. Because it gave her the chance to sleep with Gopi in their secret place. It allowed her to witness the night prayers of Madhuban and the other girls. It bestowed upon her the opportunity to bless the renewed devoutness and devotedness of Chintamani who came every night to pray to the goddess and to ask for forgiveness of any wrongs she may have done.

But most of all being with Gopi in the mouth or on the bosom of Durga Kali gave her the edge and the advantage of secretly observing the night doings of Mahisha Narayana. At nights the demon would stalk into the crater. Sometimes he would walk lost in circles. Sometimes he would stand the entire night lost in thought—sometimes Saraswattee felt his mind just go blank. At other times he would circle the sacred orifices, study them, scoop out mud, cup out water; or poke shiny metal things into them. But most of all he would stand in the middle of the courtyard and stare up at the cauldron eyes of Durga Kali.

Then Kali and Saraswattee and Gopi beheld his true demonic nature because he would become obsessed; possessed: and pure evil lust for vengeance would become the mirror of his face and eyes. Then Kali—not Gopi nor Saraswattee—would hear the screams of his mother echo in Mahisha's ears as the flames of the funeral pyre ate into her flesh while her husband, Pundit Mahesh Narayana, stood by and watched his pregnant wife burn alive to death—by his own decree. Those screams of his mother as the flames tore at her flesh—it was those screams that helped Kali most as she searched for the true identity of Mahisha. When she got lost in the genealogy of the past, those screams brought her back to the moment of Mahisha Narayana's mortal birth. Then one night Kali Durga realized what a fool she had been. She had overlooked the obvious. In her madness, in her delirium to discover Mahisha's true identity, she had discarded the most natural starting point —the mortal birth of the demon!

But this night, the moment she realized this, Mahisha walked into the volcanic crater and came upon Chintamani, she who knew the legend well; she who knew better than to come out at night to pray while an evil man stalked the shrine. Chintamani stood before Kali and her voice rose in prayer, and just as Kali conceived the moment of Mahisha's mortal birth and was about to shriek in delight and rouse her cobra lingam, in walked the demon and he saw Chintamani alone in the courtyard. As Mahisha sneaked up behind Chintamani, Saraswattee jumped to her feet and was about to scream. Gopi pulled her down and clasped a hand over her mouth and bid her be quiet. Gopi slipped down the back of the goddess.

Then Chintamani turned and there he rose. Out the vapors of the most sacred orifice. On the opposite side from her. Chintamani gasped but could not move. Mahisha stared at her, laughed, glanced at the most sacred orifice, to Chintamani, and back and forth. And once again he experienced the lust in his genitalia—lust for a woman which began to burn through his body and he began to sweat and walked around the most sacred orifice and confronted Chintamani. The sweat leaked from his body and he felt his penis tug at his guts and lengthen. Chintamani backed away, clutched her hands to her breasts, and dropped her head. Gopi slid behind the temple. Mahisha laughed, said: "How beautiful. So young. So beautiful. Ha ha. A wife—and a virgin—ha ha ha!" Then he reached out a hand and Saraswattee clamped her jaws together and as the hand of the demon touched Chintamani under her chin, Kali, in a quiet fit of vengeful anger, transferred the entire weight of the ten tons of her granite head to Chitamani's head. And Mahisha tried to lift that head. But could not. He blackened and pushed up. The girl's head would not budge. The sweat oozed out of his own body and leaked from his head and his eyes. He pushed up against the chin. The girl's chin felt cold like granite and seemed to weigh ten tons. Mahisha's heart pounded and his temple plates throbbed and his body trembled. But as he forced against the granite head of Kali his penis suddenly shrivelled into a bud and Kali realized that Mahisha Narayana—the demon was himself a virgin! Forty-five years old; and a virgin! Then the laughter of Kali echoed in Mahisha's ears and he too came into the same realization: forty-five years old and a virgin. Born of a woman, he had never had a woman. Never felt, never smelt, never tasted the body of a woman; in all its sweet intangibility: its obtuse clarity. He had remained chaste by virtue of distaste—the demon! Ha ha ha, Kali laughed in the ears of the demon as he pushed against her granite head—with his haunting abstinence, his languid asceticism, his secret sweating piousness. He; a demon. Had never known mortal passions as she Kali had. Man of science—the empiricist down to basics! He, Mahisha Narayana, Mahisha Durga, a sweating ascetic; a panting mystic: a shrivelled virgin—and she, Kali, with an especial sweet luscious delight for virgins of lust!

Then and there, instantaneously, Mahisha Narayana got his first glimpse into his true demonic nature.

Then and there, instantaneously, Kali realized that Mahisha Narayana didn't know he was Mahisha Durga.

Irony of ironies: he who had come to wreak the death and

destruction of a demon didn't know he was a demon. And paradox of paradoxes: she who was the disillusioner and purified mortals of their delusions and brought them to truth: she now had to keep Mahisha Durga deluded: keep him from the full realization of the truth about himself: because it is only when a thing recognizes itself can it become itself. She, the disillusioner, had to keep Mahisha Durga from coming face to face with his demon identity because she had first to discover how he came to be reincarnated. Only then could she confront him. Come face to face with him again. Myth to myth. Legend to legend. Goddess to demon. Man to woman—whichever; whatever—for such a time it had become.

With a cry of disgust Mahisha Narayana pulled his hand away from Chintamani and he clasped his hands over his ears to stifle the laughter of Kali and he stalked away in the darkness to stalk the legend of his genealogy.

Gopi came out from behind the temple and walked to Chintamani. The girl looked at the boy with tears in her eyes. Gopi glanced up. Chintamani followed his gaze. And there, under a universe of stars, her hands across her chest, Saraswattee towered up into the abode of the gods.

THIRTEEN

Iɴ ᴛʜᴇ morning Saraswattee awoke terrified. Her
body was wet with sweat. Her heart pounded. She awoke to find
herself alone in the cave of the red mouth. Gopi had risen early,
and had gone out into the mist of the desert.

But it was not waking to find herself alone that terrified
Saraswattee. What frightened her was the change she felt in her
own body. She remembered the night before how she had risen up
into the abode of the gods and stared down at Chintamani and
Gopi in the courtyard after the demon stalked away. Then she
had experienced an awesome power, and a powerful vision. It was as
if she had seen to the ends of the universe—as if *she* could bring the
universe to a quiet and impartial end.

Now, awake and alone in the red cave of the mouth, she felt
herself a little girl. Just a little girl. This frightened her. But what
terrified her was the change she experienced come over the body of
Durga Kali. Saraswattee sat up, clutched her chest, sweated. Her
wet hair and wet bodice clung to her body. She looked around.
Yes. Kali's mouth had changed. The floor of the mouth felt
soggy—spongy. So too the walls. Spongy; and more raw—and
spotted with cankers. The teeth had changed colors, become
greenish yellow. And the throat had tightened. Or darkened. And
the light from within the chest cavity reflected not red: but deep
purple.

Saraswattee got to her feet, stared at the darkened throat,
listened. She tried to quiet her own heart, filter the vibrations of her
own body from the vibrations of Kali's body. She wanted to hear

197

the sounds in Kali's chest and belly. But there came no sound—yes yes, there echoed a sound: the sound of listening. Someone— something within Durga's bosom listened too. Listened to the sounds of Saraswattee. The pounding of her heart. Her breathing. The sound of the ooze of her sweat. The sound of her terror. Who or what waited and listened down there?

Saraswattee jumped back, glanced up at the cave of the dark skull. The smell came different. But again no sounds. No echoes of the hisses. But that smell, of—of fresh blood. Silence in Durga's head. Silence in Durga's bosom. Yet she had changed. What was the transformation? The girl spun around and climbed out the mouth and eased down the necklace of skulls and jumped down into the stone cleft. No sooner had her feet hit the hot stone, she spun around and glanced up at the face of Kali.

Slowly she studied each cauldron eye. As if she were some ancient practitioner of some ancient medicine. Durga Kali stared back at her daughter. Saraswattee studied the tangled knot of hair, the bouldered cheeks, the tusked mouth, the regurgitated tongue. Durga's tongue, like her eyes and the inner walls of her mouth, showed the most change. The tongue had changed color, had become bluish white—and was spotted with cankers too.

Saraswattee spun around, crossed her arms over her bosom, surveyed everything as far as her eyes could see. It was early dawn. The sun didn't show yet. There blew no desert wind and the clouds of white vapors spread lazily. The courtyard lay empty. At peace. No humans about in her secret universe. She studied the sacred orifices of Durga Mata. She began with her eyes, shifted to her ears, her nostrils, her mouth. She thought the teeth there had the same greenish yellow color as the mouth. But she wasn't sure. She fixed her eyes on the largest and most sacred of the sacred orifices of Durga Kali. She studied the bouldered outer edges, the inner walls of red mud, the clouds of fine vapors, the colors—yellow, crimson, pink, red, vermillion. She inhaled the smell of hot sulphur. Her eyes fell on the cobra lingam and she quickly leaned forward. Again it had moved—or appeared to have moved! And had the red vein of blood in the solid dark glass body thickened? Saraswattee glanced from the cobra lingam to the sacred orifice and back to the cobra lingam. And again she felt small and defenseless and vulnerable. In all that vast universe of her world she was only a little girl. She. Saraswattee. Curious child. Stubborn girl. She who didn't know the legend. Not all of it; anyway. But was learning it. As she was learning about herself.

The sun rose slightly, shot its rays of light through the mist of the desert. Durga's jewels glistened with dew. With the light, Saraswattee saw the air all around hung thick with dust. She looked at the pilgrims. Their tents and huts and hovels. She looked at the village. Only the dogs and the goats and the sheep about. She glanced at the jeeps and the trucks and the tents and the workshops and laboratories of Mahisha and his technicians and soldiers.

Mahisha Narayana. What if he should step out of his tent and walk into the courtyard and look up and see her? What would he do? She knew what she would do. She would jump down on him and dig out his eyes. That was what she would do. Saraswattee studied the earth around. The walls of the crater. The rocks. Boulders. The slums. The shanties. The village. Outside those: the wheat fields and the plum orchards. Beyond them the gullies and the canyons and the gorges and the pink plateaus. The ruins. Of ancient kingdoms. Of ancient legends. And beyond them, all encompassing, the desert. And the sands of the desert. On the earth. In the air. Fine and red and pink and crimson and brown in the yellow rays of sunlight. As far as her eyes could see. A universe of desert. Ever in expansion. With no boundaries—nothing to hold the sand in. It was—yes, indeed! Kali had gathered in her mighty hands the seven worlds of the universe and crushed them with all the vengeance in her frothing blood and flung the debris away from her with all the surfeit of her disgust such that the universe, the earth, the desert, scattered far and wide in the scarred light: the universe drifting away: blowing away: sand grain by sand grain.

Thus Saraswattee, curious child, stubborn girl, beheld her world. And it saddened her. Filled her with a great sorrow. And it was with this sadness and this sorrow she turned again to the goddess and examined the eyes and the cheeks and the hair and the skulls and the bosom. Her eyes flashed from the left breast to the right breast and back to the left breast again. There was no doubt. The two breasts were now of different colors. Quickly Saraswattee climbed up on the right breast. She ran her fingers over the knuckled granite. She inspected the cracks, the crevices—moist with dew and moss. Where the breasts were grayish green before, now the right breast was mostly gray and spotted white. Saraswattee jumped off the right breast into the cleft and from the cleft she leapt onto the left breast and her feet immediately sank into the breast as if the breast was nothing but a bulge of molten black lava. Quickly the girl leapt back into the safety of the cleft. Her terror returned. She stared at her footprints on the left breast. The soles of her feet had been scorched. She lifted her feet one at a time and inspected the soles. They were covered with patches of the black molten lava.

Suddenly terror took control of the girl and she began to rush over the body of the goddess. She crawled over her hair, looked into the eyes of the tangled knot of the serpents. Some of the eyes beamed light at her. Most stared at her leaden: dead. Same with the eyes in the armpits and on Durga's back and bottom and belly. The body was firm; hot: but most of the eyes of the serpents stared dead. From the shoulders Saraswattee crawled down to the right breast, made her way down to the navel. From there, as if she was an acrobat, a gymnast; she let herself onto the cobra lingam, and like a monkey she flipped upside down, crooked her feet over its back, clasped her hands around its throat as if to choke it, and thus she eased herself forward until, stretching her head upwards, she peeped into the tiny black eyes there. They were alive. Saraswattee gasped. Naga, serpent of serpents, sullen but patient, subjected himself to the scrutiny. Besides, the girl wasn't that heavy and she didn't cause him any pain—not like the claws clamped on his tail.

The girl glanced around, saw that the desert had gotten brighter, knew that some of the people would be about. She pulled herself up on the cobra lingam, crooked her feet over it again, swung herself on its back. From there she scrambled up to the bosom and stood, her chest heavy as she breathed in and out.

Saraswattee thought. She wanted to know what was the best thing to do. Go for Gopi, or not? But she knew that by the time she got to Gopi and brought him back it would be daylight and they wouldn't be able to get up on the goddess. Without further hesitation the girl turned and began to climb up to the mouth when she suddenly stopped and turned back to the courtyard. Her face became serious, and her eyes pensive. She studied the orifices as if she had never seen them before. She studied their positions. Their forms. Their patterns. It was then she noted a shadow over the crater. A great dark shadow. Triangular. Pyramidal. The apex shot through the east end of the crater between Kali's eyes. Saraswattee had seen that shadow before. Many times. Many many times. As many times as she had seen the sun set. The sun set—but it was dawn! The sun was coming up in the east. Yet Durga cast her shadow as if the sun was behind her. Quickly the girl climbed up the shoulder and peeped west. There was no sun there. She climbed back down and indeed the sun rose in the east. Still Kali cast her shadow as if she stood with the sun behind her. For a moment Saraswattee studied the shadow, and again her eyes moved over the orifices, charting their configurations. Suddenly, Saraswattee, curious child, stubborn girl, she who knew not all the legend, she who had not heard told about the sacred orifices, what they were and what they meant, suddenly the girl made the connection— made the connection with herself and with Durga Kali—discovered the configuration of her own body.

Then she stood up straight, put her hands on her waist. Slowly the shadow on the ground seeped into the earth and disappeared. The courtyard became clear again. The shadows on the land again lost their appropriate perspectives. Saraswattee climbed down to the ground.

She knew where she would find Gopi and ran through the desert until she came to the cyprus tree. The boy sat in the shade of the tree and she went to him and threw her arms around him and clung there as she wept. Gopi hugged the girl as he whispered, "Hush, Little Mother, don't cry, hush, hush, what is it, Little Mother, what has frightened you so? What has troubled you so?"

"Gopi, Little Husband, some of the eyes of the serpents are going blind."

"Yes. I know."

"You know?"

"Yes."

"Since when?"

"Some time now."

"And why didn't you tell me?"

"I was going to."

"Little Husband, have you seen her breasts? They are changing colors. One is soft as mud!"

"Yes. I know."

"But why Gopi, why?"

"I don't know."

"You do know!"

"Maybe."

"Is Durga sick?"

Gopi didn't answer her.

"Little Husband," the girl said, "Kali is dying."

Again Gopi kept his silence, looked past the girl far into the glare of the desert. Saraswattee sat down on the ground beside him, watched the ants busy themselves.

"Little Husband, is Durga dying?" the girl asked after a while.

Gopi chose not to answer her.

"What will happen to us if Kali dies?"

Once more the boy kept his wisdom to himself.

"Why don't you answer me?" the girl commanded, letting her impatience burst out. "Answer me when I ask you something!"

"Little Mother," Gopi said, "some answers you must find for yourself. Tell me, do you think Durga is dying?"

"Yes. I thought she was coming alive. But I was wrong. She is dying."

"And what will happen to us if she dies?"

"Your father will whip me. The world will end. I do not know, Little Husband."

"Then that you must find out."

"You may have to slay your father after all. Sometimes I *feel* Kali. Then at times I don't know her at all. Her body didn't shake with the earthquakes. And because of Kali that evil man couldn't hurt Chinta. Maybe it was just me. Such knowledge the evil one has. I am learning—but you have to teach me first. What about the noises?"

"What are you talking about?"

"In Durga's belly. Sounds like a beast in there."

"Don't worry. They are only noises."

"Something is happening inside Kali, Little Husband. In her heart?"

"Yes."

"What?"

"Pain. Sadness. Confusion."

"Me too. I too am confused. And I feel sad, Little Husband, I feel very very sad. Have you been inside Durga?"

"Yes."

"*You have?*"

"Yes, Little Mother."

"And why haven't you taken me in?"

Gopi himself became troubled, impatient.

"Why, Little Husband, why?"

But Gopi didn't respond.

"What did you see?"

"Everything to see."

"Everything? The whole world?"

"No, no, Little Mother. Only what a body has inside it."

"Nothing more?"

They became pensive, silent. Gopi became evasive.

"Little Husband, is everything the evil one said to you true?"

"Not everything is true, Little Mother."

"But is everything he said true?"

"No."

"Is it all lies?"

"No."

"What then?"

"Some of what he said is true."

"Like what?"

"Like some of our ways are wrong, some of our customs are evil."

"The whipping of Chintamani and girls?"

"Yes."

"And bride price?"

"That too."

"What is not true?"

"The Engineersab."

"I knew it! I am glad to see you come to your senses! How do you know the demon is not true?"

"He doesn't know himself—his true nature."

"Does not know he is a demon?"

"Does not know if he is a man of truth. Or just a man."

"He is a demon—I know! Do you know about the shadows?"

"Yes, I do."

"Why haven't you told me?"

"When it is time for you to know you will know."

"Know what?"

"Truth. Kali. You. What makes the difference."

"What makes the difference? Little Husband, *what makes the difference?*"

Gopi made no answer.

"Little Husband!" Saraswattee pressed. "What makes the difference? What makes the difference between one truth and another? And what makes one truth greater and higher than another? What makes the demon's knowledge true, and Kali's knowledge truer?"

"Do you know the knowledge of Kali to be truer?"

"I do."

"How?"

"I feel it."

"Well, Little Mother, then why do you question me?"

"Because I want to. I want to know more. All my life I heard the words of the pundit. Now I too have learnt the words of the evil one. But you teach best. What makes the difference?"

"Look here, Little Mother, see my hand, the one the evil man pushed into the hot mud?"

"Yes, I see it. Let me hold it. I like to hold your hand. Ayi! how it must have hurt you. I too felt pain, Little Husband, ayi ayi! Did I make a nice poultice for you?"

"Yes."

"Did I rub it on good?"

"Yes, very good. My hand felt better right away."

"Did it?"

"Immediately, Little Mother. But what do you see, Little Mother?"

"It is healed, it is better."

"What else?"

"*What else?*"

"Yes. Tell me."

"It is healed, well healed, very much healed, Little Husband."

"But is that all you see?"

"I see your skin and your hands and fingers and your fingernails—I see your pores."

"What don't you see?"

"I don't see your bones—but I feel them!"

"But what else don't you see?"

"Adhey Gopiwalla! What are you doing? You think I am a fool? You think I like going in circles? What do you mean?"

"The mud, Little Mother."

"The mud?"

"Yes."

"What about the mud?"

"You tell me."

"Nothing. It is gone."

"Yes, it is gone. Where?"

"Where mud goes."

"And where is that?"

"Mud goes where mud goes!"

"Alright. It has gone into my flesh."

"*What?*"

"It has become my skin, Little Mother."

"Adhey Gopi, what nonsense are you talking?"

"Not the mud itself, Little Mother."

"What then?"

"Why did you put the mud on my hand?"

"Because your hand was scalded."

"But why?"

"Because mud is good to put on burns."

"Yes. Why?"

"Because mud heals."

"Mud heals?"

"Something inside mud heals."

"Ah yes, Little Mother. But what good is mud by itself?"

"It grows flowers!"

"Yes, but then it is not by itself. It has a seed—a flower seed. What good is mud by itself? No good. By itself it is just mud. But with a seed in it it blooms into a desert flower. What makes the difference?"

"Gopi, I asked you to teach me, not confuse me."

"What makes the difference?"

"Something inside mud, what heals?"

"But that thing inside mud, what good is it by itself itself?"

"No good."

"What makes the difference?"

"When I put it on your hand?"

"Yes, Little Mother, yes. What then makes the difference?"

"You are taking me in circles!"

"The mud is on my hand, it has something to give, what makes it give? My hand is in pain. Mud gives my hand healing. With the mud on my hand it is no longer mud and my hand is healed. What makes the difference?"

"Your hand?"

"Only partially."

"You?"

"Yes, Little Mother, I make the difference."

"*You?*"

"Yes."

"Are you sure?"

"I am."

"And me?"

"You make a greater difference."

"*I? Me? I do?*"

"Yes. You. Saraswattee."

"*I? You mean me? I do?*"

"Yes, you, Little Mother. You are the seed."

"Good! Good! HOW?"

"*You* put the mud on my hand."

"I did? Yes I did! Didn't I? I did!"

"You did, Little Mother. You are the seed in the mud."

"And that made the difference?"

"You made the difference. What good is the mud by itself?"

"Nothing."

"What good is the seed by itself?"

"No good."

"But what is this seed inside the mud?"

"Me?"

"Yes. You. You are."

"I am?"

"You are mud, Little Mother. I am mud. Chintamani is mud. Madhuban is mud. Your father is mud. The pundit is mud. The evil one is mud. Kali is mud. But we are the seed of each other."

"I am the seed of you?"

"And the seed of Kali."

"Adhey, Gopiwalla, how wise you are—but I am not the seed of the evil one!"

"No, you are not. Neither is Kali. The evil one is his own seed, his own mud."

"Adhey, Gopiwalla! *How very wise you are!* "

"All is mud. But Saraswattee makes the difference."

"Tell me more—don't stop!"

"But Saraswattee by *herself herself* makes no difference."

"What? What?"

Gopi became silent, Saraswattee got up. Then she smiled. After a while she laughed. Then she took the boy's face in her hands and looked into his eyes. She said, "What beautiful eyes you have, Little Husband."

Gopi said nothing, became serious. Saraswattee beheld his mood change and she said, "Don't stop now, Gopi. Keep talking. I want to know more. I want to know all about the desert. Teach me about the desert. Let's go into the desert. You and I, let us go and live in the desert and never come back here, come come, let us go!"

Saraswattee grabbed the boy's hand and pulled him up and Gopi asked, "Where shall we go?"

"There. Out there. Anywhere out there. Come let us go. I want to learn more."

"Ask then."

"Ask what?"

"Anything."

"Is the world round? I heard the evil one say such. Is it? Is the world round?"

"Yes, Little Mother."

"Ayi! Truly?"

"Truly."

"How do you know? Can you prove it?"

"I discovered it one day by myself."

"Adhey, Gopi, how wise you are. Show me. I want to discover the earth is round!"

"Okay. You see this tree?"

"Yes."

"Look at it."

"I am looking at it."

"Okay look out there, over the sand, across the desert. Look as far as you can see."

"I am looking."

"What do you see?"

"Adhey, Gopi, don't play the fool!"

"But what do you see?"

"I see sand."

"What about the sand?"

"It is red."

"And what else?"

"It is sand, it is red. Believe me. I am telling the truth."

"And nothing else?"

"Gopi!"

"How is it? Is it hilly? Is it flat?"

"It is flat."

"How flat?"

"Flat flat."

"Are you sure? Look closely. You have to be certain."

"I am sure it is flat."

"How flat?"

"Not as flat as your head when I am done with you—flat flat!"

"It is not curved?"

"Believe me—it is very very very *flat*."

"But are you sure? It is important."

"I am sure. I am getting angry too."

"Okay, look at the tree again."

"Okay, I have seen the tree again."

"Alright, Little Mother. Keep it as a reference point. We are going to walk in that direction as far as we can go. Alright? The tree is your marker."

"Yes! Yes! Let us go! What are you wasting time for?"

Saraswattee grabbed the boy's hand and pulled him forward and when Gopi began to walk she ran ahead of him, jumped and skipped, the rag-doll she was.

Gopi walked slowly. Saraswattee ran ahead, ran back, ran around.

Then she stopped, looked back at the cyprus tree.

As they went along the sand became drier, the desert hotter, their shadows became shorter. The sand became coarser, gravelly. They went on for hours in silence.

Saraswattee stopped, glanced back at the cyprus tree, turned and walked on again. Suddenly, abruptly, in a straight line, the sand ended and the desert turned into a desert of black stones. Saraswattee stood on the edge but would go no further. She looked back at the tree. Gopi crossed into the desert of black stones, told her the heat and the dew and the wind caused the stones to turn black.

Now for a while Saraswattee followed Gopi. She didn't run, or jump, or skip. After a long silence their shadows disappeared. Saraswattee walked slower, Gopi walked on. Then the desert of black stones changed abruptly into a desert of gray stones. Gopi waited for Saraswattee and she glanced back at the cyprus tree. They walked on together. Gopi explained how the desert came to be. He explained about the heat in the day. He explained why the desert turned cold at night. Their shadows returned, Saraswattee looked back at the tree. After a while longer Gopi said, "Stop, come back, look around." She spun around and said, "I see stones."

"Look again, more closely."

"I see more stones."

Then Gopi knelt down and looked at three oval pebbles. Saraswattee joined him and inspected the stones. "Eggs!" she shouted.

"Yes," said Gopi, "eggs of the sand grouse."

They walked on. The shrubs grew smaller. The wind picked up. The sun grew hotter. They sweated. The desert of stones gave way to a desert of sand again. Saraswattee looked back at the tree. Gopi didn't stop. Saraswattee ran and caught up with him and took his hand. Sometimes in silence they walked, sometimes the girl asked questions, sometimes Gopi talked without being asked anything. Once the girl saw a pebble, picked it up and screamed: Aye! It was not a pebble, but a locust. Then Gopi told the girl about acclimitization and how some animals survived their environment, like that locust, Little Mother you thought it was a stone, but the locust can disguise itself very well, it can take on any shape or form it finds itself in, it can look like a stone, it can look like a leaf, it can even look like a bird with beautiful colors. Saraswattee listened, resolved not to pick up things so carelessly again and said she was thirsty. Gopi stopped, looked around, went close to a chunk of weeds, and dug a hole. Water sprung up and they drank and when they moved on again Gopi told the girl how to find water in the desert. And food? she asked. Gopi told her about plants, and about roots, where to look, what not to eat. Gopi found a round stone as big as a goat's head and he picked it up and held it out to the girl. She took it, expecting to find it heavy. It was not, as if filled with air. Gopi showed her a hole and told her to look inside the rock. She did. Light shone inside. Light? Oh! It is hollow Gopi, how? Then Gopi told her what strange things the wind could do, how it could hollow out stones like that one. Saraswattee put the stone to her ear and listened. Inside, the wind whirled around. Saraswattee put the stone down and it exploded and she jumped and ran and caught up with Gopi and they walked on in silence for another celestial day and Saraswattee looked back but the cyprus tree was gone. *The cyprus tree had disappeared.*

"Gopi!" the girl shouted in alarm and wouldn't budge a step further. *"The tree is gone!"*

"That is because the earth is round, Little Mother."

"It disappeared because the earth is round?"

"Yes."

"How?"

"Think about it. If the earth was flat would that tree disappear?"

Saraswattee glanced all around. It was then she realized they were alone. There were no trees, no dunes, no shrubs, no rocks. Only sand. Everywhere. And as far as she could see. Suddenly she became acutely fearful and called Gopi closer to her.

"We are alone," she said.

"Yes. And the earth is round."

Then the girl realized the infinite possibilities for getting lost.

"We can get lost," she said.

"Yes, Little Mother, we can."

"Will we?"

"It depends on you."

"On me?"

"Yes. From now on."

"No, Gopi, no. Come back. The tree is that way. Let us go back. Why did the tree disappear? Because we walked too far?"

"Because of the curvature of the earth."

"The curvature? What big words you know! The curvature of the earth?"

"Yes. The earth is curved. If it was flat the tree wouldn't disappear."

"Is that so?"

"That is so. Think about it some more. True, if the earth was flat and we walked far enough it would vanish. But we haven't walked that far."

"But why did it only disappear now?"

"Because it is only after a certain distance you can see the curvature. Look closely."

Saraswattee bent, shielded her eyes, looked.

"What distance?" she asked.

"About five miles."

"If we go back a little ways, *will the tree appear as if by magic?*"

"Not by magic."

"It will reappear? Because the earth is curved?"

"Yes. If the earth was flat at this distance we would still see the tree."

"Then come let us go and see. This *I* must discover!"

"You go."

"Come! Let us go together!"

"Alright. But watch closely. Try to see when the tree appears. You will feel yourself on a very very small hill."

Together they retraced their steps and suddenly Saraswattee cried out: "There it is!"

Far in the distance the tree rose. Saraswattee was delighted. But she wasn't satisfied yet. She stared at the tree, she turned, stared far into the desert. Doubt and wonder both tugged at her heart. So far into the desert they had walked. Made such a long journey. Almost to the very horizon—the end of the universe. And she was about to discover the curvature of the earth. She, Saraswattee, curious child, stubborn girl, stood poised to make the greatest discovery of her life: that the earth was indeed round!

"Come," she said, "let us go back where we were. *I must see exactly when the tree disappears.*"

"You go."

"COME WITH ME!"

Gopi obeyed her and the girl began to walk backways. One step at a time. Slowly. Deliberately. She counted. One. Two. Three. Four. Five—AHA!

The tree was gone. As if by magic.

"I saw it go!" Saraswattee shouted. "Gopi. It is true. THE EARTH IS ROUND! It is true! It is true! I see. I see. I DISCOVERED IT! Oh Durga Mata, if you could only see this. Why, Gopi, the earth is round. The earth is round like a turtle's back! The earth is not flat. If the earth was flat the tree wouldn't disappear. But since the earth is curved, since the earth has a curvature, if you walk in a straight line from a reference point, because the earth is round, *your marker will disappear.* Oh! Gopiwalla, how wise you are, oh Durga Mata, how wise Gopiwalla is! *It is true. The earth is round.* AND, I, SARASWATTEE, DISCOVERED IT!"

All the girl's doubts became dispelled. She became filled with wonder. Marvel. The earth. The universe. All the possibilities. To be a girl—and still be able to discover things. Despite being a girl. To discover things. To know things. *To feel things.* What a thing was knowledge. How wise it was to have wisdom. To learn. From books. From brahmins. From people. From the earth itself. Only a moment ago she was foolish. Now she had such wisdom. She had made such a discovery. *And she a girl!*

Then once again Saraswattee became aware of how alone they were and she looked around and again saw the infinite possibilities to go wrong.

"But it is easy to get lost," she said. "So easy to get lost. If you lose your marker—your point of reference. Not so, Gopi?"

"Yes, Little Mother."

Then Saraswattee looked down, drew an invisible red line on the sand.

"Gopi," she said, "you see that invisible red line? Over here, on this side, is my home. On the other side, if I go any further, I get lost."

Gopi fixed his eyes on the sand and looked at the red line. "Is that so?"

"Is it not? Here is home. Over there all is invisible."

"Like your red line? Why is it such?"

"Because over here I am real. Over there I am not real."

"How did you arrive at that?"

"Over here is the truth. The truth of me, the truth of you. Over there—what?"

"Don't you want to find out?"

"And get lost?"

"Not if you don't lose your point of reference. Or not if you find another reference point."

"Are there markers in what is invisible?"

"Just as there are many ways to get lost, so there are many ways to find yourself. Besides, I see your red line in the sand."

"No, babu, no, I don't want to get lost too many times!"

"Then, shall we return?"

"Shall we?"

"You answer."

"Why me?"

"Because you make the difference."

"You make the difference too!"

"Here you make the difference—and the decision."

"Little Husband, I am afraid. We are so alone."

"And is that bad?"

"It makes me more afraid."

"It makes me afraid too."

"Then why do you want me to be alone?"

"I don't want you to be alone. *I want you to discover what being alone is.*"

"What will that teach me?"

"It will teach you how to be alone, if you ever have to be alone. It will teach you to live alone, if you ever have to live alone. It will teach you not to be afraid of being alone. It will teach you not to be afraid of loneliness."

"And if I learn all these things?"

"You will learn who you are."

"And then?"

"Then you can be who you are."

"Alone?"

"Alone. Or with someone."

"Someone I love?"

"Yes. Best of all—to be with someone you love. Next best—learn how to be alone. But learn how to be alone first. Then fall in love. Are you still afraid?"

"Yes."

"Over there, one step, is your home. Go."

"No! Come with me!"

"If you want. Let us return."

"No! Let us go some more."

"Alright, you lead. From now on you take us. And you bring us back."

"And if I don't bring us back?"

"Then we are lost together."

"I don't want us to be lost."

"Then don't lose us."

"Little Husband, I am afraid. We are all we have. I don't want to lose us."

"You want to learn, Little Mother. Learn."

"I am so afraid. You lead the way."

"You lead the way."

"Which way?"

"Any way. Pick a point. But remember, if the point is important, *the way there is more important*. And more important than the way there is *the way back*. Pick a marker."

"You are my reference point!"

"Then we are lost already."

The girl became exasperated and stomped her feet and said: "Adhey, Gopiwalla, don't be so wise! You are not so wise you know. And even wise people get lost!"

"Now, you are wise."

"I am wise!"

"Then let us go."

"Well, stay close then."

They looked at each other. The girl studied Gopi's face. His eyes. His hair. His lips were parched. A film of salt lay on his eyebrows. She thought of how much she liked Gopi. Slowly she looked around. Again there was only sand as far as she could see.

She made a mental check of where the tree was. Gopi watched her, saw her eyes. Then Saraswattee made one step forward and stopped.

Quickly she glanced up and saw the sun. She gasped. It was as if for the first time in her life she saw the sun. Then she realized that all day she had not paid attention to the sun. Had not really been aware of it. She further saw she had left everything up to Gopi. Had totally depended upon him. Abandoned herself and her life to him. She realized she was not only wrong. She was also very stupid. Then she laughed at herself.

Saraswattee laughed at herself and her stupidity. The girl held on to her little belly to make sure it didn't burst. All the while Gopi watched her. Saraswattee looked at him, saw his severe face. Slowly her laughter died away. Because she wished the boy would laugh too. Sometime. And if not—smile. Someday she would make him smile.

But they stared at each other and Saraswattee realized she was alone in the desert only if she thought she was and if she got lost it would be not only because of her stupidity but also because of carelessness and mostly because she didn't think. She looked around and discovered in the desert one lived in it with the sun and the moon and the stars and the wind and the trees and the sand and the so many things one passed by in one's stark naked blindness. Yes. In the desert one lived by and with the desert. By, and with, and for, Gopi; if there was a Gopi in the desert. And what if there was a Saraswattee in the desert? Then that Saraswattee had to know that Saraswattee. Had to live for Saraswattee. By her. With her. Because if there was no Gopi in the desert for this Saraswattee, then this Saraswattee was all she had. Saraswattee; and the desert. But luckily, in this desert, there existed a Gopi for this Saraswattee.

Then, as they walked on, the girl ran again. Skipped. Jumped. She pointed out this, pointed out that, showed Gopi this, showed Gopi that. And she talked—discovered new words. Gopi told her the earth had a crust fifty miles deep and if they walked fifty miles in the desert they would come to the center of the earth. Saraswattee laughed and said she wasn't such a fool. But she knew from then on it was she who kept track of the time and their position. She found water. Found food. Found shelter. She asked questions. Gopi answered. Even in a sandstorm as they trudged on. He took her to see a desert crocodile and the girl sat for hours and looked at the dustblown and mudcaked animal, fascinated, saying over and over, I never knew there were crocodiles in the desert!

Then Gopi asked her if she wanted to see ghost rain.

"Ghost rain?" she asked.

"Come," said Gopi.

Then he led her to a plain where they sat down and looked at the sky. Every once in a while some faint wisps of clouds would form and then immediately blow away. Disappear. Then more clouds came. Again evaporated. Then a huge cloud appeared overhead. When it blackened Saraswattee held on to Gopi. Suddenly the clouds exploded and rain began to fall. Saraswattee jumped and began to run about with her hands held out to catch the drops. She ran wildly, and in circles. Then she stopped. No drops of rain fell. Yet she could see in the sky not far above her, rain. She was sure. She was certain. Gopi assured her it was so. Then he explained to her that it was so hot where they were, the rain fell, evaporated before it hit the earth, and went up in clouds immediately. It was because of the heat he had dug a cave in the belly of the earth so that they too wouldn't be burnt up and die. Saraswattee looked at the wonder with wonder and thought how wonderful it was there were wonders and for a long time they walked on in silence into one sandstorm after another and then after a while even the wind died out and the silence became all consuming and Saraswattee realized they had never been that alone before. Yet, even then, she didn't draw close to Gopi for her reference point.

What seemed to Saraswattee an age and more they stood alone and without words. Then Gopi said, "I will stand here, Little Mother, you go on till I disappear and you discover the curvature of the earth by yourself."

"No, Little Husband, no!"

"Alright, Little Mother, alright."

"Yes! Gopi! Fine!"

Then Saraswattee looked and drew another imaginary line. For a long while she stood in thought. Then she crossed over and faced Gopi. There they were. He on one side. She on the other. Was Gopi her point of reference? Or her invisible red line? She began to cry. Gopi looked at her. Said nothing. After a moment Saraswattee stared at her invisible line. How long did it take for her to make that first step? What power did she have to lift her foot, push it forward? But lift it she did, through the ages, and through the ages she put it forward and when it landed it landed on firm ground. Again she moved her foot. One step at a time. She moved through the ages one step at a time, counting the seconds, the minutes, the hours, the days, the weeks, the months, the years, the decades, the centuries, once upon a time a long long time ago there was a girl named Saraswattee who had never known there was a girl named Saraswattee and who had only answered to the name Saraswattee out of habit and one day this same girl named Saraswattee, curious child, stubborn girl, one day she went out into the desert far far away and was alone and walked on alone counting each step as she moved forward celestial day by celestial day and she walked on seeing the sand, seeing the steps, being nothing, wanting to know all; most of all to know the girl named Saraswattee, wanted to become the girl Saraswattee, just the girl Saraswattee; and she walked and she walked and she walked and felt the wind and the sun and many times so many times she wanted to turn back cry out but she forced herself on forward forever and kept on and on and on a long long time ago and after a long long time she looked back and was alone and then she wept, cried out, saw an imaginary line, stood on one side knowing that on this side she was safe and yet she didn't step back: she stayed where she was and wept and felt pain because she was absolutely alone. But she would go on once upon a time and become this girl Saraswattee. She lifted her foot up to the sky and pushed it over another imaginary line. When she brought it down to the earth again she grew in height and then with each step a celestial day passed and as each celestial day passed she grew and grew and grew and loomed up from the desert into the abode of the gods and the sun vanished and after that the moon and the stars vanished and then the earth under her feet fell away and with that vanished the very last of her external reference points but she didn't weep anymore, didn't feel pain anymore, didn't feel alone anymore; even though as she walked on through time and space her arms fell away and her feet fell away and then her breasts and her head and her entire body evaporated and all that was left in the vast universe of time and space within her were her eyes and with these eyes she walked on and on and on until even internal time and internal space and internal sound all evaporated and then she discovered she wasn't alone. She who was in her was with her. She; Saraswattee; she wasn't alone. She was herself by herself in herself with Saraswattee. Then came a discovery greater than the discovery of the curvature of the earth; a discovery greater than the discovery that Gopi was her point of reference: she discovered that she—Saraswattee, girl, woman—she was the first and foremost reference point to herself and by herself and for herself: she: Saraswattee.

Immediately upon this discovery, the girl felt the beating of her heart. And she felt her lungs and her liver and her kidneys and her spleen and her hands return and so too her feet and then her body came together and the earth formed beneath her feet and with the earth came the sun and she beheld the imaginary line on the red sand and she jumped back across it and there stood Gopi. Saraswattee spun around and beheld the red imaginary line in the sand and she jumped over it and turned. Gopi disappeared. Saraswattee spun around again and began to run through the desert.

FOURTEEN

Gopi sprinted and crashed through a mirage of the girl. There she stood. Beyond her imaginary line. Unable to control her laughter. The boy realized the girl played with him and hadn't meant to run away into the desert. He turned and began to make his way towards their village. Saraswattee caught up with him and teased him: "Aye, Gopi, you thought I was going to leave you alone in the desert, not so? You were afraid, not so? You didn't want to be lost in the desert without your Little Mother. Ha ha ha. I fooled you, didn't I? I know you love me!"

Saraswattee was happy to see Gopi wasn't withdrawn into the desert of himself. He heard her words. Her frivolousness pleased him. She was in touch not only with his soul but his heart. When she was through teasing the boy she began to display her mastery of the desert and her new-found knowledge. She pointed out things and gave descriptions of desert features and made comments. "Look at that escarpment there," she shouted. "And that plateau. Huh, what is a coal bed doing here? Gopiwalla, this metamorphic thing, could it change anything into anything else? A dust storm one mountain high is going to blur out the sunset later and tonight—tonight there is going to be a thunderstorm! Aye, Gopi, you feel the change in the wind? That was a fresh wet wind—and now again, hot wind! Whee! Gopi, after the second summer and the rainfall, I think we are going to have a long cold winter. We must paste more dung in the walls of the house to keep out the cold. And we must gather a lot of phog root for fuel. The soil here is very saline Gopi, you know, very high salt content. And here Gopi, look, a mixture of sand and clay and salt—loam! Aye a toad, adhey baba! Go your way toad! Shoo! The desert is changing again Gopi. From rocky to stony to sand. Sand dunes. Parabolic sand dunes. And there—pyramidal sand dunes. Aye, Saraswattee, you know so much! Gopi, I can tell a gully from a gorge, can you? Ha ha ha! Here is a cassia bush. I will collect some pods of cassia—give you a purgative this winter. Ha ha ha. Aye, what a cold winter. Did you see that gerbil? And a sand grouse? But we must store a lot of wheat to make atta flour for chapatis. And bajra and safflower seeds and sesamun. And a lot of pulse—tur and urd and mung—I know you like mung best of all. And I am going to knit you some new wool shirts, Gopi, and maybe I will make us two woolen blankets and possibly a floor mat while you do some wood carving and make jewelry for me and for Chintamani and Madhuban—you will have to make a lot of jewelry! Aye, we are getting close, Gopi. I see ghand trees. And kumat and kikar. We are almost there—look!"

But Gopi had seen it all long before Saraswattee did. The girl ran up to him next to their cyprus tree. They stared at their shrine. Ahead of them, on the eastern path to the shrine walked a group of five men. Strangers, Gopi knew. And not pilgrims. From the size of the belly of the short fat man in the center he could tell they were a rich man and his brothers on a journey from desert village to desert village in search of suitable brides for his sons—in search of bride price.

Gopi looked at the rich man and his brothers in order not to look at the shrine. But the rich man and his brothers made their way among the ruins, climbed the eastern steps, and halted on the east wall. There was no way he could avert his eyes and he stared fully at the transformation. A new civilization had sprung up in their absence. Within the ruins; upon the ruins. Over their village: over their holy and sacred shrine. A new civilization had been erected. Mahisha Narayana's universe of the twenty-first century. But already that universe had collapsed into ruins. Or so it seemed to Gopi. A new civilization collapsed on old civilizations collapsed within ancient civilizations—and all were ruins. All around the crater; in the crater. Jeeps. Trucks. Red cranes. Yellow cranes. Tractors. Bulldozers. Platforms and rigs and all kinds of drilling equipment. A network of steel scaffolding. And all around too: soldiers with guns.

And were it not for Durga Kali, the shrine might have looked like a mining camp or an oil field. Yet there she loomed to the massive height of twenty mortal men with her hair of serpents wrestled and knotted about her head and with her body of granite and cast iron and necklace of skulls and with her tusked mouth—and with what cauldron eyes she herself beheld the scene. She: Durga Kali. Such wrath twisted her face as Gopi and Saraswattee slowly climbed the eastern steps and pushed their way among the rich strangers to the front on the east wall.

And such a rage consumed Gopi when he beheld the transformation of the crater. The temple courtyard lay a wreck—a ruin. Mahisha had his instruments and heavy equipment littered everywhere. Small cranes. Hoists. Forklifts. Steel frames and platforms. Bulldozers. Ropes and chains and cables. Everywhere tractor marks lay like broken ribs or the remains of skeletons. The sand and the pebble paths were stained with oil and grease. Instead of the smell of sulphur, the air hung heavy with the stench of the desecration and defilement of Mahisha Narayana. A wreckage. The shrine. An ancient wreck. Upon which lay the recent wreckage of the twenty-first century civilization of that man of science.

And there was blood everywhere. This Gopi now beheld. He looked at the menfolk. Their hoes and lathis lay scattered about them. They had rioted. And the soldiers had beaten them. Many stood with their heads in bloodied bandages. Some had their arms in slings. Chintamani was on her knees, her father's head cradled in her lap. And next to her stood Padma and Matti and Madhuban.

In the middle of the courtyard, before the temple, there rose up the mighty form of Mahisha Narayana. He faced the most sacred orifice, his back to Gopi. Next to him on his left stood Kahar. On his right, almost shrunken and doubled over: Pundit Ayer. The pundit looked utterly devastated. But he still tried to focus his eyes. As all the other eyes were fixed. On the gigantic elongated steel drilling bore poised in the air directly above the most sacred of the sacred orifices of Durga Mata. In the sun the steel shaft glistened. Vapors from the most sacred orifice had condensed on the steel bore. It was wet. Hot. Poised; erect: about to penetrate. And above this steel lingam of the twenty-first century towered the ravisher of evil men. She full of wrath; still impotent: herself about to be ravished. And Mahisha Narayana stood poised; about to give the order to have the bore enter the most sacred orifice.

In that moment Gopi knew exactly the real intent of Mahisha Narayana. Yes, destruction. That bore was not meant to enter the most sacred orifice to tap the geothermal energy trapped there. That bore was about to penetrate the most sacred orifice only for defilement and desecration. That was how Mahisha Narayana intended to effect his destruction of their goddess. Destruction by desecration and defilment. Symbolic destruction. The worst kind of destruction ever. Such betrayal of scorn and contempt. Such betrayal of the lust for vengeance—futile vengeance. Such betrayal of pettiness in the name of science and of the twenty-first century. Mahisha Narayana had not come to tap resources and energy for the future of the land. He had come to destroy the energy of that land. He had come to destroy the people of that land. Those people. His people. For whatever it was they had done to him—done to his mother. *Mahisha Narayana had not come to create the future: he had come to destroy the future.*

Mahisha Narayana raised his hand to give the signal and Matti cried out: "NO!"

And it was the cry from the heart of a woman to stop the physical defilement of her physical body.

All eyes flashed to the old woman with the worn face and the bright black eyes and that cry pierced every heart there—most of all the ogre heart of Kali, she who had failed to break the barrier of her past with the speed of her memory and arrive there in that place one step ahead of her future to stop that future and turn it around and vent it on the demon Mahisha Narayana who himself fixed his eyes on Matti.

"NO!" cried Matti again as her wrinkled black face crumpled up and squeezed long lost tears out of her eyes.

"No!" hissed Padma.

Suddenly all the womenfolk lost their passivity and forgot their places and became consumed with their own rage and indignation and moved forward and thronged the most sacred orifice of their goddess and shouted: "No! No! No!"

Gopi then understood that every woman there beheld Mahisha's intent not as symbolic: but as a real and physical and vile act of desecration and defilement: *rape.*

"No! No! No!" the womenfolk protested and thronged closer to the edge of the sacred orifice. Mahisha glanced at the sergeant in charge of the soldiers but the sergeant made no move. It was clear to him, as to everyone else, that before they allowed Mahisha to violate the body of their goddess those hundred or so womenfolk were ready to throw themselves to their death down the most sacred orifice.

"No! No! No! No! No!" the womenfolk vented their rage and their indignation.

"NO!"

And Mahisha Narayana spun around and came face to face with Gopi. Who again shouted: "NO!"

"Nahi! Nahi! Nahi! Nahi!" the womenfolk shouted.

"No!" Gopi shouted at the demon Mahisha. "You are an evil man. You are up to evil. You are not here for geothermal energy. You are here to destroy us and our way of life!"

"Ha ha ha," Mahisha laughed. "So you have returned, Gopi. My assistant. You who are so eager for new knowledge and new wisdom. Where have you been, O champion of Durga Kali? I know where you have been, Gopi. In the desert. A sadhu. Gone into the desert to seek more desert wisdom to return to do battle with me—the demon Mahisha!"

"You are indeed a demon."

"Is that the new wisdom you have gained?"

"Yes. And more. Much more."

"So you think you are now better equipped to defend your deity and to defeat me?"

"I was always capable of defeating you!"

"Ah! What a boast. Great. Wonderful, Gopi, wonderful. And how do you propose to defeat me?"

"Sab, what have you to gain by this your vile intent?"

"Ah, I see. You are going to appeal to my reason. You are going to appeal to my sense of decency—the goodness of my heart. Good. Because that is exactly what I intend to appeal to, Gopi. I will appeal to your reason. Your sense of decency. I will appeal to the goodness of your heart. In other words, I will use your very own weapon against you."

"Answer me! I know what this action means. It is only symbolic. And very crude and vulgar symbolism too!"

For a moment Mahisha's face puffed up and his red eyes bulged out but then he calmed down and said: "Ah Gopi. I keep forgetting what a formidable adversary you are. Crude and vulgar symbolism. Indeed. So obvious. But what do you expect from someone with a base and demonic nature as myself?"

"What is your knowledge, Sab? What is your science? Can't you use it for good—to really help us, help our people, our land?"

"Our land and our people are beyond help!"

"And what about your talk of launching us into the twenty-first century?"

"What would a primitive and barbarous people like yours do in the twenty-first century?"

"Why not help us become less primitive and barbarous? Why not use the geothermal energy I know that exists underground here to help us become more wise and more educated? You do not need to drill for geothermal energy right in this spot. This shrine is only a surface indication that the region is rich in geothermal energy. You can do your drilling half a mile from here and get all the energy you need to launch us into the future and make us less barbarous and primitive."

"Why Gopi, you astound me. Not only do you have the wisdom of the desert. You have already learnt all my science! And how right you are. The entire region for miles around is rich in geothermal energy. Only simple drilling would be necessary. You are so right!"

"Then why do you insist on your destruction here?"

"Because this is the source!"

"The source?"

"Yes."

"Of what, Sab?"

"The source of the sickness of the land!"

"What do you mean?"

"The source of the sickness of the soul of the land and the sickness of the soul of your people!"

"Sab, what do you mean? We are simple peasants—ignorant, yes, but simple human beings!"

"Not simple human beings. Primitives! Barbarians!"

"Then help us. Make us better. Teach us to become educated and modern."

"You think that is possible?"

"Why is it not possible?"

"Ha ha ha, Gopi. I warn you. I will use your very own weapon against you."

"Use it then."

"Then you yourself will destroy your people."

"If I see that they are helpless and do deserve destruction, yes, I myself will destroy them."

"Don't say I didn't warn you. Ah, look! What have we got here? Strangers. Rich and handsome strangers. Villagers, have you forgotten your manners and your hospitality? Rich and handsome strangers have come among you. Such a good omen! Greet them. Welcome them. Ask them why they have come to your village!"

In that one moment Gopi beheld Mahisha immediately triumph over the villagers. Their defiance disintegrated. At the sight of the rich stranger and his four brothers in their midst. As Gopi had recognized the mission of the strangers, thus Mahisha recognized their quest. As Mahisha recognized their mission, so too did the villagers. And as Mahisha so instantaneously triumphed over the villagers, thus instantaneously they forgot his intent of destruction against them and the menfolk bustled around the strangers and ushered them in and erected a tent and the womenfolk abandoned their defense of the most sacred orifice and rushed about to obey the orders of their menfolk to bring tea and water and sweets and fruits and quickly quickly hurry hurry dress up all our marriageable daughters and bring them out for the rich and handsome strangers to inspect—and to select as brides.

As another transformation was wrought over the shrine, Gopi lost heart. Became distant again. Withdrew within the desert of himself. Saraswattee took advantage of the diversion and climbed up the goddess and slipped into the cleft where she hid.

The womenfolk rushed through the village and hurried their daughters before them. The menfolk congregated around the strangers and humbled themselves and offered tea and refreshments. The rich man and his brothers might have been a mirage. Because though they ate and drank everything, even the obsequiousness and pandering of the villagefolk did not seem to touch them.

"Remember, Gopi," Mahisha whispered, "your very own weapon—and your very own way of life. You tell me if we can stop all of this. Child-marriages. Bride price. Whipping to exorcise evil spirits in girls. You untouchables—the spit in the gutters of the land. Behold your customs and your rituals and your ceremonies and your superstitions—blood sacrifices! Look at those five strangers. Only one of them, that short fat one, only one has sons—maybe just one son! But behold his power. What power he possesses. Look how he makes the other fathers—men!—whimper and grovel and kiss the dirt on his feet. Look at that! See them actually kiss the dirt off his feet? Wash the dust off his feet with their tears? Are they men? Are they fathers to be proud of? Is this a people to be proud of? Look at all those young girls with big bellies. How old are they? Twelve? Fourteen? With big bellies and with children crawling at their feet! Look at all those child beggars. So young. Maimed! And what about all your temple prostitutes, eh, Gopi? See them slink away in their huts and hovels? Soon even those five strangers will be offered a chance to purify their lust in the bodies of your temple prostitutes. Is this a people to be proud of? Is this a race to launch into the future? Is this a land to belong to?"

"Sab, it is noble to destroy the wrongs of society. Is it necessary to destroy the society itself?"

"If there is no other way—yes! And there is no other way. Because the society itself is sick. The very soul of the society is sick! Temple prostitutes! Gopi. Just think about it. Here is your holy shrine. There is your holy temple. Right there looms your deity. Attended by her temple prostitutes. So that at nights, your menfolk can sneak into the temple courtyard and purify their lust in the bodies of your temple prostitutes—even the pilgrims, the holy ones, who come to bathe in the breath of Durga Mata and obtain eternal bliss, as the legend says, they, the holy ones sneak behind your goddess to relieve themselves of lust!"

"At least they have the decency to sneak behind Durga's back. But you would have violated the girl Chintamani in front of her very eyes!"

Then, it became Mahisha's turn to behold the anger of the boy Gopi.

"Ha ha ha," Mahisha laughed. "Why look, you too have a touch of evil in you. You should see it in your eyes. But then I understand. She is your wife—ha ha ha!—but Gopi, I can't help myself—ha ha ha—I am a demon!"

"Sab, if our society is sick to its very soul, you are the disease in that soul!"

"Look what is unfolding before our very eyes."

Gopi followed Mahisha's outstretched hands and he saw the womenfolk hustle their daughters to be paraded before the fat strangers. Doolwah and Amakutty and Roopa and Phooloo and Sirju. They had been whipped along with Chintamani. Whipped by his father to exorcise them of their evil spirits. Had they been exorcised of their evil spirits? As Chintamani had been and a match made for her and she married on the very day? Did all of that really happen? Who knows? Who can tell? Such a time it was then, as it is now, when memory was so short and misery so so long and to comprehend the future was to know despair.

The villagers stood around and waited on the strangers who took their time to eat and drink. When they were satisfied, the fattest stranger said, "I am Mr. Nathuni, and I have five sons to marry." A sigh went up in the crater and Mr. Nathuni puffed up his chest and beamed all the praise showered on him. He asked, "Have you marriageable girls in this village?"

Badraj ran forward, bent down, touched the feet of Mr. Nathuni, touched his hands to his head and cried out, "Malik! Malik! I have two daughters to marry, please accept my daughters."

"How much do you offer for each?" Mr. Nathuni asked. Badraj seemed to turn to skin and his mouth flooded up with his sour spit. He sat on the ground, stared blankly at the sand. Around him the villagers watched. In the group of women, Padma began to cry. Madhuban dropped her eyes. Chintamani looked at Gopi. Mahisha laughed at Badraj, the untouchable.

"How much are you paying for each?" Mr. Nathuni asked again. "What is the bride price offered? What sum? How much rupees?" Badraj made no reply. He began to cry. "How much money? Any jewels? Silver? Gold? What do you offer? I have five sons!" Badraj got up on his knees, threw himself forward, put his face on Mr. Nathuni's feet, kissed them, washed them with his tears, and cried, "Malik, Malik, I am a poor man, I have no land, I have no crops, I have no goats or sheep. I have no jewels, no rupees. I have two daughters, Malik Malik accept my daughters, have mercy on a poor man, have mercy on a beggar, free me from this bondage, Malik! Malik! wash this stain off my forehead and I will make you my god!"

"What?" Mr. Nathuni asked as he pulled away his feet. "What, is this the custom? Is this our way? You offer no bride price and expect me to accept your daughters? Away! What?" Badraj rolled on the ground and threw dust over his face and beat his head with his fists. "Are there other marriageable girls in this village?" Mr. Nathuni asked. Then Nandass and Akpar and all the fathers with unmarried girls ran forward and prostrated themselves and praised Mr. Nathuni and blessed him and offered up prayers to him and those who had nothing else to offer pleaded and begged but those who could offer something ran back and forth from the courtyard to their homes, imploring their womenfolk to produce things, as if by magic—money, jewels, grain, sheep, silver plates, brass goblets, earthenware, blankets, personal clothing, promissory notes; anything, whatever; and the bride prices were laid out before Mr. Nathuni's feet and he picked this brass goblet up, inspected that silver plate, valued the worth of a bag of grain and the temple courtyard became a marketplace and the fathers of daughters bartered and begged and haggled over their shame and disgrace damning their fate that they should have had daughters born unto them and that they should be nothing but summer shadows to their own daughters.

The daughters wept; summer shadows to themselves: for such a time it was then, as it is now, the second summer of the year, when gods got the deaths they desired and came to their destinies; when in the sudden flash floods of this season the land became washed clean of all shadows and other strangers: and when mortal nights blew clear and brought rain to the earth and only the spirits of the desert, bedraggled creatures, knew mortal future and the mortal futility of that future.

A rich and handsome stranger with five sons had come and all the girls fortunate enough, had matches made for them. When the harvest is over, and at the harvest festival, the fathers of girls with matches will cease to be summer shadows and will rise up from the marriage mound: men.

But the unfortunate girls. Those without matches. They will face yet another unmarried winter. And they will face it very much as the land will face this season; the land itself like a gigantic desert-beached fish, gutted and salted and stretched out in the wind to freeze into a crust; its scales the color of gray lime. They will face this season of the unmarried, very much as their fathers will face this season of yet another shame: winter shadows to their daughters. And the daughters: winter shadows to themselves.

Unless, of course, some stray luck befell them and some lucky fellow rose out of quicksand—on his horse.

Or they were fortunate enough to be exorcised of their evil spirits.

Saraswattee got to her feet and fixed her gaze on the wrecked crater. In that very instant everyone became aware of a miracle and all eyes fell on Sutnami. Chintamani was astounded. Her father beamed with his old dignity. He no longer stood a bedraggled creature. He no longer was broken—her father had not approached the rich fat stranger with his five sons and prostrated himself and begged and grovelled to have his daughter Madhuban accepted as a bride without bride price. Her father had at last refused to allow himself to be a victim of the evil practices and the vile customs of his society. Her father had refused to be told by some pundit or by anyone that his unmarried daughters, Madhuban and Saraswattee, were a shame and a disgrace on his forehead. He fathered those daughters. He loved them all. They were not sins. Most of all, they were not the sins of his wife. Even with three unmarried daughters he was a man!

Chintamani had succumbed to the match with Gopi only for this miracle. And it didn't happen then. For whatever the reasons—all of which she was sure had to do with her ugly uncle. But all that was changed now. Her prayers were answered. She was not a sore. Madhuban was not a sore. Saraswattee was not a sore on her father's head. May Durga Mata forgive her for whatever wrongs she may have committed and though the cross-eyed pundit still had asthma, may Durga's blessing be on the lucky fellow on his horse and may he not fall in quicksand but go the other way. All praise to Kali Mata for bringing her to her senses and exorcising her of her evil spirit and for defending her that night against the evil man Mahisha Narayana.

As for himself, Mahisha saw once again who his real enemy was. If the villagers looked to Sutnami before, now there he stood before them already a folk hero—already a god! A god in Gopi's eyes too. Mahisha looked into those eyes of Gopi and he beheld the sense of pride. The sense of triumph. In Mahisha's eyes Gopi beheld the defeat. Gopi said: "Sab, can we not be made better? Can we not be taught to be modern and educated? Right before your eyes, you saw a primitive and a barbarian rise up a man! Is this not cause for hope? Will this not help you change your mind? Teach us. Help us rid ourselves of our wrong customs and vile superstitions. Put your science to aid us, to brighten our ways, to lighten our burdens. Use your science and your knowledge and your wisdom to guide us a little at a time into the future so that when we get there we are ready for the future and can cope with it. There is no need to destroy our legend. No need to destroy our deity. Behold she has wrought a miracle before your eyes! There is hope for us. We can learn. We can become a better people. I beg you, in the name of Durga Kali, forgive our parents whatever wrong they may have done you and forego your desire for vengeance and if you will not give us the enlightenment of your science then at least give us the honor of your blessings!"

Mahisha Narayana stared at Gopi and his heart beat in unison with the ogre within Kali's bosom and Kali too looked at Gopi and marvelled at his words and thought they indeed did have an effect on the demon and she thought Gopi Gopi how can a demon save you when I your god failed you but, my love, my god, let your wisdom and your words triumph over that demon and I myself shall worship you in atonement for the wrongs I have done humanity and you my children!

Such a time it was then, as it is now, when gods are fools and demons are your most constant companions. Does the folly of gods know any bounds? Who knows? Who can tell?

But Gopi could tell that his words had exactly the opposite effect he wished them to have on Mahisha. Sutnami had proven him wrong. *Sutnami had defeated him.* And from the look in his eyes Gopi could tell that Mahisha would concentrate all his evil energies on the destruction of Sutnami. Because Sutnami had become the symbol of a live god in the eyes of the villagers—even above and beyond Kali Durga.

In this sudden twist of fate, Gopi saw that Mahisha had a crude and vulgar ally in his father Kahar. He watched Mahisha whisper something to Kaharsab and then he watched his father hop over to confront Sutnami. Gopi became on edge. Mahisha smiled at him. Gopi wished he knew what Mahisha was up to; what Mahisha had set his father to. The boy remembered when Saraswattee asked him to slay his father. Suddenly he was confronted with this agony again. Without knowing what he would do, Gopi moved quickly beside his father-in-law.

"So?" Kahar said to his brother. "You have finally risen up a man. Your sin has been lifted from your head. That sin which kept you on your knees all your life. Suddenly it has disappeared and you are on your feet—a man!"

"Father—"

"Shut up!" Kahar shouted and brought his whip across Gopi's mouth and blood burst out from his lips. Chintamani tightened her fists, prayed that her father would stand up the man he was and fight back.

"Brother," Sutnami said, "we are both old now and have both suffered much. Soon we will die. It is time we make peace between us. I ask of you, forgive me for the wrong I did you."

"Please brother," Padma begged, "my husband has suffered enough. It was such a long time ago. We were young. Now it is the time of our lives to make pilgrimages and rid ourselves of our grudges and burdens of sin. I beg you in the name of Durga Mata, forgive my husband."

"My husband—"

Again Kahar swung his whip and again he drew blood. Gopi saw his mother's mouth rupture and he lunged at his father but Sutnami caught him and both landed on the ground. Sutnami got up and pulled Gopi to his feet and said: "No no. What is between my brother and myself is between my brother and myself. You mustn't interfere. You children must not interfere. I did my brother wrong. I will make atonement."

Sutnami began to walk over to Kahar and both Gopi and Chintamani knew he was going to fall on his knees before Kahar and neither wanted Sutnami to undo the manhood he had gained but a moment ago. In desperation Gopi pointed at Mahisha Narayana and shouted: *"This Mahisha Narayana is that Mahisha Narayana!"*

Then all looked at Mahisha Narayana and Pundit Ayer asked: "But how can that be?"

"He is! He himself told me so!"

"But how could that be? That Mahisha Narayana is a saint by now—most probably."

"He is that Mahisha Narayana. And he has come for vengeance on you all for whatever you did to his mother. He told me so!"

The villagers began to press around Mahisha Narayana to have a closer look at him. To see if he had any resemblance to Pundit Mahesh Narayana. The priest who had pronounced death by burning on his own pregnant wife. Again there was no sign of resemblance. But what became an even greater astonishment, no one could remember what the rich and handsome stranger who walked into their shrine as a good omen looked like. Mahisha Narayana beheld their befuddlement and he laughed and the ogre within the bosom of Kali tightened his claws on Naga's tail and Naga felt the claws slice through his flesh as the pain shot through his body and his vision became all blood. Thus he lost his impartiality and abandoned his liege to Kali and he decided to take his own course of action. Before long the claws would slice through his body and cut his tail off. He would be free. What was left of him. Then he would fly through the air and sink his fangs between those demonic red eyes.

"Yes punditji," Mahisha Narayana said, as he walked among the village men who now cowered in guilt, "this Mahisha Narayana is that Mahisha Narayana!"

"But how can that be? That Mahisha Narayana is a saint—"

"This Mahisha Narayana is a demon!" Chintamani shouted. "Father, look at his face. When he first walked into our village he was tall and handsome. Now look how black and ugly and hairy he has become. He has changed right before our eyes!"

"But how can that be? That Mahisha Narayana is a saint—most probably!"

"Chintamani is right," Gopi shouted. "He is a demon. *He is the demon Mahisha Durga!*"

"Yes Gopi, have it your way. You tell me who I am, and I will tell you who you are. Sutnamiji, shall I tell your son-in-law who he is? Shall I tell the world what your sin is? *Your sin is this boy here is your son!*"

None of the elders showed any emotions but Chintamani gasped as Padma and Matti rushed into each other's arms and began to weep. On the bosom of the goddess, Saraswattee was beside herself. Again she had been so foolish! As when the match was made for Chintamani. She had allowed herself to be trapped on the bosom of the goddess—and Gopi her brother! Gopiwalla. *Her brother!*

"Is that not so punditji," Mahisha said, "is not the boy Gopi the son of Sutnami?"

"It is so," Pundit Ayer muttered.

"Ha ha ha," Kahar laughed. "My elder brother. He should have respected my wife as his daughter. He should have protected the honor of my wife as if she was his very own daughter! He soiled my name and my honor. Took away my dignity and manhood. Made me the vile joke of our village. Well I have had my vengeance. I made you heap sin on sin and forced you to marry your own daughter to your own son!"

Gopi and Chintamani looked at each other. But he, dark-skinned boy, withdrew into the desert of himself. Who was he? What was he to Chintamani? Who was Chintamani? What was Chintamani to him? But Chintamani suffered. She suffered the sin of her father and shrivelled up as he once again shrivelled up. The girl stared at her mother and Matti. So that was the secret of their secret. What did it matter how come they bore her father's sin as if it belonged to them both? What did it matter that Padma bore Matti's sin as if it was her sin? Two people had been weak. Three people had fallen in the wake of that weakness. That was all. Such was life. Such was fate. And what did it matter why her uncle extracted such a penalty? What did it matter that brother wrought such a vengeance on brother? What did it matter that no bride price had been paid? Not even blood would have sufficed. She had once considered her choices. Actively succumb to the match—and what would become of Saraswattee? Rebel and refuse the match and be beaten and still be married off—and what would become of Saraswattee? Or kill herself and damn her father's soul—and still: what would become of Saraswattee?

Chintamani laughed. And everyone thought the girl had gone mad. How could they know why she laughed? What would become of Saraswattee? Not only she, Chintamani, had married her brother. But Saraswattee had forced her own brother to marry her. And she had made her brother pledge to marry his very own sister too! So Chintamani laughed. Because had it not been for Saraswattee's matchmaking, she, Chintamani; she who knew the legend well; would have had no alternative but to kill herself.

And how was Chintamani to know her laughter would drive Mahisha Narayana to distraction? He, Mahisha Durga; son of the demon Durga who had the power of illusion and the power to transform himself into any shape or form he chose. Mahisha Durga shared his father's powers too—in that he cherished devious ways and did his evil through the creation of diversion so that he could stay ahead of those he wanted to destroy and bring that destruction down upon them. Chintamani's indifferent laughter began to subvert the effect he had hoped for when he exposed Sutnami's sin. Quickly Mahisha went over to Kahar and again whispered and Kahar shouted: "THAT GIRL IS AN UNFAITHFUL WIFE! SHE IS AN ADULTERESS! SHE HAS COMMITTED ADULTERY WITH MAHISHA NARAYANA! I SAW IT WITH MY OWN EYES!"

"Daughter!" Sutnami shouted—and it was with the very same terror when Matti cried out against the steel bore poised above the most sacred orifice.

"Pitahji!" Chintamani screamed, now in her own terror, her eyes in betrayal of true insanity. "Father!"

"No!" Gopi shouted. "No. That is a lie. My father is telling a lie!"

"Aye bastard. Don't call me father. And don't call me a liar."

"You are a liar! My wife is no adulteress! You lie!"

Saraswattee dropped to her knees and beheld Padma and Matti throw themselves in the dust and began to pound their heads and their breasts. All the women threw themselves on the ground and covered themselves with dust and moaned and grieved. As if each one had committed the most grievous sin. The women beat their heads, beat their chests, beat their hands to the ground. They pulled their hair, rent their clothes. They wailed and grieved as if all their husbands had died. Of all the womenfolk and girl-children only Chintamani stood on her feet. And she stood as when they had whipped her. Her hands clutching her breasts. Her eyes glazed over. She: an ancient and disgraced beggarwoman. Demented.

"What did you say?" Pundit Ayer asked.

"It is true. She is an adulteress!" Kahar said.

"That is a lie!" Gopi shouted, as his eyes begged Mahisha.

"Nahi," Chintamani whispered. But she spoke only to herself.

"Ugrrrh!" Sutnami muttered.

"Shame shame shame!" Pundit Ayer shouted. "An adulteress! An unfaithful wife! A disgrace to all women! Disgrace disgrace disgrace!"

"Ugrrrh!" Sutnami choked.

"It is not true!" Gopi cried, hopeless before the treachery of Mahisha.

"I saw her with my own eyes," Kahar insisted, "many times —even on the very day she was married!"

"Nahi," Chintamani whispered in her demented state. "No. No, mother. No, father. I have not sinned. All I wanted was a horse."

"Ugrrrh!" Sutnami spluttered.

"An adulteress!" Pundit Ayer shouted. "An unfaithful wife? A shame on all women. Beat her! Beat her! For atonement all the women must beat her!"

Before Gopi could do anything Pundit Ayer rushed at Chintamani and spat at her and the womenfolk threw themselves on the girl and grabbed her by the hair and spun her around and beat her to the ground and tore her clothes and covered her with dirt and dust and spat on her. They tore the thali from her neck and flung it away. Then they threw themselves around Chintamani and continued to beat her and themselves. Saraswattee wept.

If Kahar had gotten the ultimate vengeance on his brother, Mahisha got the explosive moment he wanted. Sutnami continued to gag and choke. He frothed at the mouth. Chintamani talked to herself in a state of dementedness. But Sutnami did indeed become demented.

With his demonic eyes fixed on the demented Sutnami, Mahisha pointed at the girl Madhuban and said: "That girl has committed the most hideous sacrilege. She has touched the body of your goddess. I have seen her climb all over the sacred body of your goddess. She—a girl!"

And as it did once, so again it fell upon the volcanic crater: the utter silence of the seven worlds of creation just after the moment of dissolution.

All eyes flashed up to Durga Kali. And in that moment Sutnami grabbed a hoe and hacked Madhuban to pieces.

FIFTEEN

Over and over the demented Sutnami brought the hoe down on his daughter. In her terror Madhuban screamed: "Nahi! Babu nahi! Pitah nahi! Deedi! Sister!" But Sutnami heard no sound and hacked his daughter to pieces and as the hoe sliced through the vapors, tufts of hair and clumps of flesh and blood splattered over the temple courtyard as over all creation.

Kali beheld the horror as at that time when she first awoke and her eyes fell on the slit throat of the sheep. Revulsion paralyzed her. But not Saraswattee. Saraswattee heard the cries of Madhuban and they became her own screams and she ran in circles in the stone cleft. Chintamani neither saw nor heard anything. As on the day of her exorcism the girl reentered into a nucleus of dementedness and, secure in there, she stumbled around the crater and mumbled, a horse, all I ever wanted was a horse, a small small tiny tiny horse.

The villagers and the pilgrims scattered. Sought cover in chaos. But even in chaos they could find no refuge and the blood showered all over them. Kali stared at the hoe. But not Saraswattee. She. Curious child. Stubborn girl. She saw her father murder Madhuban, heard the screams, beheld the blood swamp the people, became seized by greater terror and scrambled up the necklace of skulls and into the cave of the mouth and then her screams were the screams of Kali.

Mahisha laughed. Mahisha laughed as only a demon could laugh. He grabbed Gopi and shook the boy and shouted: "Behold, Gopi, behold. Behold your people. See your religion at work. Blood sacrifice. Human blood sacrifice! Ha ha ha ha ha ha

Hahaha! This is your life, this is your land. These are your people, this is their way. Behold your legend come to life. Behold your religion come to life in death. The flesh of humans, the legend said, delighted Kali, and the blood of an evil man satiated her lust for vengeance and pacified her one thousand years. There. Blood. Human flesh. Why? Because of superstition! Ha ha ha! It is forbidden for the hands of a girl to touch the sacred body of your deity. So Kali! Drink your blood! Eat your human flesh! You a cannibal and no less a barbarian than your faithful devotees! Behold Gopi, can you save them? Do you want to save them? I warned you. Do you believe me now? Will you destroy them now? This is what I came to destroy. Behold my vengeance and my destruction at work. See your father hack your own sister to death because of superstition. Destroy them, Gopi, destroy them!"

Gopi leapt in the air, grabbed Mahisha by the neck, the eyes of the demon bulged out, and then his body slackened. Gopi glanced around. The demented eyes of Sutnami leaked blood but were fixed on Mahisha. Pundit Ayer's eyes ran amok as Sutnami faced Mahisha and raised his red hoe high in the air. As Sutnami brought the hoe down, Gopi himself became paralyzed as he choked Mahisha. He watched the hoe rake vapors in its descent. Then in one swift blow Kahar Saheb cracked the wooden handle of his whip on his brother's head and smashed his skull. Sutnami crumbled to the earth in the bloody heap that was his daughter Madhuban. Mahisha grabbed Gopi and flung him through the air and Gopi crashed against the wooden foot of Kahar. He glanced up and beheld the murderous eyes of his father. Mahisha laughed and shouted: "There Gopi. Look at the smashed skull of your father. Smashed by this evil creature. He is not your father. Just a greedy evil man who coveted the jewels of your deity. He joined forces with me to help me wreak my destruction so he could possess the wealth of your Kali. But see he has murdered your father. Kill him, Gopi, kill him! Destroy, destroy. There is evil in you too—if only you could see your eyes—your lust for vengeance. Hahaha. Well take vengeance. Kill that evil man. Destroy them, Gopi, there is no hope for them—destroy!"

Gopi scrambled to his knees, grabbed the hoe, jumped to his feet, and swung the hoe through the air only to find his mother in its path. Matti. She who had sinned to give birth to him. She who lived her fate as if she was his shame, his daughter; and he her father. Mahisha laughed as the hoe swung through the air but the shock of the black bright eyes of his mother caused Gopi to let go of the handle. The hoe tipped downwards and the handle struck Matti across her left breast. Kahar Saheb turned to run. Gopi lunged at him and got hold of the mortal leg. Matti, immune to the pain in her ribs, pulled at Gopi and begged: "No son, no. Do not condemn your soul as I have condemned mine!" Kahar beat Gopi and Matti off his leg and freed himself and whipped his way through the throngs as he hopped in escape.

As Kahar ran, Mahisha put his hands on his waist and his laughter echoed everywhere. Kahar made it to the southern entrance, his wooden foot hopped up one step, his foot of flesh and blood landed on the whip, and Kahar tripped. He crashed face forward across the flight of steps. His head hit the topmost stone step and his eardrums split. Blood oozed out his ears. He became dizzy. A great desire for sleep engulfed him and he would have fallen asleep except his penis moved under him. Kahar Saheb became astounded. He felt his penis thick against his belly. What, an erection? At such a time? But then Saheb Kahar became terrified. Because while his elongated penis crawled up under his naked belly, at that very same time, it also crawled down and curled around his legs. What? How could that be? Did he have two penises? Or did he split his penis in two? So that one half curled around his testicles. While the other half had lengthened all the way up to his chest—oh Durga Mata! Help! What have I done? I have crushed my testicles! Oh Kali, help me, I have ruined my manhood! I am wet with blood. All over my legs. All over my chest—what, cold frozen blood? Cold frozen blood! Kahar Saheb panicked and was about to jump up when from under his chest emerged the jewelled head of a mighty cobra serpent.

The serpent was in no hurry but he became a bit annoyed when the body of that creature turned colder than his own. The cobra didn't care too much for the cold. The eyes of Saheb Kahar bulged. The serpent slithered beneath his neck, slid against his chin, crawled up the stone step. In respect, Kahar held his breath. The cold tail of the cobra shook his frozen testicles, slithered over his dirt-clogged navel, oozed through the dirty hairs on his chest. But Kahar kept his eyes on the head. The serpent crawled up the top step, spiralled around with grace, coiled up on seven curls of its mighty bejewelled body, faced Saheb Kahar, and transfixed him with its tiny jet eyes.

Kahar Saheb scrambled up. With instant humility and penitence. And with perfect knowledge of proper etiquette. Such that he got on his knees on a step well below the serpent. He seemed well-versed and knew enough not to rise above the cobra but should be in such a position that his eyes looked up. Kahar Saheb quickly checked himself to make certain he was in absolute observance of all matters concerning such a delicate interview. When satisfied, and with the proper respect and humility, he clasped his hands before his chest and shouted: "Maharaj!"

It always tickled Naga's pride the way his *conferees* would instantly recognize him when he came to have a little chat with them. But at this particular moment he was a bit short-tempered and his impatience reflected off the glistening scales of his face and he said: *Wait! Wait wait wait. Hold it right there. Why speak in the language of mortals, eh? I have a very bad migraine and I am in a bad mood and I don't want to lose my temper and slip up. So why don't we talk in the language of our ancestors, eh? You know, let's just bounce our consciousness off each other—but real nice and easy, okay, nice and easy does it.*

Of course, Maharaj. As you wish. Excuse my bad manners.

Bad manners are excusable. But a bad man?

Yes yes, Maharaj, I am a bad man!

Don't raise your consciousness! Keep cool! I have a damn headache and I don't want to lose my temper more than is necessary!

Forgive me, Maharaj. I am an ignorant peasant. You know us low-born—

No one is low born, Kaharsab. The born make themselves low. But tell me, are you a bad man?

Yes, Maharaj. A very bad man. In fact, a very evil man.

That is so sad to hear—ah, I see you have noticed my deformity. Ah, yes, I lost a piece of my tail. An unfortunate tragedy but—here we are, me without a piece of my tail, you without a leg. Both of us deformed.

But I am more deformed than you, Maharaj. In fact, I am positively hideous. While you don't look so bad.

You think so?

Would I lie to you at this moment, Maharaj?

How true. You are done with lying. Only truth for you from now on. So, I don't look too bad with a piece of my tail missing, eh?

Positively not, Maharaj!

Keep it down. Keep your cool. Ah, what a despicable creature you are. You know, Kahar, the worst job I ever had to perform was when I had to bite your leg off. It was positively distasteful to me—I mean your flesh, your blood. I had to rinse my mouth with ambrosia for weeks! But here we are again. You know this is a unique experience for me.

How is that, Maharaj?

I never get to meet the same man twice.

I am honored Maharaj.

The honor is mine.

Forgive me. There I go again with my bad manners. I am glad you are happy to meet me again.

I am positively delighted. But, come now, Kaharsab. We don't have much time—

Maharajji, forgive me for my evil ways. Find it in your kind and gentle heart to pardon me. Give me your blessings and send me on a pilgrimage. I will do penance, I will make atonement, I will take you as my own personal deity. I will become your most devout and faithful servant.

You speak with such conviction and sincerity. You really mean what you say, don't you?

You know I do, Maharaj. You can see into my very heart.

Of course. You are right. Your heart has turned white—why you are purified. I'll be damned! Why Kahar you have purified yourself by your instant repentance. I have never seen anything like it. Why, it's a miracle! Amazing. Even in my old age, I never cease to wonder. I love wonder! So you will make me your own personal deity and worship me alone with your newfound purity?

Yes! Yes! Yes—

Please! Keep it cool!

Forgive me, Maharaj, I won't do it again. I will enshrine you in my very heart—

Indeed!

—and I will serve you without the skip of a heartbeat. Why Maharaj, I will see to it every single day you have fresh milk and pure wild honey and clarified butter and fresh vegetables—

I hate vegetables.

For you no vegetables, whatever your heart desires, you are the greatest!

You really think so?

Absolutely. Would I lie to you at a time like this?

I guess not. Anyway I always thought so myself. But it is good to hear it from the likes of you. Tell me, Kaharsab, what manner of creature are you?

Vile disgusting loathsome revolting despicable—dung Maharaj, dung!

The dung of the gods?

The dung of men!

Keep it cool!—anyway you said it—not me. Ah, what is life?

Indeed Maharaj, what is life.

No no. I asked you a question.

Me? You mean what is life? You mean you asked me what is life? I may talk in my sleep, but I don't talk to myself!

Maharaj, what do I know about life? How can I answer such a question?

Kaharsab, every single creature born to life must be able to answer that question.

Forgive me, Maharaj. I can't answer—I don't know the answer.

Sad. Very very very sad. You know the boy Gopi harbored thoughts in his heart to kill you?

He almost did Maharaj!

Ah! My head! Damn migraine! Kaharsab, shall I put a stop to our little chat?

Forgive me Maharaj, I won't do it again. I just meant he was an unnatural son.

How so?

You know all, Maharaj.

Indeed! I do know all! That is why I can tell you the boy Gopi is your son.

Gopi? My son?

Yes. True your brother wronged you. Sutnami was just a weak man. If he was not he wouldn't have allowed you to force what

*would have been an unholy marriage. Anyway, despite what your
brother did, Gopi is your son.*

Gopi. My son!

*Look how proud you have become. Next thing you know you
will be demanding bride price.*

No Maharaj, not me. Such an evil practice—but my son didn't
marry his sister?

No.

Then the marriage is a good one?

It's possible.

Maharaj we must tell them.

We? No. Nothing is to be done about it.

But why Maharaj?

*Such is life. You can't tell them. You have run out of good deeds.
And I can't tell them.*

But why?

I only chat with evil men.

Oh, I see. What about Durga Mata?

Look at her. Kali has her own problems.

But the children should know. Let me go and tell my son—

*I admire your new-found zeal for good deeds. But it's too late.
Besides it's all up to Brahma—and to tell you the truth, in my
opinion, Brahma is one of the biggest bunglers around creation.*

I think so too—

At your own risk. I could hold such opinions—

I retract that opinion.

Good for you.

But the children will never know?

*Who knows? Who can tell? Anyway, enough of this talk. We
don't have much time left. Look, look behind you. Describe for me
what you see.*

Kaharsab turned his head and fixed his eyes on the temple
courtyard and the vision of the serpent of serpents bore through his
head and set his brain on fire and Kahar beheld the crater through
lenses of blood. He saw the people in their terror. On their knees.
Or in the dust and dirt. He saw the body of his brother; the heap
that was Madhuban. He heard the cries. The wails. That scream.
He beheld his son strike out at Mahisha as the demon grabbed the
boy by the throat. Tears ran down the face of Kahar Saheb. And as

the flames engulfed his brain, so too that scream. From the ruptured mouth of Kali.

In this instant too, all became aware of that scream. The crater became silent. The villagers and the pilgrims rose to their feet and looked up at Kali. Mahisha dropped Gopi and he too became chilled into silence and fixed his eyes on she of the awe-inspiring coutenance.

Inside the mouth of Kali, Saraswattee ran about wildly as she screamed. The girl didn't know what to do. In the desert she had drawn an imaginary line. Crossed it. Felt Saraswattee become Saraswattee. Once upon a time. A long long time ago. But now the girl saw some real lines held more terror than imaginary lines. Some real lines led into horror. She was never going to set foot out of the mouth of Kali ever again. Never, never. As long as mortals crawled upon the land she would abandon the earth—as a matter of fact not only was she never ever going to step out of Kali's mouth; she would take refuge deeper within Kali: in her bosom.

In her terror, Saraswattee forgot about the sound of someone poised within the chest. She strung the rags of her bed into a long rope, tied one end around a tooth, and threw the other end down the throat. That done, the girl descended inside the body. Dense wet red clouds of vapors rose and swamped her but she let herself down and then hung in the middle of the vast chest. The girl was stunned to discover Kali didn't have a heart.

Then came the sound of ambush. The sound of the hunter; and the hunted. As when Kali herself stalked the demon Durga through the seven worlds. Simultaneously, Kali and Saraswattee realized the danger. Saraswattee didn't know what to do in her new terror. Should she just let herself fall into Durga's guts and disappear? The girl stared down at the bloody stew of steam and vapors. The stench suffocated her, she sweated; wept. Was that a real line, or an imaginary line?

But if Saraswattee didn't know what to do, Kali did. She fixed her cauldron eyes on Mahisha. It was time to rid Mahisha of his delusions. The moment of truth for he, Mahisha; the moment of truth for she: Kali. She had to bring the demon face to face with himself. Before Mahisha could move and wreak his final destruction, Kali inflicted her memory on his and gathered his mind in a knot and left an illusion of the demon there in the temple courtyard. Then, his mind like an umbilical cord, Kali dragged the demon through his genealogy. And as the ogre stalked Saraswattee, so now Kali caused Mahisha to stalk his father. Celestial day by celestial day by celestial day she leapt back. And with fury she ravished her memory and the memory of mankind. With dementedness she plundered the genealogy of the demon and her genealogy and the genealogy of all humanity. Epoch by epoch by epoch. Pyre after pyre after pyre. And as she did, generations of the dead and the deceased fell out of the cells of her brain and cascaded down her chest cavity and around Saraswattee as she hung on to her cloth rope. Millions and millions of dead bodies fell all around the girl and disappeared into the stew of Durga's guts. The vapors thickened, the stench rose. Funeral pyres exploded. Skeletons and bones and ash rained down around Saraswattee. Sparks scattered. The girl clung to her rope, wept. But Kali ravished and plundered as she stalked the demon Durga, and then she too almost decimated the seven worlds of creation. And it came down to two. Kali and Durga. Goddess versus demon. Woman versus man. Then Mahisha Durga beheld the demon Durga change shape after shape. Form after form. Now a serpent, now a swift deer, now the feces of animals. The seven worlds became a maze of one buffalo foot and one big toe. But the relentless Kali stalked on. Until all that was left of her soul was the passion for blood. Until all that was left in the blood of the demon was his lust for carnal fulfillment.

This Kali sensed. She stilled her footsteps. The demon Durga headed for his favorite corner of the earth—where he hoarded his most precious wives: the buffalo women. Kali caused a great silence to descend upon the demon's favorite resort. She gave the demon the illusion she had abandoned the hunt; gave the demon the illusion he had eluded her. When she heard his grunts Kali kept even greater stillness. She poised her spear. The grunts became more reckless. More frenzied. The earth where Kali hid vibrated. When she sensed the demon had completely abandoned himself to his lust, Kali stepped out her hiding place and confronted the demon Durga. Came face to face with him there in the field. As he mated with his buffalo wife. And she slew him right where he copulated, stuck on to his wife's buffalo behind like a gigantic black toad.

In the temple courtyard Mahisha clamped his massive hands to his ears and closed his eyes and screamed: "NO! NO! NO!" But even with his eyes closed Kali forced him to experience that death again as she re-created it to discover where she had erred and how Mahisha Durga came to be reincarnated.

There she stood. At one end of the field. In all her armor and her wrath. And there. At the other end of the field. The demon Durga. On his wife's bottom. Like a big black monstrous toad. And in copulation. She could hear his grunts echo. She could feel the ground vibrate. And then. The look of shock and surprise in those clots of red eyes as the demon glanced up and beheld her. And then. Through the air. Devoid of motion or insects. Her spear. And in the next instant. Before even his shock and surprise could disappear. With no time to dismount. With no time even to lose his erection. The spear split his throat and his hands grasped his neck as the blood gushed out and swamped the land, and still stuck on to the buffalo's behind like a big black toad his body shook in convulsions as he entered the throes of his demon death.

No mistake. There was the demon. Stuck in the throes of death. Her spear out the back of his neck so that even he with his power couldn't pull it out. His body in convulsions. And yet. Here he was. Reborn. How?

"NO! NO! NO!" Mahisha screamed.

It was then Kali's mind flashed forward to the moment of the mortal birth of Mahisha and as quickly she flashed back to the moment of death of the demon. Suddenly she realized her error. She had slain the demon in copulation with his buffalo wife. Now as she beheld him in the throes of death; as she beheld him in convulsions: *Kali suddenly realized he was simultaneously in the convulsions of an ejaculation and in that very moment of his death he scattered his demon seed like a sudden rash within the womb of his wife.*

There she caught him. There she slew him—he who enjoyed a boon from the gods that no mortal or demon not even an immortal could slay him; only a woman could slay him: and he knowing delightfully well there existed no where in creation a woman who could slay a man—let alone a demon. But she slew him. Took his identity. Took his name. Became: Durga Kali!

There too, in the convulsions of his death, the demon had sown the seeds of his evil reincarnation. And here he stood. In her beloved abode. Come for vengeance. Not knowing he was a demon. Desirous of being a man. An evil man. As if there was a difference between an evil man; and a demon.

What a fool she had been. How careless. Surfeited by victory she became haughty and vain. Became famed and renowned. And turned her back on the pleas of the buffalo wife of the demon. She; Amba: buffalo wife. Amba had called out to her. Ran after her. Begged her. To tell her what had happened. And to ask a boon. But she, now Kali Durga!—she turned deaf ears to Amba's cries.

As it had happened once before, thus it happened again. Amba, the buffalo wife of the demon Durga, as the demon himself had done when he stood on his one big toe: Amba got down on her two front knees and performed austerities and big crystal tears rolled out her buffalo eyes. And where the demon had set the world on fire by his austerities, Amba's tears now flooded the earth and Brahma was again forced to get up from his bed of lotus flowers and ask: "What do you want?"

Amba asked: "Why are we who are born ugly or black, why are we either demons or called demonic or even barbarians?"

And Brahma, the Supreme Creator, had no answer. Like a fool he stared about creation with his perplexity. He beheld the things of creation and all were beautiful and pleased him—even those creatures that were of the blackest color.

Brahma looked down upon the buffalo woman and said: "It is folly. Folly of the mortals. And folly of the gods. What do you want further?"

Amba said: "I want no creature or thing, animal or human, because of its dark skin or its blackness, to be called demon or evil or pagan."

"Granted. What else?"

"If there are to be demons in this world, let either gods or mortals be demons. Let demons be demons. But never permit an animal, however ugly or black or hideous, to be a demon or even called a demon."

"Granted. From this day on only demons and gods and mortals are to be demons if they choose. From this day, all animals of creation are deemed wonderful and delightful and sacred."

And Amba was well pleased and her heart became happy and Brahma asked: "Anything else, Mother?"

Oh! what delight Amba knew then. *Mother!* She said: "Indeed, I am to be a mother. But I carry the seed of a demon. Withhold the birth of this child in my womb for such a time when evil has been eradicated from this world, a time when humanity is good and righteous and worshipful of creation and of the things of creation. When such a time is come, transfer my child into the womb of a mortal woman, let my son be born of a mortal woman of the brahmin caste so that he may become a priest and serve you as my gratitude for all you have granted me, O Supreme Creator."

"It is done, Mother," said Brahma, and Amba got up and went through the fields and the forests the pride of the buffaloes and all the animals of creation. And she roamed through the seven worlds until it came that time. Then her son was reborn in the womb of Amba: the wife of Pundit Mahesh Narayana.

And Mahisha Narayana could not deny the screams of his mother as the flames of the pyre ate through her flesh. He sweated as if he himself was being consumed by those flames. He screamed and his heart pounded and with each beat of his heart his forehead bulged out and Gopi and Chintamani and Pundit Ayer and all the villagers and pilgrims and soldiers stared in horror as Mahisha's forehead bulged out with each beat of his heart until his forehead became transformed in shape and size to that of the belly of a pregnant woman—became like the pregnant belly of his mother Amba, whose womb, as he the son of Durga lay coiled inside it, he Mahisha Durga, sewed shut so that Amba could not give mortal birth and for six birth spans he held his mother's womb shut while the poor woman suffered the ridicule and the scorn of her villagefolk until her husband Pundit Mahesh Narayana condemned his wife to be a witch and decreed she be burnt alive and as the flames tore through her flesh her demon son could not shut out the echoes of her screams and they reverberated in his ears and he drew the womb tight over him to protect himself from being consumed by those very flames.

Amba was burnt to ashes. The pyre collapsed. Night came. The sparks died out. Then at midnight the village was terrified out of sleep by the shrieks of a child and all flocked to the warm pyre and there in the coals lay a handsome baby boy who played with his toes in his mouth.

Even right then, the young Pundit Ayer pronounced the child a saint. And indeed the boy showed every indication of saintliness and before he was five knew all the verses of the scriptures by heart. But Pundit Mahesh Narayana couldn't live down what he had done to his wife and when Mahisha was eleven he moved far away and lived on the banks of the holy river Ganges and taught his son the scriptures until one day, when the boy was thirteen years old, he grabbed his father by the throat and dragged him into the holy river Ganges and strangled him under the sacred waters and threw all the sacred books after the floating body and then went away to seek for himself his own myths and legends.

Until he came into the legend of himself. With his forehead bulged out like a pregnant belly. Mahisha clamped his hands to his head; felt his deformation. The villagefolk stared in fear and horror. Naga and Kahar watched. Chintamani became shocked out of her dementedness, and now terrified, she ran to Gopi who now looked up to Kali to find Saraswattee. But the girl was not in the stone cleft. Had she gone inside the bosom? Gopi became alarmed. But not as alarmed as Saraswattee. The silence outside the bosom became the silence inside. Where the girl hung suspended by her cloth rope. What had happened? Had everyone come to their senses? Had the demon slain villagers and pilgrims alike? Or had Kali destroyed the evil one? But Kali had little time to help Saraswattee. In the courtyard, evil was coming face to face with evil. The demon was coming face to face with himself. Kali had to act fast. Any moment now his memory would be complete; his past stretched out before him as his future. He would regain his identity. Take his name. Become Mahisha Durga. Then he would retake all the power and the might she took from him. Then what would she be? Would she be a goddess trapped in a body of granite and cast iron? Or would she herself become Kali? Or, once he retook his name and regained his power, would she be less than a goddess? A body of granite and cast iron? Or a woman? No she had to act fast and just at the moment evil became evil she had to destroy the demon for all eternity and an infinitesimal moment more.

Saraswattee felt the anger sweep through Kali's body and she began to scramble up her cloth rope when a rustle caused her to spin around. Something squeezed itself out from behind the left lung. Saraswattee watched the lung twist and warp like a gigantic bellow made of gray sponge. Then claws sliced the edge of the lung. The girl scrambled up as fast as she could. The ogre burst out from behind the lung and grabbed ligaments and veins and slid through the chest to get at her. Saraswattee froze. The ogre stopped; stared at the girl. He was hideous to behold but Saraswattee stared back. All this time. A monster. Within the bosom of Durga Mata. No heart, that creature. A beast of flesh the size of Kali's head. Twin-bodied. Two-headed. But one neck was broken and this head rolled around with one eye gouged out and the other eye dead white. The other head was tiny and raw and had raw eyes. How many times she had heard that heart beat dhoom! dhoom! dhoom! Only now the monster was silent and slid towards her. Saraswattee came to her senses and hauled herself up the rope like a terrified scarecrow. The claws caught her green straw skirt but ripped through it and Saraswattee pushed herself out the throat and tumbled into the mouth. She rolled to her feet and rushed to the front but stopped. She beheld what all eyes in the courtyard beheld: Kahar Saheb on his knees on the stone steps. With a mighty serpent erect above him.

Kali fumed. The crater trembled and the orifices puffed up huge clouds of vapors. Kali fumed not only because her faithful servant disobeyed her: he who prided himself serpent of serpents was about to be seduced—and forgive. Because Saheb Kahar had been bleached of all passions and lust. So purified by the sight of the serpent of serpents had Kahar become that at any moment that once evil creature was about to be transformed into a sage more saintly than the old rebellious viper himself. Kali coiled up her wrath and it exploded in the serpent's head as she commanded: *You old vile viper! Bite!* In that very instant, the serpent found himself almost poisoned by a surfeit of pity and he lashed out and dug his fangs between Kahar's eyes and squeezed the ages of venom into the veins of the dung of men and drew back and stood erect and watched the despicable creature before him writhe and convulse as the venom inflicted his every cell and his every pore with death and the serpent of serpents thought, ah, indeed, he must have gotten very old, he was almost fooled, because such a time it was then, as it is now, when humanity went beyond the threshold where repentance lost its effectiveness; when forgiveness of sins became impossible: and when even an evil man transformed into a saint in the nick of time found nirvana null and void in the very next nick of time. Such was the nature of the moral universe. It will not always be possible to save humanity, the wise and venerable Naga, serpent of serpents, remembered. This made him sad. With that he slithered back into the vacuum of his impartiality and disappeared.

The people blinked their eyes but no mighty cobra coiled on the steps. Only Kahar frothed and writhed with the poison in his veins. Saraswattee beheld those eyes—those dead sheep's eyes—and she looked for Gopi to tell him not to be sad but her eyes fell on Mahisha and she saw his hideous forehead and Mahisha glanced up at Kali and Saraswattee stepped back and she and Kali and all beheld Mahisha reclaim his identity as his bottom delighted him with an itch but he didn't have time to enjoy this pleasure because suddenly the mighty cobra lingam of Kali came alive and Naga coiled back to strike and Mahisha Durga became paralyzed and stood and watched the rusty fangs drip venom and before he could move the fangs nicked the bridge of his nose and the vicious breath of the serpent of serpents scorched his skin and burnt his eyebrows when suddenly the serpent of serpents snapped back in midair as the ogre clamped his claws around Naga and pulled Naga into the belly of the goddess with such force the walls of the pubis shaved off his skin and the bejewelled glass scales scattered in the air like a quiver of lightning.

Then Naga, idle serpent—who had dared challenge the ogre to do battle—did battle. The ogre struck dhoom! dhoom! dhoom! Poisonous hisses vibrated throughout the crater. The cast-iron body of the goddess cracked and splintered and blocks of granite split and crumbled. Roars and hisses entangled the ears of all present but Mahisha laughed and beat his chest and spat on his hands and rubbed the spit on his scorched skin and burnt eyebrows as his behind pleasured him even more. And again, Saraswattee found herself trapped in Kali's mouth. The roars and the hisses terrified her. She ran to the throat. She ran to the front of the mouth. Now there were no imaginary lines. She knew what waited for her within the bosom of Kali. She knew what waited for her in the temple courtyard. Which real line led to greater terror?

Which real line led to her death? She could throw herself down the throat. Or she could rush out the mouth of the goddess in full view of the villagers and have them sacrifice her for her sacrilege. She saw what the women did to Chintamani. She saw what her father did to Madhuban. She saw her hated uncle kill her father—but Kali had slain that monster. And Gopi. Her beloved Gopi. What would become of Gopi—her husband—her brother! If she was to die she wanted to die with Gopi. If Gopi was to live, she wanted to live with him. In the desert that was Gopi; or the oasis —whichever, whatever.

But now she knew the legend—she had discovered so much of the legend, same as she had discovered the curvature of the earth and *maybe* once upon a time there existed this demon who enjoyed a boon from the foolish gods that no mortal or god could slay him, only a woman could slay him; and he quite unaware there existed a girl called Saraswattee stubborn enough to do battle with the very foolish gods and if so then what of a big-headed demon?

Saraswattee rushed out the mouth of Kali and jumped down into the stone cleft. Her hair sprouted wild and her body was splattered with blood. But her eyes were black and fierce. She crossed her arms over her chest, and thus she towered up into the abode of the gods the dizzy height of Kali. And at last. Come face to face with the demon Mahisha.

SIXTEEN

ND come into the legend of her own self, the girl.

"Ho!" the voice of Saraswattee echoed through the crater. "Buffalo boy! Virgin buffalo boy! I slew your father! I will slay you too! Ho, virgin buffalo boy! Behold Kali!"

The battle within the bosom of Kali ceased. Mahisha bawled. Mahisha bawled as only a buffalo could bawl. His handsome hunter-style khaki clothes with the flap pockets turned black with sweat. He became dizzy and staggered backwards. But he couldn't take his eyes off the girl—no no, no girl she. An apparition. A mirage. No girl could she be. No mortal. And yet. Those eyes. Those tiny black eyes. How many times had he beheld them before? A hundred times? A thousand? And if not a girl—a goddess—*the goddess*? Kali? That girl the reincarnation of the bloodvexed and bloodlusting Kali? The reincarnation of the legend. Out of a body of granite and cast iron. In a body of mortal flesh and mortal blood: Kali! But if that girl was a reincarnation of Kali, then he was indeed a demon—and the legend was true. No lies. The legend true? He, Mahisha Narayana, a demon? And Kali reincarnated? Come to slay him? As she had slain his father? No no, he was no demon—he was Brahma! Suddenly the screams of his mother reverberated in his ears as the flames tore through her flesh and Mahisha bawled: "NO NO NO!"

"Ho!" Saraswattee taunted Mahisha. "Buffalo boy. Virgin buffalo boy!"

"Why," mumbled Pundit Ayer, as his eyes raged at each other, "he *is* a demon."

252

"NO NO NO!" bawled Mahisha as he himself relived his mortal birth in the ashes of his mother's pyre.

"But how could that be?" Pundit Ayer asked. "After six rebirths in his mother's womb? Why, if he had one more rebirth he would have attained godhead—seven rebirths and you are the Supreme Creator—so the holy scriptures say. But how could that be? He withheld his own birth. He is a demon—his mother was a saint—most probably! Why, we didn't kill his mother. *He* killed his mother. His father condemned his mother—and he most probably killed his own father too! But how can that be? With six rebirths he is more mortal than demon. One more rebirth—and godhead. But with six rebirths he is more mortal than demon—more of the brahmin caste than the demon class!"

Mahisha saw Kali's spear split his father's neck, beheld his father in the convulsions of death. He fixed his demon eyes on Pundit Ayer. Gopi became hopeful. He said to Mahisha: "Sab, is the legend true?" The demonic eyes flashed to Gopi. "Is the legend true, Sab?" the boy asked. Mahisha became demented and his body shook as when he strangled his mortal father under the waters of the holy Ganges. "Is what the pundit says true, Sab?" Gopi begged. "If so, then you have no right to vengeance—but enough destruction has been done. Even if you are more demon than mortal spare us. You have knowledge and wisdom. You have science. Forgive us. Let us rebuild our lives, help us change our evil ways—"

"FOOL!" Saraswattee thundered. "Adhey, Gopiwalla, are you a fool? How can you reason with a demon? How can you appeal to evil nature? Is there goodness in the heart of a demon? He is a demon. And I will slay him. Ho, buffalo boy are you ready to taste my wrath? *I am Kali!*"

"How can that be?" Pundit Ayer asked.

"You wait," Saraswattee said, "you will surely find out!"

"Sab," Gopi said, "it is only because you failed as a human being you turned to your evil nature. And with your evil nature you have turned your science to death and destruction. Maybe for once the pundit is right. Maybe you are more mortal than demon. And we didn't kill your mother. You came for vengeance on us because of your own evil act. Sab, we did you no wrong. You wreak death and destruction because you failed as a man—you failed as a man of science. You are no demon! What do you really want?"

"IMMORTALITY!" Mahisha shouted and grabbed Gopi by the throat and lifted the boy in the air and shook him: "Immortality. Can you grant me that? You with your desert wisdom? But you are right. I am no demon. I am Brahma. I am the Supreme Creator! I will not allow you to belittle my vengeance. I will not allow you to undermine my doom and destruction. Dissolution, that is what I want. I killed my mother. I killed my mortal father. I will kill you. Then I will destroy your goddess. You, Kali, behold. You want human sacrifice? You want human flesh and human blood? Behold your most faithful devotee Gopi, behold in propitiation I snap his neck for you! No goddess will slay me. No woman will slay me. I will destroy you. Behold—DISSOLUTION!"

Saraswattee and all saw the eyes of Gopi bulge as he kicked the demon in his chest and monstrous forehead. Then Saraswattee leapt. From the abode of the gods. From the dizzy height of Kali. Through all time and all space the girl leapt. From a height greater than the height she had attained when Gopi led her into the desert so that she could achieve the wisdom of the things of the desert and as she swept through the ages once again Saraswattee became Saraswattee. And in the instant Mahisha glanced up, the girl landed on the back of his neck with her knees crooked onto his shoulders and she grabbed his ears and pulled with all her vengeance and the ears of the demon stretched out into scabbed and hideous buffalo ears. Mahisha shrieked in pain. He dropped Gopi and grabbed for his ears. But Saraswattee wrung his buffalo ears as in a grindstone. The demon bawled in pain and spun around to fling off the girl. She held fast and ground those buffalo ears—for indeed she meant to wring them off. "Ho!" she taunted the demon. "Buffalo boy! I will wring off your ears. Ho, virgin buffalo boy! I will gouge out your eyes. Ho, virgin demon! I will rip out your heart and eat it raw."

When Mahisha couldn't dislodge the girl, he glanced up at the steel bore poised over the most sacred orifice of Kali. Then he laughed and shouted: "Brahma. I am Brahma! I had six mortal rebirths and one demon rebirth—seven rebirths—I am Brahma!" Mahisha grabbed the pundit and asked: "Not so, punditji?"

Pundit Ayer's eyes ran amok as he said: "It is possible—most probably." Mahisha flung the crossed-eyed pundit aside and before Gopi could stop him, he began to run between the outstretched legs of Kali while Saraswattee wrung his ears and banged on his forehead. Gopi lunged at the demon and entangled his feet but Mahisha dragged the boy through the sand as his demon laughter echoed. The demon forgot Saraswattee but she didn't let him forget her and kept on banging his head and wringing his ears. As Mahisha dragged Gopi past the ninth sacred orifice, the boy begged: "Sab. Please forgive us. Do not destroy our goddess. You have knowledge. You have wisdom. You have learning. You know the science of the twenty-first century—help us design a new future."

"Ha ha ha!" Mahisha laughed. "Ah Gopi, what an adversary you are. You wouldn't give up, would you? You love your people to such an extent? Such is your belief in the humanity of your legend? Ah, a shame. You would indeed have piloted your land into the future. But there is no future—behold dissolution!"

The dust settled on Gopi and he and Saraswattee followed the outstretched hand of the demon. They beheld the drilling bore Mahisha had erected over the ninth sacred orifice of Durga Kali. With horror, Gopi beheld the true intent of the demon. Violation of the vilest kind. Desecration of body to defile soul. Thus he would destroy the legend. The bore over the most sacred orifice was only a diversion—a diversionary ploy. Gopi stared in disbelief. Saraswattee too realized what the demon was about to do and her little fingers went for those evil eyes. But the demon didn't care and he mounted the drilling platform and grabbed the operating levers and shouted: "Behold, Gopi. No symbolic desecration this, no symbolic defilement. But doom and destruction worthy of a demon. Ha ha ha! You want to know what I am about to do, Gopi? Not what you think—such blind faith. No, not what you think. You remember what I taught you Gopi? About the earth and its core and about volcanoes and steam and geothermal energy? You remember I told you it is your goddess who squats on the future? Well, a simple explanation. Only a few feet within this hole—the ninth sacred orifice—there is a cap of rock. This cap of rock leads into a subterranean passage—the Saraswati—ha ha ha—the lost river Saraswati—she runs underground here in a vast subterranean cave. With such swift currents of water. With such swift currents of air. A powerful suction—a mighty mighty vacuum. Ha ha ha. Ah, Gopi, I see you understand. Such a bright boy. A seeker after truth. Well, here is simple scientific truth. Underground, your other Goddess Saraswati swirls through the bowels of the earth with a mighty vertigo of a vacuum. All I have to do is shatter this cap of rock and that vacuum will suck down into the bowels of the earth this entire volcanic crater together with temple and courtyard and!—your famed and renowned goddess!—ha ha ha—all will crumble and fall and be sucked away into the bowels of the earth. Your goddess. Her breath and her wrath—myth, shit and primitives! Ha ha ha. Look at it this way Gopi. I am only using one legend to destroy another legend—all legends. I am using your Saraswati to destroy your Kali! Ha ha ha. Legendary enough for you Gopi?"

"Please, Sab," the boy pleaded as Saraswattee stared at the steel bore.

"You cannot reason with a demon, Gopi," Mahisha said. "Unlike a human, a demon isn't blessed with a good side and a bad side. A demon is all demon—all evil. So you can't hold a demon responsible either—besides if I am no demon the legend is a lie—"

"The legend is a lie!" Gopi shouted. "I don't believe in the legend. And you are no demon. You are a man—just an evil man. You failed as a man. You failed as a man of religion. And you failed as a man of science. That is your true reason for your vengeance—this your death and destruction. You are human because only humans can be inhuman. You are a man because only a man can be homicidal. And you have turned your science homicidal. Just an evil man. Not Brahma. Not even a demon! The legend is a lie. I don't believe in the legend. I don't believe in you—not as a demon—not even as a man!"

Mahisha bawled. He raged. He became the most hideous and vengeful Gopi had seen him. It was as if he wanted to terrorize the boy into belief of him as a demon. He beat his chest and his ugly face twisted and his demon eyes bulged out. Saraswattee became paralyzed by fear. But Gopi didn't budge, didn't betray any fear. Unable to control his lust for vengeance Mahisha shouted: "Can a mere mortal man bring about dissolution? You don't believe, right? Well maybe you will believe in this. Behold—dissolution!" Mahisha shot the bore through the ninth sacred orifice and Kali screamed.

Kali screamed. And came alive.

Suddenly her immense body of granite and cast iron became transformed into an immortal body of flesh and blood and out of every pore and over her head the thousands of serpents sprang to life and struck out. The far and purple horizons bounced back the din of hisses upon the temple courtyard. The serpents lashed out in a maze of lightning. Dark clouds blew in, thunder erupted; then came ghost rain. The people heard the sound of waterfalls. Outside the crater, the pillars of the limestone valley collapsed into dust, the desert tore open in gorges and canyons, the ruins of ancient palaces tumbled further into sand. Inside the crater the sacred orifices clouded the air with vapors, the temple cracked down the middle, the foundation of the courtyard crumbled and the crater dropped three feet.

Then came silence; and from her dizzy height of twenty warrior men, Kali looked down upon the abode of mortals.

The dust filtered out the air, a mighty wind blew in. Kali pulled in her regurgitated tongue and the grimace of terror disappeared from her face and her mouth looked no longer tusked or hymen-ruptured. Her necklace of skulls became transformed into a sparkling necklace of precious gems. Her cauldron eyes of blood became vast pools of tears. The wind blew in, spun the many serpents out into glass-scaled strands of silk and wove them around the body into a splendorously embroidered and bejewelled sari and Kali towered up into the abode of the gods the most radiant and most beautiful of all the goddesses of creation.

Thus the people beheld her. And tears filled up their eyes, because they knew, such a time had come upon the land.

Behind the goddess Gopi got to his feet and glanced at Mahisha. Like Saraswattee on his shoulders, the demon stared in wonder. Gopi followed the sparkling eyes of Saraswattee and together they beheld the body of the goddess they had climbed up so often— taken refuge in at the time of the exorcism of Chintamani.

Kali beheld Chintamani, the most beloved of her devotees. Chintamani returned the gaze and knew instantly she was the favorite of Durga Mata. The girl felt the strength of that body, remembered how the demon had tried to lift her chin but couldn't. And the cross-eyed pundit still had asthma but Kali didn't mind her thinking such.

Kali moved her gaze to Padma and Matti. She recalled Matti's

sin; made no judgment. She shifted her eyes to Badraj and Nandass
and Akpar and the other menfolk. Again she made no judgment:
felt no pity. She saw the fat rich man and his brothers, the slain
Saheb Kahar; the murdered Sutnami. She beheld the young girls
with big bellies; beheld the maimed children turned into beggars:
beheld the temple prostitutes. She saw Phooloo and Amakutty and
Sirju and Roopa and Doolwah.

Her eyes skipped over the cross-eyed pundit and she fixed them
on the heap that was her daughter Madhuban. Then tears fell from
her eyes; fell down the sky: fell like ghost rain. The people heard
the sound of rain, felt the heat of the desert sun, longed to have
those tears gush down in torrents upon them and wash them clean
of the dust and the sand. But the tears of Kali did not fall upon the
earth. The clouds disappeared; Kali's tears evaporated. The goddess searched for Gopi and for Saraswattee.

This Saraswattee knew and tried to jump off Mahisha. The
demon grabbed her legs, laughed; ran before the goddess where his
laughter again erupted as he faced Kali. Kali fixed her eyes on
Saraswattee, saw the girl wring the buffalo ears, pound the demon
on his forehead. Then Gopi came and stood up before the goddess
and Kali shifted her eyes to him as he glanced up at her. Gopi,
dark-skinned boy; desert boy. Defender of she: Kali—but god to
Saraswattee, curious child, stubborn girl. But no sacrilege that. No
idolatry. When gods desired death and demons made pilgrimages
to sacred shrines, the children had to create their own cosmogony.
And if they turned to each other and held each other dear; that was
more than what their elders or their gods did for them. Such a time
it was.

But Gopi. What a defender he had been; what a champion.
Through him she had come again to experience love for a mortal.
Through him she had come again to experience the worship of
gods. Through him she had come again to experience the emotions
of a mortal woman. And as she looked down upon the boy, Kali
suddenly became overwhelmed by the power of those experiences
and a mighty desire to make amends and set things right possessed
her and she tried to bend and pluck Saraswattee off Mahisha and
destroy the demon for all eternity and for an eternal infinitesimal
infinite moment more but she couldn't budge.

Mahisha laughed. It was then Kali became aware of her doom

and her destruction. She glanced at Mahisha. The demon rolled his head, rolled his eyes, kept Saraswattee helpless on his shoulders. The girl struggled. Kicked. Banged on his head. Wrung his buffalo ears. Scratched at his red eyes. But all in vain, she couldn't free herself; because the demon pulled on her legs with his great black hands.

And as Mahisha pulled down on the girl, so too the immense underground vacuum beneath Kali pulled on her to suck her down into the bowels of the earth. Such force—greater by ten times the evil power with which the ogre of her heart had reversed her respiration and the circulation of her blood. The pull—the vacuum—tore at the soles of her feet with the fangs of serpents and her insteps snapped and as her ankles cracked and collapsed the volcanic crater shifted and sank five feet. Mahisha laughed and shouted: "Behold your doom. Behold your destruction. Your legend is truth. But I am no demon—I am not the son of Mahisha Durga. Behold your dissolution! I am Brahma!"

Kali fixed her eyes on the vain and boastful Mahisha. Oh, how demons were notorious for their false claims! But Brahma. And the gods. The gods; and the folly of gods. The folly of she, Kali; once Devi: the fearless and the formless and the sexless one. Creator of creators. Who had caused the body of the creator Narayana to ripen. And from whose vital fluids she had created Brahma and Shiva and Vishnu—the supreme triad: who the last time she could remember came to her and wailed and whelped like babies and then squabbled among themselves while the demon Durga ravished and plundered the seven worlds of creation. How long ago had it been? What did it matter?—she had been a fool.

Mahisha rolled his eyes and laughed. Saraswattee struggled to free herself. Gopi kept his eyes on the goddess, knew she beheld her death. In desperation the boy glanced around. What could he do? How to destroy the power of the underground vacuum before it destroyed the goddess? His desert wisdom seemed inadequate. But so too the knowledge of science he had acquired. But he had to prevent the death of the goddess because if Kali died, then what would become of the legend—the land?

Gopi glanced up at Kali and she beheld his despair and helplessness. She beheld to what fate she had indeed abandoned the children. Again tears flooded her eyes, as the demon laughter echoed throughout the desert. As the tears gushed to her eyes, so too now the memories swamped her brain and even if she wanted to she couldn't stop the torrent of the past and she journeyed through the ages and Brahma created the seven worlds and all the gods and mortals and animals and things of creation delighted in creation until the demon Durga wrought his death and destruction and Devi reincarnated herself in the body of Parvati, beloved of Shiva; and she slew the demon: became Durga Kali.

Then great civilizations sprang up throughout the seven worlds and Parvati journeyed with her consort Shiva as he kept his eyes on creation. And she Devi, now famed and renowned as Durga Kali, roamed the hills and valleys of the abode of mortals in the sensuous and seductive body of Parvati. Neither did Parvati know this nor her lover Shiva. In the body of Parvati, Kali became enchanted by creation and the things of creation; she became enamored of the body of a woman: became delighted by the emotions of a woman. Such that she thought she would idle a while in the luscious body of Parvati and have some fun. Until they came to Mount Nagar and Shiva turned blue.

Parvati saw the anger consume her beloved. Humankind had driven the Goddess Saraswati from the abode of mortals and had taken to evil ways. They had abandoned books and learning and music and poetry. They had abandoned the seasons of the gods and had taken to the seeds of slaughter and carnage and condemned their children to war. But Durga Kali caused Parvati to look kindly upon the abode of mortals and Parvati intervened on behalf of humankind and pleaded with her consort not to destroy that place. She prevailed upon her lover to let his anger subside and to lay under a tree and rest for a while. She would go in search of water, bring him succor for his ache—quench his thirst. Shiva was consoled by his lover and became pacified and lay down to rest. Parvati went through the hills and valleys in search of water. In her body went Durga Kali.

The excursion delighted Kali. She ran and skipped and jumped. She hummed a song. Smelled flowers. Chased after a butterfly. Never had she felt such freedom—such ecstasy. She was thrilled to be a human—*thrilled to be a woman*. To feel a woman's body. To experience the emotions of a woman. She had never smelled a flower before, never ran barefooted on the earth, never saw the sky, never felt the wind and the heat of the sun. Never had she tasted the juices of berries. Her fingers leaked the juices, her lips and tongue became stained purple and blue. Kali stuffed her mouth with berries and fruits and poor Parvati wondered if she herself might be pregnant. What! Such a craving for fruits she felt! So ravenous an appetite! She ate up everything. She hadn't forgotten her beloved Shiva but so far she had come upon no water. Then she stood before Mount Nagar. She stood higher than the mountain. Way up into the abode of the gods. Then a thought struck her and she knocked down the mountain. She got on her knees and with her hands she scooped out a crater. In the crater she dug a hole. She knew in the center of the earth there was water and she would fetch some for her lover and as she thought this Shiva called: "Parvati."

Then Parvati instantly became possessed by the passions of a woman and her eyes lit up and Durga Kali found herself in the strangest of situations ever. What was this? What was happening? Why was her body feeling so? Never before had she experienced such things. Her fingertips blazed afire. Her head felt dizzy. Her heart beat uncontrollably. Her entire body became hot and she sweated and didn't know what was happening—and yet she was delighted. Ecstatic. Eager to explore. Eager to experience more.

Shiva called, "Parvati."

Parvati smiled; and Kali was beside herself with anxiousness and curiosity. What was happening? What were these feelings? What were these emotions? She had never known such. Never felt such. Indeed were all these delightful emotions and passions in the body of a woman? And yet, how far dare she go? How more dare she explore? Experience? So these were the passions felt by humans and their gods!

Kali wondered what next and Parvati chuckled. Bit her lips. Held her throat. Rolled her eyes as she tried to hide and tease Shiva. Shiva again called, *"Parvati"*; and Durga Kali heard the bushes rustle and twigs snap. Her own eyes rolled. She watched and waited for what was to happen next. What ought she to do? Maybe she ought to clear out, evaporate herself away and yet so delightful it was to feel those emotions, to feel the passions of a woman, to want want—oh! Parvati laughed. When Shiva sounded close she looked around and bit her lips more and giggled and she slipped into the hole she had made and disappeared into the belly of the earth and then Kali herself laughed—this was fun! such fun! she was ready to play this hide-and-seek! and she giggled with Parvati as Shiva came up to the mountain and saw the wreckage and called, "Parvati! Parvati!" and Kali had all she could do to keep herself from bursting out into laughter, such fun it was! such a delight, hide-and-seek! and from inside the belly of the earth she watched Shiva, his face in a smile: he knew Parvati played with him, teased him; and he feigned anger and displeasure but Kali could see he was pleased and wondered what he was thinking and what in all creation was Parvati up to? But Parvati could no longer contain herself and burst out in giggles and Durga Kali whispered shoo! shoo! but Parvati laughed and Kali could no longer restrain herself and laughed too and Shiva looked down and saw the orifice. He beheld the body of his beloved as she lay there. Sweated. Consumed by desire. Enflamed by passion. Eager for him. Then Shiva rose up high into the abode of the gods, he too now in the ambrosia of his passions; and Durga Kali stopped laughing and her eyes bulged because from out of the heavens Shiva's lingam stretched out, stretched down, and Parvati giggled; and Durga Kali froze in her sweat as from the heavens to the earth Shiva's lingam came at her and she stared in a frightened wonder but before she could think or do anything the lingam entered her body and she felt the weight of Shiva on her and she cried out *hai*!

The earth shook. Shuddered. Shattered. From its womb burst lightning and thunder and hot steaming molten lava—and Durga Kali moaned in the convulsions of an infinite moment of mortal pleasure and then it was over.

She lay still. Shiva on her. She; Durga Kali; her eyes in a trance. Her hair dishevelled. Her body dripping sweat. Her breathing slowly levelled out. She felt Shiva's weight on her and put her arms around him and held him tightly and felt pleased with herself—and good.

And though in the back of her mind she knew she was now forever trapped in the body of a woman, that didn't disturb her very much. How long they lay there she didn't know. Many times she saw the sun and the moon pass before her eyes—but she, Kali, in the body of Parvati, held Shiva erect in her for many a celestial day.

The wind came cool. Blew on the sweat on her body. She felt her body. Her breasts. Her thighs. She felt Shiva's body in her. Then for a long while she had no thoughts—became pure bliss.

After a while Shiva got up. Stood naked. He reached down and pulled Parvati up. She clasped her hands around him and rested her head on his shoulder. Durga Kali looked down on that place. Everywhere she saw the jewels scattered, saw how their sweat had turned to sand, saw how her cosmetics had stained the earth. She beheld the imprint of her body: beheld the images of her orifices. That place was pleasing to her. Was precious. Sacred. If she was forever trapped in the body of a woman this was where she wanted to be. Here her home. Her heart. Yet she was not herself. She was in Parvati. She was Parvati.

And what of Devi? What of she who was formless and sexless and knew not of such things as emotions and the passions of humans and their gods? Was now that limitless being limited? Was now that indescribable entity described? Was now that formless soul given body? Was the immortal now mortal and to die even though a god?—even the Supreme Creator Brahma came to his dissolution. He came to his dissolution and all creation dissolved and nothing existed but Devi. From out of Devi was again created Brahma and from Brahma came new creation. But there she was. Devi. As Durga Kali. In the body of Parvati. And had experienced passion. Lost her sexlessness—her virginity—godhood.

Kali, in her mortal configuration, could no longer comprehend it all. She became saddened. Wept secretly. What an oversight she had been guilty of. For a fleeting moment of ecstasy, she had lost ecstasy itself. For a mortal form of existence, she had lost the immortal form of life. Yet she didn't feel she had exchanged one thing for another. Her sorrow was not at her own mortality. Her sorrow was for the mortality of all things. Because of what she had done there was to be a dissolution of dissolution itself. Because without Devi, the formless and sexless one, there could come no re-creation.

And yet, would she change things? Would she give up passion— the love of a god or even a mortal man? No. The loss of godhood was the gain of love. And one thing she knew: she did not want to return to the abode of the gods. Not as Parvati. Not as Kali. Not even as Devi. This was her home. Earth was her desire. The abode of humans. Maybe with them she might help them change their ways, loathe evil, love goodness and truth and all humankind. Maybe she had exchanged one being for another. But if all was not to be lost, she had better find a way to depart from Parvati's body. Find her own form. Her own shape. Durga Kali again looked around and knew where she wanted to be. To live. Love. Thus she caused Parvati to look fondly upon that place too. Parvati told Shiva that Mount Nagar was holy to her. She decreed it sacred. She asked that her body be reincarnated there. So that humankind may know the gods exist.

Shiva said: So be it.

Then he put one foot on Parvati's shoulder and ascended into the heavens. Durga Kali caused Parvati to face east, straddle the earth, breathe in, and be at peace. From out of the skies Shiva reached down a hand, grabbed Parvati by the hair. Then, as Shiva pulled Parvati into the abode of the gods, Durga Kali pressed down on the abode of humankind. Shiva pulled Parvati upwards by her hair. With an equal force Durga Kali pushed down upon the earth, pushed on her belly; pushed on her womb. And in the instant Shiva pulled the soul of Parvati into the abode of the gods; in that very instant Durga Kali gave birth to the temple of Shiva and her immortal body became transformed into a massive body of granite and cast iron; and now, ages and ages past the future of that ancient time to this day: here she was again reincarnated into flesh and blood and towered over the abode of mortals the most radiant and most beautiful of all goddesses of creation.

And the most sad. The most brokenhearted. Doomed to death and destruction. Wrought by the demon seed of the demon Durga whom she had slain where he mated with his buffalo wife—no no: doomed by her own doing. Her own choice. And yet she didn't want to die. Didn't want to suffer oblivion. Didn't want to abandon the abode of mortals—abandon Gopi. He who had taught her to pray again. He who had taught her to care again. He who had taught her to love again. As he loved Saraswattee, curious child, stubborn girl; who refused to give up her struggle to free herself and had her fingers sunk deep into the eyes of the demon.

Again in his desperation Gopi sought a way to strike Mahisha and forestall the death of Durga Kali. Then Mahisha reached back with his long arms and clamped his hands around Saraswattee's waist and squeezed her belly and the girl cried out. Mahisha glanced up at Kali and she knew his intent. The demon laughed: "Ha ha ha! Behold! Kali reincarnated in the death of her own body!"

As Mahisha was about to rip Saraswattee off him and fling her into the most sacred orifice, Gopi plunged at him and sank his teeth around his navel. Mahisha bawled. Saraswattee dug her fingers into his eyes. Chintamani picked up a lathi and began to beat the demon on his back and on his buffalo behind. Kali beheld her children fight the demon and she knew she had to help them because they were no match for Mahisha and even though her knees snapped and the volcanic crater shuddered and sank and the walls collapsed, Kali gathered her viscera in a knot and inhaled a mighty breath counter to the evil power of the vacuum beneath the ruptured soles of her feet and as she felt her knees unravel, she pulled and overpowered the suction of the bowels of the earth, when suddenly Pundit Ayer erupted: "All behold Kali. Behold the power of her priest. Om namah namah namah! Sacrifice to Kali. Give blood to Kali that she may become her old vengeful self and slay the demon in our midst. Become again, O Kali, blood drinker! Bring a sheep, cut its throat, offer its blood to she who delights in blood, lawba dandayi namah! reng! deng! beng! spleng! greng!"—in that instant Kali flashed her eyes and fixed them on the pundit and the wayward ligaments in the sockets of the eyes of the pundit snapped and the pupils became stuck to the bridge of his nose and the pundit straightened up as if struck by lightning and his gaze became fixed on Kali and he beheld Kali become Kali indeed, he beheld Kali become the bloodvexed and bloodlusting slayer of evil and of evil men: and the serpents tore themselves alive from the radiant and embroidered sari and hissed and struck out from every pore of her massive body of naked flesh and mortal blood and her hair became a tangle of live chaos and the jewels on her necklace turned into skulls and Kali grimaced as her face twisted in rage and her wrath exploded in the ears of the pundit: RENG! DENG! BLENG! GRENG! SPLENG!—*is that right punditji? You will offer me blood will you? Good. Then I will have your blood! I thirst for your blood! If you will torture and torment my children with your misconceptions and misinterpretations, if you will strangle my legend with the sins of your soul and your warped mind, if you will make me into a cannibal, then I will have your flesh and your blood—punditji*

punditji, when will a match be made for my daughter Saraswattee,
what evil omen lurks in my daughter's stars—chee chee chee, such an
old girl, so close to her monthlies and not married yet, shame shame
shame, a sore on her father's forehead, such a disgrace, so close to her
monthlies and not married yet, chee chee chee—slang! rang! grang!
blang! dang!—BEHOLD:

Thereupon, Kali inflicted her death on the cross-eyed pundit. As
she was to experience this death. Caused by the evil power beneath
her ruptured feet and unravelled ankles and collapsed knees. As it
sucked her into the bowels of the earth. To her doom and
destruction. Every atom of agony she experienced, every molecule
of misery she underwent, every particle of pain she knew: this
death she caused the pundit to live. Such that his insteps snapped.
His ankles unbolted. His knee joints unravelled. The pundit felt the
weight of all creation pull down on him and he tried to cry out to
Durga Mata to spare him. But Kali had not known such lust for
vengeance even when she faced the demon Durga. The pain burned
out the pores of the pundit but he couldn't scream, couldn't cry
out—then Kali unstrung his eyes and let them run amok so that he
could behold his own doom and destruction. The people stood in
silence and watched Pundit Ayer's eyes scramble around the
volcanic crater. He seemed to see everything at once. The shattered
walls. The thick white clouds of vapors with hisses of steam. The
cracked temple. The now irregular and misaligned sacred orifices.
The cranes and the tractors and the hoists and the laboratories
with the scientific instruments—all of which he had sanctioned and
blessed and misunderstood as he had misunderstood and mis-
applied his ancient Sanskrit with its ancient mantras—*reng!*
deng! bleng! the voice of Kali echoed in Pundit Ayer's ears. *Clang!*
Rang! Bang! Grang! The pundit sucked in sand and dust. His ribs
expanded outwards like the skeletal remains of the gills of a
landlost fish. The bones lost their elasticity, locked; and
atrophied—distended. Inside his chest his asthmatic lungs ruptured
like wet spiderwebs. Then the pundit felt the suction pull his guts
to his anus, pull his heart down into his belly, pull his tongue down
his throat, pull his brain loose from his skull and he suddenly
broke wind and created so tremendous a vacuum his ribs snapped
and his skull collapsed and his viscera together with his eyes got
sucked out his anus but his eyes became stuck there: still crossed.

Then Kali caused the pundit to see *the manner* whereby he had always seen things: ass backwards.

Thus too she caused him to behold himself—and all like him: pilgrims and brahmins alike: parasites on the land. Kali made the eyes of the pundit run amok throughout his own genealogy that he might see how he and his kind thwarted humanity; entangled humankind into such a helpless and hopeless convolution of genealogies that there was no way out: no future. Then she made him behold what was to be his fate and the fate of his kind: doomed to eternal rebirth as shit cleaners. Thus he had lived, ass backwards; thus he had seen things; ass backwards: thus he died: ass backwards.

And the people beheld the manner of the death of their high priest and they understood. The children beheld the manner of the doom of the priest and they understood even more. Mahisha beheld the destruction of the pundit and understood it was the vengeance of Kali and his demise came next but not if he moved fast and as Kali shifted her gaze to him, Mahisha ripped Saraswattee off of him and held the girl high in the air above his head. But the wrath of Kali now knew no bounds and her throat expanded and her head became distorted and her face, even more twisted and warped. Mahisha laughed and shouted: "Death to Kali! Death to all her devotees! Destruction to her legend! Doom to her future! Here—I sacrifice to myself—I am Brahma!"

Gopi swung away from Mahisha, snatched up the bloody hoe, and swung around with the momentum of his revolution. The breastbone of the demon split like lightning. Mahisha staggered backwards. The hoe split his demon heart in half and the thirteen valves and the thirteen chambers ruptured and his demon blood gushed out his massive chest like molten lava. Mahisha looked at the hoe, looked at his blood, looked at Gopi. He stared at Gopi with human eyes of disbelief. The crater shook, shifted, hurled up a great storm of blackness. Mahisha blinked his eyelids; felt the blackness engulf him. His arms sagged, Saraswattee dropped, Mahisha forced himself to stay on his feet; raised Saraswattee high above his head again. Gopi kept his eyes on Mahisha, moved back towards the most sacred orifice. Then he stood on its molten edge and could feel the hot steam on his back. With his eyes Mahisha calculated the distance between himself and the most sacred orifice—between he and Gopi. Such a universe, it seemed; between he and Gopi; and his evil power gushed out of him with such rapidity—he had journeyed backwards in space and time and had come into the legend of himself and did he have the strength to fling that girl to the very end of the universe way past the oasis of that boy?

"Gopi," Mahisha said, "what faith. Ah, what an adversary. Tell me, Gopi, tell me the legend is true—tell me I am a demon!"

From deep within the desert of himself Gopi returned that gaze. But he kept his silence.

"Tell me Gopi!" Mahisha shouted. "Tell me the legend is true!"

"The legend is not true, Sab."

"I am a demon. Not so, Gopi? Tell me I am a demon!"

Again Gopi kept his silence.

"Tell me I am a demon!" Mahisha screamed.

Then Gopi beheld Mahisha gather his strength and squeezed his split chest shut tight and choked off the spillage of his blood and Gopi knew Mahisha had enough might to fling Saraswattee high over his head and down to her death into the most sacred orifice. The boy glanced up at Kali, saw her distended throat, her deformed head, her warped face. She seemed choked—about to vomit. Mahisha looked up at Kali but no terror seized him. Gopi returned his gaze to Mahisha.

"Tell me the legend is true!" Mahisha screamed. "TELL ME I AM A DEMON!"

"The legend is not true," Gopi said. *"You are just an evil man."*

Mahisha flung Saraswattee through the air. As the girl flew towards the most sacred orifice, Mahisha snatched the hoe out his chest and glanced up at Kali to laugh his demon laughter in her face. Kali vomited. The ogre that was her heart, she vomited on the demon. Who watched the great blob of a beast hurl down on him. Woven through it, like a thick knotted vein, bulged the mighty body of the cobra lingam; wise and venerable sage Naga: he who prided himself the serpent of serpents. Built for delicate social intercourse and not for strenuous mortal battle, he had waged a valiant fight; Naga. In his old age. Exchanged hiss for roar; bite for blow: and had vanquished the ogre with a mighty hiss. And now his lidless eyes paralyzed the demon Mahisha, who beheld the serpent come at him through all his genealogy and from the very moment of his conception where Kali slew his father in the throes of ejaculation: his death born in the very moment of his conception. And as his father watched Kali's spear come at him and could do nothing, so too Mahisha stared at the live eyes of the serpent of serpents and stood paralyzed and the red raw blob crashed down upon him like a far-flung meteor and impaled him on his feet; such that from the mouth of the ancient cobra stuck out this handsome face of a rich and handsome stranger welcomed to the sacred shrine as a good omen.

But try as she might, Kali couldn't withhold her nausea and she continued to vomit. With pain in her eyes she glanced at the most sacred orifice. Gopi had Saraswattee by her feet and struggled to drag her out the orifice. And Kali would have pulled with him. But she didn't even have the strength to suppress her own nausea. Thus, helpless, she vomited. While Gopi dragged Saraswattee out of the most sacred orifice and the girl spun around and rushed to Gopi and he hugged her and Chintamani went to them and together the children and the people stood and wept as Kali vomited back upon the face of the earth its entire genealogy of humankind. Then Saraswattee beheld the millions and millions of dead bodies that had fallen around her as she hung on her cloth rope within the bosom of Kali now tumble down into the sand and dust of the volcanic crater. Kali looked down at the people and could not suppress her feelings of disgust and revulsion at this: the human race of mortals. Such creatures. Of blindness. Of vileness. So infested with murder and rape and war. With such evil for one another, human to human; society to society: civilization to civilization.

Such a time it is now, as it was then, the eternal dissolution of creation: and a time to purify oneself and depart the evil abode of humankind. Thus Kali purged herself. Graveyard after graveyard after graveyard. Pyre after pyre after pyre. Logs and coals scattered. Ashes clouded up the sky. Sparks exploded. The people watched. The children watched. Mahisha Narayana, his handsome head out the mouth of the cobra, watched. All the calcuttas of her womb Kali vomited back upon the face of the earth. And when she was done her body felt clean and purified. Her vision became clear. The dust and ash settled out the air. Kali fixed her eyes on Chintamani and Gopi and Saraswattee.

The three children walked past the head of Mahisha Narayana and stood before the goddess. Saraswattee stepped forward, put her hands on her waist, and transfixed Kali with her tiny black eyes—such venomed eyes her daughter cast upon her! And where Chintamani prayed—where even Gopi stood in worship—Saraswattee rose in anger.

"Saras," Chintamani whispered, "why do you look upon Kali Mata with such eyes?"

"She knows," Saraswattee said.

"Brother, tell Saras to be humble. Tell her not to look at Durga Mata such. Tell her to ask a blessing."

But Gopi held his silence.

"Saras," Chintamani pleaded, "why don't you ask a blessing?"

"Kali knows," Saraswattee repeated.

And indeed Kali knew. Knew the heart of Saraswattee, curious child, stubborn girl. She desired death and hers was death. Then Kali had the folly to ask herself: What was to become of the children?

Instantly Kali turned into stone. And cast iron.

The volcanic crater shook, shifted, shattered. The sacred orifices exhaled massive clouds of vapors. Dust and sand clogged the air; muffled the chaos of prayers. The walls collapsed. The laboratories ignited and exploded. The cranes and the bores and the alien apparatus of the science of Mahisha Narayana all tumbled and crashed. The volcanic crater rocked the desert with violent eruptions but the horizons closed in and bounced back the vibrations and waves after waves of concentric circles of earthquakes converged on the shrine and the gigantic body of the goddess together with the sacred temple of Shiva shattered and crumbled and crashed into the most sacred orifice.

The dust blacked out the sky and the sun, and the earth became its own shadow.

Slowly—celestial day by celestial day? who knows? who can tell?—but the dust filtered through the air and silenced the tremors of the desert. As slowly, the sun spiralled through the shadow of the earth to reveal the millions and millions of creatures on the face of the land. In bafflement they stood, and in transition. Without hope; but in a hurry. Windblown: and echoless. Like the desert.

And the things of the desert. All sandcovered and dustclogged. Such that you could not tell villager from pilgrim nor pilgrim from spirit.

Thus they stood; *bedraggled creatures*—when suddenly the spirits of the desert came to their senses and recognized themselves and realized they were among the living and would have none of that and quickly they began to depart in all directions and abandoned the living where they stood: shadows upon the land.

As the great migrations of the spirits of the desert fanned out in all directions the dust settled down—remember, ghosts neither are dust nor disturb dust.

The sun filtered through. Together with their villagefolk, Chintamani and Gopi and Saraswattee glanced at their shrine. The volcanic crater could not be told from the desert. The precious jewels of Durga Kali crumbled to dust. The pebble walkways dissolved into sand. The vapors—the breath and the wrath of Durga Kali, legend said—died out; the sacred orifices closed in on themselves: became like scars upon the land. Padma and Matti and Nandass and Akpar and the other villagefolk rushed about in search of their goddess and her sacred orifices. But there came not even the smell of sulphur on the wind.

Gopi caught Saraswattee with her venomed gaze fixed on the handsome face of Mahisha Narayana. The boy walked to the demon and Chintamani followed him. But for his head, Mahisha Narayana was buried in rubble—where was Naga, that serpent of serpents? Who knows? Who can tell? But for now Mahisha Narayana was still alive. Again he stared at Gopi with human eyes—this time with human eyes of supplication. Gopi knew what the demon wanted. To be told the legend was true. To be told he was indeed a demon. The boy looked around the crater. Beheld the cranes and the tractors. The workbenches and the laboratories. Of Mahisha Narayana. And of the science of Mahisha Narayana. The goats and the sheep hopped and climbed over the laboratories and the pipes and steel scaffolding. Such an ancient wreck upon the land lay the twenty-first century civilization of Mahisha Narayana. You would have thought that civilization collapsed even before the civilizations of legend-honored kingdoms. Such that the goats and the sheep knew those ruins intimately. So they climbed the scaffolding and the drilling platforms with ease—though also with indifference. And they foraged, not for shadows, but for whatever briar or bush not sucked up by that wreckage.

Gopi returned his gaze to Mahisha Narayana. He thought of what he had said to him. Only humans can be inhuman. Man was homicidal; man made his science homicidal. To use knowledge and wisdom to wreak death and destruction when he failed as a human being. When all that was necessary was the ability to distinguish right from wrong. The innate capability of humans to distinguish wrong from right. The inherent instinct in humans to know good from bad. Because all things have an innate wrongness; all things have an inherent rightness. And all that was necessary was the human ability to know—*to feel*—right from wrong.

Mahisha Narayana knew right from wrong. He might have been born a demon—but even demons have choices. Besides, Mahisha Narayana had had the benefit of art and science and of rebirth and reincarnation. He might have chosen to be mortal, and fail. That, Gopi could understand. Instead he had chosen to become his demon nature—and he still failed. Not people, but creatures like Mahisha Narayana caused civilizations to collapse, thought Gopi.

Now the eyes of Mahisha Narayana begged the boy to tell him he was a demon—to tell him the legend was true. Gopi knew the legend well; knew the legend to be true. He knew of the buffalo woman Amba and her plea to Brahma. Poor Amba. She had asked that her son be given birth at a time when humankind was good and loving and peaceful and worshipful of creation and all the things of creation. As it was, Mahisha Narayana was born at a time when mankind was most evil—the age of the triumph of wrong over right; the era of the triumph of evil over good: the yuga of the triumph of war over peace. Such a time it was then, when demons were scarce and begged for recognition if not for immortality—as if there is a difference betwen recognition and immortality—and mortals were more demons than human. And the folly of gods and their good intentions. As you see, once more, Brahma had bungled.

Gopi withdrew into the desert of himself and said not a word to Mahisha Narayana. Saraswattee beheld the handsome face of the demon twist with rage. As if it would fly at Gopi and devour him. The girl stepped forward, put her hands on her waist, fixed the demon with her black eyes. In a strong distant voice she said: "I am the Goddess Saraswati. Fair and beautiful. The rays of the moon are my hair. The sun is the tikka on my forehead. The stars are my eyes. I am the river of knowledge and wisdom and learning. I am the goddess of speech, of intellect, of memory. I am the goddess of poetry and truth and literature. I dwell in the heart of all those who would know me. I dwell on the tips of the tongues of all those who utter my name. Thus says the legend and thus am I."

Mahisha did everything he could to make his head jump at Saraswattee and devour the girl. He rolled his head, rolled his eyes, blinked his eyelids, twisted his face, stretched his neck, stretched his tongue. And as he fought to get at the girl; and as she spoke: pore by pore he turned into sand and vanished.

As he disappeared, the desert became unburdened of all premonitions and the sky rose high and the sun embraced the grains of sand and the far-flung desert *like a serpent* journeyed into a place and a time with a promise where things might grow.

The shadows upon the land took up their proper perspectives. Then with the desert at peace with itself and with the spirits of the desert, Chintamani and Gopi and Saraswattee drew close to each other. They looked at the villagefolk, who staggered around dazed in a land they didn't recognize. Matti and Padma. Nandass and Akpar. Phooloo and Amakutty and Doolwah and Sirju and Roopa. The children. The beggars. The temple prostitutes.

Saraswattee could care less where the people went.

But Gopi realized how lost the villagefolk were. He knew he and Saraswattee and Chintamani should not turn their backs on them.

How far ahead had Saraswattee journeyed?

Gopi looked at the girl and she glanced down and shouted: "Look!" She bent down, rustled the sand, held up Chintamani's gold thali. The gold thali glinted in the sunlight. Gopi and Chintamani shifted their gaze to Saraswattee's chest. The girl saw she still wore the homemade thali of desert shells Gopi had tied around her neck as they sat on the shoulder of the goddess on the third day of the exorcism.

"So," Saraswattee said, "Gopi you are my husband and my brother."

Gopi said nothing, withdrew into the oasis of himself, his dark eyes chiselled in the sunlight.

"Sister," Chintamani said, "how can that be?"

"And you, Chinta, are you not married to your brother?"

Chintamani looked at the thali and remembered her wedding day. She remembered being beaten and spat upon. As an unfaithful wife. An adulteress. She remembered when they had decorated her body and dressed her in a richly embroidered sari and held up the mirror to her and she had caught the first glimpse of herself. She hadn't asked them where the sari came from. To whom did the jewels belong? Who in the village owned a mirror? She who had not known there was a Chintamani but only answered out of habit to the name Chintamani, then, as she looked in the mirror: she saw Chintamani become the beautiful Chintamani. That beautiful Chintamani. Who didn't look anything like this Chintamani. Who stood there covered with dust and with her clothes torn and ragged and her hair ruffled and rumpled. On the day of her marriage, before the mirror, she had asked Durga Kali to let her be true. This again was her prayer, as in her mind she beheld the transformation of Kali Durga into the most radiant and most beautiful of all the goddesses of creation. That reincarnation would always be with her and as long as there was life in her Kali lived.

But she wished she was as certain of her own future as she was certain about the future of Kali.

Saraswattee beheld the sadness come over her sister and she said: "Don't worry, deedi, you did no wrong."

"What do you mean?"

"To marry your brother."

"And you?"

"Me? I did no wrong whatever."

"Then are you going to keep your thali?"

"Of course."

"But you cannot! That is wrong! Gopi, remove that thali from Saraswattee's neck!"

Both Chintamani and Saraswattee looked at Gopi and Saraswattee said: "Chinta, Gopi and I, we are married in a special way."

"What special way?"

"In a spirit way."

"Sister, I don't understand. But you must take that thali off!"

"No. I am going to keep it. Gopi is my brother. We are not married married. We have a spirit—a marriage of spirits. And even though you were married to Gopi you did no wrong. You didn't know. Gopi didn't know. The marriage is null and void. I absolve both of you!"

And again Saraswattee beheld an even greater sorrow come upon Chintamani. Chintamani looked at Gopi. Saraswattee became confused. "Chinta," she said, "you did no wrong."

"You must take that thali off," Chintamani said, the tears in her eyes a mirror to the sorrow in her heart.

"No."

"Sister. You must. Why won't you take it off? Why will you wear it?"

"To keep pundits away from me—pundits and other evil spirits!"

"WHAT?"

"That's right. I have a brother. But I have no evil spirit. And no pundit will tell me so. With this thali around my neck I am free."

"Sister, what are you talking about?"

Saraswattee fixed her eyes on the gold thali while Gopi and Chintamani watched her. The girl said: "I will keep the thali my brother Gopi tied around my neck. Because he loves me. And I love him. With this thali Gopi and I are married to the desert. But this gold thali. No one will tie such a thali around my neck. Because no bride price will ever be paid for me. No bride price will ever be paid for me because I will never become a bride. I will offer no one a thali to ensure him a long life. It is not my responsibility nor my right to ensure anyone a long life. I will accept no thali from anyone that he might give me a face. It is not the responsibility nor the right of any man *to presume* to give me a face. I already have a face—and a beautiful face at that!"

"Sister! Why do you speak that way? What vanity!"

"No vanity, deedi—just Saraswattee."

"Sister, are you not afraid of offending the gods?"

"No. The gods had better beware of offending me."

"Deedi. Have you forgotten all that has happened to us? Our fate? Have you forgotten what has happened to our father? Have you forgotten what has happened to our sister—"

Suddenly all three remembered Madhuban and turned. A mound of sand had formed over Madhuban. Quickly the sisters rushed to the hill of sand. Chintamani began to cry. Gopi walked over and studied the mound. There was no sign of blood—all was earth. The desert bore the blood well, thought Gopi, and gave instead: life—from the peak of the mound of earth sprouted a growth of tulsi.

Madhuban. Child of the desert. Who was she? What was she? Who knew her? Who touched her hand? Who saw her face? Who beheld her tears? Who felt the fear of her heart? Who said, Madhuban Madhuban, my daughter, my child? What is to become of the children of the desert, when some petty poet will sing of a god who attained nirvana? None will sing of Madhuban. But what does it matter anyway? Madhuban is killed, Madhuban is dead; the world will go on: and poets will lament their own sorrows.

"Little Husband," Saraswattee said.

"Yes, Little Mother?"

Saraswattee held out the gold thali in the splintered rays of the desert sun. She said: "Fulfill your promise. Offer this thali to our sister."

"Saras," Chintamani asked, "what do you mean by this?"

"Gopi made a promise. He must keep his promise."

"Madhuban is dead!"

"Madhuban is not dead. Here, Little Husband, take the thali."

Gopi took the thali, watched the rays of the sun swing on it.

"Brother, what are you doing? Why do you let Saras order you around like that? You are the oldest. We must do as you say. When will Saras learn her place? What does she mean that Madhuban is not dead?"

"The legend."

"The legend?"

"Our sister means if the legend is true, then Madhuban is alive."

"Now you too are confusing me."

"Chinta, do you believe the legend?"

"Deedi, you know I do!"

"Then why don't you understand?"

"I just don't understand!"

"The thali is only a token. A gift from the three of us to Madhuban. To bless her on her new pilgrimage."

"I still do not understand," Chintamani said and burst into tears. Where once she knew pain; now she knew heartache. And she wished she understood. Wished she understood her heart. Its configurations. Why such a fate—what was to become of she, Chintamani? Why did Gopi have to be her brother? And he was not an ugly brother. She didn't mind his black skin. Besides she liked his desert eyes. He was not rich—didn't have a horse. It did not matter. She would not have minded being married to him. At least—not anymore. To tell the truth, she wanted to be married to him, because, because, she liked him—she, Chintamani, had fallen in love with Gopi; he dark-skinned boy.

Hate or love, her mother had said, would come later. In the beginning there was hate; in the end came love.

Chintamani wept. Saraswattee studied her sister. Gopi kept his eyes on the gold thali. Slowly the far and purple horizons eased the sun closer to the earth. The sheep and the goats drifted towards the village. Gopi glanced at Saraswattee; caught her with her eyes on Chintamani. Chintamani kept her head down; continued to sob. Then she felt the eyes on her and glanced at Gopi. Together they faced Saraswattee. In that instant, Saraswattee knew Chintamani was in love with their brother.

This she knew. As she knew the confusion Chintamani suffered. Then Saraswattee could have condemned the soul of her father to eternal rebirth for his sin. But she did not damn her father's soul. Nor did she forgive. As she would never forgive the cross-eyed pundit. His eyes. All three knew those eyes were still with them. Those eyes would be with them for a long time. But Saraswattee would realign her cross-eyed cosmos. This thought the girl. And Brahma?—what the girl thought about that bungler cannot be told.

Such a time it was then. As it is now. The gods inhale. The universe expands. The winds blow in from the oceans; the seasons unfold their secrets. Spring comes, a shower falls, a seed germinates, a plant grows, a flower blooms, a man sins, a child is born, a girl sheds tears, the gods sleep, you dissolve. In all of this, where is the *humanity* of humanity?

"Little Husband."

"Yes, Little Mother?"

"The thali. Madhuban waits. We must offer a gift, bless our sister on her pilgrimage."

Gopi leaned forward and tied the gold thali around the brush of tulsi.

Chintamani sobbed.

Saraswattee crossed her arms over her chest. Gopi turned his head, glanced up, beheld the girl in the oasis of prayer, she; curious child: stubborn girl: *Saraswattee*.